M000309681

Advance Praise for
Behind the Lens

A gripping Afghan tale starring a strong hero wielding a camera.

Kirkus Reviews

A powerful, heartbreaking story of an American woman seeking redemption after exploiting a photographic moment in an Afghani village. Jeannée Sacken's artistic gaze is unflinching as Annie Hawkins' tale plays out against the perilous backdrop of the war in Afghanistan. Swift-paced, with deft characterization and cross-cultural savvy, this vivid novel is an absorbing read.

Shauna Singh Baldwin, author of *What the Body Remembers, The Tiger Claw*, and *The Selector of Souls*

From page one of *Behind the Lens,* Jeannée Sacken plunges her readers headlong into a foreign and often hostile culture—total immersion. With every turn of the page, the tension slowly ratchets up to its explosive ending. Sacken's main character, war photographer Annie Hawkins Green, allows the reader to hitch a ride to Afghanistan in her camera bag. And it is a hair-raising ride beginning to end. If Annie doesn't find trouble, trouble finds her. Add a touch of romance and *Behind the Lens* will top your list of unputdownables.

Jennifer Trethewey, author of the Highlanders of Balforss series

I dare you to read the first chapter of *Behind the Lens* and put it down. It can't be done. Before you know it, you are in for a great ride all the way to the end. Jeannée Sacken's writing is that good.

Judy Bridges, author of *Shut Up & Write!*

From the moment Annie Hawkins Green slaps a piece of duct tape with her identifying information on her flak jacket, the reader is thrust into the exciting and dangerous world of a photojournalist who covers conflict zones. Annie is courageous and resourceful—racked with guilt and plagued by PTSD. She's a good—though flawed—mom and a good—though flawed—friend. And that, I think, is what I love most about Sacken's writing: she creates multifaceted characters in high-stakes situations, and she never resorts to the "easy out." In *Behind the Lens*, Jeannée Sacken reminds us of the steep human cost of war and the deep human connections that can be forged there. This book will stay with you long after you finish the final page.

Kim Suhr, Director of Red Oak Writing and author of
Nothing to Lose

Behind the Lens by Jeannée Sacken is the story of Annie Hawkins-Green, war photographer, who is determined to return to Afghanistan to fulfill her vow to a young girl who died in her arms years before. Annie's journey to teach photography at her friend Darya's school for girls in Wad Qol is filled with conflict, secrets, and lies that create a danger to friends and family. All intricately entwined with the culture of the country, it's a story you'll savor from beginning to end. So, make yourself comfortable because you can't put this book down.

Roi Solberg, author of *The Caretaker* **and** *Spirit of Archetypes*

Behind the Lens is an unbiased exploration of the struggles women face from a patriarchal system in society, religion, education, and profession. Jeannée Sacken writes a poignant and riveting work of art with vivid characterizations and honest dialogue, pulling readers inside her landscape. Her book reveals prejudices, ignorance, and intolerance inherent in mores and customs that favor men and withhold opportunities from women. To overcome these controversial differences, she shows us how sincere and forthright communication is necessary for successful mutual understanding and respect.

Heba Elkobaitry, Muslim Cultural Advisement Consultant

Behind the Lens by Jeannée Sacken is a superbly written novel, with intertwining threads, including violence and terror that are ever-present in a country that has experienced the same for centuries, and intrigue and duplicity worthy of the best of the international spy thrillers. Anyone interested in examining other cultures will also appreciate the accuracy with which Sacken presents many of the complexities of a country with a mix of cultural traditions, all of which are contending with—in sometimes violent ways—their own interrelationships and the inescapable involvement with modern, Western society. Readers will be eager to know when the sequel will arrive.

Myles Hopper, author of *My Father's Shadow*

In *Behind the Lens*, Jeannée Sacken introduces us to Annie Hawkins Green: photographer, activist, and mother. In this hard-to-put-down story, from the war in Afghanistan to the war with her teenage daughter, Sacken takes us into Annie's world and keeps us rooting for her from beginning to end.

Carol Wobig, author of *The Collected Stories*

When photojournalist Annie Hawkins Green returns to Afghanistan to teach photography at her best friend's school, she's haunted by memories of a deadly Taliban ambush. After several close calls, Annie wonders: are these ghosts or is the Taliban hunting her down? Not only does this story take readers on an adventure *Behind the Lens* and into Annie's life, it transports them to the heart of Afghanistan and into a battle for equality, freedom, and justice. This riveting new debut from Jeannée Sacken will keep readers turning pages until they reach the satisfying ending.

Rochelle Melander, writing coach and author of *Mightier Than the Sword: Rebels, Reformers, and Revolutionaries Who Changed the World through Writing,* writenowcoach.com

BEHIND
the LENS

JEANNÉE SACKEN

Ten|16
PRESS

www.ten16press.com - Waukesha, WI

Behind the Lens
Copyrighted © 2021 Jeannée Sacken
ISBN 978-1-64538-233-1
Library of Congress Control Number: 2020950269
First Edition

Behind the Lens
by Jeannée Sacken

All Rights Reserved. Written permission must be secured from the publisher to use or reproduce any part of this book, except for brief quotations in critical reviews or articles.

For information, please contact:

ten16press.com
Waukesha, WI

Cover design by Kaeley Dunteman
Editing and interior design by Lauren Blue
Chapter image obtained via iStock: 2C03AK7

This book is a work of fiction. Names, characters, places, and incidents are the product of the author's imagination or are used fictitiously. Characters in this book have no relation to anyone bearing the same name and are not based on anyone known or unknown to the author. Any resemblance to actual businesses or companies, events, locales, or persons, living or dead, is coincidental.

For Michael

and

for the girls and women around the world
who bravely struggle to get an education

Afghanistan, Kandahar Province - November 2006

PRESS - ANNIE HAWKINS GREEN - B NEGATIVE

THE FIRST THING I DO ON any new assignment is print my identifying information on a piece of duct tape and stick it on the front of my flak jacket. Which sounds kind of morbid, but makes sense considering I'm a war photographer embedded with the coalition forces in southern Afghanistan. Except, ten days ago, the base commanding officer *reassigned* me far away from the front lines. Now, I'm sitting in the back of a Humvee that's churning along an unpaved, sandy road to yet another 'safe' Pashtun village where Marines will hand out bottled water and ready-to-eat meals. I get to document these feel-good forays. Not what I was expecting, but when you're a photojournalist, you find the story and you tell it.

"SAY, MA'AM?" CORPORAL SEAN Murphy smiles at me in the rearview mirror. "That little girl you liked so much last week—doesn't she live in that village up ahead?"

I follow Murphy's gaze up the road to the cluster of mud-brick houses. "Yeah, that looks like Khakwali." I haven't exactly been quiet about wanting another chance to photograph these kids. Especially Malalai. She looked to be about ten years old, and her green eyes absolutely sparkled when I showed her how to use the Polaroid camera I lug around with the rest of my gear. People love to keep the pictures of themselves, so it's a good way to make friends. She took charge, posing her mother and sisters, her grandmother and heavily bearded grandfather, aunties and cousins, yelling when they wouldn't stand still. Then she started in on the goats.

I lean forward. "Thanks, Corporal. This is great! But I'm kind of surprised the CO's sending us back this soon."

Murphy keeps driving. "Maybe we didn't tell him where we're going."

Riding shotgun, Private Manny Lopez shoots him a look. Seriously pissed.

"Murphy!" I clap my hand on his shoulder. "We could get in some serious trouble."

Murphy's hands tighten on the steering wheel. "Hey, how's he gonna know? We're all in this together, right? Me and Manny'll win some hearts and minds. You'll get some good pictures. It's a win-win."

And the guys in the second vehicle of our mini-convoy are okay with this? I look behind me, but there's no Humvee bringing up the rear. What the hell? "Murphy? What happened to Hicks and Johnson?"

"They're taking care of the last village for today."

So we can go to Khakwali. Damn. I know the rules. Murphy does, too. Convoys don't split up. Full stop.

Under the towering black clouds, the village looks even smaller and poorer than I remember. It's also strangely quiet when we pull up to the crumbling wall out front. But as soon as Murphy turns off the engine, I hear the kids. "*Ah-nie!*" A loud, giggling, happy chorus. They sprint across the sandy stretch in front of the houses, Malalai in the lead, dressed in a brown and white *shalwar kameez*. Shrieks of laughter and nonstop Pashto chatter. The bleating of goats and hens *tuck-tuck-tucking* as they skitter wildly among the kids. One of the boys pulls at the back door, eager to open it for me.

Lopez glances back at me, nodding toward my flak jacket on the seat. "Your jacket, ma'am. And do me a favor? Keep your helmet on today."

"Thanks, Corporal." I pull on the jacket then slip the Canon strap around my neck and grab the Polaroid along with some packets of film. While Murphy and Lopez set about unloading crates of MREs and flats of bottled water, the kids swarm me, pulling me to my knees, their arms encircling my neck, their lips pressing against my cheeks.

"*Assalâmu alaykum!*" Peace be unto you. I say it over and over, my smile broad, my heart warm.

"*Wa 'alaykum assalâm,*" says each child in return, clearly delighted that I can say something so important in Pashto.

They finally let me load film into the Polaroid, which Malalai immediately grabs out of my hand. One of the older kids speaks sharply and slaps her wrist. Hard. For a second, she looks ready to slap him in turn, but then meekly gives him the camera. The joy in her eyes is that suddenly gone. I want to snatch the Polaroid back for her. But this is the way of their world, and I'm not here to change their culture. The Marines have made that oh-so-clear.

The boy has a firm grip on the camera. Ghazan, that's his name. Tall and skinny with wisps of facial hair, he could be about sixteen. Last week, he told me he's usually tending the village's sheep and goats in the upper pasture several hours away. I watch him for a minute while he orders the younger kids around until I realize Malalai has disappeared. Scanning the houses, I finally catch sight of her half hidden behind the village's one tree and head toward her. I smile and wave, but she's in a deep sulk.

"*Ta tsanga yei?*" I hope I'm saying 'How are you?' in Pashto instead of the Dari greeting I offered last time. The kids roared with laughter—the *Amrikâyëy* was mangling their language. Thanks to my college roommate and best friend Darya, I speak pretty good Dari. I can hear her now: *Someday you may visit my native country, and you must be able to speak the language.* But Pashto is what the people in this part of Afghanistan speak, and it's nothing like Dari.

Malalai starts toward me. For the first time, I notice the bruises on her cheek and around her eye. Purple and yellow, the colors fading. I'm positive she didn't have any bruises the last time we were here. My breath catches in my throat as I put the pieces together: a girl who keeps the camera from the boy who wants it. I have to work to tamp down my outrage at the man—or boy—who would do this to a little girl.

"You're hurt!" I say, reaching to touch her.

"*Na!*"

I'm not convinced. "*Har shay sam barâdar di?*" Is everything okay?

"*Ho!*" She brings her hand to her cheek, then looks behind her at one of the houses. A curtain drops back into place at the window. Something here is off. Only I can't figure out what. Malalai reaches forward and tugs at my hand. "*Lâr sha! Lâr sha!*" She stabs her finger in the direction of the Humvee. What? Running through my mental military handbook of Pashto phrases, I come up empty and shake my head. "*Zë në pohezham.*" I don't understand but want to cheer her up. So, I do something I never do because letting other people handle my gear can easily end up in a broken camera. I lift the Canon and offer it to her to take a picture. Maybe this will bring back the Malalai of last week.

"*Na!*" She shies away.

Someone has made sure she'll never take another photograph. I try what I hope is a safer route, and lifting my camera toward my face, I ask, "*Keday shi yaw aks ye wakhlam?*" My ability to speak Pashto is embarrassingly limited, but the first thing I made sure to learn: May I take your picture?

Malalai bites her lip, glances back toward the house, then braces her shoulders and nods. "*Ho.*"

That quick look stops me. I'm torn. I want to take her picture but don't want to get her in trouble. Again. *Just do it!* I tell myself. Take a shot or two, then let Malalai get back to her life here.

The perfect golden light from this morning is long gone. I'm dealing with dead, flat gray, and deep dark shadows. I meter and press the shutter. Then, I kneel in the sand and capture an image of her looking down at me—sharp features, a strong girl.

Unexpectedly, Malalai's eyes light up, and she kneels next to me. Using her index finger, she haltingly swirls letters in the sand, then looks at me. Through the viewfinder, I see the pleading in her eyes.

But I don't read Pashto at all, much less the word Malalai is scrawling. My finger freezes on the shutter. Malalai is writing. Pashtun girls in remote villages don't write. Under Taliban rule, they weren't allowed to learn to write or read. Education for girls still isn't allowed in many areas. But Malalai is most definitely writing.

I come up onto my feet and frame the shot: Malalai hunched over her letters. Her face tips up toward me. The word below her just visible. This time when I click the shutter, my fingers begin to tingle. The world drops away, and I'm in my moment, the place I feel best.

Fighting the darkening sky for some light, I shift my position. Malalai doesn't move an inch, but her eyes follow me. Another click of the shutter. This is the shot.

I'm moving a little closer to the tree, when I hear a *crack* in the distance. I snap the shot just as Malalai's left hand jerks into the air and she collapses facedown in the sand. Bright crimson begins to flow from her left temple, down her battered cheek. A second *crack*, and a bullet rockets into the tree next to me.

The camera slams against my chest as I dive to the ground. Then, rolling onto my side, I fling it over my shoulder and pull Malalai into my arms. Cupping my hand over the wound in a desperate attempt to staunch the blood, I feel the odd softness where her skull used to be.

The children's laughter dies. I imagine they freeze for a moment, then scramble out of the line of fire. The goats and chickens are scattering every which way, not sure where to run to save themselves.

You bastard! Take it back! Take your fucking bullet back! I want to scream at the gunman. I want to shake my fist at the universe, at the God who let this happen. But instead, I hum notes to a song that has yet to be written. As if that could make a difference.

All this in the space of a few seconds.

A third gunshot screams past my head. Hell, those first two bullets were meant for me. My arms tremble. My heart pounds against my ribcage. I'm completely exposed out here, but I can't move. And Malalai. I've got to hold onto this little girl. I've got to save her.

Lopez. Lopez trained as a medic. If I could just get her to the Humvee. I move my head a little and look. Too far. Too open. We'll never make it.

But the tree. It's just a few feet behind me. I cradle Malalai tight against me. Digging my heels into the sand, I try to push us to the far side of the tree. Some shelter at least. But I can't do it—she's dead weight. Then, she's sliding out of my arms, onto the sand, her head lolling at an impossible angle. I try to pull her closer, but I can barely move her.

"NO!" A scream slices through the thickening air. My scream.

God, oh God, no. She can't be dead. Not Malalai. I can't let this happen. Closing my eyes, I try to think but come up empty. Damn it all, why did we come here today—of all days? Why did I take her picture? I knew something was off. Is that why they shot her? Because of me taking some pics?

Then comes a fourth shot. A fifth. A hail of bullets. Too many to count. The roar of gunfire pounds into my ears.

The firefight lasts a lifetime and is over in five minutes.

Then silence. A silence as loud as the shooting. I don't know what it means, what I should do.

A wail cuts through the thick quiet. Not me this time. Malalai's mother? Then comes the sound of a slap against flesh, echoing across the open space like a gunshot. The keening stops as suddenly as it began.

I've got to get back to the Humvee. To Lopez and Murphy. Away from Khakwali. Murphy can get us out of here, back to the base. I just need to get to the Humvee.

Right. These pieces of shit probably have me surrounded. A pretty simple equation: I move, I die.

Get in the zone, my cross-country coach says from across the years.

Zone? There's no time to get in the zone. Pretty damn soon, one of those shooters will come out and finish things. Finish me.

Breathe! Use your anger. Don't let it defeat you.

Hey, Murphy. Lopez. I call silently, willing them to hear my thoughts. *I'm alive out here.*

Nothing. Maybe they think I'm already dead. Maybe everyone thinks I'm dead.

Element of surprise. They won't be looking for a dead woman to sprint to the Humvee.

Do it! I tell myself. *Get up and run!* No. I may be cross-country slender, but I'm tall. An easy target. Imagining my sprint to the Humvee, all I can see is a hail of bullets, my hands shot off, my body bleeding out in the sand.

In the roar of the silence, I hear a faint *splat.* Then another. Footsteps? I breathe deep, ready to pummel the shooter with my camera. Something pings my leg. Not a bullet. Another sharp ping on my hand. Wet. Then the sky, black as night, opens and the rain pours down. Rain? In the middle of the dry season? Un-frigging-believable. It's so heavy, I can barely see the houses. I can't see the Humvee at all. Sheets of water. A total monsoon.

And maybe, just maybe, the shooters can't see me.

I'm on my feet, a split second to find my balance, and then I'm running flat out toward where the Humvee should be. Except that with each stride, my military boots plunge deep into the wet sand that sucks hard, not wanting to let go. I fight for each step. *Zig*, I tell myself. *Zag. Keep it random. And don't fall over what's left of the wall.* The rain pelts my face, making it impossible to see where I'm going. More gunshots. Too late, I realize that Murphy and Lopez won't be able to tell who I am. They'll think I'm an insurgent and shoot me. The Humvee looms in front of me. Sliding feetfirst under the tailgate, I furrow through the sand right past Lopez.

I lie next to him, struggling to catch my breath. Then, I look. He's not moving, not breathing. My heart clenches. Oh, God. The bullets have cut him nearly in half. Just below his armored vest. Sweet, polite Lopez, who always, without fail, reminded me to put on my flak jacket. Taking a deep breath, I feel for where his carotid should be. My fingers climb up and down his rain-slicked neck while I pray to find a pulse. Then, after another look at his shot-to-hell body, I pray I won't.

I don't.

Lopez. Dead.

Where the hell is Murphy? I've got to find him, and we've got to haul ass out of here. "Murphy?" I call as loud as I dare, hoping he can hear me over the thundering rain. No response. I ease out from under the Humvee and belly crawl along the sheltering side of the vehicle, the camera thumping against my back as I go.

"Murphy?" *Answer me!*

I find him slumped over the steering wheel. "Oh, God, Murphy. Not you, too." But then I see his eyes are open, watching me. "You're alive! They got Lopez. Look, we've got to get the hell out of here."

"Can't."

I get to my feet and run my eyes the length of his contorted body, down to the floor of the Humvee. Sloshing with rainwater and—blood. Murphy's blood. Holy shit. I look back at his face, lock eyes with him.

"Down," he says.

Dropping to my knees, I search my pockets for anything I can use as a tourniquet. And come up empty. My camera strap. I pull at it but can't get the end through the eyelet. Too wet and slippery to unbuckle. "Tell me what to do!"

"Take. Picture." He can barely get the words out.

"No, that's not how we're playing this. I'm getting you out of here. So, shut up and tell me what to do!"

"Ma'am." I have the weirdest feeling he'd salute if he could. "Can't. Sorry." His voice is so weak. I strain to hear him over the pounding of the rain on the Humvee roof.

He reaches for my hand and holds on tight. "Cold." Then he smiles—he frigging smiles. "Annie, ma'am. You think. Maybe me and you. Could've—"

I squeeze his hand. There's absolutely nothing I can do except agree with him for once. "Yeah, Marine, I think we could have." I stay kneeling next to the Humvee, until Murphy's hand slips from mine.

There's no point feeling for a pulse, but I hold my fingers to the side of his neck anyway.

"Dead," I say out loud. Now what? I'm soaking wet and scared and angry. Those fuckers out there want me dead. Somehow, I've got to get out of here before they come looking for me. Right. I've got two dead Marines, a Humvee that's sunk up to its wheel rims in wet sand, and a minefield of IEDs between me and the base.

"Damn it, Murphy. Why? Why today of all days?" Murphy's lifeless eyes stare back at me. "You had orders." And now, I'm stuck here waiting to die. I wipe the rain off my face. Or maybe it's tears. Then, I punch my fist against the side of the Humvee as hard as I can. Again, and again. Until my hand aches.

"Stop it!" I hiss. "Find a weapon, the key to the Humvee." No key in the ignition. Steeling myself, I search Murphy's pockets. Then, closing my eyes and holding my breath, I drag my fingers through the trough of his blood. "Murphy! Where did you put the key?"

I don't see his rifle either. But I grab his Beretta from the passenger seat and check the clip. Empty. Still, it's a gun. Maybe I can use it to bluff my way out of this mess. Or get myself shot.

I sit in the sand, huddled next to the Humvee, and stare at the mud-brick houses. What looks to be a woman in a periwinkle blue *burqa* stands in one of the nearby doorways. Her hand beckons. Peering through the rain, I try to decide if it really *is* a *burqa*. It's got to be—nothing else in Afghanistan is that color. But is it really a woman?

The hand beckons again, the gestures bigger, more demanding.

Then suddenly, whoever is wearing the *burqa* is running through the sheets of rain to the Humvee. My fingers curl tightly around Murphy's gun.

A woman's hand, callused, the nails embedded with dirt, grabs my wrist. Her other hand covers her heart. "*Anaa,*" she says softly. "Malalai."

"*Anaa.*" I repeat the word. Grandmother. Malalai's grandmother. I met her the first time we were here. She smiled at me and held my hand because I let Malalai use the Polaroid—which made the girl so happy. Oh God, Malalai. "*Bakhshana ghwârëm.*" I'm so sorry. Hoping that's what I said, I look through the netted eyepiece of the *burqa* into green eyes—just like her granddaughter's. Young eyes, determined. This *anaa* is like many Pashtun grandmothers—barely pushing forty.

One sharp nod, the woman taps her chest, then rattles off a string of angry-sounding words I can't begin to understand. Of course she's upset. Her granddaughter's just been killed. And even though I didn't pull the trigger, it was my finger on the shutter.

I shake my head. "Na. Zë në pohezham."

She points back toward her house, then pulls at my wrist.

Oh my God. Does she seriously think I'll go to her house so she can turn me over to whoever shot Malalai? I mean to say "*na*," but "*ho*" comes out of my mouth instead. What am I thinking? What I'm thinking is I don't have a whole lot of options. I jam Murphy's gun into my jacket pocket and take off after the woman, trying hard to run my zigzag pattern through the rain. But the sand is winning again, sucking my boots up to my ankles and holding fast. It takes all my strength to cross the open yard to her house.

Anaa slows as she approaches Malalai's crumpled body. A quick touch—a promise to return—and then she's running again, past her house, around to the back. She keeps going. One more minute, and I spot another house—very small. When we get closer, I see it's not a house at all, but a crumbling hut the goats and chickens use as a stable. With the roof partly caved in, it's not much of a shelter. I crawl in among the animals, breathe in the cesspool of mud and animal excrement, and gag. In the far corner, I find a small pile of wet, moldering straw, then my legs give out.

Malalai's grandmother comes closer and pushes her *burqa* to the back of her head. I study her face, a tiny crescent moon and stars tattooed around eyes swollen from crying. I hear Darya telling me about the old days when Pashtun grandmothers tattooed their pretty granddaughters to protect them from evil spirits. Or from men who might be tempted to have their way with a girl too pretty for her own good. Then, the Taliban banned tattooing.

She raises her hand. I flinch, ready for her to hit me. But instead, her fingers gently comb my wet hair away from my face. "*Khäesta*," she says softly.

"*Khäesta*." I know that word. Pretty.

Her fingers continue combing my hair. "*Weshtë*," she says.

"*Weshtë*." I repeat. Hair!

"*Ho!*" She smiles and cups her hand to my cheek. Then, lifting her index finger to her lips as if in promise to keep my presence here a secret, she pulls her *burqa* back over her head and steals out of the stable.

No, I want to say, *don't leave me*. But she's gone.

I huddle as far back in the corner as I can, away from the water cascading through the hole in the roof, and try to steal some warmth from the goats pressing against me. I can't hear a thing over the pounding of the rain and the bleating of unhappy animals. No sucking of footsteps. No loading of guns. No pulling of triggers. For a little while, I let myself believe *Anaa* won't tell anyone where I am. But then I realize she doesn't have to. Every single person in Khakwali knows, and they know I'm stuck here with nowhere to go. They'll wait for the rain to stop. Then, they'll come for me.

And do what? asks the frightened voice I'm doing my best to quash. *Kill me? Or rape me first, then kill me?*

Maybe I'm more valuable to them alive.

Right. Then why have three journalists been killed so far this year?

"I don't know," I whisper. "Why is anyone dying?"

I picture two Marines, navy blue dress jackets, white slacks with knife pleats, standing at our front door in Wisconsin. My husband, Todd, opens the door. Realizing why they've come, he staggers against the jamb. Why are they there? Because I'm a hostage? Or because I'm dead? What the hell does it matter. Either way, he'll suffer.

There's no way I could've known this would happen, I say to the Todd of my imagination, my teeth chattering from the cold, from my fear of what's going to come.

I knew. We both knew.

"Okay, you're right. Something like this is always possible," I whisper as a goat licks the side of my face. "Oh hell, I'm sorry, Todd, but I still would've come. I had to."

How the hell could you do this to Emmy? Six years old, and you've condemned her to grow up without her mother.

Oh, God. Emmy.

I shut down the conversation with Todd before it saps all my strength. The goat stops licking me and starts nibbling the camera strap. I push him away, but he's back a minute later. Another push. Harder this time. Then, I pull the camera over my head and get my first good look at it. The lens is at a sickening angle. The glass shattered. With any luck, the SD card is salvageable. I pop it out of the slot and slip it into the front pocket of my sodden camo pants.

Damn, it's cold. I rub my arms and lean against the goats, desperate for warmth. One of them ducks its head under my arm. I work my fingers deep into the springy hair all the way to its skin. Warm. But I still can't stop shivering.

My eyelids drift shut.

I. Just. Want. To. Sleep.

The goat is nibbling my hair, nosing me back to consciousness. I push it away, and vowing to stay awake, I pull Murphy's gun from my pocket and take aim at the darkening gap in the wall.

Hours must be passing. I check my watch. Too dark to see, and the dial won't illuminate. Dark. Maybe I could sneak out of this godforsaken village. And go where? Out into the desert with all those IEDs buried in the sand? Step on one, and my body parts will go sailing out every which way. Or stay here, waiting for the assholes who shot up Murphy and Lopez and Malalai to kill me, too? I'm too cold, too tired to think straight. So tired, I'm almost ready to give in to whatever's going to happen. I close my eyes and doze. My dreams are full of bullets and Taliban insurgents and leave me fighting to wake up.

Then, suddenly, I *am* awake. On high alert. The skin on the back of my neck prickles. Each hair stands on end, rigid. People are near the stable. Their voices carry over the spattering of the rain. Their footsteps suck in the wet sand.

My hands tremble as I clutch the gun, training it on the night. But no one comes.

A LIFETIME LATER, I WAKE up again. A goat butts my shoulder. Eyes still closed, mind not yet in gear, I swat at him, then open my eyes to total darkness. No bleating. No rain drumming overhead or splashing in front of me. Just my blood pounding in my ears.

Behind me, a faint rustle. One of the goats, eating some hay. I reach for him, more to reassure myself than anything else. A hand snakes around my neck and clamps down hard over my mouth. An arm holds me tight.

Fuck! This is it.

I buck against the body behind me, kicking out as hard as I can. Pulling one hand free, I scrabble through the straw for Murphy's gun.

Gone. I go slack, then twist with all the strength I can muster, trying to wrench away from the arm holding me. They're not going to take me. Not like this.

He tightens his hold. "Don't scream!" the voice breathes in my ear. A man's voice speaking English, American English, with a Boston accent. "I'm Commander Finn Cerelli, U.S. Navy SEAL, and I'm going to get you out of here. Are you with me?"

Still trembling, I nod. He takes his hand off my mouth, and I try to imitate his barely audible whisper. "Murphy and Lopez—"

He puts a finger to my lips and breathes into my ear. "Questions later, ma'am. Right now, we've got about two minutes before all hell breaks loose. Can you run?"

"Yeah." If you call wading knee-deep through the quicksand out there *running*.

"Then let's get the hell out of Dodge." His hands find mine and pull me to my feet.

We're off. This is cross-country at its worst. Cerelli sets a mean pace, but I'm right with him. I've run my whole life—5Ks, 10Ks. Preferably not in boots packing ten pounds of wet sand. Not to mention wet camo pants that are chafing my thighs raw and this damn flak jacket.

We're maybe a mile from Khakwali when an explosion lights up the sky. A few minutes later, a group of men surrounds us, all of them bearded and dressed like Taliban, except for the night vision goggles. I grab Cerelli's arm. That's when I notice he's dressed like them—a big overcoat, tunic, baggy pants, and brown *pakol*. How could I have missed that?

"Not to worry," he whispers. "This is my team." He turns to the man in the lead. "Any trouble?"

"Smooth as twenty-year-old scotch. Sawyer blew the Humvee."

"Just how much C-4 did you use, Chief?" Cerelli asks.

"You know how it is, Commander," says one of the biggest men I've ever seen. "I had one chance and wanted to make sure it blew."

"It did," says Cerelli. "Half of Kandahar probably knows we're here."

I shuffle my feet, desperate to get back on the trail and put more distance between us and Khakwali.

"We got the remains," says another one of the men somberly.

The remains. Murphy and Lopez. I look past Cerelli and see the body bags slung fireman-style over two SEAL shoulders. This is too fucking real. I blink back the tears that are threatening. They're really dead. Because the CO assigned us to win hearts and minds. Because Murphy wanted to make me happy. Because even though I knew something was wrong, I went ahead and took Malalai's picture. I swallow a sob and wipe away a tear.

Cerelli's hand is on my shoulder. "No time for crying, ma'am."

"Sorry."

A moment later, we're back on the trail, the same pace as before. This time, the other men are up front and Cerelli is behind me, bringing up the rear. I keep up, but how the hell are these guys able to shoulder Murphy and Lopez? They are—they were—big guys.

We've run maybe three miles when the point man stops, his hand in the air. In front of me the others drop to a knee. Cerelli pushes me down. No one says a word. Far up the trail, I can just make out a line of dark shadows moving single file across our path.

It must be a half hour later, long after the last of the shadows have disappeared, when the point man stands and motions us forward. I rise from my crouch, knees and ankles screaming in protest, then force myself into a jog to keep up with the man in

front of me. We run until my lungs burn. We run until the hand at
the front of the line goes up again, and we all freeze in place.

The guys scan the eastern horizon where the dark of night
is quickly fading to gray. Then I hear it, too—the *thwamping* of
helicopter rotors. A few minutes later, there it is, coming to ground
fifty yards in front of us, showering us with hard grains of sand. As
soon as the chopper lands, the men move fast, gently loading the
body bags containing Murphy and Lopez. A dust-off, in military-
speak: land, load, and take off as fast as possible. A minute, two, max.

Cerelli boosts me aboard and hands me my camera. Trashed.
"You're good to go," he calls to the pilots, making a circle above his
head with his index finger.

"Commander, you and your team, too, sir!" one of the pilots
yells back. "You're coming out. Orders."

Fury flashes across Cerelli's face as he climbs into the chopper,
followed by the rest of the men. "Then, let's get the hell out of here,"
Cerelli yells to the pilots. "We ran across some tangos a few klicks
back."

As we lift into the air, Sawyer and one of the other guys take
up positions by the open doors, weapons at the ready as they
scan the ground. Both men have traded their *pakols* for helmets,
their Taliban coats for camo jackets and flak vests. The helicopter
moves fast away from the extraction point. The pilots are kicking
ass to get across the border to Pakistan, or someplace safer, before
sunrise.

My eyes lock on Sawyer's. Damn, if the helicopter shifts at all,
he'll go sailing out into thin air, and it's a long way down. The last
thing I want is another casualty on my tab.

"No worries." Sawyer grins and fist-bumps the SEAL across
from him. "Centrifugal force. We're not going anywhere."

Cerelli turns to me. "You all right, ma'am?" His anger seems to have dissipated.

"Annie. Please. And I'm okay. Cold, but okay."

He doesn't look away. "Annie. I apologize. I should have blanketed you up back there, but you seemed good to go. You did great by the way." He drapes his heavy coat over my shoulders.

"What happens now?" I ask.

"USS *Bataan*, North Arabian Sea." Cerelli leans his head back against the fuselage. "A debriefing. You'll probably be in for a long day."

"Debriefing?"

"Standard procedure when Marines die, ma'am." He closes his eyes.

"Malalai died in that village, too," I whisper. With the roar of the chopper, I'm not sure he hears me. But my thoughts pound loudly in my head. Malalai died. *Malalai died.* I shiver. And *Anaa.* Oh, God. What are they going to do to her when they discover I've gone?

I pull the coat around me—the smells of sweat and musk, tobacco and male are overpowering. Cerelli has probably been wearing this coat every day since he's been in-country. I sneak another look at his long, stringy, dark hair and full beard. He looks as filthy and exhausted as I am. I study the planes of his face, his patrician nose, and the complex emotions playing across his face even as he sleeps. Anger. Frustration. Grief. And wish my camera were intact—I'd like to photograph him.

Turning away, I pull my knees to my chest and tent his heavy coat around me. But it doesn't do much to block out the cold. I pat the still-wet pockets of my camo pants to make sure the SD card is there. Yesterday's images of Malalai. A few pics of children from other villages and my Marines. All the other images are on cards in my pack—now incinerated by Sawyer's C-4 mega-explosion—or back at the base.

Malalai *dead*. Lopez *dead*. Murphy *dead*. I get to live. How can anyone's God call that just? Anger seethes inside me, wrapping tightly around my heart. I bury my face against my knees and whisper to Malalai: "I'll come back. I promise. And next time, I'll bring enough cameras for all the kids to have one."

2

Bay View, Wisconsin – May 2015

WHEN THE UBER DRIVER STOPS in front of my duplex, I see lights on in the second story. It should be dark. Mel, I assume— my fifteen-year-old daughter who insists she's outgrown the name 'Emmy,' short for Emmeline. Todd and I have joint custody, but given my insane travel schedule, she lives mostly with him. She likes to help herself to my apartment—the no-boys-allowed rule notwithstanding—when she isn't getting along with Todd or, more often, her stepmother Catherine Elizabeth.

I drop my old, faded and fraying USMC duffel, stuffed with dirty laundry, onto the front porch and ring the bell. Bonita, my downstairs tenant and good friend who makes my crazy life possible, answers immediately. Finn, the black lab we share, charges past her. He runs around me in ever-tightening circles, until he stops abruptly, stands on his hind legs, and wraps his front legs around my waist. The full weight of his overfed body leans against me until I almost lose my balance. I rub his ears and kiss his offered nose. We go through this every time I come home from an assignment, and I choose to believe he's overjoyed to see me. But I know he's just as happy with Bonita. Probably happier, because she comes home every day. She's reliable.

Three oversized Pelican cases are stacked just inside Bonita's door, CANON and FRAGILE labels plastered on each. Twenty-four Canon Rebels nestled in foam, a printer, and a laptop—ready to accompany me to Afghanistan.

"Welcome home," says Bonita.

I smile and nod at the cases. "I see Canon came through."

"You're leaving next week?"

"Right after Mel's dance recital."

Bonita raises an eyebrow. "It's been rescheduled—three weeks from now."

"You've got to be kidding."

"There was a fire at the theater on the UWM campus—right after the girls' dress rehearsal."

My breath catches in my throat. "Mel? Is she okay?"

"Mel's fine. Nothing to worry about. It happened in the middle of the night. No one was there."

I exhale.

"Anyway, they had to move the performance. And reschedule. Let her tell you about it."

Oh, God. I promised I'd go. No matter what. Because over the years, I've missed just about every important event in my daughter's life. But this new date puts the recital right in the middle of my trip to Afghanistan.

A solid thump overhead. I glance toward the ceiling.

"She showed up a few hours ago and checked in with me, just like she's supposed to."

"She's alone?" I hope.

Bonita shakes her head. "But you didn't hear it from me."

Damn. So much for the no-boys-allowed rule. I take a deep, steadying breath. Then, leaving my duffel on the front porch, I unlock the door to my second-story apartment and trudge up the steep staircase, my backpack of camera gear about to dislocate my shoulder. Finn presses against me as we climb, making sure I stay put at least for tonight. I hear the grating squeal of the back door's rusting hinges. Finn pricks up his ears.

At the top of the stairs, the door flies open, and the faint smell of marijuana wafts out. A second later, Mel, her long hair a rumpled mass of purple, bursts onto the landing. "Mom!" Her smile is just a millimeter too wide.

"You were expecting someone else?"

Finn bolts ahead of me and disappears into the apartment.

When I get to the landing, she slides my pack off my aching shoulder and carries it inside. "You must be so tired." She bounds down the stairs to retrieve my duffel. Making nice. Or trying to delay the inevitable. A few seconds later, she's back, setting my duffel on the floor just inside the door.

"I missed you, Mom." She dances into my arms and nestles against me, her head on my shoulder.

"I missed you too, sweetie," I whisper, tightening my hold, wondering when she got to be as tall as I am. My fingers comb her purple hair away from her face, smoothing it into place. "Love the color."

"Really? Daddy hates it. So does C.E." She sounds pleased and twirls halfway across the room so I can better appreciate her purpleness.

Finn trots back into the room, a Milwaukee Brewers baseball

cap in his mouth which he dutifully drops at my feet. The three of us stare down at the bright blue cap with the scrolled white and gold M. I debate whether to focus first on the marijuana or the boy. I opt for the boy.

I pick up the cap. "What's his name?"

"What do you mean? That's mine."

"Really? You hate baseball."

"So? Oh, whatever." She grabs the cap and tosses it back to Finn, who accepts the offering, lies down at my feet, and starts to chew. "Chance. His name is Chance."

"Tell me about him."

"Why?"

"Because I'm your mother, and I'd like to know."

She shrugs. "We . . . uh . . . go to school together. He's a senior, and he likes me."

Oh, daughter-of-mine, he likes you, but how do you feel about him? "What were you and Chance doing here?"

"You know, hanging out."

"Mel, your shirt's on inside out."

"I like wearing it like this."

Clearly, she's going to make me *ask the question*. "Are you sleeping with him?" I say it quietly, hoping that will somehow soften what I've just said.

It doesn't.

She plants her fists on her slender dancer's waist and yells, "I *told* you we were just hanging out! But no—you think I'm screwing my brains out! Why can't you trust me?"

"Maybe because you seem to have forgotten that we have a rule. Remember? No boys allowed." I trace my index finger down the exposed side seam of her shirt.

"But we weren't *doing* anything. Chance wouldn't—he's a great guy."

"He's an eighteen-year-old boy." With hormones.

"Yeah. So?" She grins. "You'll like him, Mom. He'll be at my recital. Oh, and by the way, there was a fire at the UWM theater. I was so stoked to dance there. But anyway, our director was able to book us at the high school, only—" She stares at me, narrowing her eyes as if she knows what I'm about to say. Of course, she does. It's been the story of her life. TNN calls, and I drop everything to fly off to photograph another conflict.

I take a deep breath. "Sweetie—"

She holds up her hand. "Don't say it! You *will* be there. You promised!"

I hate myself for the hurt I see in her eyes. "Look, you know I arranged my schedule so I could be there. But I didn't expect the date to change."

Chin quivering, she stamps her foot. "NO! You swore. No matter what."

And this definitely qualifies as 'no matter what.'

I reach for her. "Let me explain."

She slides away from me. "Explain what?"

I lower my voice, do my best to stay calm. "This is the photography workshop at Auntie Dar's school. Remember? Sweetie, we've been planning this—"

"How could I possibly forget?" she sneers. "You made some stupid promise to *Malalai*. Obviously, you love a dead girl more than me. God, you always have some lame excuse." Sounding aggrieved and betrayed and furious, she stomps into the back bedroom and slams the door.

I wince. As her absentee mother who flies in to see her for a few days, a week, between assignments, how the hell am I going to fix this? Or convince her to stop sleeping with Chance? Then there's the marijuana. Not only illegal, but it's stinking up the apartment. I can't wait to start in on that.

Finn looks up at me, his eyes letting me know what he thinks of my role in Mel's eruption. Rebuke given, he goes back to eating his way through the Brewers cap. I should do something. Talk to her. Rescue the baseball cap before it clogs up Finn's GI system. But after forty-eight hours of traveling home from Chibok, Nigeria, I'm too exhausted to do more than sleep. Except, Darya will be Skyping any minute to make sure we're good to go, as soon as she can get a connection in Kabul. I pull my laptop out of my pack and set it up on the coffee table. Then, I open every window in the living room and kitchen. Chilly, but I've got to air out the place. I pour three fingers of Wild Turkey into a glass and finally let myself sink into the too-soft cushions of my ratty old sofa.

And wait. And remember.

Eight years ago. That's when Darya and Tariq and Seema came to Milwaukee for a surprise visit. To celebrate my birthday, I thought. I was wrong. They came so Darya, my best and oldest friend, could break the news to me.

"DARYA, YOU CAN'T BE SERIOUS! Good God, Seema's only nine years old. You're moving her to Afghanistan?"

"Yes," said Darya, her voice taut as she beat the batter of my favorite apple-walnut *roat* so hard it was running the risk of separating. "That's exactly what we're doing."

"Why the hell are you doing this? It makes no sense."

"What part don't you understand? Tariq and I want to help rebuild our country. And that has to be done from the inside. By Afghans. I'm going to open a secondary school for girls which will give them a chance for an education, help them learn to think for themselves and become real citizens of the twenty-first century. It's that simple."

"Come on, Dar. It's not that simple, and you know it. In case you've forgotten, I've been to Afghanistan, and it's frigging dangerous there."

She didn't back down. "Give me some credit, please, for knowing what's going on. Yes, parts of the country are still dangerous, but the Panjshir Valley is relatively safe. Probably safer than parts of Milwaukee."

"Don't give me that! Last time I looked, there weren't very many IEDs in Milwaukee. Or Taliban. Anyway, what about your work with the UNHCR? *That's* having an impact all around the world. You're helping a lot more people than you'll ever reach in one Afghan village."

Darya shook her head. "You know as well as I do that my work with the UN is transitory at best. We fly in for a few days, poke around, fly home, and make recommendations that often go nowhere."

I wanted to protest, to say it wasn't so. But it *was* true. The times I'd gone along as the photog on fact-finding missions with her, that's exactly what happened. And any recommendations we made got bogged down in bureaucratic red tape. Still, I wasn't about to acknowledge that truth. Instead, I asked, "What about Tariq? You mean to tell me he's giving up his job at Mass General?"

"He already has. He's going to work at the local clinic."

I was dizzy at the thought. Tariq was a brilliant surgeon. And he was giving up his career? So Dar could start up a high school for girls? What the hell would he be doing at a small, backwater clinic that could possibly keep him fulfilled?

"And Seema?" I asked, knowing damn well that the girl I loved second only to my own daughter wouldn't be happy about this move. She was all about school and movies and writing plays where princes rescue princesses. A little girl living a fairy-tale life in the U.S. Moving to Afghanistan would rock her world. And not in a good way.

Darya scoffed. "Of course, she's coming with us. This will be good for her. She needs to learn about the larger world—not just books and movies—but her culture, her heritage. And she'll see how girls in some countries struggle just to get an education. It's not good for her to think she can have everything she wants at the snap of her fingers."

It was insane. Dar was the poster girl for immigrants to the U.S. From almost the moment she'd walked into our dorm room the first day of freshman year, she'd made it clear she was American, that she no longer considered herself Afghan and had no interest in going back. Ever. Hell, she even told me she wouldn't date any guys from the old country. And then all of a sudden, she and Tariq were moving back there? What were they thinking?

But, of course, it wasn't sudden. A human rights attorney for the United Nations, Dar never did anything without thinking it through. To the very last detail. As it turned out, she'd been in Pakistan—Islamabad—for a meeting. From there, she'd flown to Kabul and on to the Panjshir Valley to scout the terrain.

She'd found what she was looking for in the sleepy village of Wad Qol.

"A Shangri-La," Darya said. "Really, it's amazingly safe. Tourists even go to the valley to ski. We'll be doing good work. We'll be making a difference. Please, Annie? This is something we have to do. I need to know that you support me."

My heart was thudding in my chest. I hated the idea of Darya moving halfway around the world. But she was still my best friend. "Of course I support you."

"Thank you. And you'll come to visit, won't you? I'm depending on that. Plus," she smiled coyly, "this will be the perfect opportunity for you to make good on your vow to Malalai. You can come teach a photography workshop at the school."

In the end, after a long and stressful weekend of arguing, I caved. Of course, I supported her. She was and still is my best friend. How could I not? Besides, I truly believe the only way to a peaceful future is by making sure girls get an education. From the pictures she showed me, the building she'd bought wasn't a complete wreck, but pretty close. So, I helped, taking money from my personal account for a roof and windows. Then more for tables and chairs. Books. A steady flow of cash that Dar and I kept strictly between us. It wasn't something I wanted Todd to know.

NOW, I'M FINALLY GOING TO see this miracle of a school Darya created. And make good on my promise to Malalai. Am I as crazy as Dar? Stretched out on the sofa next to me, Finn snores like a Mack truck, but even that's not enough to keep me awake.

Sometime later, I swim to consciousness through a riptide of gray fuzziness. Finn is licking my face, the smell of doggie breath overwhelming. I don't know how long I've been asleep, but not long enough. When I'm on assignment, I can wake up on a dime, even after forty-eight hours of no sleep. But now, home, I just want to sink back into oblivion.

Except that confounded *bing-bong-bong-burble* sound won't let me.

My eyes fly open. Skype. Darya.

I push myself upright in front of my laptop and answer her call. Finn curls up next to me, his head in my lap. A moment later, Dar's on the screen. The periwinkle headscarf she's draped loosely over her hair takes me back to 2006. This was the color of the *burqas* I saw everywhere. But seeing Dar in it throws me. Since moving back to Afghanistan, she's been dressing more modestly, wearing a headscarf, but I know she doesn't like it. So, why the hell is she wearing it inside?

"I was beginning to think you weren't going to answer." Darya peers over her shoulder as if someone might be listening and tugs at the edge of the scarf, pulling it forward a fraction of an inch to hide more of her hair. She's at her *Hama* Bibi's apartment in Kabul where the internet reception is more reliable.

"Sorry. I fell asleep. It's been a long couple of days." I smile. "So, what's with the *hijab?*"

Darya sighs, then lowers her voice. "Lately, Uncle Omar has become more . . . let me say, extreme. In fact, he's almost fanatical. I think it began around the time he was elected to the National Assembly."

"What? I've met Uncle Omar, remember? He was hardly *fanatical.*"

"He is now."

"What happened?"

"I'm sure it's to appeal to his constituency. And he wants *Hama* Bibi to wear a *burqa.*"

"Seriously?" *Hama* Bibi is one of the most progressive women in Kabul, a professor at Kabul University, and last I knew, would never wear the *burqa*.

"She hasn't acquiesced, so things here are a bit tense. Uncle made it clear I am also to wear one while I'm here. This is my compromise."

"Even in the house?"

"Even in the house." I see the annoyance wash across her face. "You see, *Hama* Bibi is my father's sister, and Omar is her husband, so strictly speaking, he and I are not blood relations. But that's ridiculous. And he knows it. I realize I'm making things harder for Auntie because Uncle refuses to be in the same room with me and sometimes leaves for hours at a time. But there are some things I will not do."

When we were in college, Dar had told me, "There is nothing in the Qur'an that says women have to cover themselves, just that we should dress modestly. And, of course," she added firmly, "that goes for men, too." She's always been all about women working and fighting in the trenches with men. "Islam teaches that women are twin halves of men."

There's a sudden blip of static on the screen, reminding us we don't have much time before the satellite moves out of range.

She puts us back on track. "I think it might be better if you stay at a hotel rather than with my aunt and uncle."

"No worries. I'll make a reservation at the InterContinental." I don't want to deal with ultra-conservative Uncle Omar either.

Darya nods. "On to a better subject. All the girls at school and the teachers are excited about the workshop, although the lower girls aren't happy to be missing out. The upper-level girls have already put up some of your photographs. Of course, their favorite is the one of Malalai."

"Of course."

"Don't be like that, Annie. It's a stunning photograph, possibly your best. There's a reason why it won the Pulitzer, and you know it. No matter, the girls love it."

"And I appreciate that, Dar. I really do. But it's hard to be associated with just one image—as if it's the only thing I've ever done."

Darya's heard me complain about this before. She waves her hand in front of the screen. On to the next topic. "I want to make sure everything is set for your trip. No last-minute problems?"

A good question. I'm determined to keep the promise I made to Malalai so long ago. This workshop is going to happen. But at what price? Can I really see my way clear to miss the recital? After my no-matter-what promise to my daughter? Oh, hell. I take the plunge. "To be honest, something *has* come up. My schedule at this end has gotten totally screwed up. Mel—"

"Mom, no."

Startled, I look up from my laptop to see Mel standing a few feet away. She's been listening? Of course, she has; that's what fifteen-year-old girls do. A second later, she pushes Finn off the sofa and plops down next to me so Darya can see her, too. "Hey, Auntie Dar."

"Hello, Mel. Interesting hair color."

She fluffs her hair. "Thanks. So, how's Seema? Is she there?"

"She's at home in Wad Qol studying for graduation exams."

"There are high school *graduation exams*? For real?"

Darya smiles. "Indeed, there are."

Mel dismisses the exams with a major eye-roll. "Well, she can't be worried. She's got to be the smartest girl in the school. Probably in all of Afghanistan. Anyway. Look, Mom doesn't need to cancel.

I'll have lots more recitals. There's one next winter she can come to. Besides, Bonita always records them for her. It'd be crazy for her to cancel just to watch me dance for all of twenty minutes."

I shake my head. "Sweetie—"

"S'okay, Mom. Really. Those girls are expecting you. They're all excited, and besides, if you wait until next year, the senior girls will miss out."

Darya smiles. "That is very generous of you."

Mel combs her fingers through her long, purple hair. "That's it. I have spoken. Later." She waves, pushes herself off the sofa, then heads toward her room, Finn trotting alongside.

I turn back to the laptop. Dar looks perplexed. "Well?" she asks.

"I guess I'm good to go. I've got three cases of equipment from Canon. My tickets. An appointment with the Afghan consul to get my visa." I yawn. "In the meantime, I've got to catch up on some sleep."

"You had a rough trip?"

"Very rough. Nigeria. Chibok. Land of Boko Haram."

"A nasty group." She grimaces. I can see the concern in her eyes.

"Very nasty. But hey, don't worry about me. I'm fine." Maybe it's not me that has her worried. Wait, this is Dar. As I well know, even if she *is* worried, she never shows it. "So, what's going on?"

She waves away my question. "It's the end of the school year, which means a lot of paperwork. There are several grants I'm working on. And I am dealing with a very moody daughter."

"Seema? Moody? What's the problem?"

She shakes her head. "When I try to talk with her, she either explodes or gives me the silent treatment. It is most likely her exams. All the girls are nervous."

"Ah, the teenage years. A joy to live through them yet again." I grin and lift my eyes to heaven for some divine intervention. "Our reward for making it through the first time—we get to experience them again with our daughters."

Darya looks puzzled. "I don't recall acting like that when I was seventeen."

I laugh. "I'm sure you didn't. But I absolutely did. Most girls do."

"Not in Afghanistan. Would you do me a favor? Please talk to Seema while you're here. She has always trusted you. Maybe you can get her to open up and tell you what is bothering her."

"You bet."

"But enough of that. I am so happy that soon you will be here."

"I leave next weekend, which means I should get to Kabul the following Tuesday. But with travel in that part of the world being what it is, I'm more likely to arrive on Wednesday."

Darya smiles. "Tariq could drive down on Friday. How would you feel about spending a couple days in Kabul?"

"That would work. I can do some shopping on Chicken Street."

She frowns. "Ah, be careful—" And just that quickly, the satellite moves out of range. Darya's face pixilates into thousands of tiny bits of color which fade to a blank screen.

Looking up, I see my daughter is back. Listening. She smiles brightly. "So, what's going on with Seema?"

I shrug. "According to Auntie Dar, she's moody."

She wrinkles her brow. "What does that even mean?"

"Hormonal? Hell, I don't know, but she's taking it out on Darya."

"That's kinda weird. Not like Seema at all. I wonder if she's got a boyfriend."

I shake my head. "That's not a great idea in Afghanistan."

"Why not? It's not like Auntie Dar and Uncle Tariq would force her into some kind of arranged marriage or something."

"No, but Afghanistan is a very conservative country. The boyfriend-girlfriend thing is still very different over there. I'll talk to her."

"Like that'll help."

"Thanks for the vote of confidence." Another yawn, and I push myself off the sofa, ready to get to bed. "I'll see you in the morning."

"Wait, Mom. Your boots?"

"What?"

"Your boots. If I wore them in the house, you'd kill me."

I look down at my boots. And then to the front door. Sure enough, there's a trail of dirt pellets from the lug soles of my military-issue boots that I wear in the field. Not chic, but they've saved my toes more than once. I usually change out of them for the trip home, but my running shoes managed to disappear from my hotel room. "Snakes," I say, feeling the need to explain. "On this trip, I had to stomp on a lot of snakes."

3

I WAKE UP TO SUNLIGHT streaming through the window. It takes me a full minute to figure out where I am. Chibok? Lagos? London? New York? This is what I go through after every long assignment. Sometimes it takes a few days to catch up to where I am. Sometimes I don't find myself until just before I take off again. I roll over and lock my eyes on my favorite of all the black-and-white portraits I've made over the years, the one that's always beside my bed at home—Mel at age seven (back when she was still Emmy) and Seema at nine. Their shining eyes and laughing faces were utter perfection. Pure innocence. They had no idea their worlds were about to spin off their axes. That within a few months, Seema would be living on the other side of the world. That a few months after that, Todd and I would be heading to divorce court.

Noise in the kitchen rattles through my door. The Vitamix whirring. Finn's bark of approval. I swing my legs to the floor, make sure I'm decent, and go join the party.

Finn barks again, then catapults himself the length of the galley kitchen to lean against me.

"Hey you," I say, roughing his ears, "what's with abandoning me?"
Finn gazes at me with total adoration.

"It's almost noon, Mom. He had to go out." Mel swings around with a glass of Green Power in her hand. "Oh, and by the way, there wasn't anything here to eat, so Bonita and I went shopping. Want one?"

I take the drink and sip. God, I've missed these. "You make the best smoothies."

"I do a lot of things well," she says smugly.

Looking at her over the edge of my green-veggie-coated glass, I decide that I've done one thing right as a mother after all: my daughter definitely has a positive sense of self. I catch myself. I may have planted that seed, but it was her stepmother and her father who've nurtured that self at least as much as I have. Fuck it. I've done next to nothing except promise to be there for her and then break my promises.

I take another sip of Green Power. "Did you say noon? You sure that's right?"

"Yeah." She drags out the word. "So, Mom, about Chibok."

"What brought this up?" I say warily.

"I was listening last night when you told Auntie Dar you had a rough trip."

"Thanks for the privacy."

She sets down her glass. "Well, that's the only way I can find out where you go. It's not like you *tell* me."

She's right, of course. I don't tell her. Or Todd. Because I go to frigging dangerous places. And I've got this crazy idea that if they don't know, they'll worry less. Which is probably stupid on my part. Obviously, she wants to know. To buy time and figure out what to say, I take a long drink of my smoothie.

"That's where you went to stomp snakes?" she asks.

I nearly snort Green Power out my nose. "There were definitely snakes, literally and figuratively." I see the question on her face and stop. "Real snakes—nasty ones like puff adders, vipers, and my personal favorite, spitting cobras—and people—"

"I get it—a metaphor—people who act like snakes. Like Boko Haram."

I set the glass on the counter. "How do you know about Boko Haram?"

"There's this whole 'Bring Back Our Girls' thing on Facebook with profiles of the girls Boko Haram stole from that school." She holds up her phone. "Anyway, this morning I Googled you to see your pictures from Nigeria. This really great shot you took came up with a story about the girls. Ohmygod, Mom, those men are horrible, evil. They've killed so many people, and those poor girls—I mean—"

"Which is why we stayed as far away from Boko Haram as possible."

"So, what were you doing there?"

"Interviewing the girls' mothers, to see how they're coping." My mental video of our time in the village runs through my mind. "And it just so happened that while we were there, one of the girls escaped from the Boko Haram stronghold with her 'husband.'" I make exaggerated air quotes.

Mel's fingers dance across the screen of her iPhone until she finds the pic she wants. She enlarges the image and holds up the phone. My photograph of the girl returning to her village featured on the TNN web page.

I study the image, too small to convey the magnitude of that moment. I was photographing one of the mothers when an army jeep pulled up. The girl climbed out of the back seat, her baby in a cloth sling, all the while keeping an eye on the man standing next to her, the man claiming to be her husband. She said she'd been sent to gather firewood, her husband as her guard, and just kept walking, for days, until they walked out of the forest. That's when a patrol of soldiers found them.

"She married one of her captors? That's gross."

"It's not like she had a choice, sweetie. They 'married' her off. Sometimes the girls are given to rebels as a reward for bravery. Sometimes they sell the girls to raise money. What got to me was later, after the army took her husband away, she told me she missed him."

Her eyes widen. "How much?"

"How much did she miss him?"

She rolls her eyes. "How much do they charge for the girls?"

I stare at her, incredulous. I do *not* want to be talking to my daughter about this. But she's not backing down. Hell, maybe this is something she should know. "The last I heard, $165."

She turns away and walks to the sink.

Too much. I told her too much. I circle my arms around her, feel her stiffen for a moment, then relax. "It's okay, sweetie. You're safe."

"Those girls aren't. And, Mom, $165? That's less than my iPhone." She turns and leans her head against my shoulder. "What if something like that happens to Seema?"

"Seema hasn't been kidnapped."

"But it could happen. The Taliban are in Afghanistan, right?"

I hug her tighter. What has happened to this world that my fifteen-year-old daughter has to worry about such evil? I refuse to lie. "Yes, but not anywhere close to Wad Qol."

"Mom, this is serious." She pushes me away. "After you teach your course, you've got to bring her back. She could live here for the summer—until she leaves for college. We'll share my room. It'll be fun."

"And what would the two of you do?"

"Hang out. Go to Summerfest. The beach."

"And you're going to get around how? As I remember, Seema never took to the bicycle we got her."

"Well, uh, Dad's getting me a car for my birthday."

"He's *what?* You haven't even taken drivers ed yet. Is he paying for your insurance?" Well, shit. Todd couldn't have discussed this with me? So much for co-parenting. I bite my lower lip and remember to keep my daughter out of my disagreements with her father. But that doesn't keep me from adding lamely, "Don't forget, learner's permits have restrictions."

"Like I don't know that. The point is we could have fun. More fun than she's having in Afghanistan. If you'd get Netflix, we could watch movies."

Oh yes, Seema loves movies. Sappy teen romances were high on her list last time she and Dar visited. I wonder if I *could* convince Seema to come back with me. Something to think about.

Just then, a cacophonous noise erupts from Mel's phone. "No!" she groans. "It's C.E." A second later, she manages to sound completely pleasant. "Hi!"

"Emmy. Nice of you to finally answer." Catherine Elizabeth's fingernails-on-chalkboard voice ricochets around my kitchen. Mel must have pressed the speaker button. "Where are you? You said you couldn't go up to the lake with us because you have a paper due tomorrow. Your sisters were so disappointed, they begged to come home early, and, surprise, the house is empty."

Clearly, I'm not the only one who has trust issues with Mel, but I really don't like the tone Catherine Elizabeth's taking with my daughter. I'm about to say something when I remember that this woman has been raising Mel, without a whole lot of help from me. So, I cut her some slack.

Mel looks to me for help. I raise my eyebrows and shrug. *You're on your own, kid.* Then I lean against the counter and slowly savor my Green Power. Next to me, Finn cocks his head as if to say, *You're going to let her talk to our girl that way?*

"Sooorrryyy. I guess I turned off my phone." Mel sounds admirably contrite.

Lame, I mouth to her.

"We've talked about this before, Emmy. If it happens again, we'll confiscate your phone. So, where are you?"

"Okay. But see, yesterday, Chance asked me to go to the beach. After that, we got some burgers. Then, my mom got home, and I came over to her house, and we've sort of been talking."

I nearly choke as I listen to her version of last night's events. Is Catherine Elizabeth savvy enough to figure out the truth?

"Chance? Oh, good, I'm glad you're seeing him again. Are you with *her* now?"

'Her.' As in 'me.' Catherine Elizabeth prefers to ignore the biology of Mel's past.

"Yeah."

"I'd like to speak with her, please."

Mel hands me the phone. "Catherine Elizabeth, it's been a while." I steel myself and make a mental note to back up Mel as much as I can—without actually lying.

"Has Emmy been with you all night?"

So much for social niceties. "Why yes, she has."

"Oh, well, good." She sounds disappointed.

"If that's all—"

"No, there's one other thing. You never sent last month's support check—" I fumble with the phone for a couple seconds before I can turn off the speaker.

Trust Catherine Elizabeth to piss me off before I'm in the country for even twenty-four hours. I struggle to keep my voice civil. "By any chance is Todd there?"

"I keep the books in our family—"

"Is he there?"

I hear a muffled exchange, and then Todd is on the line. For Mel's sake, I press the speaker button again and tell him about the workshop at Darya's school.

"You're telling me now? How long have you and Darya been planning this?" he asks.

He's never going to understand a promise I made to a dead girl eight and a half years ago. So, I don't even try to explain. I just wait.

Finally, he asks, "What about Emmy's . . . dance thing?" Which makes me wonder if Catherine Elizabeth is prompting him.

Damn, he still knows how to push my buttons.

"She's okay with me going." I sneak a look at Mel, who's looking pretty satisfied with her sacrifice. I owe her big-time.

We listen to him breathing. I can almost hear his lungs shudder.

Another trip to a crazy, dangerous place. The Panjshir Valley may be safer than most parts of Afghanistan, but 'safe' is still relative. Anything could happen. Especially since I won't have my TNN crew with me. Or a fixer. Todd may or may not realize that. But he's not going to hear it from me. We've both made our choices. I chose TNN eight years ago, and he chose Catherine Elizabeth not long after that.

Finally, he speaks. "It's insane. But that never stopped you before. Even when we were married. I won't try talking you out of it."

Thank you. Thank you for not making a big deal out of this, especially with Mel listening. "Okay then. Just wanted to let you know."

"And Annie? Take care of yourself. Don't make me have to tell Mel you didn't make it."

"No worries."

I'm about to power off when I hear Catherine Elizabeth, her voice barely audible. "I can't believe she's skipping Emmy's recital again. You know as well as I do how disappointed she's going to be." Clearly not meant for my ears. Or maybe it was. With Catherine Elizabeth, you never know.

I put down the cell and catch the scared look in my daughter's eyes. "Look, sweetie, about what your dad said just now? Nothing's going to happen to me."

She picks up her glass of Green Power and tries hard to look blasé. "I *know* what you do, Mom, and it's okay. Just don't go getting yourself dead."

Dubai

ANOTHER DELAY.

A disembodied voice echoes throughout Concourse C at Dubai International Airport, speaking first in Arabic, then in French, and finally in English. "Attention, please! Gentlemen and ladies. We regret greatly to inform passengers that Emirates Flight 1385 to Kabul is delayed." I seriously doubt the 'regret greatly' part.

Hard to believe this is the fastest way to get to Afghanistan without going the military route. Just my luck, the first-class lounge is closed. I squirm on the ridiculously hard metal seat, trying to find a semi-comfortable position. Finally admitting defeat, I slouch down and prop my booted feet on one of the Pelican cases arrayed in front of me. A definite perk of flying first class is that there are no limits to carry-ons. Closing my eyes, I do my best to tune out my fellow passengers.

"It's like the third or fourth goddamn delay!" a woman nearby yells into her cell. "I don't care what you have to do, just get me on another flight."

I wince. Someone, please find this woman another flight.

"Well, if *you* can't do it, find someone who can."

"Buck up, Piera!" A man's voice. "We're all in the same jam. It'll get sorted."

That voice. I know that oh-so-proper Cambridge accent. Forward Operating Base Masum Ghar, November 2006. I open my eyes and scout the room as unobtrusively as possible. There he is—three rows behind me. Nic Parker Lowe. In the flesh. What did I do to piss off the airport gods?

He looks older—his face craggier in person than on TV. The man has done some hard living. The white at his temples looks good, though, distinguished. Back in the day, he was at the BBC. I wonder if he's still there. Odd that we haven't run into each other before now. Or lucky. He's definitely not someone I want to see again. Ever. I pull my black-checked *keffiyeh* forward to shield my face, tuck in my hair, and hope for the best.

But I can't tune out my memory. For eight and a half years, I've done my best to keep what happened during the embed at Masum Ghar buried deep inside me, so deep I could almost forget. Almost. Which has been the only way I could get on with my job. And my life. But hearing Nic's voice conjures up that day of the sandstorm. The day that set everything else in motion.

OH-SEVEN-HUNDRED. IN THE mess tent. The place was packed. U.S. Marines. Afghan military. Some Brits. Plus, a few journalists who'd won embed slots, like me—Dan, Josh, and the renowned Nic

Parker Lowe. But I was the only photog and the lone female. Even though I'd been working conflict zones as a stringer with the AP for years, as far as they were concerned, I was the new kid on the block. And they weren't about to let me forget it.

Dan was still holding forth when Nic pushed back his chair. "Well, lads, I'm off." A few minutes later, I was getting a refill on my coffee when I saw Dan and Josh head out. Something was up. I grabbed my pack and charged out of the mess. It took a minute, but finally I saw them by the Humvees. A Marine was standing next to the open driver's door.

I jogged over, but they acted like I wasn't there. "Hey!" I nudged Nic's arm as he opened the front passenger door. No way they were scooping me. If they were going off base to cover a story, hell, I was going with them.

Nic looked at the others. Josh shook his head. Dan shrugged.

"Look," said Nic, turning back to me, "we got wind of a spec op that's going down. We want to get something before the military sanitizes the bloody hell out of it."

"Are you frigging crazy? You're going out there without an escort?"

"We've got the corporal here. He's armed." Nic's hand wandered down my back, found its way to my butt, and fondled me in a slow grope. I slapped it away. God, what an asshole! Dangerous or not, I wasn't passing up a chance for some authentic shots. I yanked open the rear door and climbed into the Humvee. It didn't take much for the corporal to talk his way past the guards, and then we were outside the wire.

It was a miserable ride. The road was unpaved and deeply rutted, and the corporal drove way too fast. I wanted to ask where we were going, but the tension was palpable, so I kept my questions to myself.

Finally, Josh asked, "How far are we going?"

The corporal didn't say a word. It was Nic who answered, "Not too much farther."

A few minutes later, the wind picked up and sand started pelting the vehicle. Another kilometer, and the Humvee swerved sideways, coming to a stop in the drifting sand. We were in the middle of a barren moonscape. There was nothing, *nothing*, but rocks and sand. Not a single Marine. Nothing.

"This it?" asked Josh.

"Yes, sir." The corporal nodded, then stared pointedly out the side window at a pile of rocks about fifty feet away.

"Then let's get on with it!" Nic sounded almost gleeful.

We all climbed out of the Humvee, and I plowed through the blowing sand toward the rocks. When I turned my back to the wind, expecting one of the guys to be standing nearby, I saw the rear lights of the vehicle—tiny pinpoints of red in the distance. I stared in disbelief at the retreating Humvee, then ran after it, expecting any second they'd stop and be all 'Ha ha, gotcha.'

Only they didn't stop. I couldn't fucking believe it. They didn't stop.

I fell for the oldest hazing trick in the books. It'd been way too easy getting off base. Which meant those assholes at the guard tower had been in on it, too. Damn, I should've known. If something had been going down, if a story had been breaking, the military minders would've told all of us, brought us out here. It wouldn't have been a secret.

LET'S GET ON WITH IT! All these years later, I can still hear Nic's glee as he set me up. I can still feel the terror churning in my gut while I slogged through the sandstorm. It got even worse when three Humvees appeared out of nowhere and surrounded me, guns aimed out the windows, ready to fire. Back inside the wire, the CO let me have it but didn't send me home. Of course, there was no way I could tell him it was hazing. Sure, ratting out the guys would have gotten them one-way tickets home, but it would have gotten me blackballed out of the brotherhood. Or my gear could've gone missing. I might've come down with a mystery illness. Maybe even fragged by a live grenade. I never did get the chance for payback. The very next day, Nic and the guys went to the western front with the Marines. I stayed behind visiting villages and photographing deliveries of MREs and bottled water. My penance.

I'm still pissed. Nic knew exactly how to play me, and I was so eager to prove myself that I fell for it. And now here he is. With any luck, he'll stay where he is and won't notice me.

"Listen to me. You have *got* to get me on another flight. I will *not* sit in this hellhole another three hours waiting for Emirates to get their act together." The woman Nic Lowe called Piera is back on her phone.

Piera McNeil—of course. The news diva. Last I heard, she had a show on FOX. She usually came off as opinionated as hell and often downright wrong. *That* Piera McNeil targeted her interview victims like a piranha. Then ate them alive.

I shift on the metal seat, still trying to find a position that won't leave me aching and sore. Long-distance hauls are brutal. Finally, I give up trying to rest and sit up. The loosened *keffiyeh* slides off my head.

And there is Nic Lowe towering over me. "Annie? Annie Hawkins Green? I can't believe it."

"Hey, Nic." So much for staying incognito.

"It's been what, ten years? No. November, 2006."

"It's been a long time." But not long enough. I brace myself for a snarky comment about how much older I look.

"You haven't changed a bit. Pardon my non-PC commentary, but you look as smashing now as you did back then."

"Why, Nic, I had no idea you cared."

"Come on, old thing. How could I possibly forget you? We had a great time at Masum Ghar."

"Not so sure I remember it quite that fondly."

"What's a little hazing? We do that to all the rookies," he chuckles. "You know, welcome to the club, and all that. And, as I remember it, you put on your big-girl knickers and managed just fine. We were all quite impressed."

Yeah, Nic, what you *remember* is that I kept my mouth shut and didn't give you and your buddies up to the CO. As *I* remember, you assholes left me out there to fend for myself. Or die.

Nic doesn't dim the wattage of his camera-ready smile one iota in the face of my silence. "Where've you been all these years? One minute you were trying to play with the big boys, and the next we heard you were in the middle of that mess with those Marines who died. Then you were gone. Never came back to base. Rumor was you didn't even show up to collect your Pulitzer." He helps himself to the seat next to me. "That was a great shot by the way."

I flinch at the words. A great shot. It's the picture of Malalai he's talking about, of course. Her eyes wide with fear, but her mouth set in determination. I got the prize for a few of the photographs I had taken during my visit to Khakwali and another village—the whole impact-of-the-war-on-kids thing. But it was the shot of Malalai— the one that landed on the front cover of *Time*—that got all the attention. I try not to think about the Pulitzer.

Nic's mention of the Pulitzer gets Piera's attention. Suddenly, she's standing in front of me, reaching across the Pelican cases to shake hands. "Hi, I'm Piera McNeil. Al Shabakat. I think we should talk."

Al Shabakat. So, that explains her disappearance from FOX. I extricate my hand from her grasp. "Really, there's nothing to tell."

"Oh, I don't believe that for a minute," says Nic. "There's a story here, and I'm betting it's a good one. There was a lot of talk back then, but no one's ever said what really happened out there. This has spec op written all over it."

"Think again." I laugh. "If any of those rumors had been true, I'd have written the story." In fact, my editor at the AP was all over me to do exactly that. But there was Commander Finn Cerelli threatening to haul me in front of a tribunal, maybe even charge me with treason, if I talked. Then, there was the fact that I'd crossed the line with those images. Because of me, Malalai *died*, and I became part of the story. No journalist wants that to happen.

Piera squeezes herself into the space between Nic and me. "Oh, I *do* smell a story here, Annie. It's all right for me to call you Annie, isn't it?"

I smooth out my *keffiyeh*, then wrap it around my neck. "I think what you're smelling, Ms. McNeil, is me—I've been holed up here for the last ten hours."

"So, you're going back in-country," says Nic, his eyes running the length of my body. "Curious, don't you think, that this is the first time we've met up in all these years?"

"Guess we're just in different places at different times." Or I've been lucky.

Nic taps one of the Pelican cases. "That's a lot of gear you're toting."

"It gets the job done." With their Canon labels, my cases scream *camera gear*. Just the lead they're looking for.

"You know, Annie, it seems to me you're either onto a big story—or maybe you *are* the story." The adversarial tone in Piera's voice belies her smile. "It won't take me long to dig it up, so why not just tell me. Journalist to journalist."

"Google away, Piera." What she'll find are the basics—birth, college, divorce. And copies of some of my more noteworthy images. As for Khakwali—the military scrubbed the entire episode.

IT'S ANOTHER FIVE HOURS before we finally board. I relax into my soft leather first-class seat and savor the glass of chilled champagne the flight attendant hands me. God bless champagne. God bless my camera company for covering my plane tickets. I told them to give the money to the school instead. The Wad Qol Secondary School for Girls needs everything. The girls sit three and four to a table and have to share textbooks. There's heat and light when there's fuel for the generator, and then only what's left over after the boys' school gets its share. So, the company came up with a donation for the school, too.

"What an amazing coincidence!" Piera McNeil stands in the aisle, looking smug, then sidles past me to the window seat. Did she bribe someone?

I flag down the flight attendant who helped me shoulder the Pelican cases into the overhead bins. "I'm sorry to bother you, but is there *any* other seat available? Anywhere? Even in coach?"

"There is something wrong with this seat?" He's clearly puzzled.

"I can't sit next to this woman." I don't lower my voice.

The attendant looks past me to Piera, taking in her wavy, dark hair, perfectly applied makeup, too-tight shirt stretched across voluptuous breasts. He'd clearly give his left nut to sit with her.

"I *am* sorry, Madame, but the plane is completely full." The attendant watches Piera as she adjusts her bra strap. "There is nothing available, except for an attendant's jump seat, and that is against regulations." His wistful tone says *he'd* trade places with me if regulations allowed. Instead, he hands me another glass of champagne. I down the drink.

Piera jams her carry-on under the seat in front of her, then helps herself to part of my space for her laptop. "Excuse me, Annie, or would you prefer I call you Ms. Green? I think we may have gotten off on the wrong foot. What if we start again?"

"I repeat, there's nothing to tell."

The plane backs away from the gate and taxis to the runway. First in line for take-off, the pilot announces. Two minutes later, I curl my fingers around the ends of the armrests as we race down the runway and lift into the sky.

Piera starts in again. "I just want to help you. An interview on Al Shabakat could do wonders to raise funds for the girls' school where you'll be teaching."

Shit.

She keeps talking. "We could do a great promo: Pulitzer-winning photographer remembers girls of Afghanistan. Imagine the money it could bring in to help educate those poor girls."

"I don't know what you're talking about."

She smiles coyly. "Well, that's what your daughter told me you'll be doing in Afghanistan. Mel, right?"

I can barely contain my urge to slap this woman across the face. "You. Talked. To. My. Daughter?" I measure each word precisely.

Anyone who knows me would realize how close I am to losing it. This woman doesn't have a clue.

Piera leans in closer. "And Mel said—"

"You fucking talked to my fifteen-year-old daughter?"

"Only fifteen? I didn't realize. Frankly, she sounded older."

"Just who the hell do you think you are? Calling my family, questioning my daughter. Any reputable journalist knows that's totally off-limits." Oh God, what did this woman pry out of Mel? The last thing I need is this bottom-feeder trailing me to Wad Qol for a feature story. The media will have a field day.

"You told me to Google you," she smirks.

"Me. I told you to Google *me*. Not my daughter. Let's get this straight. As far as you're concerned, my daughter does not exist."

Piera's smile freezes across unnaturally whitened teeth.

Overhead, the intercom buzzes on. The captain from the flight deck. "Ladies and gentlemen, I would like to inform you that in five minutes, we will be entering the air space of the Islamic Republic of Iran."

"As if there's anything we can do about it," I inadvertently say out loud.

"You could do what I do—get a Canadian passport," says Piera. "The Iranians seem to like them better."

A Canadian passport—the thought has actually occurred to me. But instead, I say, "Does the State Department know you've got multiple passports from different countries?"

AN HOUR LATER, THE captain is back on the intercom. "Ladies and gentlemen, please be advised that we have just left Iranian air space."

Behind me, in coach, applause erupts. The travelers in first class try to look blasé, but it's clear they're relieved, too. What were the pilots thinking—telling us about Iranian air space? Do they worry Iran could actually scramble military jets and force us to land? Or are they trying to create drama?

Afghan air space. Thirty-five thousand feet down, it's Afghanistan. This time, I'm truly on my own in Kabul. At least it's only for two days, then Tariq will pick me up and we'll drive up to Wad Qol.

"Are you all right?" Piera leans in close and touches my arm with a gentleness that surprises me. "You're looking pretty white."

I ignore her. How well I know Piera McNeil's ploy of enticing her victims to talk, then moving in for the kill.

5

Afghanistan - Kabul

AS SOON AS WE LAND in Kabul, I break away from Piera
and head toward Immigration. She catches up to me at the all-
important Foreign Registration desk. Skip this step, and you end
up spending hours at the Ministry of the Interior completing even
more paperwork. Or the police haul you in, forcing you to pay a
hefty bribe.

I curl my arm around the form I'm filling out, doing my best to
block the Piranha's view. Handing over two passport photos, I get
my card and move on to Baggage Claim, where I pile my duffel on
top of the cart loaded with the Pelican cases. Then, I make my way
through Customs.

"Annie, wait up!" Nic's voice rises above the din, causing a
momentary silence as people turn to look. "Annie!" he shouts again.

No way I can pretend I haven't heard.

He hurries to my side. "You're staying at the InterCon?"

I nod. There's no point lying. The InterContinental is the securest hotel in the city, and many journalists transiting through stay there. Especially those on expense accounts. Nic will certainly see me around the place.

"I am, too. Let's share a cab." Nic reaches for my cart.

"That's okay," I say, keeping my hand on my stuff. "I've got a driver."

We stop in the meet-and-greet hall where two drivers are holding up signs for their passengers. Neither one says GREEN, or even HAWKINS. But after the long delay in Dubai, I can't say I'm surprised. And I'm not naïve enough to wait around on the off-chance he might show.

Nic crooks an eyebrow. "About that cab?"

"Thanks, but no. I can get my own."

"Sorry, old thing, but I'm not leaving you on the sidewalk at the airport. I don't want that on my conscience." He balances his duffel on top of my gear and heads toward the taxi zone. "When were you last here, anyway?"

I shrug. "It's been a few years."

"And I'll wager you had a crew and a fixer. Well, take my word for it—it's not safe for a woman to take a cab on her own."

"Give me a break." I stare at this man whose *cojones* I once threatened to roast.

"Believe me or not, but I'm not leaving you here."

Seriously? He was perfectly willing to abandon me in a desert planted full of IEDs, but not at an airport?

"Annie! Nic!"

No. Please, no. I look behind me and see Piera hurrying toward us, leaving her crew in her wake.

"You're both staying at the InterCon, I assume?" she says,

pulling even with us. "Good. I'll ride with you. I'm not about to be squashed into a tiny car with my crew and all that gear."

I look pointedly at the cart Nic's pushing, but Piera is already walking toward the cab at the front of the line. Nic doesn't object, and I'm too tired to argue. The young driver wrangles my cases into the trunk of the rusted, twenty-year-old vehicle, then wedges the duffels and backpacks onto the passenger seat next to him. The three of us crush together in the back. No seat belts.

Our driver speeds away from the airport and veers out onto the congested highway, accelerating to swerve around vehicles, leaning on his horn to warn others to give way. It makes for a terrifying game of screeching bumper cars. I hold my breath as we slide between two trucks, missing both by inches. The nauseating smell of exhaust mixed with too-sweet air freshener and stale cigarette smoke doesn't help.

Piera starts in again. "So, Ms. Green, you certainly have a lot of gear. How long will you be staying in Afghanistan?"

I'm instantly on alert. Piera's innocent smile notwithstanding, it's clear she's dug up something else.

"Oh, should I be calling you Ms. Hawkins?"

"Where are you going with this, Piera?" Nic sounds annoyed.

"You're divorced now, aren't you?"

I wave her off. "Aren't we all."

"Interesting that your daughter lives with your ex-husband and his new family. Don't Wisconsin judges usually award custody of children to their *mothers*? Unless the mother is deemed *unfit*?"

"Ease up, Piera." Nic sounds downright pissed. He might leave me to die in the desert, but he sure knows when a fellow journalist is veering out-of-bounds.

Burning acid and a lot of guilt rise into my throat. I'm rarely sick on the road, but if we don't get to the hotel soon, I'm going to throw up. I reach for the knob to roll down the window. Missing.

The cabby takes the next exit, then careens through impossibly narrow streets until he's stopped short by an accident, what looks to be a couple of cars that tried unsuccessfully to squeeze past each other. Now they're wedged in and not going anywhere. Backing up at a reckless speed that does nothing for my nausea, he pulls onto a wide boulevard where congested traffic forces him to inch slowly past an enormous mosque. Its façade makes me gasp—a stunningly intricate mosaic. The domes and minarets a turquoise so vivid, my heart would ache if I weren't feeling quite so crappy. Finally, we enter the sprawling grounds of the Hotel InterContinental, stopping at the first of three security checkpoints. I heave a sigh of relief.

We hand over our passports and registration cards to the tall guard with gold stripes on his epaulettes. He checks our names against the guest list. When he opens the third passport, he looks at his clipboard, then speaks quietly into the radio attached to his collar. Two other guards, who've been lingering over cigarettes nearby, jog toward us, shifting their guns into position.

My stomach clenches.

"You will get out," says the tall guard, our passports in one hand, a semi-automatic in the other. He points to the driver, too, who climbs out of the cab, hands above his head, fear distorting his face. I'm guessing this isn't the usual protocol for taxis dropping off guests at the hotel.

Piera obviously thinks so, too. She's out of the cab and in the guard's face. "What's going on? I've stayed here plenty of times, and there's never been a problem."

"You will stand back," he says, using his gun to point to a spot a few meters away.

Piera doesn't budge.

The guards search the duffels and packs quickly. My Pelican cases are a different story.

"These! Which one of you?" shouts the tall guard.

I step forward. "They're mine."

"You will remove them from the trunk," he says, pointing his gun at me.

"Annie, wait!" Piera steps in front of me and jabs her finger at the guard. "For God's sake! This is insane! Look at the labels on those cases. It's obviously camera equipment."

My stomach clenches tighter. Oh, God, Piera, would you shut up! There are trigger-happy men with big guns here.

The guard whispers into his radio. A little louder this time, but I still can't make out what he's saying. Whatever he said brings the chief of security at a run. The other guards and the taxi driver, his hands still above his head in surrender, back away from the cab. Seconds later, what seems like a battalion of boots pound down the driveway toward us. They, too, stop at a distance, guns at the ready.

Oh, shit. Just what we need: more men with guns.

Piera backs up and stands next to Nic and me. Nic looks distinctly amused. Piera finally looks nervous.

Using his gun, the tall guard motions me forward to the trunk of the taxi.

I heave the cases up and out of the trunk. Pelican cases are so durable they could probably fall out of a plane and still be intact. But I want the cameras in good working order for the girls in Wad Qol, so I place each of the three cases as carefully as possible on the ground. Which I'm sure makes me look guilty of something.

The chief of security takes over. "You have the keys?"

I root for the keys in the deep front pocket of my cargo pants.

Then it hits me. *Bamb-e-motor.* That's what the guard said into his radio. He thinks I'm going to blow everyone up—that I'm a suicide bomber. *Slow and easy,* I tell myself. *No sudden moves. Let's get this done without anyone getting dead.* Hands trembling, I carefully unlock the cases to reveal two dozen digital cameras, a laptop, and a small printer. The guards take aim—at Nic, Piera, and me.

"Cameras," I say the obvious, working hard to keep my voice steady, my eyes on the security chief. "I'm a photographer."

"You are only one photographer. And you have this many cameras?" He tries to stare me down.

I return his stare, despite the sweat streaming down my back.

"Passport."

The tall guard hands my passport to the chief, who scrutinizes every entry and exit stamp. Starting with South Sudan and ending with Nigeria—which should raise his suspicions.

Instead, he surprises me. "You have a work visa in Afghanistan for the next six months." His finger stabs the visa the Afghan consul in Chicago glued into my passport just seven days ago. "That is a very long time to be in the Panjshir Valley. What is there that will interest you for all that time?"

"Yes, well, I probably won't be there that long."

Wrong answer.

"I mean, I got an extended visa in case I'm asked to stay longer."

The chief holds out his hand. "Your press credentials, please."

I always carry my TNN press pass, but since I'm not here on assignment, using it could cost me my job. "I'm not here with the press corps."

His thick eyebrows knit together.

Damn. I do not want Piera McNeil to know any more than she already does. But I don't have a choice. I hand the chief the letter from Darya, written on official letterhead from *Hama* Bibi's university.

The chief reads it to himself. "Darya Faludi," he says quietly. "A good woman. So, you will be teaching at her school in Wad Qol." I hope Piera didn't hear that.

But just as quickly, all consideration vanishes. "Show me the cameras!"

Lifting a camera from its foam bed, I show him the empty slot awaiting a SanDisk card. I show him the cards. The batteries and chargers. The printer and the laptop. Boxes of spare ink cartridges. Photo paper. Then all the rest of the cameras.

The chief assesses the twenty-four cameras in front of him. "That one," he says, pointing to one in the middle. "Show me how it works."

The guards and the driver shuffle farther away from the cab and the cases. So does Piera. Nic stays by my side. I owe him big-time. Same goes for the security chief. I'm guessing he'd rather join the rest of the crowd, but he's opting to save face. I figure his men won't shoot with him standing next to me, but then again, in Afghanistan, who knows?

"Take it nice and slow," Nic whispers. "Those AMD-65s are known for their hair triggers."

"You bet," I whisper back, slipping an SD card and a battery into the camera, then turning it on. First, the click, then the fast *whir* clearly startle the chief, who takes a quick step back. He was expecting an explosion?

"Would you like me to take a picture?" I try to sound sweet and innocent and cooperative as hell.

The chief stares at me for two seconds, then answers. "You will take a picture of him." He points at Nic. "A close-up."

The guards click the safeties off their guns. No pressure here. I line up the shot. Nic, bless him, looks completely relaxed. Leaning back against the car, he offers his trademark you-can-trust-me smile that keeps him in front of television audiences. A nice side light eases the cragginess of his face. I press the shutter button. Damn, this is going to be a good shot. I'm sure it's Piera who exhales a loud sigh of relief. What a piece of work. Did she really think I was going to blow them up?

The chief is back at my side.

I flip the camera to show him Nic's image. It *is* a terrific shot.

Nic cranes his neck to see, so I turn the camera toward him. "I could use a new publicity still."

The chief raises his eyebrows. "Not bad. He is a handsome man, your husband."

"You mean Nic? No, he's not my husband." I shoot a look at Nic, who has the decency to look wounded.

"We're friends," he says. "Going back years. We were on the same flight into Kabul and shared a cab."

The chief steps away for a prolonged back-and-forth on his collared radio. Minutes later, he waves the guards back to their posts. He returns our passports and registration cards and claps his hand jovially on Nic's shoulder. "You are a brave man, sir." When he turns to me, his eyes linger on my breasts. "Thank you, Madame. You pack these up now. Perhaps you will take a picture of me before you depart the hotel." He raises an eyebrow in case I didn't quite pick up on his innuendo.

Finally, he speaks to the cab driver, this time loud enough for me to hear. "Proceed to the front door, but next time you see cases like these, you have the police at the airport search them. You understand? Do not bring trouble to this hotel."

I'm kneeling in front of the open cases, tucking everything back in place, when Nic squats beside me. "They had some action here a couple years ago," he says quietly. "And recently, there's been a spate of attacks all over Kabul."

"I figured."

"So, thanks for not blowing me up."

"Maybe next time."

A few minutes later, the taxi drops us off at the palatial entrance. A bellman loads my gear onto a cart. Nic carries his own. Piera probably figures her crew will take care of whatever she brought and hurries ahead of us into the opulent lobby.

"Madame, your name?" The clerk at the spectacular gold and brown marble registration desk directs his questions to the computer monitor in front of him instead of looking at me.

Is it because I'm a woman? Because I'm American? *My hair,* I chide myself. I pull my *keffiyeh* from my backpack, drape it over my hair, then wrap it modestly around my neck. Show respect, and people will be more accepting. Critical for a photographer, especially one who wants to remain invisible.

Ornate brass room key in hand, I walk through the lobby following the bellman with my luggage. We pass clusters of gilded divans and armchairs crowded with Middle Eastern businessmen, politicians, and a couple sultans in traditional garb. I can feel their eyes assessing me. Undressing me.

"Annie!" Nic trails behind me. "Wait up."

Great. More men watching me, and now they know my name. When Nic catches up, he slings his arm across my shoulders. That's better. Our audience will think he's my husband, or better yet, my boyfriend. Just so long as they think I'm taken. And just so long as Nic doesn't get the wrong idea.

"How about we meet for dinner at the café out by the pool? Less formal than the dining room."

"Thanks," I say, "but I'm going to call home, then call it a night."

"Oh, come on, Annie. We've got some catching up to do."

"Sorry. Besides, I don't think I can deal with being around the Piranha anymore tonight."

Nic laughs. "Perfect name. Does she know?"

"God, no, and don't you dare tell her. She's already on my case."

"I wasn't planning to invite her."

"That's optimistic, don't you think? She doesn't seem the type to wait for an invitation."

"You really tell it like it is, Annie. I always liked that about you. Look, I'll be by the pool around eight o'clock. If you want to join me, that would be smashing." He waves his key over his head and strides ahead to the bank of elevators.

6

MY ROOM IS NOTHING LIKE the gilded opulence of the lobby. A double bed with a dip in the middle the size of a canyon, a nightstand with a gooseneck lamp, and the ugliest brass and crystal ceiling fixture I've ever seen. No dresser, not even a chair. Hard to believe that all the rooms in the InterCon look like this. But over the years, I've stayed in much worse. Besides, two days from now, Tariq will pick me up, and I'll be on my way to Wad Qol.

I sit on the edge of the bed and count back the hours to Milwaukee time—4:30 PM here, 7:00 AM there. Which means Mel is up and getting ready for school. A good time to catch her. I pull up her name on my smartphone and wait for the international connection to click in. Counting to sixty, listening to the static on the line. Finally, a recorded voice: *All circuits are busy. Try your call again later.*

I'm on my feet, pacing the small room. God, my legs are tight. Too much sitting on planes and in terminals the last few days. I lean against the bathroom doorjamb to stretch my hamstrings. I'd love to get in a run before showering and ordering room service. But running outdoors here is impossible. I leaf through the portfolio of services looking for an indoor gym and find *Men's Fitness Center*. *Women's Fitness Center* has a tattered note pasted over it: *Coming soon!* I can just imagine what would happen if I show up in my running tights and sports bra at the men's gym.

It takes another three tries, but I finally get an international line. One ring and halfway around the world, Mel answers. "Mom?" The line is crystal clear.

"Hey, sweetie."

"Ohmygod, Mom, it's really you. I mean, I knew you were fine and all that, and I've been watching the news so I know nothing's going on in Afghanistan."

"But?"

"Well, you were supposed to get there yesterday, and I've been waiting, but you never called, and I've been kind of worried . . ." Her voice peters out.

Mel worried? She never sits around waiting for me to call. I almost never call when I'm away from home, but when I do, I inevitably end up leaving a message on her voice mail. So, why this trip? Sure, I'm in Afghanistan, but I've been to other really dangerous places, and she shrugs them off. *Annie?* Todd's voice. *Take care of yourself. Don't make me have to tell Emmy you didn't make it.* Damn, I don't want her worrying about me. Todd and C.E. better not be stoking her fear.

"I'm sorry. I should've called. There were a ton of flight delays. That's just what happens in this part of the world, especially in and out of Kabul."

"Yeah, well, no biggie." I can picture her shrug, her diffidence returning. She surprises me when she says, "But, uh, next time let me know, okay?" I can hear her disappointment that I'm not sufficiently appreciating how worried she's been.

"You bet." Please don't let Catherine Elizabeth and Todd find out she's worrying. That will be just one more thing for C.E. to hold over my head. "So, how are *you*?" Which is code for: Please tell me about Chance. Please tell me the truth about whether you're having sex with him. Better yet, please tell me he's out of the picture. Please, *talk* to me.

"Good."

Except she doesn't sound good. And she's definitely not picking up on my code.

"So, what's up?"

"Nothing."

"You and Catherine Elizabeth getting along?"

"I guess."

Right. "Tell me, please."

"Mom, no. Look, I don't want to screw up your trip."

"Sweetie."

"Okay. It's . . . well . . . last week C.E. said she didn't get your check."

So, she *did* hear that. I take a breath. "It's nothing for you to worry about."

"Don't tell me that, Mom. I asked her what she meant, and she told me you're paying child support."

I clench my fists. Tell myself to breathe. "Of course, I am. I'm your mother. Your dad said he could handle it, but I insisted."

"Mom, that's so unfair. Daddy makes a fortune. We live in a mansion. Plus, there's the lake house. C.E. drives a Mercedes. You've got furniture with holes. Why should you have to pay them? And *then*, she told me you have to pay half my college."

And just that suddenly, I'm walking through a minefield. "That's not exactly true. I don't *have* to pay. I *want* to pay."

"No."

"No? What do you mean 'no'?"

"I'm not going to college."

"Yes, you are. Period. Look, is your dad still home?"

"Yeah."

"Could I talk to him, please?"

"Jeez, Mom, this is what you always do—you talk to *him* about me, instead of talking to *me*."

"That's not true."

"It sure seems like it."

"Well, it's not. This actually has to do with C.E. saying things to you she has no business talking about."

"Like she always does."

I wonder how true that is. Definitely something I need to investigate when I get home. "Could I please talk to your dad?"

"Whatever." I picture Mel thrusting the phone at her father and storming out of the room.

"Annie." Todd's voice comes on the line, a bit out of breath, but so close that he could be in the room with me. "I take it you got there safe and sound."

"The usual delays, but I'm here. Did you hear any of what Mel said?"

"It was kind of hard not to—she's pretty riled up. Look, if it's about the support checks, don't worry. I've told you that before."

I try to keep it light. "Catherine Elizabeth doesn't seem to have gotten that message."

"I'll talk to her." Todd sounds tired and maybe a little besieged. An ex-wife, a current wife, a teenage daughter, seven-year-old twin daughters. He's juggling a lot and trying to keep us all happy. "She loves Emmy, you know. She treats her like her own daughter, the same as the twins."

I don't for one minute believe that. "But regardless, she absolutely should *not* be discussing support checks with *our* daughter. Or who's paying for college."

I wait for Todd to answer, but instead I get an earful of static. The connection's gone. A twinge of regret takes me by surprise. Strange that it still hits me sometimes, even this many years after the divorce. *I love you, Annie, but it tears me up when you go to those insanely dangerous places. I can't . . . I can't live with you doing that. Not anymore.*

I flop across the bed, and not for the first time wonder if I should've stayed. Tried harder to make our marriage work. But if I'm honest with myself, there was nothing I could've done. Except give up a big part of who I am. Todd and I turned out to be two different people who wanted very different things. He wanted a beautiful home, happy kids, and a loving wife—everything and everyone safe and sound. He's got that now. Just not with me.

THE ROOM IS DARK WHEN I wake up, Mel and Todd and Catherine Elizabeth still very much on my mind. I finish my pity party in the shower, scouring away my guilt over having abandoned my daughter to her stepmother. Then, surveying the small, nearly empty room, I decide that room service and eating here aren't going to cut it. I need company. So, I braid my wet hair in a single plait, use my *keffiyeh* as a headscarf, and head down to the poolside café. Maybe Nic will still be there.

Pink and white fairy lights flicker in the trees around the pool. Off to the east, the city lights of Kabul dot the deepening sapphire night sky. It feels like pure magic, a world away from the decades of war and suicide bombers and religious police that have plagued this country.

I circle the pool and find Nic at a table by himself. He smiles at my approach and, like the gentleman he wants to think he is, stands and pulls out a chair. A waiter is next to me in an instant, draping a pink cloth napkin across my lap without coming close to touching me.

"You just missed the Piranha," says Nic.

I look around. "You're kidding."

"No such luck. She helped herself to a half hour of me."

"And here I thought you two were an item."

"She certainly thinks so. She tried pretty hard to crawl into my bed."

"Seriously?"

"Oh, yeah."

I lean back in my chair and study him. Really a good-looking man. And, to be honest, Piera is a stunningly beautiful woman. So, why isn't Nic hopping into bed with her? Too high a price to pay? Doesn't cheat on his wife? Yeah, I definitely remember talk about a beautiful wife and a daughter back in the day. "And here I was wondering if you were going to hit on me tonight," I tease.

He gives me a 'come hither' look. "Do you want me to?"

God, no. The last thing I need is to hook up with Nic Parker Lowe. Or anyone. A series of post-divorce no-strings-attached visits to my bed has totally turned me off men. They're a complication I most definitely do not need. I nod in the direction of the buffet tables. "Have you eaten?"

"With the Piranha? Perish the thought."

I laugh and push back my chair. "Let's."

The aromas are enticing. I lift the silver domes of the serving dishes to discover European and American food: sirloin tips, *coq au vin, pasta carbonara.* A sous-chef is grilling steaks to order. All the food I try to avoid when I'm on the road—the surest way to get sick.

The chef directs me to the Afghan dishes at another table where he spoons *Kabuli pulao,* the national dish of rice and lamb, flavored with raisins, almonds, and grated carrot, onto a plate for me.

"*Borani banjân, lotfan.*" I point to the eggplant in yogurt sauce.

"*Balê, banjân.*" He smiles broadly as he slathers even more yogurt sauce on top of my eggplant slices.

Back at the table, Nic looks up from his steak and baked potato mounded with sour cream and chives. "That's quite a meal. My grandfather would have made a comment about 'going native.'"

"It's delicious," I protest. "Probably better than your dinner."

"Not to mention that it earned you the undying gratitude of the chef. Didn't know you speak Dari. You sounded pretty fluent back there. Spook-fluent."

My fork stops halfway to my mouth. Damn, Nic's right. Most of the Americans who speak Dari or Pashto are military or CIA. An affiliation I most definitely do not need. I glance toward the buffet tables where, yes, indeed, the chef is looking my way, pointing me out to the servers. Just great.

"Not to worry. I think the old guy's smitten. And speaking of smitten—"

I put up my hand. "Look, Nic. About before, I was kidding."

"So, you *don't* want to go to bed with me?"

"Nic—"

"No, look, that's a good thing."

I wait for the put-down.

"It's not what you think. I'm . . . in a committed relationship. Have been for years. Perez—that's his name, Perez Mopantokobogo. We've got a place in South Africa. Cape Town."

Nic, gay? I look at him. Really *look* at him. Haloed by the lights, he makes a nice image. I reach for my camera. Which I left in my room.

"For obvious reasons, I don't tell many people. Haven't told my colleagues. And I certainly haven't told Piera."

"So, why tell me?"

"You didn't give me up to the CO at Masum Ghar. And whatever the hell else happened—and the pictures that won you that Pulitzer tell me something big did happen—you never said a word. That takes guts."

"Speaking of Masum Ghar, what the fuck were you thinking? I could've died out there."

He has the decency to look chastened. "We do that to all the newbies. Especially the women. Some outdated notion of chivalry we men have."

"Chivalry?" I snort. "Is that what you call it?"

"The women-shouldn't-be-in-a-war-zone kind."

"That's hardly chivalrous."

Nic raises an eyebrow. "In a medieval way, it was definitely chivalrous. And, I should point out, you were hardly a lady."

"I should have run you through with a sword."

"Probably. Never understood why you didn't. One word from you, and we would've been out of there. You would have been golden."

I grin. "Oh, believe me, the thought crossed my mind. Let's just call it *chivalry*, shall we? Although I don't think there's a statute of limitations on payback."

He laughs, clearly dismissing the possibility. "It all came out right in the end, though." Nic inserts a tiny question at the end of his statement, then studies me intently, as if he's waiting for me to tell him what really happened that day in Khakwali. "You didn't die. You won the big prize we all covet."

I stare at him for a long minute. Because of his stupid-ass hazing, I spent my brief embed taking pictures of kids playing and villagers stockpiling tasteless MREs. To be honest though, for me, telling the stories of the living is just as important as documenting the war action. But then suddenly I *was* in the middle of a war zone. And people—my people—died. Lopez cut in half by bullets. Murphy bleeding out. Malalai dying in my arms.

After what seems like an eternity of silence, I move the conversation back to the previous topic. "So, why come out to me? You could've just laughed off my uncharacteristically bold, and may I say, poorly timed come-on."

"A couple reasons." The smile is gone from his eyes.

Damn, he's serious. I let him talk.

"It's open season on journalists out here in Afghanistan. They've gotten three of us so far this year. It's a dangerous business bringing the news to inquiring minds." He grins sardonically. "The thing is, no one else knows about Perez, and if it happens to me, I'd like to know someone who's been in the zone that would . . . go . . . and talk to him."

His words push me back in my chair. I look beyond him at the pink and white fairy lights until they pixilate into so many dots. Why me? Nic must have friends, close friends, who could do it. I've done this already. Murphy's widow. I don't have it in me to make another death visit: the painful phone call, the long walk up to the door. Eight years ago, I disobeyed Commander Cerelli's orders to

let the Marine Corps handle it and went to 622 Capistrano Drive
in Camp Pendleton, planning to tell Kelly Murphy her husband
died a hero. She was young and weepy and working her way
through a six-pack of Bud Light. She was also six months pregnant
with another Marine's child. Which meant she'd been cheating on
Murphy before he shipped out to Afghanistan. Cerelli had been
right all along. I had no business going there. God only knows what
I'd discover if I ever had to make a death visit to Nic's partner.

Nic leans forward. "Please, Annie? It would mean a lot."

Even though every cell inside me is screaming *no*, I reach across
the table for his hand. "Tell me what I need to know."

He does, his voice amazingly calm given that he's talking about
the aftermath of his own, probably very violent, death.

I squeeze his hand. "You said you had a couple reasons for our
intimate chat."

"I do." He studies my face, something I'm not used to. "You've
got great bone structure, you know, a lot like Nicole Kidman, but
you're looking a bit battle-fatigued. I thought you might like to talk
about whatever it is that's going on. Never fear, I won't be feeding
any scandalous tidbits to our beloved Piera. This is completely off
the record."

I wave away his real question. "Same old, same old. Teenage
daughter, ex-husband, his new wife."

"Ah. Yes." He raises an eyebrow. "Having a daughter can muck
up jobs like ours. Being away so much. Feeling guilty?"

"Always."

He pushes back his plate and signals for coffee. I order a glass
of *chai sabz*. We don't say a word until our drinks arrive.

"Lovely." I savor the aroma of the cardamom-flavored,
traditional green tea. Then munch on one of the honeyed *baklawa*

the waiter serves with our drinks, letting the delicate phyllo leaves melt on my tongue.

The silence stretches between us.

"I've been in this business long enough to know you're knee-deep in something," he finally says. "All those cameras suggest a spec op. They could get you in trouble. A lot of trouble. People are already talking."

"About me?" I try to laugh, but it comes out more like a snort. My fingers worry the cloth napkin draped across my lap. "So, who's talking?"

"The security people—they came by my room after we checked in, asking some pointed questions. The registration clerks. The Piranha." He ticks them off his fingers. "And before you got down here, a couple military types stopped by the table to chat."

"Get real. I am so not a spook."

"You're not going to tell me, are you?" Disappointment flickers in his eyes.

I shake my head. "Sorry."

"Annie—"

I raise my hand to stop him. "Hey, remember, I keep my mouth shut." Which, of course, makes it sound like I really *am* keeping some deep, dark secret. I smile and lighten my tone. "Let's just say I made a commitment to someone very important to me and leave it at that."

Nic shoots me an aggrieved look. "Fair enough. Let *me* just caution you that things in Afghanistan aren't as safe as you may think. The security chief mentioned Wad Qol this afternoon and again in my room. If you're heading up the Panjshir Valley, you need to know it's no Shangri-La anymore. There have been incidents. The Taliban is on the move. Word is ISIS is out there, too."

I manage a thin smile. "Thanks. Good to know." Thanks to you, too, Dar. What the hell have you gotten me into?

"Be careful. Those are really bad guys we're talking about, and they're not too keen on photographers. Or art in general. Remember the Buddhist statues at Bamyan? Whatever you do, don't let yourself get snagged by ISIS. They have a predilection for beheading people. Especially journalists. Especially Americans. No dispensation for women."

For a few seconds, I'm tempted to tell him. It would probably be smart to have someone here who knows how to reach me. Just in case. For some crazy reason, I'm pretty sure I can trust him. The thing is, though, this photography workshop is way too personal. A young girl gave her life for mine. There's nothing I can ever do to compensate for that. If anybody outside Wad Qol finds out about the workshop, there's going to be a ton of publicity and acclaim. And I sure as hell don't want any of it. But Nic's trusting me with his secret. Maybe I should trust him back. I look around. No one's paying us the least attention, but that doesn't mean anything. No, the very air in Kabul carries secrets, revealing them to exactly the wrong people.

We sit another hour, sipping coffee and *chai sabz*, the lights twinkling around us. Nic talks about Perez and their life together. "It's a beautiful thing, finding the love of my life. Living in South Africa is good, too. Not the best place to play for the other team, but Perez was already living there, playing football for the national team, in fact. He's still there with a job he loves, so now it's my home base. You should come sometime. Look us up."

"Thanks, Nic. I may just do that."

He puts his hand over mine and smiles wistfully. "Afraid I'm seriously done in. I'm off to bed, alone—regretfully." He pushes back his chair and stands, offering his hand to help me up. "Come on. I'll walk you to your room." It's not a question.

I shake my head, not quite ready to face my nearly barren room. "I think I'll sit here a little longer."

"Tomorrow then." He crosses the patio. When he reaches the far side of the pool, he stops to chat with a few men, and for a brief moment, they all look toward our table. I wonder if he's talking about me. Right. A little paranoid, are we? I shake my head and go back to drinking my *chai*, staring at the fairy lights in the trees.

It's been almost fourteen years since the U.S. came to Afghanistan to oust Al Qaeda. Then, later, to defeat the Taliban. So many people have died. And what's changed? I'm sitting in a hotel restaurant by myself late at night. Something no woman could've done under the Taliban. As if that really matters.

I get the sense that half the people in this country are sliding back into the Middle Ages, believing that's where the world should be. Sure, a few high schools like Darya's are open, but most Afghan girls still struggle to get an education, and they definitely aren't encouraged to think for themselves. Their fathers, brothers, uncles just want to marry them off to the first man—often a much older man—who'll pay a decent bride price. Way too many men still believe their daughters, sisters, nieces, wives are their property, and that they can dispose of them as they see fit.

Chai finished, I stare glumly at the leaves floating on the bottom of my glass. Khakwali coalesces before my eyes. Then, Lopez lying by the Humvee. Murphy bleeding out. Malalai missing half her head.

I shake the glass, and the leaves swirl. But when they stop, what I see is just as horrific.

An explosion. Bodies. Blood. So much blood.

What the hell is going on? What am I seeing? I want to get rid of the glass, but my fingers are locked fast around it, skin stretched taut. My knuckles turn white.

I can't look away, can't break the hold the tea leaves have on me.

Finally, the tea glass crashes to the concrete at my feet, the noise stopping the conversations around me. My face flames, and I feel men's stares pressing against me.

The waiter is with me instantly. "Is there anything wrong, Madame?"

Heart pounding, I shake my head. "No." I can't possibly tell him what I saw. I can't tell anyone. It's insane.

He wrinkles his brow, clearly worried. "Madame is all right?"

"Yes. I'm sorry about the glass." My hands are still trembling.

He looks at me warily. "Would Madame like another *chai*?"

"Please," I say. Then, deciding I've had enough caffeine, I shake my head. "I'm sorry. No, no thank you."

Clearly confused about what the American woman really wants, the waiter backs away.

Male voices again rumble around me, speaking Dari and Pashto and Arabic. Cigar smoke wafts over from a nearby table. I glance at one group of men, then another. They're all watching me. What are they thinking? Their eyes remind me that I'm female, that I should be home in my husband's bed. And, if I'm not, then it's open season. Damn. I should have gone up to my room when Nic left.

Pushing back from the table, I tug my *keffiyeh* over my hair and, straightening my shoulders, propel myself toward the hotel lobby doors. *Do not*, I tell myself sternly, *make eye contact*. The last thing I need is for one of these cigar smokers to think I'm extending an invitation.

I make it to the hotel lobby.

The bank of elevators.

The fifth floor.

I'm halfway down the long hall to my room when I hear the ding of the elevator. The doors swoosh open. Male voices.

I glance behind me. One of the men has turned in my direction. *Stop being so paranoid*, I tell myself, but I walk a little faster.

Heavy footfalls jog after me.

I pick up my pace. My room is just a little farther, but I hesitate. I don't want this guy to know where my room is.

"Annie? Wait up!"

"Nic?" Relief floods through me.

"Glad I caught you." He hands me an envelope with *Hotel InterContinental Kabul* etched in elegant gold script as the return address. *Annie Hawkins* is scrawled in black ink. "Wasn't sure about the *Green*. Whether you're still using your ex's name."

"This is fine."

"Thanks for helping me, old thing. While I'm at it, I'll go ahead and add your name to my emergency contact list at the BBC. Let's hope they never have to call."

"Let's hope." I swallow hard.

The elevator dings again. This time a woman gets off, looks up and down the hall, then hurries toward us.

I stare in disbelief.

Nic curses.

"So, there you two are," Piera says, a bottle of Jack Daniels in hand. "Anyone interested in a nightcap?"

Leave it to the Piranha to start off her stay in Kabul with an illegal beverage.

"Not me," says Nic. "I'm done for. Heading off to bed."

"That could be fun." Piera looks so eager I almost feel sorry for her. Almost.

"Sorry, Piera." Nic doesn't sound sorry at all. "Too tired for company."

"Annie?" Piera's tone says I'm her plan B. "This would be a good time for us to talk."

"Talk? Us? I don't think so."

Piera's eyes lock on the envelope in my hand. "Nic, I'd recognize your handwriting anywhere."

I glance at Nic. I'm surprised to see the corners of his mouth turn down. *Don't*, I want to tell him. *Piranhas feed on the least sign of weakness.*

"It's been lovely, Nic, but I'm bushed. Tomorrow night?" I turn toward my door, and for good measure, wave the envelope over my head.

I DON'T READ NIC'S 'I'm dead' letter. I don't even want to think about what might be in it. Instead, I tuck it into the hidden sleeve inside my Lowepro backpack, hoping I never have to take it out.

Peeling off my clothes, I pull on my *Take Back the Night* T-shirt. Lights off, I fluff the pillows and slip under the covers, ready to sleep for the first time in days. I try hard to relax, but my mind races with thoughts of Nic Lowe's stupid hazing stunt. As soon as I manage to shut that down, my thoughts threaten to take me to Khakwali. Malalai, Murphy, Lopez. No. I'm not going there. An hour passes. Wide awake, far from sleep, I roll onto my side and open my eyes. The red digital numbers on my travel clock reconfigure from 1:15 to 1:29 to 1:34.

"*Ah-nie? Ah-nie?*"

I freeze.

"*Lutfan!*" Please, says a small voice in the dark.

I don't even breathe.

"*Lutfan! Lutfan, mrasta râsara kawalay she?*" Please, can you help me? A girl's voice. A young girl.

How the hell could someone be in my room? I *know* I locked the door.

"*Kamrâ. Lutfan. Zmâ dë kâmre wasâyel.*"

This is nuts. There can't possibly be anyone in here. I scrabble for my flashlight on the bedside table but come up with the clock instead.

"*Lutfan? Ah-nie? Zmâ kâmra pëkar di.*"

Okay, I get that she's talking about a camera. And she wants me to do something to help her. "*Zë në pohezham.*" But I don't understand more than that. Oh God, I can barely breathe. "What do you want?" Wait, I know how to say that. "*Tsë ghwâre?*"

"*Ghwâram kâmra.*"

"Who are you?"

"*Ah-nie?*"

"*Stâ num tsë day?* What is your name?" I pull back my arm, ready to throw the nearly weightless clock.

"*Zmâ num Malalai day.*"

"Malalai?" My heart skips a beat. "No! That's impossible. You died. Years ago." I fumble with the lamp, finally managing to turn it on, only to knock it to the floor. The light is dim, but I'm able to see the room is empty.

Heart racing, clock still in hand, I swing my feet to the floor and inch my way to the bathroom. "Malalai? Where are you? Please, come out. I won't hurt you."

I check behind the door. Nothing.

The shower. Empty.

"Malalai? Don't leave! I didn't forget you. Please believe me. You're the reason I'm here." Tears welling, I slump against the doorjamb. How could I have let her die? What kind of mother lets a little girl die?

I slide down the jamb to the floor, and it's November 2006. I'm in Khakwali. The sand. The weight of Malalai's head lolling against my chest, her blood oozing onto my hands. The sound of gunfire. Deafening. Until the rain.

Then I'm running, sliding under the Humvee next to Lopez, crawling to Murphy only to watch him die.

Running again. This time I'm following Malalai's *anaa* to a crumbling hut—a shelter for the village goats and chickens—to wait through the night for morning. When the militants will come for me.

Except they don't.

Commander Finn Cerelli gets to me first. Rescues me. Only to fly me to the USS *Bataan* and put me through what he called a debriefing. In truth, a week from hell.

"Damn it, Murphy!" I shake my fist at the ceiling. "We never should have gone to Khakwali. The orders were for a different village that day, but you just had to impress me. I should've told you I was married. I should've said *something*. Then maybe you and Lopez and Malalai—maybe you'd all be alive today." Furious with Murphy, with myself, and with the fucking Taliban for killing, *still* killing, innocent people, I drop my head in my hands.

HOURS LATER, I WAKE. HEART pounding. Breathing hard. Chilled from sweating. Where the hell am I? Curled up tight on a floor. Across the room, a light burns faintly, letting me see a bed but no photo of Mel and Seema. Not home. I run through my checklist of countries and land in Afghanistan. Kabul. The InterCon. My first day back in-country, and the memories I so carefully and thoroughly buried years ago are roaring back to life. Fuck. I glance at the clock still in my hand—4:00 AM. I look longingly at the bed. But I'm way too spent to haul myself across the room.

7

TWO SHARP KNOCKS STARTLE me awake. I lift my head from the carpet in front of the bathroom. The floor? What the hell? I look at the clock lying inches from my face. 8:00 AM. Then I remember Malalai. *Dead*, I tell myself sternly. *She's dead. She was not in this room last night.*

Two more knocks. Still half-asleep, I push myself to my feet and cross the room. "Nic?" I say, making sure my T-shirt is covering my ass. Then, I break my cardinal rule when traveling: I open the door.

"Not Nic," says the forty-something man in the hall. "You really should check through the peephole before you open the door. And keep the chain on."

"Who the hell are you?"

"I take it Nic didn't tell you I'd be coming by."

I feel my face flush. No. Nic wouldn't set me up. Would he? "Look, I don't know what you've heard, but I am so not into that." I push hard against the door, but it doesn't close.

"Not into *what*?"

His gaze drifts from my face down my suddenly indecently short T-shirt to my way-too-long bare legs. *Take Back the Night* seems a touch too provocative a slogan to be wearing in front of this stranger. To make matters worse, I feel my flush expanding—from my cheeks down to my chest. Damn you, Nic!

"Whatever you're thinking I'm into. Look, just leave. Now."

The man offers a half smile and holds up his hand in a sign of peace. "Annie, I'm not here for what you think I'm thinking."

"Shit! Nic told you my name?" I push harder against the door, but it doesn't budge.

"No, he most definitely did *not* tell me your name. Nic was the total gentleman. Very protective of you, I might add. No," the dimple next to his crooked smile deepens, "I remember your name. You're hard to forget."

His Boston accent finally slides into place. "Commander Finn Cerelli." Good God, this man doesn't look anything like the needed-a-bath-months-ago, greasy-haired, scraggly-bearded Navy SEAL who rescued me years ago. Only to put me through the interrogation grinder from hell aboard the USS *Bataan*. Even in jeans, a light blue polo shirt, and a well-worn leather bomber jacket, this Cerelli is total military. Short, silvering hair aside, the bearing, the stance says it all.

"Captain," he says quietly.

"I'm impressed. Then tell me, Captain, why are you at my door," I shove the clock in front of his face, "at oh-eight-hundred?"

He firmly pushes the clock and my hand back a few inches. "Nice to see you, too."

"Yeah, yeah. You mind answering my question? I'm here less than twenty-four hours, and you show up. Interesting coincidence, don't you think? A girl could get paranoid."

"Paranoia. Not the effect I had in mind. Rough night, I see."

"How did you know?"

"Rug burn." He points to my cheek. "Been there a few times myself. Usually after a long night of drinking." He raises an eyebrow.

"No drinking. This is a Muslim country." No matter that among most journalists I know, Kabul has had the reputation of being quite a party city the last few years.

"Weeeellll," he drags out the word, "if you know the right people, you can get some nice scotch."

"I don't." I cross my arms, which doesn't do much to conceal my boobs. "Know the right people, that is. Bourbon, though, I could go for, but not at this time of the morning. That's a bit much, even for me. Now, would you please answer my question? What the hell are you doing here?"

"Security."

"*What?*"

"I want to make sure you are. Secure." He picks up the backpack resting at his feet and then looks past me into the room. "May I come in?"

Obviously not a conversation Cerelli wants to have in the hall. I study his face for a long twenty seconds. Okay, he's not my favorite person after the way we parted company all those years ago, but yeah, I trust him. I take a step back. He shuts the door behind him and scans the room. I watch him take in the lamp on the floor, my duffel, the stacked Pelican cases, and my backpack. Then, motioning for me to follow, he crosses to the bathroom and turns on the shower.

"Bugged," he says quietly. "The lamp in the bedroom. The ceiling light. The air-con vents."

"You've got to be kidding! You expect me to believe they've bugged all the rooms in this hotel?"

"Just a select few. Yours. You made quite the impression when you arrived."

"How do you know that? And how do you know this room is bugged?"

"You probably don't want to know."

Meaning, he most likely had something to do with installing the bugs. I let that roll around my brain for a moment, and then realization dawns. "You're one of the military types who stopped by Nic's table last night."

"Guilty."

"You've been listening to me? Last night? This morning?"

He nods. "I did."

"Damn." I shift my hands to the outside of my crossed arms. The mirror reflects my image. I look like I'm trying to hold myself together. Not very effectively. "You think I'm crazy, don't you?"

"What I think is you're developing a very annoying habit of telling me what I'm thinking."

"*Sorry.* I'm sure I have a lot of habits you'd consider *annoying*." In the mirror, my cheeks are still ridiculously red, and the rug burn is taking on an ugly purple hue. I glance up, and the reflection of my eyes meets his.

He breaks our eye contact to dig into his backpack. "To answer your question, I'm here to give you a satellite phone. Since you'll be up in the Panjshir Valley, I thought you'd feel safer having a phone you could depend on."

"I've got my smartphone."

He laughs. "Your cell won't be, let us say, 'reliable' up there. But the military satellite channels are. I've programmed in all my contact info." He points to the numbers printed neatly on the unit. "And this is the sat phone number."

I reach for the bulky phone, then snatch back my hand. "How do you know where I'm going?"

He shrugs. "Darya Faludi contacted me last week. Thought I should know."

Why? It's hard to imagine Darya telling Cerelli anything, much less this.

He's still holding out the sat phone. "You going to take this?"

"Yes, I'll take it. Thank you." It's bulkier and heavier than my cell. And, I really hope, completely unnecessary.

"You're welcome."

I watch him, the contours of his face—he still has great bone structure. And just like eight and a half years ago, no secrets to be gleaned there, at least none I can detect. Whatever he knows about Darya isn't obvious on his face. "Look, Cerelli, I don't get it. I'm here to teach a photography course at a girls' school. That's it. Why would Darya tell you about me? How do you even know her?"

He looks at me in a way I don't completely understand. I could almost swear that, for a few seconds, he's gone to another place. "Tariq patched me up one time."

I think about that, weighing whether to push for more details. But the Cerelli I knew all those years ago wouldn't tell me more no matter how hard I pushed, so why bother. "Why get the U.S. Navy involved with me?"

"Let's get this clear: the Navy's not involved. I'm simply doing a favor for some friends and hoping to keep you safe in the process. I'm also guessing you haven't gotten a completely accurate picture of what's been going on here since the drawdown."

"Darya didn't go into detail, no." Friends, huh? Dar, why the hell haven't you ever mentioned that you know Cerelli?

"But Nic did tell you about the Taliban?"

I sigh and look away, feeling like everyone knows something more than they're telling me. "He mentioned them. Look, I'm not a complete idiot. I'm in conflict zones all the time."

"I know that. But you haven't been in *this* conflict zone for a few years."

"How the hell do you know that?" I narrow my eyes. Then I remember: this is Cerelli. The man knows everything. Damn it. I know the Taliban's resurging and ISIS is moving in. Of course, I do—I'm a journalist. I'm paid to know. I just didn't expect it all to happen so fast. Plus, being on my own, I needed to feel safe. So, I bought into the government line that the Afghan military is up to defending the country. Even though I know it's not.

"Don't beat yourself up. The coalition forces and the politicians underestimated the opposition." Cerelli offers an encouraging smile. Friendly.

"You're a mind reader now, too?"

"Just observant. You don't exactly hide what you're thinking. A word of advice: don't play poker with me unless you plan to lose."

I laugh. "I'll have you know I play a pretty mean game of poker."

"Good to know." Cerelli gives that crooked half smile again. "So, you're still planning to go up to Wad Qol?"

"Of course," I bristle. "Canon didn't donate all this equipment just for me to bring it home. More important, I'm not going to disappoint those girls."

"If you're sure, then let's get moving. We've got a lot to do today."

"What're you talking about?"

I feel his eyes tracing my bare legs again. Funny how I managed to forget I'm half-naked. Probably not a good habit to get into around Cerelli. Then again, maybe it doesn't matter. I'm off men— at least for this trip.

"More security," he says, bringing his eyes back up to mine. Nice eyes. "We're getting you a gun."

"I don't think so. I shoot cameras. Not guns."

"Where you're going, *I'll* sleep better knowing you've got a gun. I'll also feel better if you put on some clothes."

8

KOCHA-E-MURGHA, ALSO KNOWN as Chicken Street, is narrow and crowded with stalls selling everything imaginable. Silver rings and necklaces and earrings. Gold bangles I'd love to have jangling on my wrists. Brilliantly colorful, intricately patterned silk and wool carpets. Pashmina shawls that look so soft I want one in every color to take home for Mel. Hand-tooled leather belts, the musty scent wafting around me. Long strips of white and brown and tan cotton cloth to wrap into turbans. Glistening boxes made of lapis lazuli. For enough money, I'm sure I could snag some Jack Daniels or Wild Turkey. And, given all the poppy fields outside the city, I wouldn't be surprised if there was some opium or even heroin changing hands.

Shoppers jam the street. Expats from Western countries. Afghan men mostly in *shalwar kameez*, but some wearing jeans and T-shirts. Afghan women modestly dressed in form-concealing clothes—arms and wrists, calves and ankles covered—and they're all wearing headscarves. Or *burqas* that cover them head to ankles with a bit of woven netting to see through. So many *burqas*. So much for progress. I can't distinguish one woman from another. Any sense of individuality is totally concealed. Which is the point, of course.

I'm wearing a loose-fitting tunic, my baggiest cargo pants, and my *keffiyeh*. Not that the black-checked scarf is doing much to conceal my red hair. Piera, with her body-hugging clothes, will be a cultural disaster.

Cerelli maneuvers his way around slowly moving pairs of women and groups of window shoppers. I follow on his heels. At some point, he reaches for my sleeve-covered wrist—not my hand—to keep track of me and keep me moving.

"Don't come here on your own," he says quietly over his shoulder.

"Seriously?"

"It's not safe, especially for a woman."

"You've got to be kidding." I glance pointedly at the hundreds of women crowding the street.

"They're Afghans, and it's not always safe for them either. There've been some bombings. Cars. Wagons. Trucks. Suicides. And kidnappings—a great moneymaker for the Taliban and ISIS. Just promise me you'll stay away."

I look at the stalls, the shoppers, the eye-achingly blue sky overhead. It's hard to believe such violence is happening here. So much chatter. So much life. Suicide bombers could kill a lot of people on this street. So easy to rig explosives under a *burqa*. I shudder at the thought. Definitely not safe. I'll feel a whole lot better when we get out of here. But I'm in-country for the duration, and whatever precautions I have to take, I will.

"So, am I safe with you?"

He grins. "Probably not. But stay close anyway. We won't be here very long."

His grin fades. His hand tightens its hold on my wrist as his pace slows the slightest bit.

"What's going on?" I ask.

"Just looking."

"For what?"

"Not what. *Whom.* And I'm not picking him up yet."

I stare at him in disbelief. "A little paranoid, are we?"

"Always. It's what keeps me alive."

Of course, the man is cautious. Of course, he has a finely-tuned sixth sense. It's that survival instinct that's gotten him to Chicken Street today.

"Look," he says barely loud enough for me to hear, "just because I don't see him, doesn't mean he's not out there."

"Or she," I whisper back.

He looks at me over his shoulder. "Or she."

After a few blocks, the stalls of Chicken Street give way to more permanent structures. Small shops only a few meters wide, with actual windows and doors, offering carved wooden furniture and pottery, clothing and shoes. Then a bookstore, a display of Dari and Pashto poetry books in the front window. I try to stop, but Cerelli hurries me along. His hand still unobtrusively directing me, he steps around a pair of *burqa*-clad women. Dust and the ripe odor of human sweat envelop me as I follow him into a shop.

A *burqa* shop.

This can't be right. I stop abruptly just as Cerelli lets go of my wrist. Turning to look back to the street, I see the two women watching me. Framed in the shop doorway, clad in their black *burqas*, dark socks, and worn leather sandals, the women create an image I'd love to capture. My fingers itch for my Canon.

A gun, I want to remind Cerelli. *Not a burqa.* I clench my jaw. Maybe, I think, trying to calm down, just maybe this shop is a black-market front for guns? But somehow, I know it's not. I know Cerelli has something besides guns in mind, something that's going to really piss me off.

The black-bearded shopkeeper sits sprawled on a rusting metal chair in front of rack upon rack of hanging *burqas*. Periwinkle. Rose pink. Coppery brown. Lapis blue. Black. The desire in my fingers intensifies. Another image needing to be captured. But why does it have to be an image of *burqas*?

A young boy, probably all of eight, dressed in a white *shalwar kameez* and a plaid vest, looking like a mini-me of his shopkeeper father, smiles joyfully at Cerelli. "*Kâkâ* Feen!" he shouts and launches himself into Finn's arms.

I stare at the scene in front of me. *Kâkâ?* Uncle? Seriously? The Dari language is complicated with different names for every possible family relationship. Just saying "uncle" depends on whether the uncle is the father's brother or the mother's. But unless Cerelli's got an Afghan wife lurking in the background, he's not this boy's uncle.

"Feen! *Salâm, berâdar-em.*" The shopkeeper stands and claps his hand on Cerelli's shoulder.

"*Salâm,* Arman *berâdar-em.*"

My brother. Or my good friend. There's no way Cerelli is the shopkeeper's brother. So, how does he know this guy? There could be any number of explanations. None of which he's likely to tell me.

I let the men talk and wander to the racks of *burqas*. Different colors, but all of them the same style—yards of fabric with dyed-to-match netting for the eyes and roughly made lace near the hem. All designed to conceal a woman and render her shapeless.

And protect her against men's baser instincts. Against my better judgment, I finger a bit of rosy-pink fabric. Heavy cotton, tightly woven. Coarse. Definitely not breathable. This would be a furnace in the hot summer months.

The boy approaches shyly, stopping a foot away, taking care not to touch me. "*Asalâmu alaykum!*" Peace on you, he says, adopting the formal greeting.

"*Wa 'alaykum asalâm.*" And on you, peace, I reply, watching his eyes grow large in surprise.

"*Amrikâyi?*"

"*Balê.*" I nod yes, continuing to rub the rough fabric between my thumb and forefinger. This could cause some serious chafing no matter what a woman is wearing underneath.

"*Na.*" He shakes his head, then lifts the hem of a coppery brown *burqa* and points at the long curl of red that has worked its way loose from my headscarf. "*Naswâri.*"

"Yes, the brown, it will work well for you." The shopkeeper cups his hand on the boy's head. His face radiates approval of his son's suggestion. This brown will definitely make my hair flame even more intensely. "My son has a good eye for color."

Which would seem to be a waste in a burqa shop, I think.

"No." All three of us turn to look at Cerelli, who's holding up the hem of a periwinkle *burqa*. "We'll take this one."

"But, my brother, she will be invisible in that color. All the women, they wear the periwinkle. She will be just one of many."

"Yes, my brother, that is precisely why I want it."

The shopkeeper looks thoughtful for a moment and then clearly gets Cerelli's point. "*Balê.*"

I sure as hell don't. "But of course, I'm not buying a *burqa*," I say, trying to sound pleasant, but firm.

The two men barely glance at me before they resume their dickering. A moment later, they look at me again, longer this time, sizing me with their eyes.

"*Bozorg,*" they say at the same time.

Large? Without the least hesitation, not even bothering to ask me, they both decide I wear a *large*? I sidle over to Cerelli. Barely able to control my anger, I breathe into his ear, "I. Am. Not. Buying. A. *Burqa.*"

"No," he breathes back. "I am." Turning to the shopkeeper, he adds, "And the *shalwar kameez*. Also, large."

A *shalwar kameez*? We haven't even talked about that. The light isn't all that great in the shop, but from what I can see, the *shalwar kameez* Cerelli is pointing to is a drab brown. Definite message there.

The shopkeeper beams as he carefully folds the clothing, then wraps them in two separate parcels of pristine white paper. He measures out several lengths of white cotton string. My anger mounts with each knot he ties.

As soon as we leave the shop, I'm all over Cerelli. "What the hell do you think you're doing?"

"Security," he says. "You can thank me later."

"*Thank* you?" He's got to be kidding. I want to wring his neck.

"I DON'T EXPECT YOU TO wear the damn thing," Cerelli says as we walk back up Chicken Street, then turn onto Flower Street where the pungent aromas of grilling meats and vegetables have me salivating.

"Ah, good, lunch," I say, sniffing the air. "And thank God, because I'm starving. We large women have to eat a lot."

The corner of his mouth quirks up, and he shakes his head before continuing. "Believe me, this is the *last* thing I want to see you wearing. But it might just save your life."

"I'm teaching a photography class. Two weeks, and I'm on my way home. End of story. I don't need a *burqa*."

He stops in the middle of the sidewalk and glares at me. I get the message: Go *teach your course! Just don't be stupid. Take the burqa.* The men behind us manage to walk around him but shoulder their way against me. I clench my fists in annoyance. Right. The lot of a woman in Afghanistan: to be invisible.

"Look, chances are remote that anything will happen in Wad Qol or anywhere else in the Panjshir Valley while you're there. Okay? Ahmad Shah Massoud may be dead, but he's got the five lions keeping watch over the valley—"

"Lions?"

"That's what *Panjshir* means—five lions. Massoud's brothers, his son, and thousands of loyal Tajiks keep watch over the valley. Plus, the Hindu Kush Mountains make it next to impossible for any force to get in. You *should* be safe. The Taliban were never able to get a foothold there. Neither were the Soviets. And I seriously doubt ISIS will either."

"So, if you're not worried, why—?" I point to the packages he's carrying.

"I said *remote*, not impossible. My job is to make you as safe as I can."

I think about that for five seconds, then shake my head. "No, it's not."

He looks at me quizzically. "What's not?"

"Your job. It's not your job to keep me safe."

The muscle by the corner of his eye starts to pulse.

"Hey." I almost put my hand on his arm, then pull it back. "Not that I don't appreciate your efforts, I just want to be clear about your job responsibilities. So," I sort of smile, "where to now?"

He manages a half grin. "We're going to see what Fatima can do to turn you into a believable Afghan woman."

"Fatima?"

"A friend."

Fatima turns out to be the owner of *Khosha* restaurant. Movie-star beautiful with flawless skin and lustrous dark hair, she smiles mysteriously when she sees Cerelli. "Phinneas," she breathes in an indescribably sexy voice, "it has been a long time."

Phinneas? He goes by Phinneas? Since when?

He smiles. Then, they turn their backs to me, and I can't hear a word they're saying. But I can sure see their body language. They're barely an inch apart from each other. Friend, indeed. Fatima nods toward the back door. Cerelli and I follow her out to a tiny courtyard full of potted mulberry and lemon trees, coriander and tarragon. Plus another herb I don't recognize. I stop and rub a green leaf between my thumb and index finger, then sniff.

"*Sabzi*," says Fatima. "I brought all these plants from home."

She leads us up a staircase to the rooftop patio where hundreds of pots of herbs and lettuces, radishes and chives line the two-foot-high brick-and-plaster wall ringing the edge. The spiciness is intoxicating.

The reason for our visit becomes all too clear when Cerelli opens the package containing the *burqa*. Fatima drapes it effortlessly over her head. "You will watch closely, please," she says to me. And then she glides around the rooftop, somehow managing to avoid the chairs and tables and even the pots of herbs. Two minutes later, she pulls it off and hands it to me. "Now, is your turn."

Burqa on, I spend the next hour—a very long and tedious hour—strutting back and forth across the patio, fuming under the miles of heavy cotton cloth. Damn you, Cerelli. This *burqa* is every bit as hot and suffocating as I imagined. Sweat trickles down my back. The cool, refreshing breeze Cerelli is clearly enjoying doesn't penetrate the heavy cotton. Neither do the scents of the herbs. Or the noise from the street out front, beyond the ten-foot-high wall. My world is reduced to the little I can see through the netted eyepiece. Which means a crosshatched portion of what is directly in front of me, but zilch in my peripheral vision.

As I stalk my way across the patio, I recall the periwinkle *burqa* stuffed in the bottom of my backpack eight years ago. That *burqa* was never worn. I never even tried it on, and until this very moment have taken a great deal of pride for all womankind in that small act of defiance.

"No, not like that." Fatima exhales in loud exasperation. Again. "You look like a giant peahen. And you move like a donkey. A limping donkey. Your legs, they are stiff, maybe like you are trying to get attention. No Afghan woman walks like that."

I clench my fists and look for something to pound. Damn. I'm drenched in sweat. The *burqa* is clinging in all the wrong places. And I've been doing my best to walk like an Afghan woman. But all Fatima does is offer a running critique. Cerelli's no help. He's doing what any man would—ogling Fatima.

"Fatima!" A male voice bellows up the stairs, chased by the aromas of grilling meat and vegetables. *That* I can smell. Inside my *burqa*, I'm salivating.

"Lunch is starting soon," says Fatima. "I will have to go. Ten minutes more. That is all."

Thank God. The end is in sight. But Fatima continues to stare at me, shaking her head in despair. A lame donkey. Unwomanly. Whereas Fatima with her exquisitely kohl-rimmed eyes, perfectly manicured nails, and beautifully embroidered silk *shalwar kameez* skimming her body exudes everything feminine. And lush. Plus, she's Cerelli's special 'friend.' That much is obvious, even to a lame donkey. Not that I care.

Somewhere off to the side where I can't see him because I can't see crap, Cerelli exhales. Not a happy sound.

"Look," I say, unearthing myself from the miles of fabric and holding the *burqa* out to Fatima, "could you please show me? One more time?"

"I show you before."

"Yes, but I was angry then." Cerelli guffaws. "Please? Just once more, and this time I promise to pay attention. I want to get this right." Liar.

I sit on a cushion and watch as Fatima dons the periwinkle *burqa*. She's not as large as I am, but she's not petite either. The *burqa* is huge, but she's able to slip it over her head without clumsily battling the fabric. She never comes close to tripping. And somehow, she doesn't so much walk as *glide* across the rooftop, coming to a stop in front of me. Turning, she glides smoothly away, the fabric barely rippling. Almost like she's not even inside the *burqa* at all.

Almost like she's a ghost.

I look at Cerelli. The man is completely mesmerized. A smile plays at the corners of his mouth. I know that expression. Anticipation. Cerelli must sense me studying him because he turns toward me and raises an eyebrow in question: have you figured it out yet?

"Lose the boots," he calls to me across the patio.

At this point, I'm willing to try anything, so I loosen the laces and toe off my old military-issue boots.

"No!" Still wearing the *burqa*, Fatima hurries over. "No white socks. They will arrest you or whip you for that. Must be dark socks."

"Okay. Got it. No white socks." Damn. Women get arrested for wearing white socks? A holdover from the Taliban? I tent the *burqa* once again over my head, adjusting the skullcap so it drapes correctly, hiding me.

I finally understand. I think. When they wear these shapeless tents, most Afghan women *want* to be invisible. Or their husbands, fathers, brothers, sons want them to be invisible. The Taliban wants them invisible. Al Qaeda wants them invisible. ISIS wants them invisible. The women wear the *burqa* because they don't want to draw attention to themselves, get in trouble, arrested, whipped. The *burqa* means safety and mobility. Maybe even greater independence. I think about all those male eyes undressing me at the hotel last night—their feeling of entitlement was palpable. And scary. So, if it's the only way to go out in public safely, women give in and wear this infernal furnace. And do their best to be invisible. They move, but they don't move. They hover. They float. They certainly don't walk like Western women, who believe they have every right to go wherever, do whatever, be whoever.

How to get into that mindset? *Think in Dari*, I tell myself. But all I can come up with is that proverb I used to tell Mel whenever she complained that something was too hard: 'However tall the mountain, there is a path to the top.' Which is actually a pretty accurate description of what many Afghan women have to go through in life. They have to climb some pretty steep mountains and scramble over some jagged rocks.

I take a step. Still strutting.

Think of something else, I tell myself.

Then, suddenly, I'm in Khakwali, cowering next to the Humvee, leaning over Murphy, desperate to figure out how to get the hell away from the militants who want to kill me. Someone in a periwinkle *burqa* is crossing the open space in front of the mud-brick houses, coming toward me. Is it a woman? *Anaa*. Malalai's grandmother. She grabs my hand, wanting to help me because I was kind to her granddaughter.

And now, she's here—in front of me on the rooftop patio, gesturing frantically for me to follow her. She pulls at my wrist. I follow. *Grow small*, I admonish myself. *Stay invisible. Make the shooters believe you're an Afghan woman.* I float after *Anaa*. Back and forth across the rooftop, weaving past low tables and piles of cushions. Zig. Then zag. Keeping the pattern random. Then, *Anaa* moves dangerously close to the edge, to the one place where the ledge is crumbling, and tripping over some pots of cardamom, she disappears.

"*Na!*" I scream, and with a single, large American step, tangle my feet in the *burqa* and fall face-first to the floor.

I'm fighting the humiliation of my face-plant when I feel Cerelli's hands on me, pulling off the *burqa*. "Are you all right?"

"Fine. I-I . . . I was following her and . . . and—" I look at my scraped palms, then up into Cerelli's eyes. The unnetted view of Cerelli is much better, but I'm not at all sure I like the worry I see gathering in the depths of those brown eyes.

"Not bad," says Fatima, walking toward us. "The beginning, the end, not so good—they very bad, terrible. But in the middle, even *I* could believe you are Afghan woman."

"Thanks," I say, feeling ridiculously pleased. "You helped a lot."

"Good luck," she says graciously. "Tomorrow maybe, you come back to *Khosha* for more practice." What she's really saying: you need all the practice you can get.

I'm in the middle of rewrapping the *burqa* in the paper from the shop when I glance up to see Cerelli hand a roll of Afghani bills to Fatima. My heart surprises me by skipping a beat as I watch her look up at him, smile seductively, and slide the money smoothly down the neckline of her *shalwar kameez* and into her bra. I focus back on my package, thread the string around the wrapping, and pull it into a tight knot.

Fatima leads us downstairs into the main part of the restaurant. We both order the *borani banjân*, even though I ate it just last night. Fatima serves the food almost immediately. "Phinneas," she murmurs in her low and sexy voice as she positions Cerelli's plate in exactly the right spot. She makes such a production out of it that I nearly roll my eyes. Once she leaves, I relax into the floor cushion and breathe in the aromas. When I finally look up, I see Cerelli is watching me.

"Phinneas?" I say. "What's with that? You told me your name was Finn."

He raises an eyebrow. "I'm a complicated person."

"No kidding." I tear off a piece of hot *nân* and use it to scoop up a mouthful of grilled eggplant cooked with tomatoes and yogurt. *Oh, God.* I close my eyes. This is as close to nirvana as I'm going to get anytime soon.

Cerelli looks up from his plate, his smile crooking up the right side of his mouth. "Did you just moan?"

I feel my face flush. "Afraid so." Can I possibly embarrass myself more? Might as well go for broke. Ignoring my napkin, I slowly suck each of the fingers on my right hand to make sure none of the heavenly sauce goes to waste. "Better than sex," I say, pitching my voice low and breathy, like Fatima's.

Cerelli eats the last of the *nân*, studying me carefully. "I think we need more data to make an accurate comparison."

I stop sucking and narrow my eyes. "Let me get this straight. Did you, an officer and a gentleman, just proposition me?"

He puts up his hands in surrender. "*You're* the one who moaned."

Fatima busies herself serving the never-ending flow of customers, and yet every time I look up, I see her watching us. As soon as we finish our *borani banjân,* she brings over two glasses of *chai sabz* and a plate of honey and nut sweets. The look on Cerelli's face as he thanks her makes it clear which sweets he'd prefer. The tiny clench around my heart takes me by surprise. Get real. This is Cerelli. The man has obviously slept his way through a small country of women. Not to mention that a few years ago, he accused me of fucking Murphy and was ready to stamp me a one-way ticket to Gitmo.

He turns back to me. "You mind telling me what was going on up on the roof?"

Whiplash. Damn, he's still good at catching me off guard. "I thought we were talking about sex."

"Consider this foreplay."

"Funny."

"The roof? Your final walk in the *burqa?* Tell me about it." He's looking so deeply into my eyes, it feels like he can see inside me. Which is way too claustrophobic.

I squirm on my floor cushion. "You mean when I wasn't limping like a lame donkey?" Out of the corner of my eye, I see Fatima emerge from the kitchen carrying two plates laden with food that smells delicious. How could I possibly still be hungry?

"You do have a way with words."

I sip my tea, holding the glass with both hands. "I believe those were Fatima's words."

"Really? I didn't notice." He rests his index finger on the back of one of my hands, barely touching me, but it's enough to draw me back into the conversation.

"More foreplay?" I ask.

He doesn't move his finger. "The roof."

"I was trying to get inside the head of an Afghan woman who's wearing one of those . . . *things*. They're awful, you know. Have you tried wearing one? They're hot. They stink. You could suffocate—"

"Point taken. Continue."

"So, I realized most Afghan women probably don't want to wear them either, but it lets them feel safe, protected."

He's watching me, intently. Too intently.

I drop my eyes back to the plate of *baklawa* and sugared almonds. "Well, so, uh, then I saw her—do you really want to know this?"

"I do. Who did you see?"

"Okay, this is going to sound crazy, but I thought I saw Malalai's *anaa* from Khakwali. She was there, up on the roof, wearing a periwinkle *burqa,* and she was doing that same surreal floating thing as Fatima—moving like some kind of wraith, like she wasn't really inside the *burqa*. She told me to follow her. She was trying to help me get away from the Taliban. So, I moved like a ghost, too—" Shit. What did I just say? Cerelli must think I'm certifiable.

Before I realize what's happening, Cerelli is leaning across the table, gently loosening my fingers from the tea glass. Fatima starts toward the table, but he waves her off.

I slump on my cushion, watching Cerelli watch me. The minutes tick by, but I can't bring myself to look away. It's as if his eyes are the only thing tethering me in place, keeping me from floating away.

"I'm losing it, aren't I?"

"I don't think so."

"How can you say that?"

"Because eight and a half years ago, I got inside your head. If you were crazy, believe me, I'd know."

"That was then. What the hell is wrong with me now?"

"Has this happened before?"

I take a deep breath and nod. "Last night, this morning. I *heard* Malalai in my room. I talked to her."

"I know."

"She answered me."

"No, listen to me. You *heard* her speak. That's different from *she answered me*."

I let that sink in, until I understand what he means. He's taken Malalai out of the equation. *I'm* the action figure here.

"What about last night at the hotel café?" he asks.

"Last night?"

"After Nic Lowe stopped by the table, I kept an eye out. Just in case any of those interested parties at the tables next to yours got a little too interested."

I get where he's going. "You saw me drop the tea glass."

"I did. Tell me what that was about."

I look down at my hands, stalling for time. Do I want to tell him? I should. I look up again, and his eyes catch mine. "It was the tea leaves. I saw their faces in the tea leaves—Murphy and Lopez. Malalai."

"Like what just happened up on the roof?"

I take my time answering. "No. With the tea leaves, I didn't hear anything. I wasn't caught up in it. It wasn't *real*."

He nods. "Anything else since Masum Ghar?"

I shake my head slowly. "Only that time on the ship—the first day of the 'debriefing.' You probably don't remember."

"Oh, I remember." Cerelli smiles. "Nothing since then?"

"That's it." I bunch the cloth napkin in my fists. "So far."

"They've all happened here in Kabul since you've been back."

"Yeah," I nod. "So, what are you saying?"

A smile tugs at the corner of his mouth. "Not crazy."

"Sorry to disagree, but it feels pretty crazy. What I imagine PTSD might be like."

He takes in my comment and shrugs. "Could be. I'm not saying it isn't. But I'm betting that when you get home, you'll be okay." His finger is back to resting on my hand. "Something's triggering your flashbacks," he says. "You know what they say: 'After a man is bitten by a snake, he's afraid of ropes.'"

"I've never been very fond of snakes."

"The point is, if someone has a bad experience, similar things can remind them of it. You had a very bad experience in Khakwali. But you were okay for years. Now that you're back, something here and now is making you relive that time, triggering your memories. Could be nerves, or something as simple as a sound, a smell, me."

Cerelli as the trigger? Seriously? The man saved my life, yeah, but later, onboard the *Bataan*, he was pretty much a bastard.

"So, what am I supposed to do? What if something like this happens again when I'm in Wad Qol?"

"When a big wave comes, lower your head and let it pass."

I manage a thin smile. "That sounds like something my daughter would say. Darya gave her a book of Dari proverbs years ago, and she took that as permission to tell me how to live my life."

His eyes brighten. "Emmeline, right? And you call her Emmy?"

That stops me for a second as I remember the threats Cerelli's co-interrogator made on the USS *Bataan*. Unless I confessed to aiding the Taliban, I'd never see my daughter again. I clear my throat and push that awful day out of mind. "You remember. Yeah,

Emmeline. Kind of an old-fashioned name, but it's in honor of my Grammy, her great-grandmother. She goes by Mel now. Apparently, 'Emmy' was too babyish."

"Tell me about her. Wait, let me guess. Red hair, like yours."

"Wrong." I dig out my phone and open the gallery to a recent shot of Mel cuddling with the dog. "Purple." I hold up the phone for him to see.

Cerelli takes the phone and studies the picture, a smile lighting his eyes. "For a photographer, your sense of color is wacked."

"What do you mean?"

"Her hair isn't purple. It's periwinkle. Same color as the *burqa* we just bought you."

I snatch the phone, ready to tell him he's an idiot, that I know what color my own daughter's hair is. Mel's image smirks at me from the small screen. Damn, he's right.

Periwinkle. It had to be periwinkle? *Mom, think about it.* Of course. Her favorite flower. The vines of vinca loaded with those very flowers running riot in the garden in front of my house. How come Cerelli saw it immediately, and I didn't?

He smiles. "I like it. Shows a free spirit."

"Definitely a free spirit. A force of nature." I look again at the picture. "She dances. Right now, she's doing modern, although her stepmother's after her to go back to classical ballet." Why the hell did I bring *that* up? "She lives to dance. That, and Chance."

"Chance? Is that a name? Or a game? Or what?"

"Her boyfriend." I look up from the screen. "Don't get me started."

"Tell me about the guy."

I frown. "Mel's fifteen. Chance is older—eighteen, maybe? A senior in high school. My ex and his wife think this guy hangs the moon, but I think he's too old for her. I found them in my apartment when I got home from my last assignment. Actually, I found her. Chance ran out the back door. The coward. I think he's pressuring her for sex. She says she's been saying *no*, but—"

"You're her mother. You worry. That's good."

"Yeah, I worry. A lot. My guilt over being away from her so much knows no bounds."

"You have any video of her dancing on that cell?"

"I do. Her winter recital. My friend, Bonita, shot it for me. I was—I was on assignment." I bring up the video, pass my phone across the table.

He watches until the end. "I don't know a whole lot about dance, but I like what I see. Great movement. And—spirit. She takes after her mother."

I'm determined not to blush. "I don't know about that. I love to dance, but Mel *is* a dancer." I tuck the cell back in my pocket. What a great sport he is.

"One more question."

"Yeah?"

"What's your dog's name?"

Shit. He has to ask that? This time, I can't keep from blushing. "Finn."

"A good name." He leans forward, and his voice takes on a serious tone. "Do me a favor. Give Mel the number for the sat phone. My contact info, too. She'll feel better knowing she can reach you. I think you will, too. And—"

"I know. My cell won't be worth crap in the valley."

9

AN HOUR AND A HALF to the base at Bagram, and then we're in the building that houses the shooting range. Cerelli brings out two guns. The first, a Sig Sauer P228, is the one he thinks will work best for me, but it's lighter than I expected. I assume the stance, two-handing the gun like he showed me. But something feels off, like it's too small for my hands. Maybe it's got the wrong heft. Or maybe it's just that it's a *gun*—the last thing I want to hold. Or use. I put it back on the table.

"Talk to me," he says.

"I don't know." I shrug. "It doesn't feel right. Like it could fly right out of my hand."

"Try the other one. It's a little heavier. You've got to have the right piece—it's got to feel like it's a natural extension of your hand."

"Cerelli, my *cameras* feel like a part of me. There's no way on earth a *gun* will ever feel that way."

He picks up the other Sig Sauer and hands it to me.

I balance the gun in my hand. Maybe a little better. "It's just not—I don't know how to explain it. It doesn't feel—"

The muscle at the corner of his eye twitches.

"Look, I'm sure it's me. I'm just not a—"

"—gun person. Believe me, I got the message."

"Annie. Good to see you again. Captain." Senior Chief Sawyer stands in the open doorway and grins. Damn, he looks almost the same as he did eight and a half years ago. Although his beard isn't quite so scraggly, and his hair isn't as long. He was my knight in shining armor during that week of hell on the *Bataan*. "I've got the shooting range set up and ready to go. Annie, you got your gun?"

I don't laugh. Neither does Cerelli.

"Give us a minute, Chief," says Cerelli quietly, the muscle at the corner of his eye now pulsing. "Annie, you've got to have the right gun. Your life—"

"I *know*, but these just feel wrong. Too light, maybe?"

"Hey, Captain. Why not let her try yours?" Sawyer says casually, like it's no big deal.

The muscle by Cerelli's eye looks like it could launch into a major spasm.

I step back, out of the line of fire, and raise my hands in surrender. "No need. I'll just go with this one. It'll be fine. Show me to the range."

"Okay, then." Sawyer rubs his hands together. "Through the door and to the right. Lucky booth number three." The booth is small, especially with Sawyer crowding in next to me. Cerelli stays back, doing what he does best—watching. "Annie! You with me here?" Sawyer has assumed the stance. "Eyes on me. The Captain may be an ace shot, but his form's all wrong. Now me—perfect form."

A quick glance over my shoulder, and I catch sight of Cerelli's smirk. Then focus on Sawyer and try to copy what he's doing.

"Plant your feet and keep your weight under your hips. Easy on the knees."

Check.

"Hold the gun with both hands."

Death grip. I hold on as tight as I can.

Sawyer puts his hand on my shoulder. "Ease up, okay? Don't kill the gun. Love it. Hands steady and firm—like you're caressing—"

"Caressing. Got it."

"I mean, like you're caressing your camera."

"I don't *caress* my camera."

"Well, think of something you *do* caress."

Behind us, Cerelli chokes back a laugh.

"Okay. Forget caressing. Just hold it gently. And firmly." Defeat is audible in Sawyer's voice. "Now, bring up the gun. Sight your target. Lock your elbows."

Check. Check. Check.

"Keep your hands steady and be ready for the recoil."

"Got it."

"You ready?"

I nod.

"Then release the safety."

"The safety?"

"My bad." He shows me how to release the safety, then re-engages it, and makes me do it. "Aim for body mass." Pulling my earmuffs into place, effectively plunging me into a cone of silence, he points toward the target and taps me on the shoulder, mouthing, "When you're ready."

Steadying the gun in my hands, I take a deep breath, and—wishing I were anywhere but here—pull the trigger. The Sig flies up—way up. I don't need to look at the target to know I missed it—by a mile.

Sawyer taps my shoulder. Try again.

I overcorrect, and this time the Sig drops down.

Another tap.

Another miss. Sideways.

Sawyer motions me to take off the muffs. "What's wrong?"

What? He can't see? The target's obviously still bullet-free.

Then Cerelli's next to me, taking the Sig out of my hand. "Try this one," he says, handing me a new gun.

Much as I hate to admit it, this gun feels good. A bit heavy, but the right heft. Well-balanced. Like my favorite Canon. I'm betting it's Cerelli's gun. "You sure you trust me with this?" I ask him over my shoulder.

"You planning to shoot me?"

"It crossed my mind earlier, but I'm good now."

"Then, I trust you. Go for it."

I two-hand the gun and lift it, but then freeze, trying to work through Sawyer's long checklist. Cerelli lifts the gun a little higher into my sightline.

"Forget everything Sawyer told you," he breathes into my ear. "Find your own way." He clamps the muffs over my ears.

I squint my left eye and focus my right on the paper terrorist hanging at the far end of my alley, aim for the torso, and pull the trigger. Smooth. Then, taking a deep breath and holding it, I pump six more bullets into the paper chest.

Cerelli lifts the muff off my right ear. "Did you seriously just moan?"

I laugh.

Sawyer brings the paper target up to the booth. "The Captain said this was your first time shooting a gun?"

"Yeah."

He shakes his head. "You're one scary lady."

Cerelli circles the seven holes with a red marker. "BZ with the shooting."

"BZ? What does that mean?"

"Bravo Zulu. Well done. Let's see if you can do it again."

For the next two hours, that's exactly what I do. Again, and again. Not that I bull's-eye every shot, but it turns out I'm damn good. And ready for this to be over. "How much longer?" I hear the whine in my voice and cringe.

Cerelli quirks his eyebrow, clearly thinking I need all the practice I can get. "Look, the last thing I want is for you to shoot this gun. But if you have to, I want to make damn sure you're the one who walks away."

I sigh, sight the target, and empty the clip.

THE TRAFFIC ON THE ROAD back to Kabul is bumper-to-bumper, so it takes close to three hours to get to the Inter-Continental. When we finally arrive, the security guard takes one look at Cerelli and waves us right through. Unlike yesterday. Cerelli walks me inside, and standing in front of the reception desk, we read Tariq Ghafoor's message. Just one line:

I will come to the hotel for you tomorrow at seven in the morning.

"Looks like you're off to Wad Qol," says Cerelli as we walk the length of the lobby toward the elevators. "You'll feel better once you're on the road. A word of caution, though. The highway up to the valley can be crap. Sometimes almost nonexistent."

"Like their cell phone reception."

He grins.

I study his face. He's hard to read, but I'm betting he's relieved to see the last of me. Just like when I left the USS *Bataan* for Karachi and then home. He most definitely was happy to see me go. And pissed—certain there was an SD card I hadn't given up despite his almost constant harassment. He was right, of course. I'd hidden it in my bra.

"So, are you going to ask me?" I say.

His face goes blank.

"Last time I saw you, on the flight deck of the *Bataan*, you were like a pit bull, still after me about that SD card you thought I was holding back. I've been waiting all day for you to ask."

He laughs. "Annie, I don't need to ask. I *know* exactly what happened to that card. You published the photos and won a pretty impressive prize. I was sure you had it in the pocket of those baggy pants you insisted on wearing."

"But you frisked me."

He raises an eyebrow. "Waist down. You would've unmanned me if I'd done any more. Now, would you tell *me* something?"

I narrow my eyes. "What?"

He leans in close and lowers his voice. "Why the hell you were driving around with Murphy and Lopez handing out water and MREs instead of going to the front."

"You're still thinking about that?" I ask incredulously.

"Oh, yeah. Not knowing has been making me crazy for years."

One look at his face tells me it's true. Which puzzles me. "The CO at Masum Ghar didn't tell you?"

He grins. "Oh, he told me the bullshit you fed him. And that he held you back, gave you penalty duty for going AWOL and lying on top of it. Same thing you told me during our 'conversation' on the *Bataan*. I want to know what really went down."

I think about it for half a minute. Do I really want to tell him? I've managed to keep this buried deep inside me. Until I ran into Nic a couple days ago. And now. . . oh, hell, what does it matter anymore. "Hazing," I say finally. "As in, the guys handed me a line about getting the scoop on a spec op, and I jumped. Needless to say, the only thing going on was the chance to dump me out in the desert and let me find my own way back."

His grin vanishes. The muscle next to his eye leaps into action.

"See, war correspondents are a brotherhood. Emphasis on the 'brother.' Men make the rules, and you do what you have to do to stay in the game. Or you get out. Or sometimes, you die."

"You're fucking kidding me."

"I wish I were. But it still happens. More often than I care to think about."

He turns away from me, but not before I see the dark flush of anger wash across his face. Then, he's back to looking at me, his hand on my shoulder. "You should have told me. I could have done something."

I shake my head. "That's exactly why I didn't. It would've been the end of my career."

"Meaning?"

"You tell, word gets out. Word *always* gets out. And then, they drum you out of the brotherhood, make it so bad you want to quit. In all kinds of ways. Sabotaging your gear. Not telling you to duck when there's incoming. Fragging. Same as in the military."

"So, when you told the CO you snuck outside the wire to photograph civilians, that was a lie—to save your career."

"Exactly. Not my finest moment, but I couldn't tell him the guys had hazed me."

"You going to give me a name?"

It doesn't take me long to come to a decision. "No. Let's just say it wasn't only one person. It never is. And there were Marines in on it."

"The CO know anything?"

"I don't think so."

"I want their names."

Damn it all. I shouldn't have said anything. The man really is a pit bull. "Give it up, Cerelli."

"Can't." His phone rings, and he holds up an index finger. Sawyer's voice is at the other end.

"Leaving now." Cerelli slides his cell back into the inner pocket of his jacket. "Looks like I'm going wheels up. CONUS." CONUS. Military-speak for Continental United States. He hands me the packages with the *burqa*, the *shalwar kameez*, and the gun that wasn't his but is the same model and weight, along with some clips of ammunition.

"I figured something was up," I say. "So, thanks for all your help today."

"I think you're set." He rests his hand on the small of my back. Friendly. "Look, I'll be back in-country soon. You call me if you get in trouble."

"Trouble?" I cock my head. "What trouble?"

He grins. "Funny. But I need you to take this seriously."

I do my best to look serious. "I promise if I get in trouble, I'll call."

"Thank you. And before you leave Kabul, call Mel. Give her the sat phone number."

"Done."

"Do you have sandals?"

"No."

"Tomorrow, have Tariq stop at the market in Bazarak. He knows where it is. Get yourself a pair. Leather, not those cheap plastic ones the villagers in the valley wear. Make sure you wear them and scuff them up good so they don't look brand new. And dark socks. If you have to go invisible, you need to *be* invisible."

He's dead serious. "Dark socks. Sandals. Scuffed. Got it."

"One last thing." He smiles. "You can rest easier tonight. I had Sawyer remove the bugs from your room today. And the video feed."

"Video?" I choke out the word, thinking of when I stripped down last night, not to mention *showered*. "You were *watching* me, too?"

"It was a pleasure, ma'am."

10

CALL MEL. CERELLI SAID IT twice, and I'm taking him seriously. My smartphone in hand, I stand at the window in my room, listening to the static and watching the sun set. The pollution-laden Kabul sky blazes a thousand shades of pink and orange and gold. I could lose myself in those colors. Another minute, then I tap out the full number, country code and all. Two rings later, Mel's on the line.

"Hey, Mom!"

"Sweetie. How's it going?"

She doesn't answer right away. My thoughts run instantly to Chance. Please, no. Don't let him be pressuring her to sleep with him. But she hates it when I push too hard, so I grip the cell and force myself to wait.

"Good." Her voice says otherwise.

"It's not Chance, is it?" So much for waiting.

"No, Mom. It's not Chance. God, you're so predictable. It's . . . I didn't want to upset you, but—well—it's C.E."

"What's going on?" I work at keeping my voice steady but feel it starting to fray.

"Get this. All of a sudden, she hates my hair. I mean really hates it. She's convinced Daddy that I look hideous. So, now I've got to color it back to brown or . . ."

"Or what?"

"I'm grounded till I change it back. Mom, the dance recital— if I miss rehearsals, I'll be cut from the performance. And—" She gulps. "Mom, you've got to talk to Daddy. Please?"

Mel's been dying her hair crazy colors for over a year. So, why is Catherine Elizabeth doing this now? I can already hear Todd's stupid assurances that C.E. *loves Emmy like she's her own daughter.* Right.

The sun slips below the horizon. The colors so vivid a minute ago darken to mauve and purple, then to deep sapphire blue. Here in Kabul, night seems to fall faster than back home where I can count on sunsets to linger. It never ceases to amaze me how quickly things change or totally cease to be in some parts of the world.

"Mom, please? Don't let them do this to me!"

"Is he there?"

"I'll get him."

"Wait! Look, where I'm going—Wad Qol village—I just found out you probably won't be able to reach me on my cell. Remember how Auntie Dar always has to call from Kabul? So, I, uh, got a satellite phone. I've also got the number for a friend—in case you can't reach me." I read her the numbers Cerelli wrote on the phone. "Could you program those into your cell?"

"No problem. Now, will you talk to him? Please?"

"Put him on."

It takes her a minute and a terse exchange with Catherine Elizabeth—*leave your father alone*—before Todd gets on the line.

"Annie? You okay?" He sounds worried. I wonder how Catherine Elizabeth feels about that.

"I'm fine. Look, I was just talking to Mel about . . . her hair."
I put the palm of my hand against the cool glass of the window,
my fingers spread wide. Below in the courtyard, the fairy lights are
twinkling and the restaurant is bustling to life.

"There's nothing to talk about. I agree with Catherine Elizabeth
on this. Mel's purple hair is . . . grotesque. End of conversation."

I curl my fingers into a fist. "She is *not* grotesque. Her hair color
reflects who she is—her free spirit." I make a mental note to thank
Cerelli. "You should be proud *our* daughter is able to express herself
in such a vibrant way. Oh, and by the way, didn't we agree to consult
on major decisions?"

"You seriously think this qualifies as major?"

"It's major to her."

"Annie. Her hair—it's over the top. I love her—you know I love
her—but there have to be limits. Teenagers want their parents to
set limits. Now she's got the twins pestering us to let them dye their
hair some crazy color. Look, Catherine Elizabeth has great taste.
She's made an appointment for Mel with her—*colorist.*" I hear
C.E. prompting in the background. "She'll look great for her dance
recital. Like a fifteen-year-old should look."

I give up counting his misconceptions about teenage girls.
"Periwinkle," I say, offering another thank you to Cerelli. "Her hair
is periwinkle, not purple."

Todd doesn't say a word. I wait out the normal cell-to-cell
international delay, but all I get is silence. It takes me a minute, and
then I realize the line is dead.

I quickly punch in the number again, but this time get nothing.
Not even static. Come on! I've *got* to get through. I try again. Still
nothing. Just dead air.

I use the room phone to call the front desk.

"Ah, Madame Green. We regret the inconvenience, but the towers, they are not cooperating tonight. It is likely there will be no more reception in Kabul until tomorrow. It is most unfortunate."

'Most unfortunate' isn't going to help Mel while her hair is turning brown. I look at the sat phone, wondering if this qualifies as an emergency. Yeah, it does for her. I punch in the number for the house in Milwaukee. The phone rings. And rings. I try Todd's cell. More ringing. Evidently, he doesn't want to talk. Damn, this was a mistake. This call. This conversation. Mel there. Me here.

I wander back to the window and look down at the cheery lights. Cooling my forehead against the window glass, I make a promise to Mel that first thing when I get home, I'll help her dye her hair whatever color she wants. A frigging rainbow, if that's what it takes.

Below me, the fairy lights flicker, then go out. Except for the burning coals in the brazier and the occasional cigar tip, the patio is dark. So is my room. Now, glowing cigar tips are moving fast toward the hotel lobby. Then, the coals are doused.

The darkness is total. Power outage? Kabul is known for its wonky electricity.

Or something worse? An attack? Could the Taliban actually be launching an attack? Blowing up a cell phone tower first to make it harder for the military to respond?

Hands in front of me, I feel my way through the darkness across the room to the door. Opening it, I step out into the hall and look both ways. It's pitch-black. The emergency lights aren't even illuminated. Damn! I violated my second safety rule: find the fire exits. I'll never be able to do it now.

Get back in the fucking room! Cerelli's voice thunders in my head. *Lock the door!*

"This is insane," I say as I feel my way back into the room. "You're *wheels up* to CONUS. How do you know what's going on?"

Hands shaking, I lock the door. Which isn't going to keep out any militants who want to get in. So, I pull the mattress off the bed, drag it across the room, then shoulder it up in front of the door. The bed frame won't budge. The nightstand, my Pelican cases, my duffel. Anything portable, I shove against the mattress. This paltry pile won't keep them out for long, but it's the best I can do. Then, grabbing the blanket and pillow, my pack with my camera and the Sig, I make my way to the bathroom, slamming and locking the door behind me.

Sit on the floor with your back to the door. It'll slow them down. Cerelli's voice again. *Tub's better if there's an explosion.*

"I know this!" I yell back at him. "I've been in war zones!"

Then do it!

I dig the gun out of my pack and try desperately to remember everything Sawyer told me to do. Except, Cerelli told me to forget everything Sawyer said. Shit. I'm well and truly on my own. Ramming a clip into the Sig, I hunker down in the tub. Hands trembling, I train the gun on where the bathroom door should be.

And tighten my grip.

Then, from a distance, comes the *thwamp-thwamp-thwamp* of a helicopter. Closer and louder until I can't hear the pounding of my own heart. The cavalry to the rescue?

Thwamp-thwamp-thwamp. The sound jolts me back eight and a half years. I grab for the side of the bathtub, but my hand flails in the dark. I'm in a helicopter with Commander Finn Cerelli and his team, touching down on the USS *Bataan* flight deck.

EVEN BEFORE THE ROTORS STOP, the men are on their feet, passing the two body bags down to the waiting crew. I scrunch up tight against the fuselage and watch. Then, Commander Cerelli's hand is on my upper arm. "They're gone, ma'am. You can open your eyes."

"I watched," I say, desperate that he understand. "I had to." I struggle to my feet, stiff from so many hours of flying. And the cold.

"I know." Cerelli looks intently into my eyes. "Believe me, I know. It may be war, but it never gets easier."

"It shouldn't get easier. Ever."

Hours later and even more exhausted, I sit in a small gray room at an aluminum-top table, opposite Cerelli, my last SD card buried deep in the pocket of the baggy jeans borrowed from the Navy while the laundry cleans my clothes. Despite my non-regulation extended shower of scrubbing and steaming, I can still smell blood. Malalai's. Murphy's. Lopez's.

Cerelli, though, looks unbelievably well rested, his long hair shiny clean and pulled back into a ponytail, his beard less scraggly. He taps a BIC pen on the legal pad in front of him. "Tell me what happened." He smiles, his brown eyes encouraging, making me trust that everything will be all right. Just a debriefing to sort out a bad situation.

But I don't have a clue where to begin. Without warning, a tiny pinprick of panic starts throbbing in the middle of my forehead and then expands until I'm struggling to sit upright. I stare at a spot in the center of the table. It's yawning wider and wider. Sand. So much sand. And rain, turning the sand to muck. I grip the edge of the tabletop and fight desperately to keep from being sucked in.

Cold creeps up my legs, inches along my spine, engulfs me. The smell of blood fills my nostrils. My hands, wet and stinking of goat shit, close around Murphy's gun.

Hands reach for me. Clamp onto my wrists. Hold tight.

"Murphy! No! You can't die." I pull hard, trying to break away.

"Annie!"

I look up. Cerelli is leaning across the table, his hands holding me, his eyes locked on mine.

"Breathe," he says.

Cautiously, I eye the center of the table. Nothing there except Cerelli's pad of paper. No hole. I risk a deep breath, then let it out slowly. Another breath.

"We're on the USS *Bataan*. You're safe."

Trembling from fear, shivering with cold, I look around the room. Solid steel bulkheads. Not even any windows. Safe? I'm not so sure. "What's wrong with me?"

"Nothing's wrong with you," he says quietly, firmly. "War is hell and then more hell. You watched two, no, three people die. Believe me, nothing's wrong with you." A while later. "You back with me?" he asks.

"Yeah."

"Good. Look, I know this isn't easy, but it's important. We've got to know what happened out there. I need you to tell me what you saw, heard, whatever you noticed."

I nod. More than anything, I want the SEALs, the Marines, the entire U.S. military to go back to Khakwali and get those bastards.

Cerelli keeps his hands on the table, ready to grab hold of me if he has to. "Tell me."

I tell him about Murphy surprising me with a return visit to Khakwali. About the older boy taking the Polaroid camera from

Malalai, and about her writing letters in the sand. About the bullets, so many bullets. About Malalai in my arms, her head half-gone. About running to Lopez, then crawling to Murphy. About Malalai's *anaa* leading me to the stable. About waiting through the rain and the night for the militants to come for me. But I skip the part about why the CO reassigned me to photograph the Marines winning hearts and minds. I also don't say anything about Hicks and Johnson and the second Humvee in our mini-convoy.

"Is that all?" he asks.

"Yes," I say slowly, deciding I've told him the critical facts.

The door bursts open. Another man struts in and sits down next to Cerelli. John Smith. Hawaiian shirt, khakis. CIA. I don't doubt it for a minute.

"Tell us again," says John Smith, AKA Mr. CIA.

Again? How does he know what I said in the first place? Has he been standing outside the door listening? I think about that for all of five seconds and figure out that the room is bugged. Has to be. I try to keep my voice light. "I just told Commander Cerelli. Do you honestly think I'm going to change my story?"

John Smith narrows his eyes. His expression doesn't change, except for the flaring of his left nostril. Then, without warning, he leans forward, far forward, in-my-face forward. "What I *think*, Ms. Green, is that your story has holes in it. Big holes. Holes I could navigate this ship through."

His voice pushes me back in my chair. "Holes? What are you talking about? I just told Commander Cerelli exactly what happened."

He slams his hand on the table in front of me. "You wouldn't recognize the truth if you ran headfirst into it. The truth is I've got *two* Marines shot to hell in a village that was full of Taliban. A village that wasn't on their orders. No way they were supposed to be there. And there's *one* survivor. You. I find that suspicious." He's still in my face. "Now, if you ever want to go stateside again, instead of having the Commander and me punch you a one-way ticket to Gitmo, you better tell me what the fuck happened out there."

Just that quickly, my confidence that this 'situation' will be resolved quickly disappears over the edge of the deep, dark hole that's back in the middle of the table. My mouth is desert dry. My tongue is sticking to the back of my teeth. "Could I—?" I nod at the bottle of water in front of Cerelli.

I drink half the bottle, then tell my story again. I'm nearing the end when I look at Mr. CIA. He's stone-faced, arms crossed, staring at me. Cerelli is slouched in his chair, only he's not at ease. Neither one of them has written a single note. Finally, I get it. These assholes are looking to pin Murphy's and Lopez's deaths on someone, and they've already made up their minds that that someone is me. Time to stop talking.

"Ms. Green?" says Mr. Smith. "You planning to finish your story?"

"As a matter of fact, I'm not. I'm invoking my right to an attorney."

"An attorney." His voice is flat.

"Her name is Darya Faludi—" Her Boston address and phone number are on the tip of my tongue.

But Mr. Smith leans back in his chair and laughs. "You don't get it, do you? This isn't the United States. You don't have any rights. And we're sure as shit not getting some Afghan lawyer in here to defend you."

I'm not giving up that easily. "This is the USS *Bataan*. Which puts it under U.S. jurisdiction. You can't just—"

Cerelli taps the table with his BIC. "We haven't brought charges. Yet. For the moment, this is still a debriefing."

"Then I'm out of here."

But before I can stand up, Mr. Smith is around the table, his hands on my shoulders. "No such luck," he says. "Now, enough of this crap about 'hearts and minds.' I want the truth."

"I told you the truth. I was in Khakwali because that's where Corporal Murphy *told* me we were going."

"Yeah, well, I've got a problem with that." Mr. CIA pulls a piece of paper from his shirt pocket and slaps it on the table. "Their orders were to go to Kobani that day. And Privates Hicks and Johnson— remember them?—are telling a very different story. They say Murphy had a thing for you. They say *you* wanted to go to *that* village and got Murphy to make sure that happened. Which tells me you were working with the Taliban to set up some Marines."

What? I shake my head in disbelief. And hear Murphy's voice echo inside my head. *You think maybe me and you could've?* Thank God no one heard us.

Cerelli waves Mr. CIA back to his chair, then looks at me. "Annie, here's the thing. Maybe Murphy came on to you. Marines are away from home for months at a time. They get lonely—"

"Excuse me, Commander. Are you seriously saying *men have needs?*"

Cerelli blinks. "I guess I am."

"Pig."

"So, Ms. Green, *were* you?" John Smith sneers.

"Excuse me, Mr. Smith, was I *what?*"

Cerelli stands and leans far across the table, clearly intent on breaking me. "Were you fucking Corporal Murphy?"

Before I realize what I'm doing, I'm on my feet, slapping

Cerelli's face. He takes the first slap but grabs my wrist before I can hit him again. Mr. CIA leaps off his chair, training his handgun on me and looking like he'd be happy to pull the trigger.

"Feel better?" Cerelli is still holding my wrist.

What I feel is the power in his hand. He could snap my arm in half if he wanted. "Much better," I say, searching frantically for a shred of dignity.

"Let's take it from a different angle." Cerelli lets go of my wrist, and I nearly fall back onto my chair. "Here's the thing. The other embedded journalists at FOB Masum Ghar all went to the front, but you stayed behind. Why?" Cerelli raises an eyebrow as if he already knows the answer.

Of course, he knows. Obviously, the CO has told him about my foray off base. That is, he's told Cerelli the story I fed him about going outside the wire to photograph women and children. On my own. The story I made up instead of fingering Nic and company. What I had to do to save my career. Fuck. Then came Khakwali. Marines died. Pvts. Hicks and Johnson lied about Murphy and blamed me to cover their butts. And just because I didn't end up dead, everyone's decided I set up Murphy and Lopez.

Guilty.

SOMETIME LATER, MY HEAD jerks upright off the edge of the bathtub. I look around me but can't see anything in the dark. Or hear anything except for the roar of the helicopter outside my window. Or is that blood pounding in my ears?

Stiff and sore, I shift, trying to find a more comfortable position. Everything about the *Bataan* seemed so real. Was I hallucinating? Or did I fall asleep? A nightmare. I can't risk doing that again. I've got to be awake when they come for me. I've got to be able to fight.

Rubbing my eyes, I stop short. Where's the Sig? Oh God, where did I put it? Is the safety on? I search the folds of the blanket I've wrapped around me. Carefully. I don't want to shoot myself. But find nothing. I climb out of the tub. On hands and knees, I gingerly pat the floor in widening circles until I find it. Safety on, I ease myself into the tub again. And stare into the darkness, determined not to let the nightmare of Cerelli and Mr. CIA back into the bathroom.

But now that it's unleashed, I can't keep it buried. Because the interrogation didn't end with Cerelli's question. Far from it. More days. Sometimes in the middle of the night. Anything to catch me off guard. To get me to confess to something I hadn't done. Until one afternoon, Cerelli and Mr. CIA changed their tactics.

I STAND IN THE DOORWAY of the interrogation room, staring in disbelief as Cerelli and Mr. CIA tape hundreds of photographs and Polaroids to the bulkheads. My photographs.

Behind me, Sawyer coughs. My guardian angel. A few days earlier, he overheard some of Murphy's and Lopez's buddies blaming me for their deaths. So, he appointed himself my perpetual escort just in case they decided to do something stupid—like stuff me in a laundry bag and dump me overboard. Meals, the head, wherever I need to go, Sawyer goes with me. The best part—he's nice to me. The only person onboard who is. Or maybe it's all a pile of crap. Maybe Cerelli set him up to get me to talk.

Cerelli turns around. "Good. You're just in time to help us analyze these pictures."

"What the fuck have you done?" I storm into the room. "Those are *my* images. Oh, God, tell me you saved the originals." Behind me, I hear the door close—Sawyer handing me over to the forces of evil.

Cerelli actually grins. I want to slap him. Again. "Sit down, and we'll talk." He turns his chair around and straddles the seat.

My fury ready to boil over, I jerk the chair away from the table and sit down. Hard.

Mr. CIA goes on hanging pictures.

Cerelli catches my eye and ticks off the answers to my unasked questions on his fingers. "Ten SanDisk cards were found in your quarters at Masum Ghar. Only two had any pictures on them. Three more cards were found in your pack. All had pictures. The Navy's very skilled photographers printed them, but I have no idea whether they saved your originals."

"You had no right. *No right.* I want my cards now."

"Confiscated," says Mr. CIA without turning around.

"You can't—"

"But," says Mr. CIA, "we have."

"You see, Annie," says Cerelli, "I've got this problem—"

"You've always got problems."

"And my primary problem is you." His tone goes from friendly to deathly cold in a second. "You've impeded this investigation from day one. You've withheld information. You've misled. You've lied. It ends now." He picks up a Lowepro camera backpack from the deck and slams it down on the table. My Lowepro.

"Where did you—?"

"Where you left it," says Cerelli. "In the back seat of the

Humvee. Senior Chief Sawyer retrieved it. And we found some items of interest." He pulls out a camera and puts it on the table.

"My backup."

"The card is wiped clean. You lug around a spare camera because all photogs love to haul more weight?"

"I carry a backup because sand is death on digital cameras. The few pics I took were lousy, so I deleted them."

He reaches into my pack again and pulls out a periwinkle *burqa*. "Care to explain this?"

"I take it the CO didn't tell you this is part of the required dress code for embedded female journalists. I'm—or I *was*—supposed to carry it with me at all times, just in case."

"No," says Cerelli, "he didn't happen to mention that."

"Or maybe," says Mr. CIA, turning around, "you wore it to meet your handler when you snuck off base."

Jesus. Could this hole get any deeper?

Then, Cerelli lays my pack of birth control pills on the table between us. "Care to comment?"

"I'm married. And I don't want to get pregnant." I can hear Mr. CIA's snort of derision from somewhere behind me. As if my BCPs are the final nail in the coffin of evidence against me.

Finally, my passport. Cerelli opens it, bends back the binding, then flattens it on the table and turns the pages. "Democratic Republic of Congo. The West Bank. Israel. Tanzania. Kenya."

"So? I was covering conflicts. I'm a war photographer. It's what I *do*."

Mr. CIA hangs the last picture and comes to the table. Like Cerelli, he turns his chair around and straddles it. "You just happened to be in Nairobi when Al Qaeda blew up the United States Embassy."

"Give me a break. You can't possibly think—"

Mr. CIA cuts me off. "You have a good friend who's from Afghanistan. Darya Faludi, right? Your college roommate."

I nod.

"That isn't exactly the name of the girl next door. How come you've got an international human rights attorney at your beck and call?"

"What the fuck are you talking about?" I clench my fists. "Darya had nothing to do with me going to Afghanistan. She tried to talk me *out* of going because it's too dangerous. Dar's about as American as they come."

"Prove it." Cerelli's voice is as sharp as the MK3 knife I've heard SEALs carry in-country.

"What?"

"You've lied repeatedly. Why should I believe you?" His eyes give no ground.

"I haven't—Darya, we went to school together. We were roommates. Best friends."

"In other words," Mr. CIA cuts in, "you'd lie your guts out for her."

"No!" And that *is* a lie. I absolutely would lie my guts—and my heart—out for her. Frantic, I scramble to come up with anything that will keep Dar out of this insanity, keep the FBI from knocking on her door and hauling her away. But nothing I say wipes the disbelief off their faces. Finally, I slam my open palms on the table. "What the hell does it matter! The point is Darya is American."

"Says you," Mr. CIA sneers. He frigging *sneers*. "We've got all the pieces now. We know how it went down. You were out in the desert that day to meet up with your handler and pass on whatever intel you'd picked up around Masum Ghar. Your handler told you not to go to the front. So, when the CO ordered you to remain behind, you were set. You got Murphy to go back to Khakwali. The guy had a hard-on for you. Easy pickings." He uses his middle finger to push my pack of BCPs closer to me. "The Taliban figured they'd get a couple Humvees, some guns, some uniforms. Everything they needed to get into Masum Ghar and blow up a whole lot more Marines. We call that colluding with the enemy. We also call it treason."

Holy shit! My head is ready to explode.

Mr. CIA saunters around to my side of the table, leaning in so close, his sour breath makes me want to throw up. "Here's what I want to know. How can you do this to your daughter?" He jiggles my chair. "Do you even care what this is going to do to Emmeline? Oh, you call her Emmy, don't you?"

Keep it together, I tell myself, clutching my chair. "You leave my daughter the hell out of this. You go near her, and I'll—"

"You'll what?"

"I'll cut off your frigging balls."

Cerelli exhales. "Okay, Ms. War Photographer. We'll give you one last chance to come clean. Help us with these photographs. Then, we'll let you know if we think you're aiding and abetting terrorists."

I am done. Totally and completely done. I close my eyes in defeat, wishing I could make this room, these assholes, the entire frigging ship disappear. But I'm stuck. And then there's Emmy. At home. Waiting for me. Trusting I'll come back. Only six years old. I absolutely can't let her grow up with me in Gitmo or Leavenworth or wherever they're going to stick me. Another minute, then I nod.

Cerelli slides a 5x7 black and white across the table. Not one of mine. "Recognize him?"

I look at the photograph, *really* look at it. The graying beard. The full lips. The hawkish nose. The cold, hate-filled eyes. I stop at the eyes. I've seen those eyes before. Khakwali? Malalai's grandfather?

Photograph in hand, I walk to the display of Malalai's Polaroids taped to the bulkhead. *Anaa* carrying MREs back to her house. Kids giggling and poking each other. Only one image of a man. Her grandfather. I hold up the 5x7. The eyes. Same color. Same shape. But not full of hate. Back and forth I look. Cerelli's photo. Malalai's photo.

"Sorry," I finally say. "I see the similarity, but it's not the same person."

"Keep going." Cerelli angles his chair around to watch me hunt through the gallery of images.

Making my way around the room to my own photographs, I check my images from our first visit to Khakwali. There's a whole series with the kids clustered in front of a house, Malalai standing proudly in front. The tallest boy, a teenager wearing a brown *pakol*, the headgear of many Pashtun males, stands off to one side, edging into the shadows, as if he were trying to disappear around the corner. He's the shepherd—Ghazan. He spoke a little Dari, heavily accented. He told me he'd just come down from the upper pasture. But he scowled when he saw my camera, yelling at the kids, making them cower. Then stormed away behind one of the houses. After he left, the kids giggled and made silly faces for the camera. But when he came back, they shut down. They posed, but they were stiff, self-conscious.

I took so many photos of these kids, waiting for them to stop posing, to drop their guard. They did, finally. But Ghazan never relaxed. I can see it in the photos arrayed in front of me. He's clearly nervous, shifting from one foot to the other. In one shot, I caught him looking over his shoulder. Following his gaze, I notice a blur at the edge of the pic—a man in a turban darting behind the next house. So, there *was* another man in the village. Not just the grandfather. The next photo: Ghazan's angry eyes jump out at me. So intense for a boy who can't be more than sixteen.

The last photo in this little series. And there is the man in the turban again—at the very edge of the image, staring directly into the camera. The consuming hate in his eyes. I don't need to compare him to the man in the 5 x 7 but hold it up anyway. The same guy.

"You're sure?" asks Cerelli softly, standing just behind me.

I nearly jump out of my skin. "Don't *do* that!"

"Do what?"

"Sneak up on me like that. It's like you're a ghost."

Cerelli takes the 5 x 7 from my hand and holds it up next to my photograph on the bulkhead. "You're sure?"

"No question. Who is he?"

"I could tell you, but then I'd have to kill you."

I sigh. "Don't be such a cliché."

"You think I'm a cliché?" Cerelli sounds wounded.

"You and Mr. CIA. Both of you—big-time."

"Ouch."

I pull the picture of interest off the wall and continue scanning the images. I saw this guy—or someone who looked a lot like him—in another village. Nearby. After the first visit to Khakwali and before the second. He took more than his share of bottles of water and MREs, made his wives carry them back to their houses. He kept a sharp eye on me the entire time. Scowling. Angry. Creepy. He had a couple sons. One was about the same age as Ghazan. Also a shepherd. But this boy never told me his name.

I fan myself with the picture. These two boys looked a lot alike. Cousins? They have to be.

Come on. Which village was it? I scan image after image, positive I caught father and son in one of the photos. Only I can't find it. I go back to the beginning and look again, slowly this time. And there it is. The father frowning darkly and leading his wives, loaded down like mules, his scowling son trailing behind. I suck in my breath. It's a damn good image. Great lighting that gives a surreal quality to the picture. And I'm willing to bet the Navy or the CIA or whoever's in charge isn't going to let me have this photo. What a waste.

Comparing the two photos, I decide it's not the same guy I saw in Khakwali after all. This man has a bit more gray in his beard, and he's wearing a *pakol* instead of a turban. But other than that, the two men look nearly identical. I bet they're brothers. I peel the pic off the bulkhead, then go back to Malalai's Polaroid of her grandfather and take that, too. And the image of Ghazan, the shepherd. Grabbing the 5 x 7 from Cerelli, I spread out the images on the table. Five males. Three generations.

"Holy shit!" Mr. CIA whistles. "Both brothers. Their father. And two of their sons."

"Nice work," says Cerelli. "For your sake, let's hope it pans out."

I OPEN MY EYES TO the dark. Not as thick and inky as before, it's now the charcoal gray of dawn. The *mu'adhdhin's* call to prayer at the nearby mosque echoes off the tiles in the bathroom. It must be the first *salah* of the day. I doze a little longer until the golden light of early morning filters through the window. God, I'm sore.

And stiff. My neck aches, and I can barely lift my right arm. Last night comes flooding back. The power failure. The helicopter. My interrogation on the *Bataan*. I catch sight of the Sig in my lap and pick it up. The safety's off.

Let's hope it pans out. Cerelli and Mr. CIA were obsessed with the men and boys in those pictures. I wonder if my images got them what they wanted. Not that I'll ever know.

And now here I am in a bathtub in Kabul. Hoping against hope that whatever militants stormed the hotel last night are long gone. That the hotel security force took them out. I push myself out of the tub and ease open the bathroom window. Gut clenched tight, I look down below to the patio restaurant where waiters are hosing down the concrete and setting the tables as if nothing happened at all.

11

I SLOWLY OPEN THE BATHROOM door. Everything in the bedroom is exactly the way I left it last night—the mattress and all my gear stacked up against the door. I comb trembling fingers through my hair. Did anything happen last night? Or was it all some kind of bizarre hallucination? But I *heard* the helicopter. I *felt* the pulsing of its rotors.

Yeah. And I heard Malalai in the room the night before. And saw *Anaa* on the rooftop at *Khosha*. This isn't good. Damn it all, PTSD is something I most definitely don't need right now.

I glance at the clock. An hour until I'm supposed to meet Tariq in the lobby. Then the InterCon and its nightmares will be behind me. I wrestle the mattress back onto the bed and have just enough time for a shower. Breakfast will have to be a KIND bar brought from home.

At 7:00 AM, I'm crossing the lobby, the bellman trailing behind me, the luggage cart piled with my gear. Tariq is waiting in front of the registration desk. He's considerably thinner than when I last saw him, his hair graying and shaggy. He smiles but shakes his head when I reach to hug him.

"Everyone here knows who I am. And they know Darya," he says quietly, apologetically. "They know you are not my wife."

"Enough said. Can I at least say it's good to see you?"

"It is good to see you as well." His smiling eyes warm me. "Ah, before I forget, your friend was just here. She said you forgot to give her our address."

Apprehensive, I glance around the lobby. "Tariq, I don't have any friends here."

He looks puzzled. "I am sure she mentioned you by name. Let me think. Piera. Yes. That is what she is called."

"I should have known. Definitely not a friend. I call her the Piranha. She's a journalist. The worst kind. She's been snooping around, trying to figure out why I'm here. I don't trust her, and I don't think you want your family splashed all over Al Shabakat TV. Please tell me you didn't give her your address."

"How very odd," he says, rubbing his hand against his jaw. "She knew you were leaving this morning, and she knew me by name."

Remembering Tariq's note from yesterday, I glare at the clerks behind the registration desk. I know exactly how she got her information.

"Well, not to worry." Tariq is ever the optimist. "Your Piranha hasn't done anything yet, and we will pray that she stays far away from us. Things are heating up west of here. She will soon be chasing stories out there." So, he did give her the address. I can only hope he's right about Piera moving on to something more interesting.

When I check out, the clerk behind the registration desk smiles awkwardly in response to my glare. "Thank you for staying with us, Madame. We hope to see you the next time you are in Kabul." He places an envelope on the counter between us. "This was left for you." Assuming it's from Piera, I'm ready to tell him to toss it, but then I see Nic's scrawl. Opening the envelope, I pull out a sheet of hotel stationery.

I'm off to Herat. Take care. Remember there are Taliban in the Panjshir Valley. Maybe Islamic State. Call if you need me. +44-020-1955. Nic

Herat. Where things really are heating up. Take care of yourself, Nic.

An hour later, we're on the A75 heading to Charikar. Tariq says Friday is the heaviest traffic day of the week. Today will likely be even worse because the *Loya Jirga* called by the president to discuss peace with the Taliban ended late last night, and all 3,200 delegates are heading home. But for now, despite the crazy driving, we're making good time in Tariq's aging Corolla with its disconcerting crack that reaches halfway across the windshield.

"So, tell me, how is life in Afghanistan?" I ask. "Your work at the clinic?"

He keeps his eyes on the road. "My work is quite challenging. Treating even the simplest ailments can be difficult, especially when we run short of medicines and supplies. But this is exactly what invigorates me."

"And Darya? The last time we Skyped, she seemed, I don't know, sort of tired?"

Tariq takes a while to answer and then measures his words. "Her soul needs to rest. Do you know that expression?"

"No. But I can imagine."

He seems to be trying to decide what to say next. "Coming here was her idea. She said she felt called home."

"Oh, I remember."

"But Afghanistan today is very different from when she lived in Kabul as a young girl. Even in the Panjshir Valley, life has become much more conservative. Although it is possibly the most progressive place in the country—next to Kabul."

The throngs of women wearing *burqas* on Chicken Street parade again before my eyes. Cerelli's cautions ring loud. "Things seem pretty conservative in Kabul, too."

"And you will see that it is even more so in Wad Qol." He lowers his voice, even though it's only the two of us in the car. "Then you understand why this is so very difficult for Darya. Back when we lived in Boston, she was always in charge." He laughs softly. "She was in charge of me, too, right from the start."

"It was pretty obvious."

"She knew exactly where she was going in life. Then, just when I thought I knew the direction she was taking me, she shifted course and decided we had to come to Afghanistan."

"I remember when you and Darya came to break the news," I say pensively. "Until that moment, I had always dreamed Dar and I would grow old together."

"That was a difficult weekend for all of us," says Tariq with a quick glance at me. "And possibly for Darya most of all."

"But she's the one who wanted to go back to Afghanistan."

"That is true." Tariq purses his lips before continuing. "Of course, she knew that people here might not want their daughters going beyond elementary school, that a higher education might interfere with families' plans for them to get married and have babies. But Darya believed she could change that."

"Oh God."

"Ah, my friend," Tariq's voice is heavy with warning, his right index finger raised in lecture mode, "here, you must not take the name of Allah in vain. You may give thanks and declare him great, but please do not curse him. As the proverb says, 'Bad language is the enemy of life.'"

"Of course it is. I'm sorry."

"Anything else could get you in serious trouble," says Tariq, his voice gentler. "Even in private conversation. Especially in private conversation. You never know who is listening. Blasphemy could get you jailed. Or worse."

Damn. I know this. The last thing I need is to insult anyone. Or get lashes for insulting Allah. So, major language overhaul. Best not to even *think* in my usual way.

"But, your sentiment about Darya is correct." He smiles sadly. "I cannot help wondering what Allah had in mind for her. And *that*— questioning Allah—is truly blasphemous and would definitely get me lashes. Yes, life has become more conservative in this country— again—even in the Panjshir Valley."

Oh, Dar, what have you gotten yourself into? What have you gotten *me* into? The knot in my gut tightens.

"To be fair to my wife," he continues, "once I accepted the idea of coming here, I was, as you say, all in. Of course, I knew what a patriarchal culture we were returning to, but I thought if anyone could change attitudes, she could. I encouraged her, and, honestly, I liked the idea of practicing medicine here, where so many people have so little. I am able to make a real difference."

'Make a real difference.' How many times have I heard Darya say exactly that?

"What makes it even harder is that life here has been generous with me. Just this week, a family brought me a lamb to thank me for saving their grandfather's life. In their eyes, *I* am a hero. But their daughter who spotted her grandfather's heart problem? No, she is a girl. The science teacher who taught the girl? No. Darya, who hired the science teacher? No. You see, not everyone wants girls to be educated. There have been attacks."

The headlines I've read in the last year—*Afghan Girls Disfigured by Acid on Way to School; Girls Stoned Leaving School*—scroll in front of my eyes. "But not in Wad Qol!"

"No, not in Wad Qol." His voice hangs in the air as if there's something more he wants to say.

Yet. I finish his thought for him. "So why stay?"

He smiles. "My wife is persistent. Have you ever known her to give up?"

Of course, Darya wouldn't give up. Once she commits, she's tenacious. I saw that the moment she walked into our dorm room freshman year. Brilliant, full of compassion, and determined to improve the world. I've never had a better friend. She was always there for me. My biggest supporter, especially when I was struggling to make it as a photographer on the school newspaper. Sophomore year, I definitely would have packed it in if Dar hadn't been there for me.

Tariq taps the brakes, rousing me from my daydream. Traffic is getting heavier, and with no set lanes, drivers are weaving all over the road. Both hands on the steering wheel, he's concentrating to avoid the crazies who are coming closer and closer as they cut in front of us. I guess he's used to this kamikaze driving because he's still able to talk.

"Tell me," he asks, "how is Emmy doing? It has been so long since I last saw her."

"She's fine, although she goes by 'Mel' now. And it's the usual teen problems: boys, not getting along all that well with her stepmother, her father, any adult."

"Are these problems serious?"

"Honestly, they probably bother me more than her."

"Because you are away so much?"

"You got it. My guilt knows no bounds." But not enough to keep me from my job. Time to shift the focus of this conversation. "So, how about Seema?" I say. "Darya said she's studying hard for exams. She must be excited to be going to Harvard in the fall." Last summer, I met up with Darya and Seema in Boston to tour a few colleges. During our visit, Seema confided that she didn't want to major in pre-med or pre-law. *That's what my parents want. I want to study literature and writing.* Not exactly the career path Dar or Tariq would pick for her, but I convinced Seema to talk to her mother. Dar wasn't thrilled. Probably the understatement of the year. But she's been supporting her. Much to Seema's surprise.

Tariq is quiet for such a long time I wonder if he heard me. Finally, he says, "The last month, she has been sleeping later and later in the morning. The teachers have told Darya that she sometimes even falls asleep in class."

"That doesn't sound like Seema. Is she okay?"

"She says that she is too excited about your visit that she cannot fall asleep at night. But that seems strange to me—like something a small child would say before a holiday. I checked her over." He shrugs. "Physically, she is fine."

It does seem odd. Especially added to what Darya described as her being 'moody.' What would keep Mel awake at night? Not an upcoming visit from Dar and Seema. Not even a dance recital. The only thing I can think of: Chance. But I'm certainly not going there. Not with Tariq. "So maybe she really *is* excited to see me. I'm looking forward to spending time with her. But with teens, you never know. I'd be willing to bet what she's really excited about is college and living in Boston. My senior year in high school, I couldn't concentrate on my classes or much of anything else."

Tariq glances over at me. "You are probably—"

Just then, a car cuts in front of us, way too close, clipping the front of the Corolla. I grab the armrest and brace my other hand against the dashboard. Tariq wrestles with the steering wheel, struggling to keep the car on the road. We spin—a complete 360—somehow missing the other vehicles. Then skid sideways off the highway. Finally, we come to rest at the very edge of the verge, inches from where the ground has sheared away to the valley below.

My heart racing, I look out the window and down the steeply sloping hillside. At the bottom, I see a mound of leafless trees that must have tumbled down when the earth gave way. Another inch and we would have gone over. We still could—rolling over and over to the bottom. To think about being seriously injured in Afghanistan. Few doctors. Fewer hospitals. I can't begin to imagine. Instead, I lean toward Tariq, trying to shift my weight away from the drop-off.

"You are all right?" Tariq sounds every bit the doctor.

"Fine." I concentrate on not rocking the car.

"We were lucky." He nods toward my side of the car.

My fingers white-knuckle the armrest. "I can't believe that jerk didn't stop."

"I am not surprised. But if you are all right, I will pull forward, away from the edge, and then check the bumper."

"That would be good. This is pretty steep."

"Ah, if you think this is bad, wait until we get to the Panjshir River Road."

I force a tight smile. "Sounds . . . scenic."

"It is. The Panjshir is probably the most beautiful valley in Afghanistan. At least, for me it is. I hope you find it as breathtaking as I do."

Move the car! I want to scream.

Tariq pulls forward, then gets out to inspect the damage. Traffic doesn't slow or even give us a wider berth. One driver comes so close, his tires screech as he fights to miss us. Our car rocks, and Tariq jumps out of the way just in time. After some wrenching and twisting of the bumper, he climbs back in. "Nothing to worry about," he says calmly. "It is only a crushed bumper. I was able to pull it away from the tire."

"I'm guessing insurance claims aren't real common here?"

Tariq laughs. "Insurance? That is a construct of the West." He pats the dashboard. "The car still runs. With luck and Allah's will, we will make it to Wad Qol with no more excitement."

He waits for a gap in the traffic, then pulls back onto the road. It takes a few minutes for the Corolla to sputter its way back up to speed. Actually, it feels like we're going considerably slower than before, and I'm sure I hear a high-pitched squeal that wasn't there before. But Tariq seems oblivious. I also notice the crack now runs the full length of the windshield.

"That seems worse," I say, pointing.

"Maybe a little longer." Tariq nods in agreement. "But it has been there for a while. As you have seen, the roads here are not so good, and trucks are always throwing stones. They ding the windshield, and then at night, when it gets cold, the cracks splinter. The first time it happened, we replaced the windshield. Now, we drive with the cracks."

12

WE'RE WELL PAST CHARIKAR, heading northeast on the only road into the Panjshir Valley. No signs of the promised Shangri-La yet. No alpine mountains covered with green fir trees or orchards full of mulberry bushes. Instead, Tariq points to the hulk of a helicopter, the tail and rotors long since scavenged, left to rust in the middle of a rock-strewn field of dirt.

"American?"

He shakes his head. "It is Soviet. You will see more wrecks farther up into the valley. Thanks to Ahmad Shah Massoud and the *mujaheddin*, the Soviets were never able to conquer Panjshir. Did you know that Massoud actually evacuated the entire valley three times?"

I've done a good deal of research on Afghanistan, but this last bit I didn't know.

"He was a man ahead of his time," Tariq continues. "Women didn't have to wear the *burqa*, and girls went to school."

"Al Qaeda got Massoud, though," I say quietly.

"Yes, and his assassination devastated the people here. Almost all the Tajik men in the valley attended his funeral." Tariq sounds almost wistful, like he wishes he could have been there.

"So, it was *after* his assassination that girls' schools were closed? Under threat of Al Qaeda and the Taliban?"

"Yes. Those were hard times. The Taliban made incursions. They did not succeed in taking over the valley, but everyone was terrified about what would happen if they did. Many women and girls stayed home. After Massoud's death, his brother led the fight against the Taliban. Even now, most men here are still loyal to the Massoud family."

"Quite a dynasty," I muse.

"His tomb is at Bazarak," says Tariq, steering to the right to avoid an oncoming car. "If we get through the checkpoint at Dalan Sang in time, perhaps we could stop to see it. There is a splendid view of the valley."

"I'd like that. Plus, I need to run by the market in Bazarak to get some sandals and dark socks. Captain Cerelli's suggestion. He said you'd know where to go?"

He nods thoughtfully. "Of course. If Captain Cerelli wants us to do that, we shall. That would also be a good place to have a bite to eat and rest."

We reach the mouth of the gorge where the two ridges of the Hindu Kush Mountains tower above us. Right next to the road, the Panjshir River charges wild and muddy and high, the roar of the water drowning out our conversation. Carved into the side of the mountains, the road narrows dramatically, forcing the two-way traffic even closer together. Tariq wasn't kidding that this route isn't for the faint of heart. The lane back to Kabul runs along the edge of a cliff that plummets down to the river. No guardrail. Nervous drivers heading to the city sometimes veer halfway into our lane.

Vehicles heading up into the valley are squeezed closer and closer to the mountain wall.

This is hard to watch. I desperately want to close my eyes, but I can't.

Tariq shouts over the roar of the river. "This is snow melt from farther up the valley. When we get out of the gorge, you will be able to see snow on the mountaintops."

We follow the twists and turns of the road, Tariq constantly swerving out of the path of oncoming vehicles. It's easy to see why he wants to get to Wad Qol before dark. And despite the slower speed, it still seems like we're making good time. Then, we round a bend and slow to a crawl. More like stop, wait, pull forward a car length. At this rate, we'll never make it to the checkpoint, much less Massoud's tomb or Wad Qol.

"And now we wait." Tariq looks like the epitome of patience in the face of what promises to be a very long wait.

It is. We move forward with excruciating slowness. Another half hour, another bend in the road. Always another bend. Always inching forward bumper-to-bumper toward the Dalan Sang checkpoint.

I'm getting antsy. Rifling through my pack, I dig out my camera and turn it on. I always feel better when I have my Canon in hand, ready to shoot. But I don't feel better. Something about this long line of vehicles is getting to me. And it's not just the exhaust.

Stop being so paranoid, I tell myself.

Never stop being paranoid, Cerelli's voice sounds in my ear. *Check out who's around you.*

I focus the camera on the drivers and passengers in the vehicles I can see ahead of us. Which isn't much—mostly backs of heads and profiles. I turn and, resting the lens on the back of my seat, study the vehicles behind us, all the way to the last bend in the road, snapping picture after picture. Everyone looks just like I imagine I do—eyes glazed over and bored to death. Now, if there were someone holding up his index finger to Allah in heaven above, eyes shining with passionate fervor and maniacal intensity ... right. As if I could recognize a terrorist. I glance at Tariq—how can he be so calm?

We pull forward a car length.

Then another.

Enough picture-taking. I don't need to draw attention to myself or upset anyone. Lowering the Canon to my lap, I flip idly through the images. Heads thrown back, eyes closed for catnaps.

"Did you get any good photographs?" Tariq asks.

I shake my head. "Not really." Just trying to keep myself from jumping into the river from boredom.

We pull forward again, and then finally around the bend. Up ahead, the road widens to allow for a small stone kiosk between the two lanes. Several guards are chatting with drivers and inspecting the contents of trunks and flatbeds, even peering into the hold of a tanker truck.

"What are they looking for?"

Tariq shrugs. "It could be many things. This is a well-known smuggling route. Heroin. Guns. Ammunition. Even people."

I go back to scrolling through the images, absentmindedly magnifying faces, scrutinizing eyes. A photo essay of drivers pulling up to Dalan Sang. A study in mind-killing boredom.

Don't you mean mind-numbing? Cerelli's voice is back.

Tariq pulls forward to the checkpoint just as a bus packed full of people rolls up, heading toward the city. That will take a while. I turn off the camera and hand him my passport and registration card.

"*Asalâmu alaykum,* Dr. Ghafoor," says the guard with a brief salute and a smile. "We meet again. I see that you have your cargo with you this time."

"Lieutenant. *Wa 'alaykum asalâm.*" Tariq climbs out of the car.

The lieutenant doesn't bother with Tariq's identity card but takes his time paging through my passport. He walks around the car and opens the passenger door. "Please," he says with a smile.

I push out of the car and manage to snag my *keffiyeh* on the door, pulling it off my head. "I'm so sorry." Scrambling to cover my hair, I half expect the lieutenant to dismantle the camera hanging around my neck and put my gear through the kind of intense search that happened at the InterContinental. Then I remember the Sig Sauer in my pack. Fuck, what's he going to say when he finds that? Not to mention the *burqa.* I add these pieces together and come up with one conclusion: spy. Cerelli, what've you done to me?

He limits himself to a cursory glance at the Pelican cases in the back seat, nods, then walks back to chat with Tariq.

Really? That's it?

Nearly giddy with relief, I get back in the car and strain to hear what he's saying to Tariq. "Yes, I can see why . . . Cerelli." Whoa. The lieutenant knows Cerelli? A minute later, the lieutenant returns my passport to Tariq and raises his hand in farewell.

We're on our way again, but barely. Several vehicles ahead of us, the tanker is inching along, creating yet another long traffic jam.

"Well, that went a whole lot better than I was expecting," I say.

"Sometimes it helps to arrange things ahead of time."

"You mean a bribe? How much did you have to pay him?"

Tariq smiles. "I paid nothing."

"Cerelli?"

"The captain has helped many people over the years. He has many friends in the Panjshir."

"So, how do you know him?"

Tariq answers almost too quickly. "I patched him up a while back."

Now that's an interesting coincidence. Cerelli used the exact same words yesterday to tell me how he knows Tariq. Almost as if they made sure to get their stories straight. So, what does that mean? I shake my head. Get a grip—this is Tariq. Mr. Straight Arrow. It means exactly what he said: he patched up Cerelli.

I go back to scrolling through my snaps. I zoom in on a driver's eyes. Closed. On to the next image. This driver's looking out the window toward the river. The next image. I've magnified the driver's face only a few degrees when I see it. He's staring straight at me. No, *into* me, *through* me. He's not bored. Far from it. His long hair and scraggly beard draw my attention for a moment. But it's those piercing eyes, that tightness of his mouth. I know that look. It's almost a cliché of fanaticism. Eyes like I saw back in my Masum Ghar and Khakwali days. Fingers trembling, I crop and magnify the angry eyes.

"Tariq."

We're rounding a bend where the road is precariously narrow, but Tariq risks a glance in my direction. Wordlessly, I turn the camera so he can see the picture on the screen.

He cups his hand over the top of the image to get a better view, then looks sharply at me. "When did you take this?"

"A few minutes ago. Just before we got to the checkpoint. He's a couple cars behind—"

Tariq looks ahead to the tanker still inching forward. "They could be working together—the truck driver and the driver behind us. I've seen this before. They slow down the line of traffic, hoping for the maximum number of casualties."

He pulls the car as close as he can to the rock face and turns off the ignition. He's halfway out his door, ready to run back and warn people, when the blast erupts, blocking out the roar of the river. The car shakes, rises slightly off the ground, then drops. The air is sucked from my lungs. The cracked windshield explodes outward into a million tiny slivers. Then shards of metal and tiny chunks of burning rubber rain down on us.

I slide off the seat and onto the floor, arms over my head. Waiting. Another blast will come. That's the way these guys work. Wait for people to run to help, then detonate another bomb. Or two. The tanker ahead of us. *They could be working together.* Oh God, what if there's a bomb in that truck—with all that fuel? It will take out this section of the road. Maybe trigger an avalanche. He'll kill us all and cut off the entire valley from Kabul. That's the plan. It's got to be.

I wait.

And wait, praying Tariq is still alive.

But no second blast detonates.

I wait for the river to roar again, but all I can hear is a loud ringing—shrill and constant.

I climb over the center console and out the driver's door. Tariq is lying facedown on the road, a bloodied arm above his head.

"Tariq!"

"Get back in the car!"

"Your arm!"

"It's not mine!" he yells. "Please, get into the car."

He's obviously thinking the same thing I am. Suicide bombings always come in twos and threes.

We wait. Teeth chattering, hands shaking, I huddle again on the floor of the front seat and count to 300.

Enough time. I climb onto my seat and out of the car. Tariq is already at the trunk.

"My medical kit!" he yells. "Do you have anything we could use as tourniquets? Anything at all?"

Tourniquets? Is that what he said? His voice sounds so far away. I do a frantic mental inventory of what I've brought. Grabbing my pack, I yank the *burqa* out of its paper-and-string wrapping and hold it up to show Tariq.

He takes the string. "Do you have anything else?"

I stare at his mouth, trying to make out his words. Damn this ringing. Guessing that some Afghan men might object to strips torn from a *burqa*, I throw the yards and yards of periwinkle cloth into the back seat. I swing my camera behind me to get it out of my way. Camera straps. Canon gave me thinner straps, much more pliable than the usual ones. There's one for each of the cameras. Still in their plastic wrappings. Maybe, just maybe they'll work. I unlock and jerk open the first Pelican case.

"Good," says Tariq, stuffing straps into his kit, then setting off at a run toward the bomb site.

I collect the rest of the cellophane packets and stuff them in my backpack. Shouldering the pack, I realize it's heavier than I expected. The clips of ammo. The gun. God, I hope I don't have to use it today. I take off after Tariq, racing back to the checkpoint. The pack bangs against my hip as I cut around smoking vehicles and charred human appendages and God only knows what else. When I round the bend, the burning wreckage of the bus and dismembered bodies on the road stop me short, mid-stride. My knees turn to jello, soft and wobbly. The wreckage spins. My stomach roils. I'm going down.

When a big wave comes, lower your head and let it pass. Cerelli's voice. *Then go help Tariq save some lives. Promise you'll call me if you get in trouble.*

The sat phone. I dig it out of my pack and punch in the number Cerelli wrote on its side.

A man who sounds like a generic big and powerful SEAL answers on the first ring. "Yeah?" No Boston accent. Not Cerelli. Or maybe it is. The ringing in my ears is so loud, I'm not sure of anything.

"This is Annie!" I yell. "Annie Hawkins Green. Captain Finn Cerelli told me to call this number if I'm in trouble."

"Annie, this is Sawyer."

"Sawyer?" Is that what the man said?

"Annie. Are you all right?"

"There's been a suicide bombing. I'm standing in the middle of it. I'm okay, but I can't hear too well."

"Where?" He's shouting now.

"The Panjshir Valley. Dalan Sang checkpoint."

"Shit. Any casualties?"

I hear that loud and clear. "Too many to count. Look, I've got to go help Tariq with tourniquets."

"Choppers in the air in five. Should be with you in thirty. An hour at the latest."

"Thanks, Sawyer." But he's already hung up.

"Annie!" Tariq's voice. "I need your hands over here stat."

I turn in a slow circle, looking for Tariq, but I can't see him for all the bodies. So many bodies. I feel Malalai's head against my breast, Lopez's cooling flesh, Murphy's blood slippery on my hands. Oh God, there's so much blood. *You think maybe me and you could've—?* Then silence.

I look up the road to the east into the valley, past the smoking wrecks of what were once cars and pickups, and see a periwinkle *burqa* running away from the carnage. No matter that I'm obviously hallucinating again, I want to run after her and just keep running as hard and as far as I can. The smell of blood is wafting into my nostrils, into me. Going down.

"Annie! Now!" I follow his voice and see him, working on someone.

Put your head down and wait for the wave to pass.

No running away. Not this time.

I can do this. I've got to do this.

I cram the sat phone and the camera into my pack, then retie my *keffiyeh* over my mouth and nose. Putting my head down and doing my best to ignore all the death around me, I head over to help Tariq, who's pressing a scarf against a young man's thigh with both hands.

"Latex gloves." He nods toward his kit. I find a pair and pull them on. "Now tie a camera strap around his leg on top of the cloth. Tight. Tighter. We've got to staunch the blood flow."

Gentle doesn't matter, so I put all my strength into it and tie the strap as tight as I can. The young man clenches his jaw but doesn't make a sound. He's light-skinned, and his face is getting whiter by the minute. Come on, God, work with me here. Don't let him die.

"Now, tie a second one higher on the thigh." Tariq's voice is competent and unbelievably calm.

"I used the sat phone to call in some helicopters," I say as we work, surprised that my hands are calmly doing exactly what Tariq tells them to do. "They should be here in half an hour or so."

"Good." Tariq stands and moves to another patient.

The young man on the ground reaches for my sleeve to stop me from standing up. He can barely hold on. *Murphy, don't do this to me. Not again.*

Stop. This isn't Murphy. This is not Khakwali.

"My wife," he whispers. "She is called Nazira. Over there. I beg of you, please help her."

A young woman is lying nearby. She's on her side, knees pulled up, and covered in blood. Not moving. Dead, I think.

"Please," says the young man, his dark eyes distraught. "You must save her."

"You speak English," I say. "Does she? Does Nazira?"

"Yes."

The woman groans. Even with the ringing in my ears, I hear her. I grab a camera strap and reach for another pair of latex gloves.

"We're low on gloves," calls Tariq.

I kneel in the bloody dirt that's quickly turning to mud and run my hands down the woman's arms, her bent legs. Probing as gently as I can for a gash, for some kind of wound, I find nothing. Impossible. With all this blood, there has to be an injury, a bad one. Just then, the woman braces herself against me, trying not to move, but shuddering violently. Then I see it. More blood pours out from between her legs, saturating her baggy pants. She shudders again, harder this time. And moans. A contraction? My eyes race up her body and find the telltale mound hidden beneath the voluminous tunic of her *shalwar kameez.*

"Tariq, we've got a baby coming here," I call.

"You'll have to handle it."

Handle it? Is he serious? I've *had* a baby. I've never *delivered* a baby. Especially from a young woman who looks like she's bleeding out.

"Nazira," her husband calls out. She doesn't respond.

I ease Nazira's blood-soaked pants off her and lay them across her distended belly. Save the pants. We need as much cloth as we can get for bandages, whether or not it's saturated with blood. Nazira rolls onto her back. I drape my *keffiyeh* over her bare legs. The contractions are coming fast now. So is the blood. There's way too much blood. What the hell am I supposed to do about all this blood?

"Nazira." I take hold of her hand. "Can you stop pushing?"

A scream escapes her clenched jaw.

"Tariq, please," I call to his back, hunched over a nearby body. "This baby's coming! Now!"

Tariq doesn't even glance up. "Can't."

Nazira squeezes my hand, moaning and grunting from behind clenched teeth.

I take a deep breath and lift the *keffiyeh*. The baby's head is crowning. *The baby's head.* More blood rushes out past the tiny head. It's up to Nazira, who's losing way too much blood, to get this baby born alive.

"Nazira, your baby wants to be born now," I say in Dari. "Can you push?"

Nazira's entire body gathers for one final push.

I cradle my hands around the baby's head, easing out one shoulder, then the other. The baby slips out into my waiting arms. Pale pink and chalky white. Not blue. I glance down. A boy. A mass of thick black hair plastered to his head. I put my hand on the baby's chest. A tiny heart beating. Alive.

But he's tiny. So tiny. Too tiny?

I grab the *keffiyeh* and clean his face. Breathe! But something's wrong.

Then I see it. Blood is oozing from the stump of cord protruding from the baby's belly. Just a few inches long. The umbilical cord has already been severed. How could that happen? *How* doesn't matter. The real question is: how the hell do I keep this baby from bleeding to death? I grab a camera strap, still in its plastic wrapping. Ripping it open with my teeth, I ease off the rubber band and loop it around and around the stump of the umbilical cord. Then, I tie the camera strap on top. And hold my breath.

The bleeding slows, then stops. *Thank you, God!* I want to shout in jubilation. It worked. Something worked. I wipe the baby's face again. He opens his eyes and stares at me for just a moment, then scrunches them shut, opens his mouth wide, and lets out an angry scream. All good.

I swaddle the newborn in my bloody *keffiyeh*, lay him against Nazira's breasts, and wrap the new mother's weakening arms around him.

"A boy," I say, bringing her arms together to cradle him.

"*Tashakkor*," she whispers, her voice impossibly weak. "Thank you."

"*Mashallah*," I say. But then just a few seconds later, I catch the baby as first one, then both of Nazira's arms slip to the ground. And now I want to shake my fist at the sky. No just and loving God would let a young mother die. Not like this. Her blood draining into the dirt. A stranger cradling her newborn son.

"It is Allah's will," says the young father. His voice sounds calm, but when I look at him closely, I see the tears on his cheeks. He shifts his eyes to his newborn son in my arms. "Massoud. Tell them my son's name—"

Massoud? As in the son of Ahmad Shah Massoud, the lion of Panjshir? Tariq and I were just talking about the man, and now I'm working on his son? His grandson? I stare in disbelief at the man lying a few feet away, two of my camera straps keeping him from bleeding out.

Overhead, the roar of helicopters drowns out his voice. They cruise past the carnage and head farther down the curving road. Where can they possibly land? The gorge road becomes so impossibly narrow. It'll take them hours to hike all the way back here. I can't possibly keep this baby and his father alive that long.

They must have roped down from the helicopters because minutes later, medics and soldiers swarm around us, spreading out among the wounded, the dying, the dead. Taking charge. Overhead, more choppers *thwamp* their arrival.

I sit in the dirt next to the young couple, rocking their squalling baby in my arms. "Keep crying, Baby Massoud, keep crying," I sing to him in Dari.

"Excuse me, ma'am?" A soldier in green BDUs stands over me. "Are you Annie? The one who spoke to Senior Chief Sawyer?"

"Yes."

"CHIEF! Here!" The soldier looks back at me, his eyes wide. "Sawyer didn't say anything about a baby. Is that your baby, ma'am?"

"This," I say, nodding at the young father, whose eyes are open and fixed on his newborn son, and at the young mother who hasn't taken a breath in way too long, "is Baby Massoud, and he's about twenty minutes old."

Sawyer is standing over me now. "Did you say Massoud?"

I wipe tears and blood from my cheeks. "I did. And I think he's hungry."

"Massoud. Un-frigging-believable. And with Cerelli CONUS."

I watch as Afghan soldiers carefully, almost reverently, lift the bodies of the young parents onto litters and start the trek back around the bend and down the gorge to the waiting helicopters.

Another Afghan soldier offers his arms for the baby. "I'll take good care of this young lion, ma'am. You have my word."

Sawyer pulls me to my feet. "You still have that sat phone?" I stare at Sawyer. He looks at me closely. "Are you okay?"

"Your voice. I can hear your voice. There's been this awful ringing."

"Glad it's subsiding." Sawyer puts a hand on my shoulder. "Now, about the sat phone?"

I dig into my pack and pull out the phone. "Compliments of Cerelli."

Sawyer punches in a number and almost immediately starts talking. "She's covered in blood, but fine." He kicks at the dirt with his booted toe. "I think most of it came from delivering a baby. Get this, it's Baby Boy Massoud."

Cerelli roars at the other end of the line.

"I got a good look at the young father. He's Massoud's son all right—Ahmad—has that same long nose with the hook on the end. Must have been heading home from the *Loya Jirga*. He's hurt pretty bad. Critical, I'd say. The mother's dead. The baby is small, but he's got lungs."

Sawyer walks a few feet farther away. "No leads yet."

I take out my camera and scroll through images until I find the man with the scary eyes—the eyes that look kind of familiar—then walk it over to Sawyer. He holds up the sat phone so Cerelli can hear us talk.

"Holy shit." Sawyer studies the image. "He's looking straight at you."

"Yeah," I nod. "He saw me, that's for sure. This is maybe an hour before he blew himself up—and everyone else. I shot RAW, so you can pull out a lot more data than from a jpeg."

"Annie, you mind telling me why you just happened to be taking pictures at that exact moment?" Cerelli's voice sounds scratchy and a lot farther away than I want it to be.

"We were stuck in a long line of traffic. I was bored."

"Don't do this to me."

I stare at the phone. Did Cerelli's voice just crack?

"You stay safe." Cerelli is still talking. "Don't make me come haul you out of there in a body bag."

Sawyer puts the phone to his ear and walks away into the field of the dead and dying. Far enough that I can't hear what he and Cerelli are talking about. An Afghan officer with a gold star and two crossed swords on his epaulets joins Sawyer. I watch the man turn white with rage as he looks at the image on my camera.

When Sawyer comes back to me, he tucks the phone into my pack, then the camera, and holds up the SD card for me to see him slip it into his pocket.

"How are you holding up?" he asks.

I shrug. "I've had better days, but all things considered, I'm good."

He nods. "Sorry to make you do this, but we've got to look at every face on every single body and see if we can find your bomber. I want to make damn sure this fucker's dead."

We look.

The Afghan major looks with us.

At every single body.

Some of which no longer have arms or legs or heads. Or faces.

No one finds him.

Because, we all come to realize, he's not here. Sawyer thinks the guy abandoned his car right before it was his turn to pull up to the kiosk, then walked away, probably climbed down to the river to a waiting raft, and detonated the bomb.

I reach for Sawyer's arm. "I feel like I've maybe seen him before."

That stops him.

"Where?"

"I don't know. This is going to sound crazy—but maybe when I was here in '06."

"You remember a name?"

"I don't know. Maybe Ghazan?" I shake my head. How the hell did I come up with that name?

Sawyer's eyes widen.

"He was about sixteen when I was here before. That would put him about the right age. He lived in Khakwali. There was a cousin who looked a lot like him living in another village." I shake my head. "Sorry. That's all I've got."

Sawyer claps a hand on my shoulder. "I know who those Kandahar guys are, but I don't think the guy in the photo is Ghazan. As far as I know, they've stayed away from Panjshir. Not to worry. I'll check into it. But promise me you'll keep your eyes open. And get another headscarf. With that hair, you could be a target."

Sawyer walks me back to where Tariq is working on yet another casualty. "Doc, you're good to go," says Sawyer. "Cerelli wants you both off the road before dark."

I look at the sky. The sun is sinking toward the western mountains. 'Before dark' might be pushing it.

Tariq glances up from the man he's working on and shakes his head.

Sawyer waves over two medics with a litter. "Dr. Ghafoor, this is the last of the survivors. The medics are ready to take him to Bagram."

Tariq pushes himself to his feet, then looks slowly around at the carnage, all the bodies on the ground. "Then, I see there is nothing left for me but to obey Captain Cerelli."

"Thanks, Doc." Sawyer steers Tariq away from the bodies. "Your car in any shape to get you home?"

"The windshield is gone, but it should still run," says Tariq.

"We'll check it out. You think you'll be able to drive the rest of the way to Wad Qol?" asks Sawyer. "Or should I get you a driver?"

Tariq closes his eyes and nods. "Yes," he says, his voice strained with exhaustion. "Drive. That I can do." He suddenly seems to remember something and turns toward me. "The baby—"

"Still alive. But the mother didn't make it. Baby Boy Massoud," says Sawyer with a meaningful look.

I watch Tariq's eyes narrow as he connects the dots. Ahmad Shah Massoud—assassinated almost fourteen years ago. His daughter-in-law dead. His only son and grandson now fighting for their lives. Were they the targets?

13

Afghanistan – Wad Qol

THE NIGHT SKY IS NEARLY pitch-black. Just the merest sliver of a moon peeks through the clouds. No stars. We're down to one parking light, making our way along the winding road with its precipitous drop to the river. The windshield is gone. Even driving slowly, wind roars into the car, chapping my cheeks and lips, blasting against my eyes which ache from the strain of keeping them open. At least Tariq still has his glasses.

Teeth chattering, I wrap my arms around myself, trying to hold in whatever warmth I can. How can it be this cold in May? But I know it's more than the plummeting temperature that came when the sun disappeared behind the Hindu Kush. This is what happens when blood and death engulf me. Malalai, Lopez, Murphy. And now I have Nazira to add to the list. Maybe also Ahmad and Baby Boy Massoud.

I glance at Tariq hunched over the steering wheel, peering into the darkness. How is he able to drive? I shiver and tighten my hold on my arms.

Finally, the car slows to a crawl, Tariq turns left off the main valley road, and we cross the bridge into Wad Qol. We drive slowly along the unpaved village roads, quiet except for the chugging and grinding of the car. The houses are dark, their windows shuttered against the night. Tariq somehow manages to see the mule standing in the middle of the road and steers around it. Several turns later, we leave the village behind and drive another few kilometers north.

"Are we anywhere close to the school?" I ask.

"We are passing it now," he says. "It's on your right behind those trees, but it's too dark for you to see anything. I am sure Darya will want to show you tomorrow." Finally, he pulls the car off the road next to a one-story stone house with a flat roof and light streaming from the windows. He makes no move to get out, just sits behind the steering wheel and studies the house. "I am surprised Darya has not closed the shutters for the night."

I climb out of the car just as the front door flies open and Seema runs toward us, her long, dark hair trailing behind her. "Auntie!" she shrieks as she throws herself into my arms. I hug her tight. So much more petite than Mel. I don't think she's grown at all since I saw her last. She holds onto me as if she'll never let go. "I can't believe you're finally here!" she says between kisses on both my cheeks. "I have so much to tell you!"

We lug my gear into the house, stacking it in a corner of the front room. The lounge, as Afghans call it, is cozy with a fire in the fireplace, two low sofas and an armchair, intricately woven carpets covering the painted tile floor, a large coffee table standing just a foot high, and a scattering of large floor cushions. Black and

white portraits I've made of Seema and Mel over the years hang
on the walls. Comfortable, but far from the luxury of the Beacon
Hill town house where Darya and Tariq used to live. I turn back to
Seema, only to see her staring wide-eyed at her father and me.

"Dad! Auntie! You're bleeding!"

I look at the blood caked on my hands, rimmed under my
fingernails. My tunic and cargo pants are streaked with mud mixed
with blood. A lot of blood. Oh God, Nazira. If only I'd been able to
do something to keep her alive. The room starts to spin, and I grab
the back of the armchair for support.

"Annie?" Tariq sounds concerned.

I wave away his worry but keep my handhold on the chair.

"Seema! Draw your auntie a bath, as warm as possible. And
make her some *chai*. Strong, with sugar. Then close the shutters.
Tell me, where is your mother?"

I look around. Yeah, where *is* Darya?

"You were very late. She was worried, so she went to the school."

To the school? How is that supposed to help? I glance from
Seema to Tariq, who nods as if this were a perfectly logical thing
for Darya to do.

Tariq takes charge. "There was an explosion at the checkpoint.
Your auntie and I tended some of the wounded. We are both all
right." No mention of the many people who were beyond wounded.
He turns to me. "You are perhaps suffering a little shock. You will
feel better once you warm up. And put on some clean clothes." He
pulls the front door shut behind him. A minute later, I hear the car
cough back to life.

"Did anyone die?" Seema whispers.

How to answer. I don't know what Darya and Tariq would
want me to say. But she doesn't seem to need me to say anything. I

can only imagine what my face looks like, probably just as bloody as the rest of me.

"A bath," she says, reaching for my hand and leading me down a long, dimly lit hall to the back of the house. The bathroom clearly has been converted from some other use. A storage closet maybe? A tiny bedroom? I'm sure Darya would have drawn the line at an outhouse, which is probably what many villagers in Wad Qol rely on. Here, a basin sits atop what was once a small dresser with pipes running up the wall to the ceiling, and probably to a cistern on the roof. A toilet in the corner doesn't look all that stable. A large, chipped enamel tub has a handheld attachment for bathing. No curtain. I bet the tile floor turns into a pond.

A half hour later, my hair washed and my body scrubbed nearly raw, I'm soaking in the tub of lukewarm water. It helps relax me, but the water is cooling quickly, almost as fast as my adrenaline is draining out of me. Still warmer than the air, the water embraces me as I sink lower and lower. It rises above my breasts, my neck, to my chin. The knock at the door brings me back from the edge of sleep.

"Annie!"

"Dar?" I sputter awake.

"May I come in?" Before I can answer, the door opens and Darya slips into the bathroom. "Oh, Annie." She looks me over, grimacing as she takes in the pink-tinged water.

I push up a bit. "I'm glad we made it. It's been a brutal day."

"Tariq told me. I can't believe this has happened. Truly, this is such a safe place. There are bombings in other parts of the country, but nothing has ever happened here or on the River Road. Once in a while, the guards at Dalan Sang stop a smuggler, but nothing more. As I told you, *tourists* come here to ski." She perches on the edge of the tub and cups her hand against my cheek. "How *are* you?"

I smile, but it feels half-hearted. "Adrenaline crash, I'm afraid. It's a good thing you came in just now. I was falling asleep."

"Then out you get! I won't have my dearest friend drown in my house. Are you hungry? Seema helped me make dinner—some of your favorites—*aush* and *borani banjân.*"

"Dar—"

She holds up her hand. "You don't need to say anything. Dinner will keep until tomorrow. Maybe another cup of *chai?*"

"*Chai* would be good. Oh, and something to wear?"

"I brought you some clean clothes, and I'll go make more tea." She plunges her hand into the bathwater and pulls the plug, then scoops up my bloody clothes from the floor and looks at them dubiously. "We'll see if these can be laundered."

HOURS LATER, MY EARS ARE ringing again. On and off and on. When the shrill noise stops for a few minutes, I heave a sigh of relief and pray for sleep. I'm desperate for sleep.

Except now, I hear voices. Whispers. In the courtyard outside my window. I feel like I'm back in the stable in Khakwali, the whispers getting closer. Footsteps.

I clutch the wool blanket around me and refuse to be pulled back into that nightmare. *I'm at Darya's house*, I tell myself. *Wad Qol.* I reach to turn on the lamp. Nothing. My heart slams against my ribs, and Khakwali starts surfacing again. I grab my flashlight. Darya's house. I'm safe.

Then I remember: Dar said they have a generator that powers the house. They've turned it off for the night.

More whispers. Who the hell is out there? My paranoia sets in.

The suicide bomber from Dalan Sang? We couldn't find his body among the dead. Could he possibly have gotten away? Followed us here?

I climb out of bed and, keeping my feet on the thick woolen rug to avoid the icy-cold tiles, make my way to the window at the end of my small room. Casement windows that swing into the room, and they're not quite closed. I open them wider, then shine my flashlight into the courtyard. The beam doesn't do much, and with the thick bush shielding the window, I can't see anyone. The light stops the voices though. But at this time of night, no one should be out there.

And someone was definitely out there just now—talking. Multiple someones.

Hearing voices doesn't mean someone's actually out there talking.

Thanks for the reminder, Cerelli. And now I can't hear a thing. Shit, maybe I really do have PTSD. Not a diagnosis I want to consider, especially not in Afghanistan.

No, I'm *positive* I heard people out there. Yeah, well, I was sure I heard Malalai a few nights ago and a helicopter last night. So, what do I do? There's no point waking up Tariq or Dar for voices that might or might not be real—they're as exhausted as I am. I don't really want them to know how close to crazy I'm edging either. And there's no way I'm going outside on my own to investigate.

The kitchen. From what I remember of the quick tour Darya gave me tonight, the kitchen is on this side of the house, and there's a window overlooking the courtyard. I push the casement windows shut and slip out of my room. Opposite mine, the door to Seema's room is closed. All quiet there—no light from under the door to indicate that she's awake and studying. I scurry down the hall with its cold tile floor, through the lounge, and into the kitchen, shutting the door quietly behind me. Peering over the potted herbs on the windowsill and out into the courtyard, I see nothing. And hear nothing. The beam from my flashlight doesn't pick up anyone. I check one last time, and that's when the ringing starts up again. Shrill and singsong. I'm ready to scream. Tomorrow, I'll have Tariq check me over. Although if it's tinnitus, I already know there's nothing he can do. I'll have to live with it until it goes away on its own. *If* it goes away.

Easing the kitchen door closed behind me, I turn toward the hall and sense someone lurking nearby. Turning toward the front door, I click on my flashlight as quickly as I can. Seema stands frozen in place, clad in a floor-length nightgown and a sweater, her eyes wide, looking like she's seen a ghost. Exactly how I feel.

"Seema! You scared me to death!" I whisper, my hand to my heart. "What are you doing here?"

"Pardon, Auntie."

"Were you outside just now?"

"No!"

"It's just that I heard voices. Out in the courtyard."

"Auntie, are you sure? That doesn't make any sense. There wouldn't be anyone in our courtyard at this time of night." She sounds so sure that I start to doubt myself again. "But you know, sometimes the wind whistles on this side of the house, and it can sound like voices."

"The wind?"

She nods. "Sometimes it gets so loud, I can actually hear it in my room."

I stare at her. Yeah, but there's no wind tonight. I would have heard it rustling the leaves of the bush outside my window. Now, I see the backpack in her arms and trace my flashlight beam over it. *Lowepro.* "Is that mine?"

"I was just going to bring it to your room." The words rush out of her mouth. Almost too fast. "You left it out here. Your phone was ringing."

"My *phone?*"

She nods. "Off and on for the last couple of hours."

All this time, that ringing has been my *phone?* No. That can't be right. My ring tone is the old Carole King tune, *Natural Woman.* I take the Lowepro, and we head back to our rooms. I'm opening my door when music erupts from my pack. Something Afghan.

"Do you hear that?" she says. "It's a Nasrat Parsa song. His music is very romantic. All the girls at school love it. I'm sure it's your phone."

It takes me a couple beats and then I remember: the sat phone. "Oh *gosh,* that must be my *new* phone." Damn, I'm an idiot. But what's with the ringtone, Cerelli? You couldn't go for something ordinary?

"It's okay, Auntie. I hope everything is all right." She backs into her bedroom.

I shut my door and pull out the phone.

"Mommy? Is that you?"

"Mel—?"

"Mom! I've been so worried. I've been trying to reach you for *hours,* and the phone kept ringing and ringing, and I didn't know what to think, and I thought you really were dead." Her voice sounds weepy.

"Sweetie, I—"

"But that captain called, and he promised me you were okay, that he actually talked to you. He said the bombing would be all over TV and not to worry. But see, they keep showing it, over and over on TNN—and I've been so scared and no one answered the phone—"

"Whoa! Take a breath, then tell me what happened."

"*Mom*, don't give me that. You *know* what happened. You were *there*. The suicide bombing. They keep showing you covered in blood."

"It was on television?"

"It's on right now." She drops her voice to a whisper. "Daddy's so upset. And for once, C.E. isn't saying anything. They're parked in front of the TV in their bedroom, but they won't let the twins or me watch."

Holy shit. I pace the length of the room to the windows. Wide open. I push them closed and head back to the door. To the windows again. How the hell did *anyone* get footage of the bombing? I didn't see any media.

"Look, I'm fine. Yes, there was a bombing. But Uncle Tariq and I were already way past the checkpoint when it happened. We went back to help."

"That's what Captain Cerelli said."

"You talked to Cerelli?"

"Are you listening to me? I already *told* you that. Oh, and FYI, I like him a lot. He talked to Daddy, too."

"Oh, right. Sorry." The media coverage has me concerned. "Do me a favor, sweetie? There aren't any TVs here, so can you get to one—not the one your dad's watching?"

"Sure. I've got it on now."

"Okay, good. Is there a reporter who's calling in the story?"

"Yeah, Piera something. The same reporter who called here a couple days ago. She said she's a friend of yours. Did I tell you about that?"

"We'll talk about that later," I say. "For now, tell me what she's saying."

"She's talking about the bombing. I'm pretty sure she's in a helicopter or something. The camera's definitely looking down. Now she's talking about you. Her voice is choking up, like she could start crying any minute. She keeps calling you a really good friend, and the camera's zooming in on you. She's saying you look gravely wounded. God, Mom, you really do look *awful*. You're just sort of sitting there next to a lady. And you're covered in blood."

So, the Piranha talked her way onto a military chopper. Great. Just great. And brought a cameraman along. And all the news channels picked up the Al Shabakat feed. Knowing cable, they'll run this clip 24/7 for days. Totally freaking out my daughter and ex-husband. Can it get any better?

"Mom? You still there? What were you doing with that lady? The one who's lying next to you?"

"I helped deliver her baby."

She doesn't say anything for a few very long seconds. "What happened? To the lady, I mean."

I close my eyes. But that takes me back to Dalan Sang. All that blood. Nazira knew she was dying. She held on long enough to make sure her son was born. I blink hard. Eyes open. "She died."

"What about the baby?"

"Uncle Tariq thinks he'll make it." If stretching the truth makes my daughter feel the slightest bit better, it's worth the lie. "Now about Piera?"

"Yeah?" She sounds suddenly wary.

"She's not a friend of mine. She's trolling for a story, and—" And what the hell else can I say? That I'm afraid the Piranha will follow me to Wad Qol?

"Don't worry, Mom. I get it. Piera's a lying bitch. If she calls again, I'll tell her to fuck off."

"No! Don't. The bitch will put that on the news." I cringe, realizing that despite Tariq's caution, my language has already gone back to hell. And now Mel is sounding like me.

"Yeah, I get it, Mom. Captain Cerelli told me not to take any more calls unless it's you or him. And I'm not supposed to tell my friends, even though I know everyone will be talking about it at school. He told Daddy not to talk to anyone either, especially reporters."

"Good. That's good. Tell you what, if you can't reach me, just call Captain Cerelli and do whatever he tells you." What am I saying? That Cerelli's a good guy, and I trust him. He'll look out for Mel—and Todd.

"Sure." She sounds like she's smiling. "I kinda figured you were gonna say something like that. Hey, Mom, are you and him—"

"No!" I sit down hard on the bed. "So, uh . . . tell me, how are things going with C.E.?"

She hesitates. "Not so good. I didn't want to tell you, but she took me to Shear Design today and made me get my hair dyed."

Fuck! So, Todd let C.E. do it. Clearly, my vote doesn't count. *Refocus*, I tell myself. *This isn't about me, it's about Mel and her hair.* "And? How does it look?"

"Like shit."

"Mel—"

"No really. Like shit. It's caca-shit brown."

"Oh, sweetie. I tried. I talked to your dad." Was that really only last night? "But the main cell phone tower went down. Can you live with it? At least until I get home?"

"It's pretty awful." Her voice cracks. "I don't think I can dance looking like this."

"Tell you what. If you really can't stand it, do something. Make a statement. Go big. Go bold. I trust you."

"Really? You won't get mad?"

"It's hair. Whatever you do, you can always change it." I wonder if Cerelli has bugged the sat phone. What will he say if he's listening at SEAL headquarters or the Pentagon or, oh hell, the White House, and Mel and I are talking about caca-colored hair?

"Say, Mom?"

"Yeah?"

"I thought you should know I broke up with Chance."

I inhale sharply. *Think carefully how to respond to this,* I caution myself. I run through a thousand possible questions in three seconds before settling on, "How are you doing?"

"Good."

Please tell me why you broke up! Did he force you to have sex? Did he hurt you? But questions will push her into a cone of silence. I wait, hoping she'll trust me enough to say what happened.

"Oh, Mom, he . . . he told me my dancing is dumb. He said I'm wasting too much time practicing when I should be spending it with him. And you know how much I've been wanting to get accepted to that dance program at UWM this summer."

"Dance program?"

"OMG, didn't I tell you? Oh, Mom, it's this great course, *really* prestigious, like internationally famous, and they're only accepting one girl and one guy from high schools—in the entire country. The rest of the students are in college or even dancing professionally. I applied, and I've got an audition!"

"Sweetie, that's fantastic!" I do my best to sound excited, but it's hard because I realize C.E. has known about this, probably for quite a while, and I'm just hearing about it now. And whose fault is that? "So, what does your audition have to do with Chance?"

"He told me, practically ordered me, to skip the audition. He said he wasn't willing to wait around all summer while I'm in classes and that there are plenty of other girls who'd be happy to hang out with him."

How dare he!

"I told him to check out—that I'm not giving up dance."

"Good for you."

"Yeah. I'm totally over him."

I'm so proud of her. "I love you, sweetie."

"Yeah, Mom, I love you, too. Oh, and Mom? Could you stay away from those bombers, please?"

"I'll do my best." As I power off the phone, I hear the click of the door across the hall closing. Seema's door. Seema was listening?

14

THE AROMA OF BAKING APPLE-walnut *roat* wafts into my room. One of my favorite foods on the planet. Salivating, I swing my feet to the floor and knock the sat phone off the bed. Not good. I can just imagine Cerelli's reaction if I have to tell him I broke it less than forty-eight hours after he gave it to me. I power it on. Still working, thank God.

Then it dawns on me: last night, when I opened my pack to get to the phone, it was on top of everything else. But thinking back to Dalan Sang, I can visualize Sawyer putting the phone in first, then my camera on top. Just like I always do to make sure I can grab my camera if I need it. And I didn't take out either one after that. Which means someone else must have. Seema. She went through my pack? Damn!

The gun. I unzip the Lowepro and dig down farther. The Sig is there. And the ammo clips. Everything's accounted for. I heave a sigh of relief. So, why was she going through my stuff?

She probably heard the ringing and was trying to figure out what it was.

But the Seema I know would have told me she'd looked in my pack. Would even have apologized.

Something niggles at the edge of my memory from last night. What am I missing? Come on, think! Ah, I know. She wasn't in the front room when I made my way to the kitchen. There's no way I could've missed her.

So, maybe she was in her room. Asleep. The phone started ringing, and she went to investigate.

I picture her standing at the front door, my pack clutched to her chest, her *hijab* draped around her neck. Her *hijab*? Why would she be wearing a headscarf in the house? That doesn't make sense.

Because . . . she wasn't in the house. Because she'd been outside. She was one of the voices in the courtyard. It wasn't the wind sounding like voices. No matter what Seema said, there wasn't any wind. There were real people. Seema. Who was with her? I'm betting it was a teenage boy.

The thought of Seema sneaking outside to meet up with a boy gives me pause. Correction: a horny teenage boy with hormones that have probably shut down his rational thinking skills. And for all I know, Seema is just as eager. I sure was at her age.

I think about this hypothetical meeting in the courtyard until I start to shiver. And realize that it's freezing in my little room. A lot colder than last night. Rummaging through my duffel, I find the woolen sweater Darya told me to bring. My old copper-colored cardigan. *It can be very cold in the valley until late morning when the sun finally warms things up.* No kidding. I stuff my arms in the sleeves and wrap it around me. Better, but then I see the open windows. I could swear I shut them last night. Maybe I didn't latch them securely. Or maybe Seema was right: there *was* wind and that pushed them ajar.

I shake my head. The fact that Seema was wearing a headscarf tells me she was outside. I know she was.

Four steps and I'm at the open window, looking into the dense, shiny, dark green leaves of the overgrown bush, one small branch starting to poke its way into the room. Leaves in the shapes of hearts. Heavy with hundreds of dark red berries about two inches long and curved just so. Mulberries. Up close, the swollen berries look almost sexual—ripe and succulent. I pop one in my mouth, and the sweet, raspberry-like juice literally explodes, then dribbles down my chin, sprinkling tiny droplets of deep crimson onto my sweater.

I wipe my chin with the back of my hand, latch the windows, and follow the still enticing aroma of *roat* to the kitchen where Darya is stirring a bowl of goat-milk yogurt. Another bowl—mulberries floating in their juice—sits on the table.

Darya looks up. "Ah, you are awake. After yesterday, I thought you might want to sleep in today."

"Not with your *roat* seducing me."

Darya grins. "You remember."

"As if I could forget?" I pull my sweater tight around me. Even though it's warmer in the kitchen, I'm still feeling chilled.

Darya studies me, then laughs with delight. "I remember that sweater! Your Grammy knit it for you. It's what? Twenty-five years old?"

"From freshman year. You said to bring a sweater, and this is the warmest one I've got. It's a little patched, but so what."

"And I still have the one she knit for me. Red, remember? You'll see. I wear it all the time. Especially in the morning when I walk to school. I'd freeze without it." She lowers her voice. "I think it embarrasses Seema, though. All the holes and badly darned patches."

"Tell me about it." I point to my own patches. "Mel is after me to get something less raggedy. And as for embarrassing our daughters, I think it's in the rule book."

"In the States, perhaps, but not here. In Afghanistan, daughters are brought up to respect their parents. Well, certainly their fathers. Their lives depend on it."

I narrow my eyes.

"Don't look at me that way." Darya wags her finger. "I'm not saying anything about you or Mel." She pulls out a chair from the well-worn and scarred oak table. "Now sit, and we'll eat."

"What about Tariq and Seema?"

"Tariq was called to the clinic early this morning but should be back soon. My less-than-energetic daughter is still asleep." Darya smiles away her annoyance then sits down across from me. "She's sleeping later and later. Some days, it's nearly impossible to wake her for school."

I nod. "Tariq said something about that yesterday." Which leaves me perplexed. Seema always loved school. She was always prepared, always did her homework first thing. I remember she even won awards for perfect attendance. In short, the student every teacher dreamed of having. What's going on? The boy in the courtyard? Hang on. I really don't know if there was a boy out there with Seema.

"I was hoping her behavior would change once you got here." She shakes her head. "But, as you can see . . ."

"That could be my fault," I say with a guilty laugh. "Apparently, the sat phone Cerelli gave me was ringing last night. I left it in my pack by the front door, and the noise kept her awake."

Darya frowns. "Odd that it didn't wake either Tariq or me. Our room is right next to the lounge, and we're not the heaviest sleepers."

I'm back to sorting through the puzzle. So, where *was* Seema in all this? My pack was by the front door. I heard the phone ringing on and off for what felt like hours. If it woke Seema, like she said, wouldn't she have checked it out sooner? My mental image of her *hijab* waves in front of me. Let's suppose she *was* outside in the courtyard. She heard the ringing, ducked in to grab my pack, and took it outside with her. Why would she do that? To keep the noise from waking her parents. Because . . . she didn't want them discovering she was outside. With a boy. Which would explain the *hijab*. And the voices. And why the phone ringing didn't wake Darya or Tariq.

"Although now that I think of it," says Darya, "the wind did pick up last night. It woke me up once or twice. Ah, I should warn you: the courtyard is a lovely place to relax—very private. But the wind can really whip around out there. I hope it didn't wake you."

The wind? Damn. Maybe Seema *was* telling the truth. Now I don't know what to think. I prop my elbow on the table, my chin in the palm of my hand, and walk through what happened last night. Again.

"Annie?"

"Sorry. I was drifting. I must be more tired than I thought."

"I was just wondering who was calling you so late."

"No mystery. Mel was worried about the suicide bombing."

"How could she have possibly known?"

"The wonders of cable TV correspondents who talk their way onto military helicopters, then upload their feed to stations around the world."

Darya shakes her head in sympathy. "No wonder she was trying to reach you. Is she all right now?"

I nod. "Actually, Cerelli got to her first and told her everything was okay."

I catch her up on the latest dramas in my daughter's life until the apple-walnut *roat* is cool enough to slice. The perfect breakfast with yogurt and spicy *chai*. And oh, God, these berries.

"Would you like some more?" Darya nods toward the empty bowl.

I look down at my fingers stained crimson. Please tell me I didn't just eat *all* the berries. "Oh, Dar—"

"Eat them, please. The bushes are loaded. We are literally squishing them as we walk in the courtyard. To tell you the truth, we're all a little tired of them."

"I can't begin to understand that." A soft moan escapes my mouth, and immediately I feel my cheeks flush.

"Are we still talking about mulberries?"

"Let's not go there. My sex life, or lack thereof, is most definitely not up for discussion over breakfast. Or at all. In fact, why don't you tell me about the school and my class? What I should expect. And what I should wear. I brought my usual baggy pants and tunics. And Cerelli insisted on buying me a *burqa*—"

"No! Definitely not the *burqa*! It's not expected for foreign women, and it can even be misconstrued."

"What?"

"It would be more respectful if you wear what you brought from home. Or a *shalwar kameez*, if you have one. And maybe a scarf over your hair."

"Fine with me. I don't like anything about the *burqa*, how it cuts women off from the world. It feels like a prison to me."

"Annie." Darya uses her headmistress voice. "You must know that many women in Afghanistan wear *burqas* because they want to, not because they're forced to. Several of our teachers wear them. It's part of the culture. They feel it is an act of honor and dignity, and also a way to show their modesty, their piety. They feel more secure and so can get around more easily. Please don't make the mistake so many in the West do and think that all these women are oppressed and need to be liberated."

"But you don't like the *burqa* either."

"I wouldn't be caught dead in one." Darya clasps her hands together. "It's just that since I've been here, I've learned that it's not so black-and-white. Wait until you meet Gulshan, our literature and English teacher. You'll see what I mean."

"The *burqa* is out." I raise my hands, happy to surrender the point, then pause, remembering the bombing yesterday and the fate of my *keffiyeh*. "Do you have a headscarf you could loan me? I'm afraid mine went to the cause of birthing a baby."

"Yes, of course." Darya has always been more than happy to accessorize me—her way of cleaning up my act and making me look more presentable. But I hear something in those three words that tells me her thoughts are elsewhere. The tone of our happy breakfast has shifted.

"What's going on, Dar?"

She looks toward the kitchen window with its shelf of potted herbs. "This is embarrassing." Her fingers are busily picking nonexistent threads off the sleeve of her *shalwar kameez*. "So far, only two girls have signed up for your workshop—Seema and her best friend Bahar. The other girls are excited, but their parents have not yet given their permission. I honestly thought they'd come around, but the workshop starts tomorrow."

"I expected some resistance, but look, it's okay. I can always start the workshop with those two. If all else fails, I'll leave the equipment and think up something to tell Canon. No problem."

"You are right!" proclaims a smiling Tariq from the kitchen

doorway, his sudden appearance catching us both by surprise. "There is no problem." He sits at the table and helps himself to a hefty slab of *roat* and a glass of *chai.* "Everyone in the village is talking about what happened yesterday. You saved Ahmad Shah Massoud's son—and delivered his grandson. You are well on your way to becoming a hero throughout the valley."

I shake my head. "But that's crazy. Nazira's the hero. She stayed alive long enough to birth the little guy. All I did was hold him."

"That is not the way the baby's father is telling the story. He says that first you saved *his* life with the tourniquets." Tariq rubs his jaw.

"Tariq, *you* saved him."

"Yes, well, not according to Ahmad Massoud. And you then saved his newborn son. I heard from the doctors in Kabul that they found a rubber band wrapped around the baby's umbilical cord?"

I shrug. "It was all I had."

"I also hear that father and son are holding their own."

"That's wonderful news!" I smile.

"Ahmad Bâz Massoud—that is what he will be called," says Tariq.

"Bâz?" I ask.

"It is the Dari word for *Hawk.* I believe there was some talk of his second name being Annie, but the family decided *Hawk* would be more appropriate for a boy. It was the closest they could come to *Hawkins.*"

I blink hard. "Wow."

"You really have become something of a legend in these parts, Annie. So, I believe you will have more young ladies in your workshop tomorrow than you know what to do with."

"Not to mention, a very important connection with the

Massoud family," says Darya. "You're one of them now. And should you ever need help, the Massoud clan would like nothing better than to save *your* life."

"Apparently, you have another admirer as well." Tariq looks a bit worried. "We received a call at the clinic this morning from a man named Nic Lowe. He said he's a journalist with the BBC and an old friend of yours."

I shake my head at this description of Nic. "*Old friend* might be stretching things, but I do know him. We were both staying at the InterContinental in Kabul and had dinner together one night."

"So, then, he is not like the woman—Piera. That is fortunate. He called because he heard about the bombing yesterday and wanted to make sure you are all right. Apparently, Piera is reporting on television that you were severely injured. I assured him you are quite fine. I hope I said the right thing?"

"Never fear, you told Nic exactly the right thing. What I would have told him if he'd called me." Tariq looks somewhat relieved, but not completely. Just like back in college when he was my tutor and quizzing me about my beautiful and enchanting roommate Darya. He was never totally sure if he was saying the right thing or asking questions that might somehow be out-of-bounds. Maybe the Piranha should take lessons. I shake my head. Nic calling to check up on me. Whoever would've thought—Nic Parker Lowe is turning out to be a stand-up guy.

AFTER BREAKFAST, DARYA FOLLOWS me back to my room, two headscarves draped over her forearm, one periwinkle, one black. "I thought one of these might work for you tomorrow. But why don't you show me what you're planning to wear. Maybe I have something else that will work better."

"I'm afraid my wardrobe is a bit thin." Especially after yesterday. I pull clothes out of my still-packed duffel and lay them across the bed. "You know me: I travel light, and I'm not exactly the picture of high fashion. Most of my stuff is khaki or black." I show her my old cotton *shalwar kameez*, bought years ago in Kabul. Baggy cargo pants. Tunics. "Oh, and there's this—"

I pull out Cerelli's package and unwrap it to reveal the *shalwar kameez* I saw in the shop. Except now that I look at it up close, I see it's not cheap brown cotton. It's amazing. No embroidery. No embellishments. Just magnificent fine slub silk. In the sunlight, I can see hundreds of red and orange, gold and brown threads woven together to create an extraordinary glowing copper. I trace a thread. Is that spun *gold*? I imagine how this will drape over my body, what it will hint at, and what it will reveal. Remembering the hidden video camera in my hotel room, I flush, betting Cerelli already knows.

"Oh my!" Darya's eyes brighten, and she reaches to rub the fabric between her fingers. "Where—?"

"Cerelli. We argued about the *burqa*. I'm guessing this is his way of apologizing."

Darya shakes her head. "Annie, this is much more than an apology." She snags the wrapping paper from where I dropped it on the bed and deftly smooths it with her hands. "Aha! You, my dearest friend, have been holding out on me."

"What?"

"Read this." She points to the lines scrawled on the inside of the paper. "Or is your Dari rusty? I could always translate, but I think you'd rather I don't."

I read slowly, taking my time to savor the Dari words, rich with meaning, and this is what I come up with:

May you be jasmine flowering by the side of the river.
I will quench my thirst and breathe your scent.

Okay, this is definitely not an apology. But what about Fatima?

"Annie, no man writes *that landay* to a woman and gives her *that shalwar kameez*, which I happen to know costs a small fortune and which I might add you will *not* wear to school, without hoping things between them will move in a more . . . intimate and pleasurable . . . direction."

"Dar, are you talking about sex?"

Darya holds her index finger in front of her lips—our signal from years ago that *little ears could be listening*. Only those ears aren't so little anymore.

"Come on. You sound downright romantic. We're not talking the 1950s here." And who knows? Maybe he meant this for Fatima. "It has to be a mistake."

"Idiot! You listen to me. I know Captain Phinneas Cerelli, and I know he doesn't make mistakes."

Phinneas? I think back to Fatima's sexy purr when she said his name. "What's with calling him Phinneas?"

"It's his name."

I shake my head. Finn, I accept. But he's definitely not a Phinneas. Suspicions raised, I cross my arms. "How exactly do you know Cerelli anyway?"

Darya bats away my question, then smiles mysteriously. "I suggest that you think very carefully how you want to respond to his invitation. Because that's what this *shalwar kameez* is." She turns toward the door, then looks back. "Oh, and tomorrow wear the periwinkle headscarf with the cargo pants and a tunic."

Holding the paper wrapping for the *shalwar kameez,* I sit on the bed and read it again. No one's ever written a *landay* to me. The thought that Cerelli took the time to scribble an Afghan poem warms me in a way my sweater can't. Which catches me by surprise.

Come on! This is Cerelli. It's a two-line poem. Don't make it into more than it is.

Yeah, well it *is* more than a poem. Dar knows it. And I bet Cerelli does, too.

I pick up the tunic and let my thumb glide over the fabric. Exquisitely soft. But it's the *landay* that holds my attention. Traditional Afghan love poems, originally composed by Pashtun women who weren't allowed to learn to read or write but wanted to create poems for men they loved. Forbidden love. Not for the husbands chosen by their parents that were mostly business transactions. Actually, women weren't allowed to express feelings of *love* either. So, they were really risking their lives to do so.

It's been a long time since I've actually heard a *landay.* Not since college, when I dragged Dar to a party at the International Student Center to introduce her to Tariq, who just so happened to be my calculus tutor. They were the only Afghans I knew, and I thought they might like each other. Later that night, I ended up hearing the first few words of my first *landay.* Except I didn't know it at the time. I thought Darya was giving a major thumbs-down to Tariq. Little did I know.

AT THE PARTY, TARIQ WAS a goner from the instant he first laid eyes on Darya. But Dar was giving off vibes that he was a no-go, even though she hung out with him for an entire hour. Then, she abruptly picked up her backpack and signaled me that it was time to go study.

"So?" I asked when we settled at a table in a far corner of the library stacks.

Darya shrugged. "A passing traveler." She opened her book and started taking notes.

Passing traveler? That's harsh.

A few days later, when I got to my tutorial session, Tariq wasn't focused on calculus. He didn't even notice when I started making stupid mistakes on purpose. "Hello! Earth to Tariq!"

"Could you tell me," he said dreamily, "did Darya happen to say anything about me?"

I stifled my laugh. Did guys really get this messed up over girls? One look at Tariq's eyes told me he was serious. A lot more serious than Darya. What could I possibly say that would let him down gently?

"Well, you know, Darya's really into her studies. She's pre-law and doesn't go out much."

Deflated, Tariq sank back in his chair. "Did she say anything?"

I had to give him some hope, but I couldn't lead him on either. "Well, she did say something about a passing traveler."

"Really?" Tariq sat up straighter than straight. "A *passing traveler?* You are certain those were her exact words?"

"Yeah. That's what she said." Okay, I was confused. Tariq didn't look upset. At all. He was blushing. Smiling. And, if possible, that look in his eyes was even dreamier. What the hell? Maybe I was wrong about him. Maybe he was really a lovesick, out-of-touch stalker.

I tapped my pencil on the desk to get his attention. "Look, Tariq, tell you what. I've got a calculus quiz this week I'd really rather not fail. So, could we focus on derivatives and getting me a B?"

"Oh, Annie, you must accept my apologies. Of course, we will now work, and then I will escort you back to your dormitory. It is getting dark, and I do not like the idea of you walking alone on campus."

Yeah, and you love the idea of maybe, just maybe catching a glimpse of the woman who dismissed you as a *passing traveler*.

Three years later, when Darya married Tariq, I accidently overheard the rest of that *landay*. Darya quietly sang it to Tariq right before *Hama* Bibi led us to the center of the ballroom to dance the *Attan* at the wedding reception.

Oh, passing traveler! Never will I be satiated by your sight.
Stay and watch me dance.

Clearly, Dar had changed her mind about never dating a guy from Afghanistan.

I RUN MY HANDS OVER the silk tunic. So beautiful, but I can't imagine when I could ever wear it. Before folding it back up in the wrapping paper, I read Cerelli's *landay* again. And take note of the little two-step in my heart. But then I think back to our day in Kabul, and I cringe. All I did was snark at him. Why would he be writing these lines to me? No, Darya's got to be wrong. This gift was meant for Fatima.

15

DARYA SUGGESTS A WALK TO the school. She wants to show it off, and I'm eager to see it. I catch Seema as she's heading out the door, her *hijab* covering her hair, a full pack weighing her down. "Seema! Why don't you come with us?"

"Oh, Auntie, I wish I could." She looks disappointed. "But I promised my friend, Bahar, I'd study with her today. Our graduation exams are in a few weeks."

Dar smiles proudly. "The girls have been working together all term. The senior girls like to study in pairs and quiz each other."

So, it's just Dar and me. We link arms and set off. Mulberry bushes and walnut trees line the unpaved road. A few houses are nestled far back in the groves—invisible in the dark last night when I arrived. Goats and a wandering mule join us for short stretches, then wander off to forage for wildflowers and berries. There's enough of a breeze to keep us cool, but also to churn up dust. We haven't gone very far before we're both filthy and coughing. Mirror images of each other, we readjust our headscarves to cover our mouths.

"The *hijab* may not be my favorite thing to wear," says Darya, tightening her hold on my arm, "but it has its advantages."

"Oh yeah. This is one of the reasons why I always travel with my *keffiyeh*. I need to buy another."

"I doubt you'll find one in Wad Qol. But you could get an inexpensive headscarf at one of the shops in the village."

"Something else to add to my list. Cerelli told me to buy some sandals and dark socks. I planned to do that yesterday, but then Dalan Sang happened."

"The shops in the village will have something. Now, let's stop talking about yesterday." Darya waves her hand in front of us, pushing away all negative thoughts. "It's pretty here, don't you think? We live about three kilometers from the school, five from the village. At first, I thought I'd miss living in the center of everything, but to be honest, I've come to appreciate the privacy."

"Hard to believe, you being a city girl." I nudge her with my elbow. "You walk this every day?" Darya was never one for physical exertion.

She grins. "Morning and late afternoon. Tariq offers to drive me, and when I work late, he insists. But I like the walk. It lets me organize my thoughts, and it's the only real exercise I get."

One of the goats is back, nibbling at Darya's sweater. When she bats him away, he starts in on mine. I swat at him, but he's not deterred. Another swat, then a stern "GO AWAY!" He cocks his head as if to say, *You don't mean that!* One more swat, then he trots amiably to the side of the road to munch on some delectable poppies.

"They're certainly dogged," Darya laughs, then pulls me a fraction of an inch closer. "Now, tell me about Phinneas. What's going on between you two?"

"Cerelli and me? Are you serious?"

"Just answer my question."

"Nothing. There's absolutely nothing between the two of us."

She laughs again. "I don't believe that for one minute. That *shalwar kameez* and the *landay* say something is most definitely going on. Or it will be soon. The question is: do you want something to happen?"

"Oh, Dar, get real." I stare at her in disbelief. "Don't you remember how horrible he was to me? I told you how he interrogated me on the *Bataan*."

"You never told me the details."

"Because he threatened to come after me if I told anyone."

"I seriously doubt Phinneas would have done that," she says dismissively. "Besides, that was more than eight years ago. Maybe it's time to move on? How were things between you two in Kabul?"

I'm starting to clue in. "You mind telling me what you had to do with setting us up?"

She tries to look affronted. "I have no idea what you're talking about. I simply asked him to check up on you. To help you get situated. If something more than that happened," she pauses for dramatic effect, and that's when I catch the smile in her eyes, "that was up to Phinneas. And you."

"And how exactly do you and Tariq know him anyway?"

She waves away my question.

"No, Dar. Come on. I want an answer. How do you know Cerelli?"

"Oh, please. There's nothing mysterious about how we know him. The expat community in Afghanistan is really quite small."

"He's not an expat."

"No, but he spends a great deal of time in-country."

I narrow my eyes.

She shrugs. "All right. He came to Wad Qol a few years ago and ended up needing some medical assistance while he was here. Tariq took care of him. After that—" She waves her hand again, evidently thinking I'll be satisfied with the little she's told me.

"And what about Fatima?"

"Fatima?" She puzzles over my question. "I don't—Wait! Does she own a restaurant in Kabul?"

"She's beautiful, voluptuous, and very sexy. It's clear they've known each other for a while. I'm guessing in the biblical sense."

"I do remember her. But all that was a long time ago." She shakes her head emphatically. "They've both moved on. Besides, Fatima's married now. To the man with whom she owns the restaurant."

All *that*? All *what*? I picture Cerelli and Fatima barely an inch apart from each other and her obvious appreciation of his attention. I seriously wonder whether either one of them has moved on.

"So, tell me," says Darya, as if she already knows the answer, "was he still as awful as he was on the *Bataan*?"

"Not at all." I catch myself smiling. "He was a complete gentleman. Actually, I really enjoyed spending the day with him. It was fun. Comfortable. Except for the fact that he bugged my room. There was even a videocam."

Darya arches her eyebrows. "Surely that wasn't intentional!"

"Really, Dar? Since when do you believe in coincidence? Besides, didn't you say that Cerelli 'doesn't make mistakes'?" I make exaggerated air quotes.

"Since when are you paranoid?"

"Paranoid? Me? I don't think so." Well, given my bizarre hallucinations since I arrived in Afghanistan, maybe I *am* a little paranoid. "Actually, there was a bit of a to-do at security when I arrived with so many cameras. The guards thought I might be about to blow up the hotel. So, they rewarded me with one of the special rooms Cerelli had rigged up."

"Oh, Annie! I am sorry. Truly. We should have expected that."

I shrug.

"So, back to this video Phinneas took of you." She raises her eyes to the sky. "Did you put on a show?"

"I didn't see the video, but he *did* thank me."

Darya searches my face for a few disconcerting moments. "My friend, I'm telling you this because I care about you. It's way past time for you to get a love interest in your life, to find a partner. You spend too much time on the road. It's all you do, and you're not the kind of person to be single."

I shake my head. "Sorry to disappoint you, but I'm not looking for a relationship. I doubt it would solve the riddle of me, and it would seriously complicate my life. The last thing I need is another Todd demanding I live up to his expectations, insisting I give up my job. Bottom line: as hard as it is for you to believe, I'm perfectly happy being single." Hearing myself say that stops me. Is it true?

She entwines her fingers with mine. "I'm not telling you to give up your work. I would never tell you that. Nor would Phinneas, I'm certain. You are too good to stop. I realized that back in college. Remember? And you *need* to be out in the field."

I squeeze her hand. "But?"

"But, I do not for one minute believe you *are* happy being single. You need some balance in your life. When was the last time you went on a date?"

"You mean when was the last time I went to bed with someone?" Which was a lot longer ago than I'm prepared to acknowledge.

She winces. "No, that wasn't exactly what I was asking, but you definitely answered my question."

"Dating is way too awkward. Not to mention, uncomfortable."

"Did you not just tell me you 'really enjoyed' your day with Phinneas?" She throws my air quotes right back at me.

"Yeah, I did say that." And despite becoming the displeased and very reluctant recipient of a Sig Saur and a *burqa*, I *did* enjoy my time with Cerelli. No awkwardness. No discomfort. Well, not much. But a relationship? My heart does its second quick two-step of the day, then I remember the twinge I felt when I saw the looks flying back and forth between Fatima and Cerelli. Nope, I'm not going there.

Dar tightens her hold on my arm. "So?"

"It's too complicated. My work schedule is insane, and I need to spend more time with Mel." I shake my head. "Nope. I've got all I can handle. The end."

"Well, then," she sighs. "So, tell me about Mel. To be honest, when I talked to you the other night, I thought you were going to say you couldn't come."

"You read that right. Mel's dance recital got rescheduled to next week."

"And you're feeling guilty about missing it?"

"Not just this one. Way too many recitals. Along with every other major event in her life."

"Surely you exaggerate."

"Believe me, I'm not. My guilt is endless. And Mel knows how to push my buttons."

"But she seemed sincere when she told you to come."

I smile. "Oh, she was sincere. But she's also milking it. I owe her big-time."

"You haven't always felt like this, have you?"

"It feels like it's getting harder, being away from her."

"How is she getting on with Catherine Elizabeth? And Todd? Could that have anything to do with how you're feeling?"

I laugh. "You always get to the heart of the matter. Truthfully, it's close to open warfare. Mel's asserting herself. Her stepmother resents it. Todd's siding with Catherine Elizabeth, which leaves Mel feeling betrayed and angry." I slow my steps. And decide not to mention that so much of the current drama has been caused by Mel's choice of hair color.

Darya stops walking and turns toward me. "This isn't your fault. Mel has a very strong personality. She always has. Like her mother. You can't take this on yourself. She'll sort herself out."

I look off through the trees at a run-down house, the mud bricks in front disintegrating, the front door and windows boarded up. "Abandoned. That's what she feels. And that *has* been my fault."

"Annie, no. You have a life and a career."

"And a daughter who needs—"

"She will be fine." Darya starts us walking again. "Come, let me show you the school that Mel has graciously allowed you to visit." She steers us off the main road onto a narrow driveway. "I promise you, the next time we Skype, I will be sure to thank her." She points ahead.

I stop mid-step and stare. It's nothing like that first photo she showed me eight years ago in Milwaukee. That building was a dilapidated wreck. Roof partially caved in. Windows cracked or nonexistent. Front door hanging off its hinges. Bricks and chunks of plaster missing. I've heard about this school for so long, and Dar's sent photos of the various improvements—the new roof and windows, the smooth plastering on the exterior. But it's not the same as seeing it in person. Now, I'm finally here, and I'm completely and totally in awe.

"May I present: The Wad Qol Secondary School for Girls." I hear the pride in her voice. She squeezes my hand. "And we built this together. You and I. Without your donations, we couldn't have done a fraction of this rebuilding."

"Oh, Dar." A smile creeps across my face. "It's beautiful. Absolutely magnificent. So much more than the photos show."

We stop in front of the main door, solid wood and painted the vivid turquoise blue I've seen on so many mosques in eastern Afghanistan. On either side of the door, there are three windows, then another group of three—all polished until they sparkle in the sunshine. Their white-painted frames are cracking, though, and in serious need of attention—I make a mental note. I walk to the closest window and peer inside to see a classroom with rows of wooden tables, red-painted wooden benches parked neatly beneath each one.

"That will be your classroom," says Darya as she unlocks the door.

"Darya!" A woman in a black *burqa* hurries up the driveway toward us. I look my question at Dar, but she waits until the woman joins us to answer.

"This is perfect," says Darya. "Gulshan, I am so glad you happened by." She turns to me. "I mentioned Gulshan at breakfast. She teaches literature and the English language. She was the first teacher at the school and has helped me every step of the way. Her daughter, Bahar, and Seema have been the best of friends since we moved here. And you will be using her classroom when you teach the workshop."

Gulshan takes a step closer to me. "Ms. Hawkins Green, it is such an honor to have you here to teach photography. The girls are so excited that they cannot concentrate on any of their other subjects." She ducks her head for a moment, then looks back at me. "I must confess that I did not *happen* by. I was sure Darya would bring you to the school today, and I wanted to be the first to welcome you." Behind the netted eyepiece, Gulshan's eyes shine.

"Please, call me Annie. It is *my honor* to be here. Teaching this workshop has been a dream of mine for many years. It's wonderful of you to allow me to teach in your classroom."

Darya motions us into the dimly lit front hall, patches of light coming from open classroom doors. "I know it's pretty dark inside today," she says to me more than to Gulshan. "But I'd rather not turn on the generator. We have just enough kerosene to last until the end of term if we're careful. Gulshan, could you show Annie the classroom? I have a few things I should check on in my office."

I follow Gulshan into the room we'll share for the next two weeks. Sunlight streams through the windows. She sweeps the front of her *burqa* back over her head, then touches my arm and points to the back of the room, where enlargements of several of my photographs have been tacked across the wall. "The girls, they were so excited to put up your pictures." The image of Malalai, bigger than life-size, is in the middle, dominating the room. My breath catches in my throat, and I turn away, not ready to see it.

"I'm glad the girls are looking forward to the workshop," I say, hoping to find something else we can talk about. "It looks like someone spent a lot of time cleaning and polishing. Everything looks so special. I feel very welcomed. Thank you."

Gulshan blushes, and I realize she's the one who has made this room as perfect as it can possibly be. "We have this school because of you, and I wanted you to see it at its very best."

My smile freezes. Darya told her? I gave her the Pulitzer Prize money and made other donations over the years on the strict condition I remain anonymous. I thought she understood—I don't want to be lauded for this. *Let it go*, I tell myself. *Don't embarrass this woman. She's worked hard to make everything right.* "So," I ask, looking around the room, "you teach literature and English to all the grades?"

"Yes. Except, of course, you'll be teaching the senior girls photography in place of their literature class."

I nod. So, that's how they're working it. "Darya mentioned the kerosene is running low. Is there anything you need for your classes? Something special? Maybe more literature books?" I've brought enough cash with me to help buy some supplies.

She smiles. "That is very kind. But we have many literature books. Captain Cerelli likes to give them to us. He especially likes Pashto and Dari poetry. Oh, and Persian poetry, too. He is a very nice man. Very educated."

Cerelli again.

I search for another subject. "Darya tells me that Seema and Bahar are best friends?"

Gulshan's smile slips, and she looks away from me for a few moments. "Yes, they used to be very good friends. They were together all the time. Sometimes it seemed that Seema was one of my daughters." She pauses for a few seconds, clearly searching for the right words. "But now they are concentrating on their studies and taking their graduation exams."

I nod. "Hence the reason why Seema's not with us this afternoon. She begged off to go study with Bahar."

A look of momentary confusion sweeps across Gulshan's face. "No, I think Bahar is working with Wiin, one of the other senior girls." Another sweep of emotion crosses her face, and then she brings her hand to her lips as if she wants to take back her words.

I think about my brief interaction with Seema as she was hurrying out the door. She said 'Bahar.' And Dar repeated the name. Didn't she? I smile and shake my head. "So many names. All at once. I clearly misunderstood. It will be easier once I start meeting the girls tomorrow and can put names together with faces."

"Of course." Gulshan is smiling again.

I weigh her words as the unsettled feelings from last night and this morning take hold again. I'm sure Seema said 'Bahar' as she left the house. But if Bahar is studying with this other girl, where was Seema going? And Dar is definitely under the impression that the two girls are best friends and study partners. What kind of secrets is Seema keeping?

16

IT'S GOING ON MIDNIGHT BEFORE the house grows quiet. I punch Cerelli's number into the sat phone. Please let him answer. Not Sawyer. It takes some minutes for the satellite far overhead to home in on the phone in my hand. Finally, I hear the connection click. Then the ring.

"Cerelli."

Oh God, what the hell am I doing?

"Annie? Are you there? You all right?"

"I'm here, and I'm fine." But my voice sounds shaky. My hands are actually trembling. How can I be nervous?

"You sure about that?"

"Much better than yesterday."

"Yeah, well that was a definite clusterfuck. I'm glad you had the sat phone and thought to use it in the middle of everything."

"I'm lucky you gave it to me." My voice still sounds stiff.

"You sure everything's okay? What aren't you telling me?"

For a second, I feel like I'm back in the interrogation room onboard the *Bataan*.

"Annie?"

I run my fingers through my hair. "No big deal. Just a couple interesting hallucinations."

"Talk to me."

I tell him about my last night in Kabul. "You hear anything about an attack at the hotel? A helicopter hovering outside?" I decide not to mention that my nightmare or hallucination or whatever the hell it was entailed reliving the interrogation at Cerelli's hands.

He waits a beat too long to answer. "I wish I could say yes to both questions. But this is on you. Sorry."

"Then at Dalan Sang yesterday, I imagined I saw *Anaa*, Malalai's grandmother, again. This time, she was running away from the explosion."

"Why did you think it was *Anaa*?" His voice is sharper.

"She was wearing that periwinkle *burqa*. So, I . . ."

"Lots of women in Afghanistan wear that color *burqa*."

"God, Cerelli, I don't know. I mean, why am I hallucinating at all?"

"You sure it was a hallucination?"

"Given all the insane things that have been happening and that I saw her on the rooftop of *Khosha* . . ." Why *did* I think the woman in the *burqa* was a hallucination?

At his end, Cerelli is silent, giving me time to think this through. I close my eyes and cautiously ease myself back to Dalan Sang, trying to conjure up my mental video of the periwinkle woman running away from the explosion. Wait. Something's off with this woman. I rewind the video and play it again. I watch her run. Then, for a brief moment, she slows and looks back toward the checkpoint.

Stop right there. Are those boots she's wearing? No, it can't be. *Anaa* wore sandals. I look again. Those are definitely boots. And now, she's hiking the *burqa* up above her knees. And running hard. Pounding the pavement. Like I'd be running. But not like any Afghan woman would run. That isn't a woman. It's a man. And why is he still running? Not to save himself from the explosion. He's far enough away now. So, the most important question: why is *he* wearing a *burqa?*

"Holy shit. It wasn't a woman." I walk Cerelli through my mental video.

"But was it real?"

"I think it was."

"Why?"

Good question. I think about that for a long minute. Cerelli doesn't interrupt. "Because I've only been hallucinating things that happened to me. Reliving them. Not making up new events. At least, so far."

"Good insight." He sounds pleased. And impressed.

"I don't get it, Cerelli. Why is this important?" But almost as soon as the words are out of my mouth, I start to see why.

"Sawyer thinks the bomber got away. Probably had a small boat or maybe an inflatable raft tied up somewhere close by. But we haven't found a scintilla of evidence to prove it. By the way, which direction was your *burqa* running?"

"East. Into the valley."

"Good work, sweetheart."

I smile, inordinately pleased. "Thanks. But to be honest, that's not why I called."

"Why did you call?"

I stroke the silky fabric of the *shalwar kameez.* "Look, I know I gave you a hard time about the *burqa* . . . and, well, I finally unwrapped the *shalwar kameez.* It's beautiful. Thank you."

"You like it?"

"Like it? Of course, I like it. It's gorgeous." So, he did mean to give it to me.

"Good."

Then I hear my daughter's voice. *I like him.* In the middle of everything, all that chaos yesterday, when Cerelli was probably up to his eyeballs in whatever military guys do during emergencies, he called my daughter just to make sure she wasn't frightened by what was hitting the media.

"I also want to thank you for making sure Mel was okay. And Todd. *That* was going above and beyond."

"Glad I could help. She seemed okay after I told her you weren't hurt. Your husband, though—"

"Ex-husband, actually, but it's amicable. Mostly."

"Amicable is good. But he was pretty strung out. You might want to check in with him."

"Thanks. I'll do that."

He clears his throat. "I hope I didn't overstep. I got a call from your boss at TNN. They were airing that Al Shabakat newsfeed. The one with Piera McNeil reporting that you were gravely injured, if not dead. He wanted to double-check some facts, so I passed on the info about your condition, and TNN's been running an update."

"Oh, jeez, I didn't even think to call in. My boss must have been frantic. Thank you."

"Glad I could help."

"One last thing. I, uh, read your *landay*." That could've been smoother. How to feel like an awkward teenager with surging hormones all over again.

At the other end of the line, Cerelli is quiet.

Damn. Maybe Dar got it wrong. And now I've gone and embarrassed us both.

Darya's voice. *I know Captain Phinneas Cerelli, and I know he doesn't make mistakes.*

Cerelli's deep voice reaches thousands of miles through the phone and wraps warmly around me. "Did you, now."

17

I'M SUDDENLY, INEXPLICABLY wide-awake. The darkness is heavy, weighing on me. Like in the stable at Khakwali, I'm waiting for first light, waiting for the Taliban militants to move in. My heart pounds against my ribs until it hurts to breathe. I strain to hear the slightest sound, to see a sliver of light—anything to let me know where they are, when they'll come, so I can fight. My hands scrabble across the straw, searching for the gun.

But I'm not feeling the prickly straw in the stable. Soft wool slowly brings me back. Darya's guestroom. In Wad Qol. Safe. But a cold chill still grips me. The back of my neck prickles. Someone is out there in the dark.

The leaves outside my window rustle. But there's no wind tonight. This is the sound of someone making his way through the mulberry bush. When, according to Seema, no one should be in the courtyard.

I don't move. I barely breathe until the night becomes quiet again. It could be minutes. It could be a half hour. When I'm sure that whoever was there is gone, I slip out of bed, and flashlight in

hand, cross the room to the window. Open. Thanks to Cerelli and
that golden voice he wrapped around me a few hours ago, I needed
air in the room to cool off.

Pointing the beam into the mulberry branches, I find something
that most definitely doesn't belong. Tucked between two of the
ripest berries, a leaf of white, lined notebook paper, folded in half.
I snag the paper, move back to my bed, and read a few lines in
grammatically challenged Dari, scrawled in what appears to be a
very masculine hand.

> *You promised to come. I waited into the night.*
> *One day when you want me, I will be out of sight.*

A *landay*. And since I doubt either Darya or Tariq is exchanging
poems in the mulberry bush, that leaves Seema. Who clearly has an
admiring boy in hot pursuit. Which takes me back to last night and
the voices I heard in the courtyard. Despite her denial, her *hijab*
tells me she was outside. And now the boyfriend is back.

I refold the *landay* and tap it against the palm of my hand.
Pretty innocent. I'm betting this is a first love. Sweet. Maybe a few
kisses. At least they were in the courtyard, which is screened from
the road. So, no one's the wiser. Except for Auntie, who happens
to be staying in the bedroom that overlooks the courtyard. Which
makes it too risky for Seema to sneak outside.

Still, this is Afghanistan. There are people here who'd see any
display of affection as dishonoring the family. But from what I hear,
there are also plenty of teens who are breaking with tradition and
finding their own love. Which I'm sure is what Dar and Tariq want
for their daughter. After she finishes college. I slip the note back
among the berries. I'll keep an eye on her. For now.

18

TARIQ WAS RIGHT. ALL ONE hundred girls at the Wad Qol Secondary School want to take the workshop. And they're all crammed into the classroom, sitting five and six to a bench behind tables made for two.

"Teachers and students," says Darya, standing in front of the cracked blackboard, "it is my very great honor to introduce my good friend from the United States of America, Ms. Annie Hawkins Green."

Leaning against the wall by the door, I smile, then dip my head as the girls and teachers break into wild applause. I hate being the center of attention. My place is most definitely *behind* the camera. How am I supposed to teach photography to a group of girls who apparently think of me as a legend?

The girls look back at Darya, who launches into a rather long and detailed explanation of the workshop. I study the girls. At first glance, they look pretty much alike. Each one is wearing a brown *shalwar kameez* and white headscarf. No makeup. Not a lick of lip gloss. But then, I look closer at the headscarves. There's a lot of personality in how they're wearing them. Some girls have pulled their *hijabs* low onto the forehead and wrapped them tightly around the neck—not a single hair visible. I'm surprised to see Seema sitting with these girls—each of them the picture of modesty. Not where I would have thought the only American-born girl would be and totally different from how she looked the other night when her *hijab* was draped casually around her neck. She's also sporting dark, sunken crescents beneath her eyes. Obviously, her late-night activities are catching up with her.

Closer to me, some girls have wrapped their *hijabs* more loosely, a few teasing strands of shiny, dark brown hair peeking out. From the corner of my eye, I catch two of these girls passing notes back and forth under the table and struggle to keep from smiling. These girls are just like girls everywhere.

Others are even more daring and have pushed their scarves partway back on their heads, revealing waves of hair that dip fetchingly over their foreheads. For boys they might see after school?

A few girls are super daring. Their scarves rest all the way back on the crown of the head, most of their hair on display.

The teachers are standing along the back wall of the classroom. Most wear black *hijabs*. Gulshan and one other wear the *burqa*—black. Darya's headscarf is black, too, but with a fine gold filigree embroidered along the edge that frames her face. Beautiful—if one has to wear a head covering. But what would the Taliban—or ISIS—make of that gold embroidery? Oh, hell. What would the Taliban make of the *hijabs* pushed so far back that they're not covering much hair at all? Or this school? Of Darya's determination to educate girls, to make them equal actors in their future?

Self-consciously, I reach for my headscarf—periwinkle. I can almost hear Cerelli weighing in on the color.

You want to be invisible.

But you're the one who insisted on the periwinkle *burqa.*

A burqa's different. With the hijab, everyone can see your red hair—not very Afghan.

Okay, okay. Tomorrow I'll wear the black scarf—all the better to fit in among the other teachers. I find my hair fluffed around my face. I walk my fingers back, still finding only hair, thick and curly and way too wild. Where's my *hijab?* I never have trouble with my *keffiyeh*—once I wrap it around my head, it's as good as glued on. A coarser weave and cheaper fabric than the fine scarf from Darya.

Trying hard to be unobtrusive, I continue the search. A muffled giggle, and I realize one of the girls sitting closest to me has noticed. She elbows the girl next to her, who in turn elbows a third girl. Hands cover mouths to stifle laughter. My cheeks flame. This is not how I want to start the workshop. But I smile, too, and finally my fingers latch onto the scarf clinging to the very back of my head. I try to inch it forward, but my hair is too thick and keeps bunching up. I do what I can to tuck it under the edge of the scarf but can only imagine the fashion disaster I'm creating. Damn. I untie the scarf and fix it in place as quickly and as tightly as possible. Looking up, I see almost everyone watching me. Clearly, I need to get some pointers from Dar.

Darya is wrapping up her speech. "As some of you may know, Ms. Hawkins Green won a very prestigious award, the Pulitzer Prize, for a series of photographs of village girls and boys taken right here in Afghanistan. One of those pictures was on the cover of *Time* magazine."

Malalai is in front of my eyes. Not the image, the girl. Crouching, her left hand reaching toward me, her right index finger drawing letters in the sand. Staring into the lens, she's pleading with me to take the *Amrikâyi* soldiers and leave, to save ourselves. I blink hard and push her back into her photograph on the wall. How I could possibly have failed to understand the desperation in those young eyes, the plea so obvious in the printed image? My only excuse: sometimes I don't see what I've really captured until I've played with the image after the fact. In some ways, I feel all-powerful when I crop or accentuate details or push the light. But I sure don't feel that way when I think of Malalai.

"What most of you don't know, however, is—"

No! Don't say it, Darya!

"—that Ms. Green gave the money she won from that prize to our school. That money bought us a roof, new windows, and all the tables and benches in the classrooms. Even many of the books you use. And every year since then, she gives more money to our school to pay for supplies and repairs."

The applause is earsplitting. Excruciating. Oh God, Dar. Maybe you think you're telling just a few students and teachers, but this is as good as telling the world. The last thing I want is for anyone to praise me for altruism or generosity. Because giving the money isn't either of those things. I don't particularly want to be seen as paying blood money either, although all things considered, that's probably what I'm doing. The skin on my fingers crawls. Usually that's a signal to grab a camera, but at the moment, I feel more like strangling Darya. Doing something, anything, to stop her talking.

Except Darya doesn't look like she'll be wrapping things up anytime soon. She talks on, casting a benevolent gaze around the room until she gets to me. And then, mercifully, she stops. Thank God. She gives me a quizzical look. *What's wrong?* I glance down and see that I've crossed my arms. And I'm definitely not smiling.

"All right," says Darya. I think she's directing that comment to me. She smiles at the students. "I'm sure Ms. Green appreciates your warm welcome. And now, lower-level girls, please return to your classrooms with your teachers. Senior-level girls will stay here to start your photography class."

There are twenty-three girls. They tell me their names, but the only ones I remember are Bahar, who wears a moderately daring headscarf—interesting given that her mother, Gulshan, wears the *burqa*—and, of course, Seema. I've got twenty-four cameras. I give each girl a DSLR Rebel, a charged battery, and a charger plus a SanDisk card. Then, I take one for myself. Surprise rustles through the classroom. Hands shoot into the air, and I nod at Bahar.

"Ms. Green, you will be using the same camera as the rest of us?"

"I will. I think that's the best way for me to help you learn how to use it."

Excited chatter tells me I made the right decision to leave my regular camera tucked securely in my backpack. My eyes seek out Seema. She smiles but looks like she could easily fall asleep.

The girls clutch their cameras, looking as if they'll never put them down. I'd prefer to see those cameras hanging securely around their necks, but the straps went to tourniquets, which are now probably in the garbage bin of a Kabul hospital. Maybe I can figure out an alternative, but for now they'll just have to be careful. We run through the basics to get the cameras up and working. The light is bright enough in the classroom, so I let them practice by taking a few shots of each other. Oh my, these girls sure know how to pose. And giggle.

"Okay!" I wave my hands to get their attention. "You can take more photographs for homework. For now, let's talk about photography."

The girls scurry back to their seats, secure their cameras on the tables in front of them, primly fold their hands, and look expectantly at me.

Here goes. "There are different kinds of photographers," I say by way of introduction. "I'm a photojournalist, which means I tell stories with my pictures, kind of like a reporter who tells stories with words. It's my way of communicating, of letting people know what's going on in the world. What's *really* going on, not just what some governments want us to know."

Several girls gasp, and I make a mental note to check my future comments about the Afghan government. Or any government. There's no point in making the girls uncomfortable. Besides, they're sure to report everything that happens in the workshop to their parents. I don't need to see the inside of a prison on this trip. But I won't sugarcoat things either.

"Telling the truth," I continue, "means that sometimes pictures can be disturbing, even shocking. My job is to tell the story as truthfully as I can."

A girl sitting next to Bahar slowly pokes her hand above her head. "My name is Wiin. May I ask a question?"

"Of course."

She takes a breath. "What if it is a dangerous story? One that could get you hurt or might get you in trouble?"

I grin. "Well, I *am* a war photographer. So, I take photos in dangerous situations all the time. Like pictures of soldiers fighting. Or even dying."

The girls gasp.

I point to the three pictures of Malalai and other kids in Khakwali tacked up on the back wall. "But I also take photos of ordinary people doing ordinary things while war is going on around

them. Like boys tending their goats. Or kids going to school or
playing. I just recently took a picture of a teenage girl in Nigeria
bringing her baby home to her mother's house. When I show these
pictures of life alongside pictures of people dying because of war,
all the images are more powerful. And sometimes heartbreaking."

Bahar's hand shoots up. "You mean because there is both
life and death? Someone might be alive one minute and then die
suddenly? Even if they are civilians?"

"Yes." My eyes lock on Malalai's. "Exactly."

A murmur of quiet chatter runs through the classroom.

Seema looks like she wants to say something, so I call on her.
"But aren't you scared going into wars?"

"Yeah." They all laugh. "Sorry, I didn't mean to be so glib. The
real answer is: yes, sometimes I'm completely and totally terrified.
I do my best to be careful, to take precautions. But the bottom line
is: this is what I do. It's my job. And it's important."

At the very back of the room, a girl stands up next to her bench.
"What if you do not have a story? Or maybe you have an idea, but
you are not sure how to tell the story?"

"Good question! That's where planning comes in. The first
thing is to figure out what you want to say in your photograph,
what you want your audience to see, how you want them to feel.
Then, you work on composing a shot to create that message. You
frame the picture and use lighting and shadows in different ways.
You also use depth of field to create an effect."

"Fields?" Bahar looks confused. So do the rest of the girls.

"The field is what we call the overall picture. Maybe I want the
entire image to be in focus, so you can see everything clearly. Or
maybe I want one person to stand out clearly while the background
is a little blurred, or even completely out of focus."

"Like you did with Malalai," says a girl seated by the windows. "You can see the houses behind her, but not clearly."

"That's right."

"How did you plan that picture?" asks Bahar.

"To be honest, I didn't. I just *took* that picture. I broke every rule, but as I looked through my lens that day, I *felt* the image. The composition, the lighting, the depth of field, everything. It all came together. And I knew it was right. Then, I just forgot all the technical stuff and shot the picture." I shrug. "Sometimes it happens that way."

Seema looks surprised. "But you won a prize for that picture. You became famous."

"Remember, I'd already taken thousands and thousands of pictures by that time, so I didn't need to think about the rules. They just came automatically. And my goal for you is that during this workshop you'll learn some of the rules well enough that they become automatic for you, too."

Bahar wrinkles her brow. "You mean you want us to learn the rules so well that we can forget them?"

"That's exactly what I mean."

A smile creeps onto her face. Seema's, too. The rest of the girls look a little shell-shocked, as if breaking rules isn't something to be talked about.

"Ms. Green," says Bahar, "will you tell us the story about Malalai?"

I should have expected one of the girls would ask me this, but stupidly, I didn't. I take a deep breath and slowly walk to the back of the room where the bigger-than-life-size print of my famous photograph is tacked to the wall. Can I do this? Can I tell these girls about Malalai? About that day? Without ending up back in Khakwali? I've got to try.

"She was trying to save my life. And the lives of two U.S. Marines. We were in her village handing out food and water. We'd been there before, but this day," I tap the image, "Malalai told me to leave. Except, I wasn't smart enough to understand. I don't speak Pashto, and she didn't speak English or Dari. So, she wrote a warning in the sand. See there, she wrote the letters—T A L I B A N." My finger traces the swirls and curves of the Pashto letters, letters I couldn't make sense of until much later when I printed the image.

A bench scrapes the floor, and Bahar comes to stand next to me. More benches are shoved back, until all twenty-three girls are crowded around me.

"Look at her eyes," says Bahar. "She is terrified."

"I think she looks desperate," says Seema, "desperate for you to understand her."

"Yes. She was. And one second after I took this photograph, it was too late. The Taliban fighters hiding in the houses shot her before I could figure out what she was trying to tell me."

"What about the Marines?" whispers Bahar.

"They killed them, too."

"Why didn't they kill you?"

"They wanted to, but—" My voice stays in my throat. I struggle to keep from going back to the soggy, smelly stable at Khakwali. I reach forward and touch my fingers to Malalai's hand. "The important thing is what you see in this photograph. What it says to you."

"Fear," says a quiet voice at my shoulder. "She is very afraid."

"Bravery," says Bahar. "Even though she is scared, she is trying to help you anyway. Do you think she knew they were going to shoot her?"

"I think she knew they were going to shoot *us*."

"I see love," says Seema.

"Love?" scoffs Bahar with a roll of her eyes. "That is crazy." A couple of the girls standing next to her seem to share her opinion, giggling into their hands and looking toward the ceiling.

"Yes, love." Seema crosses her arms and raises her chin to drive home her point. "I think she loved you, Auntie, I mean Ms. Green, so much that she was willing to die to try to save you. That's what you do when you love someone. Love can make you do things you never thought you'd do."

Bahar whispers to the girl next to her. Both girls smile.

Time to intervene. "Of course, there is no one correct answer. We each bring our own experience to what we see in a photograph, in any art, so we may interpret it in different ways."

Bahar and most of the girls nod, but Seema keeps staring at Malalai, as if there's a palpable connection between them. She's clearly convinced her interpretation is the right one. The only one.

I tent my fingers, pressing them hard against my lips, hoping I can find a way to tap into Seema's deeply held feelings and help her express them through the photographs I want her to take. But I'm also praying to God to keep my sorrow, my regret, my unmitigated guilt over Malalai's death locked deep inside me. Away from these girls.

19

I HANG OUT AT SCHOOL FOR the rest of the day in case any of the girls have questions about their cameras. Or their assignment for tomorrow. Not terribly hard. *Take pictures of the people in your family.* Just something to get them used to their Rebels. I'm also hoping that after school I can get Seema to walk into the village with me to buy a pair of sandals, some socks, a cheap headscarf. I want to talk to her. The night I arrived, she seemed so happy to see me—not moody at all. But since then, I've barely seen her.

When the last class is almost over, I poke my head around the door of the room I share with Gulshan, hoping to collect my backpack. She's alone, *burqa* pushed back from her face, reading her way through a pile of student essays. The overhead lights are off, and she's angled her desk to take advantage of the afternoon sunlight coming in the windows. I'd bet anything she's scrimping on the kerosene to make it last through the end of the school year. I wonder if Dar knows. Gulshan looks up and smiles.

"Sorry to interrupt," I say.

She's on her feet in an instant, coming toward me with her arms outstretched. "No, no! The girls wrote essays today. They finished early, so I dismissed them. Please, come in." She reaches for my hands and pulls me into the room toward the windows overlooking the front yard. "Tell me, how was your first day? You are pleased?"

"Well, I'm not a teacher, but I think it went okay. I just wish I could have given the girls straps for their cameras. It would be so much better if they could hang the cameras around their necks. Safer for the cameras."

"Yes, we all heard how you used the straps to save Ahmad Massoud and his infant son and many other people. It was a miracle you were there at that moment."

Time to set things right. "I really didn't do much. It was Tariq who saved people. And, of course, Ahmad Massoud's wife gave birth to her baby."

Gulshan shakes her head and smiles. "That is not the way I heard the story." So much for setting things right. She's quiet for a moment, then nods. "Many of the women in the village sew and weave. Let me see what I can do to help with straps for those cameras."

"That would be great!" I grin. "I'm also curious: have you heard from any of the girls about what *they* think of the workshop?"

Her eyes twinkle. "Oh, yes. Bahar and Wiin stopped by to see me at lunchtime. They were very excited. In fact, I always thought literature was Bahar's favorite subject, but she may have changed her mind. Her scholarship, though, is to study literature."

I note the pride in her voice and ask, "Scholarship?"

Gulshan looks modestly down at the floor, then back at me. "As you know, it is very hard for girls to get an education in this country. Not many girls from the countryside do. Very few anywhere in Afghanistan go on to university. Most parents still want their daughters to marry and have families as soon as they are old enough. But my Bahar has won a place at Kabul University. She will be studying with Professor Faludi."

"*Hama* Bibi! Oh, this is wonderful news."

Gulshan can't contain her smile. "Yes, her father and I are very proud. She has worked hard for this opportunity. And, of course, we are so thankful to Darya for all the help she has given our Bahar."

"Bahar was impressive in class today. She asked insightful questions that helped me know where to go with my lecture, what the girls needed to hear." Probably because she has Gulshan as a mother.

"That is so kind of you to say. We think she is very intelligent, but we are her parents. Our son is also at university, studying medicine. He'll look after Bahar while she is in Kabul." Gulshan leans close and says softly, "But to be perfectly honest, I don't think Bahar needs much looking after. She is very motivated. Driven. That is the right word?"

"It is the right word." I squeeze her hand. "That must be very reassuring. I wish I could say that about my daughter."

"You have a daughter?"

"Mel. She's fifteen." I dig my smartphone out of my pack and pull up the picture I showed Cerelli.

"Oh! Her hair! That is not her real color, is it?"

I smile. "Definitely not. But she's a free spirit. A dancer. And a very good student. She's definitely *driven*, but also needs a lot of looking after."

Gulshan nods her approval. "A girl needs to have spirit. You are a good mother to let her make her hair that color."

Even though I had absolutely nothing to do with my daughter's decision to go periwinkle, I'm ridiculously proud that I supported her in the battle of the hair. I'm also acutely aware of the irony of this conversation. Gulshan, in her black *burqa*, championing Mel's rebellious streak and Bahar's intellect. As Dar said the other morning at breakfast, wearing the *burqa* isn't nearly as black-and-white as Westerners think.

Enough chat. I have a reason for being here: to find out where the senior girls are now so I can rope Seema into a walk to the village. "You didn't happen to see Seema, did you?"

"Yes. I saw her in the hallway right after your class." Again, she speaks softly. "I asked for her essay, which is overdue. She apologized and explained that she was very busy with you over the weekend."

My smile contracts. That little liar. I've hardly seen her since I've been here.

"Of course, I understand. She has wanted to visit with you, so I gave her a few more days to finish. She was happy today, happier than I've seen—" She looks away from me, almost as if she's said more than she intended. Or maybe I'm just reading into her body language.

I decide to press my luck. "I'd like to ask you something, and I promise whatever you tell me will stay between us." Gulshan looks toward the open door, then back at me. I lower my voice. "Yesterday you mentioned that Bahar and Seema *used to be* good friends. I'm pretty sure Darya thinks they still are. But today in class, they didn't act like good friends. Did something happen between them?"

Gulshan cups her hand in front of her mouth, clearly trying to decide what to say. I'm guessing she knows exactly what's going on, but she shakes her head. "I have heard some talk. Only rumors. Nothing for certain. So, I should not say."

I swallow hard. "Please, Gulshan, if you know something, tell me."

"I think it would be best if you ask Seema."

At that moment, the front door of the school swings open, and girls surge laughing out onto the grounds. Groups form, everyone chatting about how to spend the rest of the afternoon. Seema stands quietly to one side, away from the groups of senior girls, clearly about to head off on her own. To meet up with her boyfriend? I wonder if her friends know.

"And now might be a good time to have that talk," I say, grabbing my backpack and heading toward the door.

"Good luck!" Gulshan calls after me.

It takes me a few minutes to work my way past the girls lingering in the hallway. When I make it out the front door, I look around for Seema, but there are so many girls wearing brown *shalwar kameezes* and white headscarves that I can't pick her out of the crowd.

"Ms. Green?" Bahar stands next to me, her *hijab* ready to slide off the back of her head. "Are you looking for someone?"

"Bahar. Hi. I was hoping to catch Seema. I want to buy a pair of sandals in the village and need to know where the best shop is."

"Oh." Bahar looks past me to the road. I'm not at all sure what to make of her frown. "I think she has already left." Looking at me, her eyes brighten. "But I would be happy to take you to the shop that sells sandals. Although, I think you could get better quality in Kabul. That is what my mother always says."

What do I say? The whole point was to engage Seema and get her talking. I can buy the sandals anytime. But one look at Bahar's eager face and I know what I have to say. "That would be great!"

We stroll arm in arm along the dirt road. Flat-roofed houses, built of stone and yellow-mud bricks, each one nearly touching the next, crowd our route. Shutters are open to take advantage of the afternoon sunshine. Mulberry bushes and walnut trees become sparser the closer we get to the village center. A couple young men herd goats and sheep down the middle of the road, the animals chattering and churning a great cloud of dust around us. A bearded, old billy goat bumps my arm in his eagerness to munch my sweater.

"*Gom shoo!*" Bahar slaps his rump.

One of the shepherds rushes over. "*Bebakhshid! Bebakhshid!*" Bowing his apology to me, he steers the billy back to the herd.

"*Noshkel naist.* No problem." I smile, enjoying the look of surprise on the shepherd's face. Clearly, I look too American to speak Dari.

"You speak Dari so well!" says Bahar.

"I had a very good teacher. Mrs. Faludi. We were roommates in college back in America."

Her eyes widen. "I did not know that. She never said. Seema never said."

"So, tell me about your plans for studying at university in the fall. Your mother said you won a scholarship."

Bahar's eyes sparkle with pride. "I haven't really won the scholarship yet. Right now, it is a promise. It depends on my final exams. So, I have to work very hard to prepare and earn high marks."

I push a little, hoping to find out more about what Seema's been up to. "Which is why Seema and you are study partners."

Confusion flits across Bahar's face so quickly that I'm not totally sure I see it. "Yes. Of course. She is very smart. The smartest girl in our class, so she helps me a lot."

Not the answer I expected. The other day, Gulshan definitely said Bahar was partners with Wiin, not Seema. So, why would Bahar lie?

It doesn't take long to reach the cluster of small shops, each one attached to its neighbor. There are more shops than I would have expected, many more. A bread store with a delicious yeasty aroma. And next to it, a butcher shop, a little general store, what looks to be a grocery store, then a shop with Western-style clothing. I can also see a shop for *burqas* and another for leather goods. It's almost like I'm back on Chicken Street.

"You could order leather sandals." Bahar points to the shop at the end of the row.

"How long will that take?"

She shrugs. "It depends on how much work he has."

We check with the sandal maker, who studies my booted feet and strokes his chin.

"A week. Maybe two," he says, handing Bahar two pieces of paper and a bit of charcoal.

I breathe in the musky smell of tanned leather as Bahar traces my unbooted feet and whispers, "It will really be three or four weeks. Maybe we should also go to the general store for you to buy a pair of plastic sandals."

"Good idea," I whisper back.

The general store is so small I can stand in the middle and almost touch both walls, so dark I should have brought my flashlight to search out the sandals. There aren't any *keffiyehs* or headscarves, but I see some wool socks—dark and heavy and scratchy—and pick up a pair, knowing if I ever wear them, my feet will be sorry.

"Ms. Green." Bahar is still standing outside the shop next to a table with a few pairs of heavy-duty brown plastic sandals. "They are pretty ugly, but probably the best you can find around here. A lot of the villagers wear them."

I step out of the shop. She's right. They're the ugliest sandals I've ever seen.

Cerelli said to get leather, but these are serviceable in case the sandal maker doesn't come through. I find a pair that looks to be my size. Damn, they stink.

"They look really uncomfortable," she whispers. "You better try them on and see if you can even walk in them."

I untie my boots and slip them off again, then slide on the sandals and take a few steps under the watchful eye of the shopkeeper. Ugly, smelly, and uncomfortable as hell. If I have to wear these when I'm running for my life, I'll never make it. But I don't really have a choice. With any luck, the leather sandals will be ready in one week, not four, and I won't ever have to run for my life.

"I am very sorry." Bahar is still whispering. "We usually go to Kabul to buy ours." She sighs, clearly wishing Wad Qol had something better to offer me.

"And next fall, you won't even have to travel to Kabul for your sandals. You'll be there already."

Bahar looks practically euphoric. "It will be so wonderful to study there. With Professor Faludi. My brother is at the university, too. I think that is why my father is allowing me to continue my studies."

And here is my opening to find out what I can about the love poem clearly intended for Seema that I found in the mulberry bush outside my window. "You'll be studying literature, right?"

"Yes. I love poetry. Especially Afghan poetry." She giggles. "Of course, there really isn't such a thing as 'Afghan' poetry. In Afghanistan, we write in Pashto or Dari or Tajik. Even Persian."

"Do you read *landays?*"

She looks puzzled for a moment. "*Landays* . . ."

"They're Pashto poems. Just two lines. Twenty-two syllables. Girls and women used to compose them, even though they weren't allowed to read or write."

Bahar's eyes brighten. "Yes, I know what they are! They are very popular now. And there are some boys who write them, too." She looks around to make sure no one is listening. "We call them into radio talk shows as secret messages to each other. Of course, we don't tell our parents. I like the romantic ones best. But I've also heard some that are more political. And there are some that are anti-Amer—" She looks stricken, clearly wishing she could take back her words.

I put my arm around her shoulder. "It's okay. I know there are anti-U.S. sentiments in Afghanistan. Anyway, you'll enjoy studying with Dr. Faludi. She's an expert in poetry."

"It's going to be wonderful. And maybe one day, I will be able to teach girls. Like my mother and Mrs. Faludi."

Oh, Darya, you really do make things happen.

"Thank you, Bahar, for showing me around the village. I've enjoyed our talk, but I'm sure you want to get home to study."

"Yes. I should go. Wiin is waiting for me." Wiin—her real study partner. Another stricken look sweeps across her face.

I pretend not to notice her slip in names and wave her off. "Study hard!" But what have I figured out? Absolutely nothing except that the girls are keeping secrets I can't begin to decipher.

The shopkeeper lurks in the doorway, watching me closely so I don't make off with the socks and sandals I seriously don't want. "Lady?" he says finally, pointing to the sandals on my feet and the socks that are already making my hands itch. "You pay." He draws his thumb across his fingers.

"Of course. I'm sorry," I fumble with the English words until I find my way to ask the price in Dari. "Cheqadar ast?"

Just as I pull my wallet from my backpack, a chill starts crawling up my spine. What the hell? Someone's out there, watching me? Turning in place, I can't see anyone suspicious, but the prickling on the back of my neck doesn't ease up. In fact, it gets worse. Damn. If there really *is* someone out there, I'm a sitting duck.

I stuff a few bills in the shopkeeper's hand. From his smile, I'm guessing I overpaid by quite a bit.

"*Mêkhâhêd ân râ bopêchânom?*" He's suddenly the picture of helpfulness.

"*Na, tashakor.* No, thank you." I try to smile. "Wrapping isn't necessary." I peer behind him and off to both sides. Not that I can see anyone besides shopkeepers and a few women running errands, but someone is definitely out there.

Don't draw attention to yourself. Finish up and get out of here. Inside my head, Cerelli's voice is loud and clear.

My boots back on and the sandals and socks stuffed in my pack, I set out on the road toward Darya's house, walking fast and churning up a lot of dust, most of which is clinging to me. Exactly the wrong way to become invisible and get myself out of the crosshairs. I can feel him, whoever the hell *he* is, behind me. But each time I turn around, the road is empty.

I'm past the turn-off to the school when I look over my shoulder again and see someone trailing behind me. My stomach clenches. Then, I recognize the brown *shalwar kameez* and white headscarf worn by the girls at school and heave a sigh of relief. No way one of the girls is stalking me. And, in fact, the prickling on the back of my neck is gone. Whoever was following me before this girl happened along has cleared out. Eyes downcast, clearly deep in thought, the girl gets closer, and I finally recognize Seema. She's pulled even with me before she looks up.

"Seema!"

"Oh . . . Auntie. I-I didn't see you." She sounds surprised. Maybe even a bit reluctant. The way she peers behind her, then up the road toward home, I almost get the feeling she's looking for an excuse to go ahead on her own.

And now I see why. Her lips are swollen, and the lower one has a small cut, the blood just beading up. "You okay?" I ask, leaning forward to get a better look.

"Of course. Why?"

I point to her lips. "They look pretty sore." Remembering the *landay* in the mulberry bush and her sudden disappearance after school, I'm guessing she may have spent her afternoon apologizing for failing to show up as promised last night. Probably with an extended make-out session. Which I trust happened someplace very private.

Her hand is instantly in front of her mouth. "It's nothing. I tripped coming out of school."

Really? "Kind of late to still be at school."

"I-I was . . . uh . . . helping my mother with a project."

Oh, please. Well, I'm not going to out-and-out accuse her of lying. Certainly not over a few kisses. So, I let it go. "Nice of you to help her. I've just been to the village to buy the socks and sandals I need. Bahar came with me."

"Auntie, I would have taken you to the village. Why didn't you ask?"

I link my arm through Seema's and start us walking home. "Well, I did look for you after school, but you just seemed to disappear. And then Bahar offered." A few steps with no response, so I try again. "She told me she's starting at Kabul University in the fall." Still nothing. "She seems very excited. She also sounded grateful to have you as her study partner."

She looks at me sideways and tries a thin smile. More blood beads up. "Yes, Bahar and I work well together. She's very smart."

And yet, Bahar hurried off to meet her real partner—Wiin. So, what's this lying all about? A way for Seema to sneak off and meet up with her boyfriend? But why is Bahar covering for her?

"You must be excited, too," I say, still digging for some shred of truth, "going to college in September."

She shrugs. Then looks away.

"Of course, Boston will be a huge change from Wad Qol. That will take some getting used to."

Not a word. This is beyond tedious, like pulling teeth, especially for a girl who swore she had so much to tell me. I can see why Darya described her as moody.

"Say, I've got an idea! Why don't you come early, maybe in August? You could spend a few weeks with Mel and me."

Another shrug. "Maybe."

"Seema, what's up? You don't sound nearly as excited as I thought you would."

She shakes her head. "I don't know. It's complicated. Maybe going to school in the States doesn't seem as great as it used to."

"Are you worried you'll be homesick?"

"I guess."

We walk up the dusty road, arm in arm, and I debate whether or not I should state the obvious. At least, what's pretty damn clear to me. With Mel, I let it ride for a while, hoping and trusting she'd do the right thing. Even at fifteen, she seems better able to handle boys than Seema.

I tighten my hold on Seema's arm and take the chance I've read the situation right. "Is it because of the boy you're seeing?"

She stops walking and whirls around to face me. "Auntie? A boy? I don't know what you're talking about. I'm not seeing any boy."

That didn't go so well. She's not exactly falling into my arms to confide in me. Certainly not like last summer's college tour when I was her trusted ally against her mom. "Sorry. Clearly, I got it wrong." I start us walking again.

Not for one minute do I think I got it wrong. Should I be worried? The whole girlfriend-boyfriend-dating thing is totally different here in Afghanistan. Nothing like in the U.S. Even though teenage girls here are starting to choose for themselves, there are also many parents who wouldn't be pleased. Far from it. If a mother here discovered her daughter alone with a boy, like I found Mel, it could lead to family disgrace. Hell, honor killings are carried out for things like that. Not that Darya or Tariq would ever—

"Hey! Wait for me." We stop. Back down the road, Darya is hurrying toward us. Joining us, she hooks her arm through mine. "I'm so glad to see the two of you together."

Seema takes a few steps back, her hand in front of her mouth. "I really need to start on my homework, so I'll let Mom show you the rest of the way home, Auntie." She practically breaks into a run.

Her swollen lips. The last thing she wants her mother to see. Likely the explanation of tripping down the school front step isn't going to work. Probably because she wasn't at school helping Darya in the first place. Too many lies, Seema. How can you keep them all straight?

But Dar doesn't seem concerned about Seema's sudden departure. "Oh, Annie! All the teachers and the students, everyone is talking about how wonderful your workshop was today. This is such a tremendous experience for the girls."

"They're very sweet and ask good questions. I let them practice with their cameras today, take some pictures of each other. From what I've seen so far, it's clear that a few of them have some real potential. I need to plan a few field trips, get them out of school to take some pictures."

"They would like that." She squeezes my arm.

"I'm also toying with the idea of a final presentation of the girls' best images to the entire school. Would that be possible?"

"Oh, Annie, the younger girls—and the teachers—would be thrilled!"

"Perfect! I'll keep planning."

Dar takes a moment to scold the goat that's trailing us before turning back to me. "Now, tell me, was Seema all right in class today? She didn't fall asleep?"

Staying up all night will do that. I've got to talk to Darya about Seema, but I need more than suspicion and mere speculation. Evidence that's solid enough to convince Dar that something's going on with Seema, something that needs attention. And clearly, I need to have another talk with Seema first. "She was fine. Very attentive."

"Good. That's probably because it was *your* class. But regardless, I'm glad to hear it." She waves her hand through the air in front of us. "One more thing." She stops us walking and turns me toward her. "Your headscarf." With one flick of the wrist, she pulls off the cloth, then rewraps it securely over my hair. "There. That should hold much better." Another wave of her hand, and we're on to a new subject. "It is so good to see you again. I've missed our talks. It's been too long since it was just *us*."

"It has." *And whose fault is that, Darya?* I swallow my ungenerous thought. "Wouldn't it be great to do something together again? Just you and me?"

Darya's smile broadens. "I know exactly the place. Farther up the Panjshir Valley. Anabah. It's an alpine town with an amazing medical and maternity center. Women from all over the northern end of the valley go there. Before you leave, we could drive up. They'd be thrilled to have you take some photographs."

"That's a terrific idea." And just that quickly, I feel lighter, relaxed.

Then I remember I need to talk to Seema again. Somehow, I have to get her to stop lying and open up to me.

20

BACK AT THE HOUSE, I HEAD to my room. Stowing my pack on the floor next to my bed, I turn and find the window open. Again. A quick search of the mulberry bush reveals no white leaves of paper. Instead, a piece of fine, pale-blue stationery, folded so small it's barely visible among the berries. I peer through the leaves, and seeing no one in the courtyard, pluck it and read:

> *Your kisses are so tender, but my lip bleeds*
> *Red on my shalwar kameez. What will my mother say?*

Well, this explains Seema's need to dash home ahead of us. Not to study, but to compose a *landay*. It also confirms that her romance has moved past the invitation in the poem I read last night. What to do.

I know Afghan teens have the same raging hormones as teens in the rest of the world. And they can't all be holding back. From what I've seen so far, Seema certainly isn't. Still, for now at least, this seems to be just a kiss. Innocent enough, but something to watch. And something I definitely need to talk to Seema about. I refold the note and slip it back among the berries.

SEEMA IS SMILING HAPPILY when she appears at dinner a few hours later. Her lip is back to looking normal—the wonders of a cold compress and a dab of the aloe I saw in the kitchen. She talks nonstop about the photography workshop, even bringing out her camera and showing Tariq how to use it. As soon as she's done eating, she takes a few shots of each of us, directing us to pose, then lurking around to take some candids. Way too many candids. The constant click of the shutter is driving each of us to distraction. I cross my fingers that the rest of the girls in the workshop are faring better taking pictures of their families. Just as Dar reaches her limit, Seema begs to be excused to finish the rest of her homework.

"Seema hasn't been this engaged by her studies for weeks." Darya smiles.

Tariq nods. "She does seem to be more energetic, and she is actually speaking with us. I think you must have waved your magic wand and transformed our daughter."

I'm not convinced. Frankly, I'm baffled by her mood swings and all the lies she's telling. This is an entirely different Seema from the girl I've known. Then again, she's not the only one keeping secrets.

21

BEFORE GOING TO BED, I SLIP out of the house to check the courtyard, hoping to find it empty. It is. At least for now. There's a gate, but I can't figure out any way to lock it, so I fully expect Seema's boyfriend will come to retrieve the *landay* waiting for him in my mulberry bush. For now, though, I'm pretty sure everyone else is sound asleep, so I sit on one of the wrought iron chairs and punch Cerelli's number into the sat phone. Then, I cross my fingers that he's not in the middle of a meeting or a training exercise or on a plane to a crisis somewhere. I hear the first ring, then the second.

"Cerelli."

"The answer to my prayers."

"I bet you say that to all the guys."

"No, tonight, just to you."

"Really."

I think I hear him smile.

"So, you called because . . . ?"

"I think a bad guy is here—in Wad Qol."

"Anyone in particular?"

"I don't know. But there's someone here. A militant, a terrorist. Maybe Taliban. Maybe ISIS." I cringe as soon as the words are out of my mouth. Maybe I'm overstating things. Just a bit.

"Did you get a visual?"

There he goes with that Navy talk again. "No, I didn't *see* him. It was more like a feeling." *A feeling?* Oh God, I sound like an idiot.

"Talk to me." He sounds serious.

"Okay. I was at the market today, the one in Wad Qol, getting sandals, and all of a sudden, this sensation swept over me that someone was watching. I *know* someone was watching me, I just couldn't see him. Then I heard you telling me to get the hell out of the shop and back to Darya's house." *Please,* I beg silently, *please believe me.*

"Did you? Go back to Darya's?"

"I did."

"Glad you listened to me. How was the walk back?"

"What do you mean?"

"Did you sense him still watching you?"

"Oh, yeah. In fact, the feeling got stronger the farther I walked from the village. Until I met up with Seema, just past the school. And that's when the prickling on the back of my neck, the cold chills stopped. It was almost like whoever was following me saw Seema and backed off."

"Any idea why?"

"Not a clue. A little later, Darya joined us."

"Did you tell her about this?"

"No."

"Why not?"

I don't answer.

"Annie? Why didn't you tell Darya?"

"Because I don't want her thinking I'm crazy."

"You're telling me."

"Yeah. So, what should I do? I feel like I've got a giant bull's-eye painted on my back."

"Can you lay low?"

"Seriously? I'm teaching a class. Which means going to school and getting the girls out in the field."

"Then keep your hair covered, don't wear makeup, and when you go to the market, make sure someone's with you."

I slump against the back of the chair. "That's it?"

"Keep the sat phone and the Sig with you."

"You want me to shoot this guy?"

"Only if you have to, but try to avoid it. Shooting people in Afghanistan upsets the authorities."

"Okay, got it. Be ugly. Be armed. But don't shoot."

"Sweetheart, you couldn't be ugly if you tried."

"Thank you, but that helps me . . . how?"

"Annie, most of the time paranoia is just that—paranoia. And sometimes what your body tells you—like yours did today—is a warning to get the hell out of Dodge."

"Okay then. Oh, and by the way, you're in my head a lot. I could use some kind of warning if you're just going to show up like that."

"I'm in your head?"

"Constantly."

"That's good. For now, keep listening to me. I'll let you know if we pick up any chatter in your neck of the woods."

"One more thing. Any luck finding the Dalan Sang bomber?"

"Not yet. So, be aware. You got a good look at the guy. And he saw you. If he's part of a network, he may come looking."

"Thanks a lot. That's very . . . comforting."

"Sorry, but comforting you isn't my goal. Just keep your head down. Please. And remember what I said about body bags."

"It's kind of hard to forget."

"I don't want you coming home in one."

"I don't either."

We both power off. Pulling my Grammy sweater tighter around me, I let myself relax into the quiet of the courtyard and the velvet dark of the night. The faintest of breezes stirs through the mulberry bushes. It's nice being out here alone with no chills creeping up my spine, no fear of being spied on.

But what if someone *is* out there? Watching me? Waiting to catch me off guard?

Damn. I'm a sitting duck out here alone in the night. I grab the sat phone and retreat back into the house, making sure to lock the door behind me.

22

I LATCH MY WINDOW SECURELY and then spend a sleepless night listening for leaves to rustle—the signal that Seema's boyfriend is retrieving her love note and dropping off another of his own. Damn, I wish they'd wise up. And soon. Before a neighbor sees this guy lurking around the house. And Seema gets into trouble. But something tells me Seema and her boyfriend aren't thinking about that.

Nothing happens until just before dawn. I'm still wide-awake, waiting. Then, I hear it. The gate creaks open, loud enough for me to hear through the closed window. I imagine I can hear the young lover's footsteps crossing the courtyard, crushing the overripe mulberries strewn all over the ground. In a moment, the leaves at my window will rustle.

They do.

All I can think of is what Cerelli told me a few hours ago: *Be aware . . . he may come looking.*

Shit. Here I've been assuming that whoever helps himself to the courtyard will be Seema's boyfriend. But what if Seema was telling the truth yesterday afternoon? What if there is no boyfriend? What if it's the bomber? Cerelli said the guy could be part of a network, which means he's probably got connections all over the Panjshir Valley, including in Wad Qol, reporting to him, letting him know where I am. He could easily be here. The bomber could be the guy who saw me in the village this afternoon, the guy who followed me until Seema happened along. There's no telling who's outside my window.

Unable to move, I wait for a flashlight to shine through my window and illuminate the room, to pick me out, and shoot.

Get out of bed, I tell myself. *Do not lie here waiting for some militant to shoot.*

Grabbing my flashlight, I slip to the floor, then hunker down in the corner next to the door, as far from the window as I can get.

The leaves outside the window stop rustling. I'm fairly sure I hear the faint tread of footsteps walking away. But I don't hear the squeal of the gate closing. Instead, a few minutes later, I hear the sound of the leaves again. Louder this time. I keep my eyes on the window. Even though it's dark out there, I'm sure I see him looming, trying to see in, see me. Then, he's gone.

I hear the metallic clank of the gate. This time, he doesn't take care about being quiet.

Flashlight in hand, I make my way across the room, hugging the wall as best I can. At the window, I cast my flashlight beam into the bush, dreading that he could still be there, no matter the closing of the gate. Oh God, what if I see those eyes, intense and angry, staring back at me? But all I see is a piece of white paper propped between two dark leaves. I open the window and quickly pluck the leaf. Then heave a sigh of relief.

Another *landay.*

The boyfriend, not a Taliban militant. I want to kick myself. Instead of cowering on the floor, I should've confronted him. Told him to clear out, to leave Seema alone.

I unfold the paper and read:

Tell her that you went to the river for water
And tripped on the sharp stones.

Seriously? I almost laugh out loud. Fetching water from the river? There's running water in this house. Seema wouldn't be going to get water from the river—not in a million years. She probably knows as much about getting water as Mel does—turn on the faucet. But I'm thinking this boy must come from a family where a sister actually does go to the river each day for water. And if that's the case, he must know that it's also a social thing. Girls go to meet up with other girls. No boys allowed. I laugh again when I realize that boys *do* go to the river. Of course, they do—for romantic hookups. In fact, that's probably where he bit Seema's lip in the first place.

I read the *landay* again. My gut tells me they're just kissing, which is nothing more than what many seventeen-year-old Afghan girls are doing with their Afghan boyfriends. As discreetly as possible.

I put the paper leaf back in place, close and latch the window, and crawl into bed. One more chance, Seema. Talk to me this time. The truth. Or—

Please, God, don't let me regret this.

23

I'M TAKING CERELLI'S ADVICE and laying as low as possible. A black *hijab* pulled far forward to cover all my hair. No makeup. And it seems to be working. For the last few days, no one has followed me on my walks from home to school or back to home. At least as far as I can tell. No more nighttime visitors. No *landays* passing through my hands. I'm not at all sure what to make of any of it, but at least I'm sleeping better.

In class, I teach the girls more of the basics of their cameras and assign them to take pictures as homework. They bring back hundreds of images of gap-toothed younger brothers. Impatient mothers and aunties. Sisters pouting in all their teenage angst. I can take only so much. Hiding out simply isn't working. We all need to get out in the field. But there's no way I'm sending them out on their own. I want to be there to coach them, to give them tips about composition and lighting and depth of field. Plus, I'm itching to get my hands on a camera.

When Gulshan comes through with twenty-four camera straps sewn and elaborately embroidered by village women, I take it as a sign we're meant to get out of the classroom. Our first field trip: the village center with all its shops. But there's no way we can do that during the single workshop hour we have each day. So, I ask Darya about taking the girls into the village after their last class.

"Of course." She smiles. "That's a splendid idea. The girls will love it."

She's right. The girls are excited. Beyond excited. Their other teachers complain the girls are no longer focusing on their academic classes. Which is exactly what I don't need—the teachers upset with me. I tell myself the girls will calm down once they realize fieldwork isn't all fun and games.

After school, I meet the girls at the front door. I'm all business. "Okay, here are the rules. First and most important: before you take any pictures of people, you must ask for permission. No means no. You say 'thank you' and move on. Second: we're representing the school, so you must be on good behavior. Don't do anything crazy. And third: if you have any questions about your camera or want advice on lighting or how to frame a shot, ask me. That's why I'm here."

With that, we set off, the girls doing their best to walk sedately. But I can see how their feet are churning up the dust, eager to be in the village and have at it. And their voices are literally bubbling with excitement.

Seema, though, glues herself to my side. I'm trying to figure out what's going on, and the only thing I can come up with is she thinks this is what I'm expecting of her. Maybe because she's the director's daughter. Or because the only other time I went to the village, I couldn't find her, so Bahar went with me. I link my arm through hers and whisper, "You don't need to hang out with me. I'm fine."

"Auntie, I *want* to walk with you." She smiles, the dark shadows under her eyes not quite as pronounced as when I first arrived in Wad Qol. "I've hardly spent any time with you."

And why is that, Seema? A secret boyfriend is more exciting than your Auntie from America? And where has the boyfriend been the last several days? Not hanging around the courtyard at night. Which could explain why Seema has been a bit out of sorts. As Darya would say, 'moody.' But I smile and hug her arm to my side all the way to the center of the village.

I gather all twenty-three girls around me and repeat the rules. Faces serious, eyes wide, they all nod. So, I let them loose. Each girl turns in place, scoping out the shops. Stacks of round *nân* piled just inside the bread store. Plastic buckets and basins in blue, green, and red mounded in front of the general store. What look to be skinned and bloody lamb legs hanging at either end of the service window of the butcher shop. Yellow plastic jugs of oil, bowls of rice and carrots, raisins and nuts on a table in front of the grocery store.

The girls stand in place, not quite sure how to begin, so I take my camera out of my pack and stroll from shop to shop, nodding at storekeepers who look intrigued by the sudden appearance of so many girls together with their American teacher. The vibrantly colored buckets catch my attention. Mid-afternoon, and the light is pretty good. It could be a fun shot, especially if the gruff and bearded shopkeeper agrees to stand next to his wares.

I nod to him and lift my camera. "*Mêtawânom aks bogirom?*" May I take your photograph? I feel the girls behind me watching, holding their collective breath, so I smile as demurely as I can and wait for his answer, hoping my overpayment for the sandals a few days ago convinces him. But in the end, he shakes his head. I point to the buckets. Could I photograph them? He looks puzzled, but nods. I snap a couple shots, playing with the shadows, all too aware of the girls behind me who have to be wondering what the hell I'm doing.

Then, he picks up a stack of buckets and grins. "*Balê,*" he says with a deep chuckle, glancing from me to the girls and back to me. Behind me, I sense twenty-three girls relax. I remember him drawing his thumb across his fingers and wonder if he's calculating how much to ask. If he does, I'll move on. I'm not going to set an expectation of payment for photographs. But he doesn't ask. My shopkeeper assumes a manly stance, stroking his beard, glowering into the camera, his bushy eyebrows angling into intimating upside-down Vs. Interesting, but weird. I take a few shots, then pause and watch his shoulders ease down a few centimeters, his eyebrows resume their natural position. He thinks I've finished. I take the last shot and smile as the familiar tingle starts at my fingertips.

The girls launch into action, racing to the bakery, elbowing each other as they stand in front of the shop snapping shots of the confused bread maker, then running on to the next shop. So many girls in brown *shalwar kameezes,* long, dark hair peeking out from white headscarves. So many Malalai's. I start to get dizzy.

Head down! Cerelli's voice, loud and clear above the girls' chatter. *Wait for the wave to pass!*

Sorry. Can't wait. I take a deep breath and grab Bahar's arm as she rockets past. "Show me what you got." I try to sound excited.

Bahar stares wide-eyed at me. "Now?"

I nod. "I'd like to see." The images she scrolls through on the camera screen fail to impress. Where do I even begin? At the beginning. "What's the story you want to tell me?"

Her eyes grow wide. "A story? I don't know."

"Take a minute and think about it. Stand here with me and look. What's going on around us?"

"Everyone is running around like crazy. They are all trying to take pictures that will impress you. They all want to get a high mark."

I whisper back, "I'm not scoring these pictures. Do you think you could stand back here, away from everyone else, and capture the craziness?"

"I could try." She giggles.

"Go for it!"

She takes a couple pictures and shows them to me. "That's good." I smile at the image of five girls charging past us, heading toward the grocery store. "They look a little blurry. What do you think that shows?"

She gulps. "That I made a mistake?"

"I think it makes them look like they're running as fast as they can. But toward what? Look around again. What do you notice?"

Bahar moves away from me and for a few minutes studies the girls standing in an awkward line in front of the hapless grocer who's holding up a large, yellow plastic jug of oil. Or water. A jug of something liquid. She brings back an image of five girls, backs to the camera, shoulder to shoulder in front of the grocer. "What kind of picture do you think you could get if you stand over there?" I point to the end of the line of girls.

Bahar considers the shot. "You mean so I get the girls from the front, holding up their cameras?"

"Think about whether you also want the grocer in the picture, posing with the jug of oil."

She's off in a flash. Then back next to me a few minutes later, Seema and Wiin in tow. All three are giggling. Bahar's picture is as funny as I thought it would be. I check Seema's and Wiin's images, then send them each in a different direction with a specific suggestion. They spread the word, and soon the rest of the girls are checking in with me. I discover it's sheer insanity to try to coach twenty-three teenage girls at the same time.

We're approaching the sixty-minute mark, when high school boys come swaggering up the street. A lot of boys. And a whole lot of testosterone. Apparently, the secondary boys' school is just a few blocks away and lets out an hour later than the girls' school. Darya, you might have thought to mention this? And like teenage boys everywhere, they're far more interested in girls than school. Equally obvious, the girls welcome the attention. There's so much flirting and posturing, I can almost smell the pheromones. At least the girls still have their cameras in action. Only now, instead of creating images of the village shops and shopkeepers, they're caught up in the urgency of teenage romance. And boys.

I abandon all thoughts of coaching and morph into the chaperone for twenty-three girls, constantly counting heads and making sure no male hands come close to touching female bodies. No surreptitious hand-holding. My latest count—twenty-two heads. Who's missing? I run through the count again and end up without Seema. Shit. She wouldn't sneak away—not in the middle of a class assignment, not with me standing right here. Would she?

I scan the periphery of the crowd and finally spot her in front of the bakery, as always when in public her *hijab* covering every strand of hair. She's taking aim with her camera at the groups of laughing teens. I'd love to join her.

Then it hits me: it's kind of strange that she's the only girl who isn't flirting. Even Bahar is out in the middle of the street laughing. I glance back at Seema, who's frowning, then aiming her camera at

Bahar and one very cute boy. Why the frown? I take another look at the boy. Could this possibly be Seema's night-visiting, *landay*-writing boyfriend? I can see why she'd have a crush on him. And I can see why she'd be pissed that he's flirting with Bahar.

Glancing back at Seema, who's still on the edge of the action, I see she's now training her camera on someone else. Wearing a T-shirt and black jeans, this guy is watching her, but not watching her. I study them both for a minute and end up not knowing what to think. This guy's too old to be her boyfriend. Is he a teacher from the boys' school? Something tells me *no*—he doesn't look the part—despite his scowling disapproval of the impromptu street party.

I bring my camera up to my eye and focus. A moment to adjust for lighting, and when I focus again, he's gone. I look, but he's nowhere in sight. In his place is a bushy-bearded older man in traditional long vest and baggy pants heading straight for me. He, clearly, is a teacher.

"*Shomä!*" he hisses. "You are responsible for this?" He sweeps his arm across the boys and girls still laughing in the street.

"*Mêbakhshêd! Mazerat Mekhwaham.*" I do my best to sound contrite and very sorry. "I didn't know the boys had a late class."

"This will not happen again!" He's not about to accept my apology. "These girls should be at home, helping their mothers. These boys should be on their way to the mosque for *salah*. They will not be able to hear the *adhan* of the *mu'adhdhin* for the noise these girls are making. This village does not need your evil Western influence."

At that very moment, the call of the *mu'adhdhin* begins to echo around the village square, propelling me into action. Rounding up the girls proves relatively easy. I put two fingers between my lips and whistle. "I think that's enough for today," I say firmly to twenty-three girls who line up in front of me, who also keep trying to catch the eyes of boys still hanging around.

Even with their intimidating teacher trying to corral them to afternoon prayers, not a single boy is moving toward the mosque.

"For homework tonight"—a collective groan rises up—"I want you to pick your best image and write the story it tells. When you present it to the class tomorrow, you'll need to explain the decisions you made to create that image. Why you photographed it the way you did." Girls are still squirming to catch glimpses of boys. "Now, shall we all go back to school together? Or are you ready to go home and get to work?" No way these girls are going to run wild on my time.

The girls stare at me in disbelief. *Seriously?*

Arms crossed, I stare back. *Seriously.*

With a great show of reluctance, girls trudge home in groups of twos and threes. Boys drag themselves toward the mosque. I wait until they all head out, then turn to look for Seema, who is nowhere to be found. The road toward the school and then home is straight enough from here; I'd be able to see her if she were headed that way. She's not.

"Bahar! Wiin!" I jog to catch up to them. "Have you seen Seema? I thought I'd walk home with her."

They glance sideways at each other. Wiin speaks up. "She's probably gone to my house to wait for us."

"To wait for you?" I finally clue in. "So, the three of you are study partners?" Interesting that no one's mentioned that detail until now. In fact, Gulshan said quite the opposite. I catch another glance between the two girls. Getting their story straight.

"Yes," says Bahar. "We should probably hurry because she will wonder where we are."

So, is this the truth? Or are they still covering for her?

I think it would be best if you ask Seema. Gulshan's voice.

She's right. And if I could get her alone and willing to answer my questions, I would. "Well, then, I'll see you both tomorrow!" I wave goodbye to the girls and begin my trek home.

I'm passing the turn-off to the school when I hear Darya call. One look at her face, her lips pressed tight together, and I know she's already heard about the spontaneous mixer in downtown Wad Qol. "Good news travels fast." I shake my head. "I'm sorry, Dar. I had no idea the boys' school—"

Darya tucks her hand around my arm. "It is my fault. I know the upper-level boys have begun staying late for extra religion classes. The rumor is their teacher has been somewhat delinquent and they need this additional instruction for their graduation exams." She raises her index finger. "But that tidbit need go no further. At any rate, it completely slipped my mind that you and the girls would be there when the boys escaped." She sighs and shakes her head. "Their director made sure it will not slip my mind again."

He *made sure?* What the hell did he say to her? "Dar, it wasn't that bad. A few chaotic minutes. Some flirting. You know, girls making eyes at boys and giggling. Boys winking back. I kept a sharp eye to make sure there was no touching, no hand-holding. And I did break it up." But not until after the boys' angry religion teacher arrived on the scene.

Dar waves her hand through the air. "Things are different here. What would seem like nothing in the States can become a very serious issue here."

Damn. "This won't cause a problem for the school, will it?"

"That's not for you to worry about." She squeezes my arm.

"Dar." I stop walking, bringing her to a halt. "The last thing you need is for me to be causing problems. You've worked too hard to get the school up and running. We can't have people complaining. Maybe trying to close down the school."

"Agreed. But I don't think that will happen." She starts us walking again. "I do think, however, that your next field trip should be somewhere the boys don't go. Perhaps . . . the river? You know, it's a part of Afghan culture that girls go to fetch water from the river."

"The river?" Remembering the *landay* that was left in the mulberry bush, I nearly choke on the word. And I can't help wondering if that's where Seema is right now—with her boyfriend. Unless she really is in a study session with Bahar and Wiin.

Darya goes on to explain. "Most houses in this area have no cistern or well and no indoor plumbing. So, it's the girls' job to fetch water. They go to a spot along the river just east of the village. They socialize with each other while they're at it. Boys are forbidden. It's strictly taboo." She smiles. "Which means, of course, that boys go there to meet up with girls. But, if you take the girls right after class ends in the afternoon, there will be no boys. The girls will be fine. And the director of the boys' school will be fine, too."

Or so we hope.

24

"IT WASN'T THAT BAD," I say to Cerelli when he calls around midnight Afghanistan time.

"PDA. Horny boys. Girls wanting romance. Afghanistan. That adds up to bad in my book." Cerelli's voice sounds tight.

"I kept an eye on them and broke it up after a few minutes." More like fifteen or twenty, but he doesn't need to know that.

"Let me guess: not soon enough. People in Wad Qol are upset."

"Well, the religion teacher certainly was. So was the director of the boys' school. He's already complained to Darya."

"Annie." I can almost see him jamming his fingers through his hair. "I thought I told you to lay low."

"I did. For a few days. But I had to get the girls out of the classroom. *I* had to get out of the classroom." Or go crazy.

"And you had to take them to the village center, two blocks from the boys' school? Knowing that at the end of term, the boys always have more religious instruction. Because boys being boys, they haven't paid attention during regular lessons."

"Or because the teacher was lax? Yeah, well. I didn't know that."

"Darya didn't tell you?"

"She said it slipped her mind."

Cerelli's silence catches me by surprise. And gets me thinking. Nothing slips Darya's mind. She never forgets anything. So, why this little detail that could've ended up causing a lot of trouble for her school?

"I take it you'll be keeping the girls at school from now on?"

"Sorry. Can't. They need to take photographs. That's the whole point."

"Damn." One little word that's packing a whole lot of frustration on Cerelli's end. "Then take them someplace safe. Look, what about the river? There's a spot where girls go to get water. No boys allowed."

What the hell? I hold the phone in front of me and stare at it. If I didn't know better, I'd think Cerelli was colluding with Dar. Except, does he seriously believe that horny teenage boys obey the no-boys-allowed rule?

"Annie? You there?"

"I'm here. Funny. Darya made the same suggestion."

Cerelli waits a second too long to respond. "Speaking of rivers, we found something."

Whiplash. How could I forget that Cerelli's a master of diversion? It takes me a couple heartbeats to follow his lead. River. Found. Dalan Sang. The bomber. Now I'm with him. "What did you find?" I'm holding my breath.

"Turns out you weren't hallucinating when you saw that periwinkle *burqa* on the run. Sawyer found some threads, actually a small piece of cloth, caught on a tree root growing out of the riverbank. Two klicks east of the bombing."

I sigh in relief that one of my hallucinations wasn't really a hallucination. But doubts quickly creep back. "You're sure it's from a *burqa?* The bomber's *burqa?*"

"Nothing's certain. But it's what we've got. That bank is steep. The bomber's probably the only person who'd even attempt to scale it. Plus, it was recent. Out there any longer, the cloth would have faded, rotted its way off the tree root."

"So, that's good news."

He laughs, but I don't hear any joy. "Good news would've been if we found his carcass. This is bad news. It means he's still out there. With a periwinkle *burqa.*"

Which means he's able to hide in plain sight. But *my* stalker hasn't been around the last few days. Everything's been quiet. Maybe he's lost interest and moved on.

"Just because you haven't seen your bad guy doesn't mean he's not out there."

"Reading my mind again, are you?"

"Whatever it takes to keep you alive."

"I'm alive. Look, when I'm not here at the house, I'm at school, surrounded by students and teachers."

"Except when you're not. When you're in the village center. A highly visible target."

"Come on. There were twenty-three girls with me this afternoon. This guy's not going after me with so many witnesses around."

"Don't bet your life on it."

Damn. Cerelli's right. "So, what am I supposed to do? I can't stay locked up in the house."

"Look, sweetheart, if you're not going to lay lower, at least don't go out by yourself. Get Seema to walk home with you after school."

"I'd love to. It'd be great to talk to her. But she's always off with her study partners preparing for graduation exams." Except I'm not so sure she really is.

"She can study after you leave. Get her or Darya to walk with you. Or get Tariq to drive you. I want someone with you." The tone in his voice startles me. He's serious.

"You really think he's out there?"

"Oh, yeah."

"Looking for me?"

"That, I don't know. We're not picking up any chatter. But I don't want you taking chances."

"Got it. I'll do my best," I whisper so quietly that for a moment I wonder if he heard me.

"Good," he says, his voice turning warm and wrapping around me. "I've come to like red hair."

25

CERELLI UNSETTLES ME. HIS worrying. His feelings for me. Mine for him. I don't know what's going on between us. Or even if I want there to be something. Yet another conundrum I need to sort out. But for now, I know he's right. I need to take precautions.

So, in the morning, I get up early and walk to school with Darya, hours before I need to be there. I make up the excuse that I should be available in case any of the girls want to ask questions while they're selecting their images from the village shoot to present in class. From the look she gives me, I'm sure she doesn't believe me. But she doesn't pry.

In class, I project each girl's village photograph onto the large bedsheet I've taped to the blackboard. Bahar's first. The rest of the girls ooh and aah as soon as it appears. I'm happy to see she's submitted an image different from any of the ones I coached her on. And it's good: the butcher is standing at the service window of his shop with lamb legs hanging on either side of him. He's looking off to the side where his toddler son is playing with a live lamb.

"Bahar, please tell us what you like about this picture."

Bahar stands next to the desk she shares with Wiin and takes a deep breath, clearly not quite sure how to begin. "I like the two sets of legs on either side of the man?"

I nod. "Very nice symmetry. And a good frame for the butcher."

She smiles, a little more confident. "And I like that he is not looking at the camera, but at his son instead."

"Yes, you captured a candid moment." I watch her repeat the word 'candid.' "And you force the observer to follow the direction the butcher is looking. What else?"

"The lamb. Yesterday morning, when I walked past the shop on my way to school, there were two, but the butcher slaughtered one to sell. It makes me wonder how long the other lamb has to live."

I swallow hard. "Yes. One lamb dead, one lamb alive—great sense of contrast and anticipation. Anything else?"

She scuffs her shoe on the floor. "This is probably wrong, but I think there is a metaphor, like with poetry."

"Tell us," I say encouragingly.

"Maybe there is also a question of how long the little boy will live?" I smile and nod, and she warms to her idea. "You see, there are a lot of bombings in Afghanistan, and many people are dying. Perhaps the little boy will also die young?"

"That's great, Bahar!"

"You think I am right?"

"I think you're absolutely brilliant!"

Bahar smiles. Her classmates whisper their congratulations.

We move through another twenty-one images featuring the burly general store owner next to his vividly colored buckets, piles of bread, and bowls of rice and lentils in front of the grocery store until we come to Seema's picture. She looks more than a little nervous. I almost hesitate to click on her image. When I do, all the girls burst out laughing. Seema, somewhat perversely, has taken a photograph of Bahar and Wiin and Chehrah eyeing four boys, who are looking back with keen interest and lascivious grins. Chehrah is pulling back Wiin's *hijab* to expose more of her hair. Wiin is sticking out her tongue at Bahar. Bahar is laughing and making devil's horns behind Chehrah. It's a terrific candid shot, but I can only imagine what the director of the boys' school would say if he saw it. Or the religion instructor. To be honest, I'm not sure Darya would like it much better.

"*Che bahaaaal!*" Wiin calls out. At least, I think it's Wiin, but everyone is laughing and talking so loudly, it's hard to tell.

"Girls! Quiet! We can't disturb the other classes." I seriously don't want any teachers coming in to complain about the noise and seeing this larger-than-life picture of girls and boys behaving badly. "Seema. Tell us why we're all laughing at this image. Why does it work?"

Seema stands next to her chair with an odd mix of emotions on her face. "Well, I was standing on the edge of the crowd, like you suggested, and I saw each girl doing something silly to the next one." She's clearly proud of her photo—and she should be—but there's something else going on in this image, a subtext I don't quite understand. And Seema looks—unhappy.

I nod. "Great movement from one girl to the next and very unexpected."

"And the boys, they look like they want to—"

"Yes, they definitely do look like that," I say quickly. The girls look at each other and giggle. "It's a great shot, Seema. You clearly struck a chord with your audience."

The tinny buzzer next to the door sounds. Time to change classes. I've just turned off my computer and pulled down the sheet when the door opens and Gulshan enters. "My, you girls seem to have the best time in this class! Ms. Green, you will have to share your teaching secrets."

The girls start laughing again. All except Seema, who seems distracted, and distanced, from the rest of the girls. Then I get it. She wasn't so much laughing with them as she was holding up their silliness to ridicule. Judging them. What the hell?

Gulshan claps her hands to hurry my girls along. They quickly grab their things and scurry out the door to their next class. Still giggling. Quickly throwing my gear together, I follow after them and manage to catch up with Seema in the hall. I put my hand on her shoulder. "It really is a good image, Seema. You caught them at exactly the right moment. That shows great patience. And good timing. Two things every photographer needs to learn."

"Thank you, Auntie."

"A favor?"

"Of course."

"Would you walk home with me after school?"

"Today?"

"Well, yes. I want to talk with you. I know you're very busy preparing for exams, but I've been here a week, and it seems like I only get to see you in class and at dinner. No time for just the two of us to chat."

She gnaws on her lower lip. Clearly, the last thing she wants to do after school is walk me home. I wait, curious to hear the excuse she comes up with.

"Okay. I'll meet you at the front door after the last class."

"Great! See you there!"

AND TO MY SURPRISE, she's there. Smiling.

It promises to be a great walk home—exactly what I need to get Seema to open up. The sky is brilliantly blue, and the breeze is refreshing—not strong enough to stir up any dust. No goats are munching on my sweater. There's not the faintest prickle on the back of my neck warning of someone following us. Seema and I link arms.

"So, have you thought any more about coming to visit this summer before going on to Harvard?"

She shrugs. "Not really. I have to pass my graduation exams first."

"With all the studying you and Bahar and Wiin have been doing, that shouldn't be a problem." I wonder what she'll say. Even though Bahar and Wiin have been covering for her, I'm guessing Seema hasn't cracked a book.

She gives me a quick sideways glance. "I don't think it's enough. I might not pass. If that happens, then I won't graduate."

I'm finally clueing in. Could it be that Seema doesn't *want* to pass her exams? "Oh, sweetie, I can't believe you'd fail. Bahar told me you're the smartest girl in the class."

"The exams are very hard, Auntie." She looks sad and confused and overwhelmed. "Maybe I'll become a photographer instead."

"Okay. There are some colleges in the States with great photography programs."

"Really? I'd still have to go to college?" Now, she looks completely deflated. Then she presses her lips tightly together and turns to look at me. "You keep talking about college. Tell me the truth: did my parents put you up to this?"

"No. Why?"

"Because that's all they talk about. College. College. College."

"Maybe because you're about to take graduation exams and go to college."

"No, Auntie. That's not why. I tried talking to my mother about maybe taking a break, you know, a gap year, or not going to college at all, but she won't even listen to me."

"So, you're saying you don't want to go to college?"

"I want them to let me make my own decisions. But they've planned out my entire life. They don't give me any choices. It's not like the way things are with you and Mel. You listen to her. You pay attention to her. My mother said you even let her dye her hair."

"She did that on her own. I didn't get a vote."

"But you see, that's my point. You let her do things on her own. My mother doesn't."

I think about the *landays* passing through my mulberry bush, how Seema has been sneaking off to meet up with a boyfriend, all the while telling Darya and me she's with her study partners. Dar may not be *letting* her, but Seema's certainly finding ways to do what she wants. "Clearly, you need to talk to her, tell her what you want to do."

She shakes her head. "Auntie, my mother is too busy helping everyone else. She doesn't have the time to consider what I want. She *tells* me what I'm supposed to want. What *she* wants me to do."

"Oh, Seema. That's just not true."

She shoots me the saddest look that clearly says, *Is too.*

There's still the matter of the boyfriend. We're dancing around a major issue, one Seema's already denied once and clearly doesn't want to talk about. The only thing I've confirmed on this walk is that she's worried about her exams. Is she really? My gut says she's not—that her 'worry' is just an excuse to justify more 'study time' with her partners. But, of course, she's never with Bahar and Wiin. At least, I don't think she is. She's with this mystery boyfriend. And, for some reason, the girls are backing up her story. All of which is still just speculation on my part. I honestly have no idea what's true and what's not. But I'm determined to force the issue and find out what's going on in Seema's life. And while I'm at it, I want to find out who this boyfriend is.

But Seema's done talking, and as soon as we get home, she retreats to her room, shutting the door firmly behind her. So much for getting her to confide in me. I wash up and head to the kitchen. Time to stop being the houseguest from hell and start earning my keep. Darya said she was planning one of my favorites tonight— qormah with chalau rice. I get the fire going in the stove, open the window to vent the smoke and cooking odors, then cover the lentils with water and set them on the burner to boil. I'm caramelizing the chopped onions when I hear the front door close.

A few moments later, Dar joins me in the kitchen. "You are truly an angel! I can smell the onions a kilometer away."

"Oh, please."

"You keep stirring. I'll get the sour plums, chickpeas, and eggplant from the storeroom. And we have a bit of Tariq's lamb left. We could mince it and make koftah. A little unorthodox, but I know how much you love meatballs."

I smile. "A woman after my heart!"

The kitchen is small, and the stove quickly heats up the room, but neither of us is complaining. We've got a rhythm going. She minces and chops and decides on just the right amount of spice. I roll meatballs and stir and check her seasoning. When I reach for a sprig of cilantro growing in a pot on the windowsill, she raises an eyebrow. "So, you think you're a good enough Afghan cook to correct me?" I step back and invite her to check. She blows the spoonful of simmering stew to cool it, then tastes. "As much as I hate to admit it, you're right. Add that cilantro. And a little more turmeric."

"A wonderful sight for my eyes!" A deep voice booms. Tariq smiles as he stands in the doorway. "I can smell the aroma of this *qormah* all the way to the clinic."

Darya taps my hand with her wooden spoon. "You see!"

"I think if this cooks any longer, we will have all of Wad Qol here to join us." Tariq grabs the spoon from Darya's hand and dips it into the pot to taste. "Annie, you may have to stay here longer than planned. We have not eaten like this in a long time."

I laugh, but Dar swats at him. "I would be pleased to have *you* cook for us."

He looks surprised. "Afghan men don't cook."

"And yet," I grin, "I remember some fantastic meals you prepared to seduce my roommate when we were in school."

"I never did that!" Tariq huffs.

"You did, too!" I protest. "I ate some of those meals."

"No, what I mean to say is that I never seduced Darya. She seduced me. From the very beginning."

"You are *deewäna*," laughs Dar, playfully cuffing his cheek. "How on earth did I seduce you?"

"Did you not breathe the same air as I did?" he asks in all seriousness.

Whoa. There's an extra person in this room, and it's me. I sidle toward the door, but Tariq blocks my way. "No, my friend, *you* are almost equally responsible. You are the one who brought us together."

"Yeah, well—"

"And now you are here. I understand from one of my colleagues at the clinic—Ikrom—that your students are very happy."

"Ikrom is Bahar's father," Darya explains.

"Oh, Bahar is a real gem. What a terrific student! And a lovely girl."

"You should have seen, or should I say *heard*, Annie's class today. There was so much laughter. The girls in the other classes are quite envious." Darya smiles.

"Then it is decided," says Tariq, turning to Darya and waving the spoon like a baton. "Annie's photography class must become a permanent part of the school's curriculum." He pivots toward me. "Each year, you will return. Girls from every corner of Afghanistan will wish to attend the Wad Qol Secondary School for Girls. Your workshop will be famous." He bangs the wooden spoon sharply against the table.

I freeze at the noise—a bullet rocketing into the tree next to me. Malalai lying in the sand, dying. Everyone will know about Malalai. Everyone will know that my photograph killed her. That . . . I'm responsible for her death.

My heart starts to pound, and the kitchen spins around me. Holding on tight to the edge of the kitchen table, I sit down hard. In front of me, in the bowl with the last of the minced lamb, Malalai's battered head lolls sideways at an impossible angle.

I look at my hands, covered with her blood, her brains. I cling tighter to the table edge. "Oh God. Not Malalai. She's just a little girl. You fucking bastard. To kill a girl over a photograph. Because she was writing in the sand. Because she wanted—"

"Annie!" Darya slaps my face.

I look up and see Cerelli in the chair opposite me, reaching for me. No, not Cerelli—Tariq. His hands are holding my sleeved wrists. I read the concern in his eyes. "Annie." His voice is quiet, calm. "You are all right. You are safe. We are in Wad Qol."

I feel Dar's hands on my shoulders, keeping me here, safe.

I watch Tariq's eyes glance upward, sharing an unspoken message with Darya.

That's when I realize that they're not surprised. They've been expecting something like this to happen. They know about my hallucinations. Only I didn't tell them. There's only one person who could have warned them.

26

"YOU TOLD THEM?" I'M SO angry at Cerelli, I can barely get the words out. "My PTSD—or whatever the hell is going on—is *mine*. Meaning it's confidential."

He waits for a moment, probably wondering if I'm done yelling at him. "You told *me*." His voice is quiet and measured and rational, clearly designed to calm me down. But I'm too pissed to let go of my fury that easily.

"I chose to tell you because I trusted you. Obviously, an error on my part. I didn't tell Darya or Tariq because—well, because I didn't."

"When we were in Kabul, you were worried about what to do if it happened again—"

"Yeah, you told me to put my head down and wait for the wave to pass. Which is what I've been doing."

"Was it working?" He's still speaking softly, forcing me to lower my voice so I can hear him.

"Sometimes."

"But not today?"

What the hell does he know about what I'm dealing with? Stupid question. I remember him holding my hands on the *Bataan* and keeping me tethered to reality at *Khosha*. He probably knows a lot. And he sure knows how to calm me down. Exactly like I used to do with Mel when she was little and throwing tantrums. "Do you have kids?"

He laughs softly. "No kids. A lot of SEALs, who sometimes need talking in off the ledge."

"You think I'm out on the ledge?"

"Something triggered a bad memory tonight."

I comb my fingers through my sweat-soaked hair, pushing it off my face. "Look, this really is strictly between you and me. You tell Dar or anyone, I'll have to kill you."

"Got it. Trust me."

"Trust you? Seriously?"

"So, kill me. I'll take my chances. But what you tell me now goes nowhere."

Something in his voice assures me this really will stay between the two of us. Just us. So, I recount the scene in the kitchen. Tell him about my guilt over Malalai's death and how I've kept it locked in my heart for the last eight-plus years. I even tell him about Bahar's photograph of the butcher with the bloody lamb legs and his young son playing with the second lamb that was still very much alive. And the minced lamb I was rolling into meatballs. The crack of the wooden spoon against the kitchen table. "I guess it's pretty obvious what the trigger is," I whisper.

"What happened to you in Khakwali shouldn't happen to anyone. And it certainly shouldn't have happened to Malalai or Murphy or Lopez. I can tell you it wasn't your fault—and sweetheart, it wasn't your fault—but I'm not sure anything I say is going to help. You got caught up in a clusterfuck that had practically nothing to do with you."

"*Practically.*"

He ignores me. "You're still carrying around a helluva lot of garbage. A lot of hurt."

He's right. I know he's right. I've managed to keep all this buried deep, deep, deep for over eight years, and now I've got some serious shit I've got to deal with. But it'll have to wait until I get back to the States. "Yeah."

"Yeah?" He clearly wants to hear more. Is this what he does when he's talking his guys down off the ledge?

"You're right. I'll see someone when I get home."

"And that will be?"

"Another week or two."

"Could you make it closer to a week?"

"Cerelli, don't try to tell me what to do."

"I'm not. I want to see you."

I play with that thought, let it take a couple turns around my brain. "Yes. I'd like to see you, too." Which, I realize, is the truth. Maybe. I imagine him quirking up the side of his mouth into that beguiling grin he has. Which tugs at my heart. I ride the companionable wave of silence between us.

Then, Cerelli's warm voice reaches across the seven thousand miles to me and wraps around me, holds me safe. "Something I think you should know."

"What?"

"The name Malalai means grief-stricken, but the most famous girls with that name are—were—warriors."

Did I know that? Somewhere in the deep recesses of my mind, I think I did.

"Back in 1880, the Second Anglo-Afghan War, at the Battle of Maiwand, when the Afghans were losing, an eighteen-year-old girl from a small village near Kandahar rallied the Afghan fighters to victory. Her name was Malalai, and Afghans have revered her ever since."

"How did she do it? Rally the troops, I mean."

"So, the story goes, when the flag bearer was shot, she rushed forward to take up the flag—some say she used her *hijab*—and sang a *landay*. Perhaps I should also tell you that the word *landay* is Pashto for 'snake'—a short, particularly poisonous one."

"I get the short part, but poisonous?"

"The women who sing these poems sometimes kill with their sarcasm."

"But not always. Some *landays* are beautiful, romantic." Especially the one you wrote to me.

"Good observation." Maybe he's thinking of that *landay*, too.

"You going to tell me the words Malalai sang?"

"I thought you'd never ask. I'm not going to sing it, and I don't have a drum for the traditional beat, but here goes:

My beloved! If you do not perish on the fields of Maiwand,
By my faith in Allah, you will shame me.

"There's a longer version," he says, "but I've always liked this shorter one the best."

"You never cease to amaze me."

I can imagine him smiling. Again.

"I like history. And poetry."

"You going to tell me what happened to Malalai of Maiwand?" I ask.

"The British shot her. She became a martyr. Islam is a religion of peace, but it has its share of martyrs. And Malalai of Maiwand is most definitely one of them."

Of course, I should have been expecting him to say that. But I wanted to imagine Malalai of Maiwand living to be an old woman, having daughters and granddaughters, teaching them to compose their own *landays*. Letting them learn to read and write.

"And for doing what she could to save your life, sweetheart, your Malalai is, too."

"Yeah." I know he's saying this to help me feel better, but my heart feels like a solid rock in the middle of my chest.

"One other thing, Annie."

"What?"

"Many Afghans call her Malalai Anna or Malalai *Anaa*. The grandmother of a nation."

I swallow hard. So, my name means the *grandmother of a nation*. Which means, I guess, that I should be brave and loving and forgiving. But all that will have to wait because I'm not completely over being mad at Cerelli.

27

I'M STILL PISSED WHEN I wake up. At Cerelli for telling Tariq and Darya about my 'episodes.' And at Darya and Tariq for—well, I'm mad at them for knowing this about me. Maybe it doesn't make sense, but if I'd wanted them to know, I would've told them. The last thing I need is them looking at me as if I'm crazy. I don't want them protecting me, feeling sorry for me. I just want things back to the way they were before yesterday afternoon.

Steering clear of Darya at school, I head home as soon as my class is over, then set myself up with my laptop in the courtyard. I scroll down to the photos the girls took during our field trip in the village, specifically Bahar's and Seema's. Really good images that speak to me. I wonder if TNN might be interested. Or my old editor at the AP. Both girls would be thrilled to see their work online. I take another look at Seema's pic of her so-called friends flirting with boys and rethink my enthusiasm. The parents of Wad Qol probably wouldn't like having their children on display, especially online. Darya definitely wouldn't, and she's probably more liberal-minded than anyone else in the village.

"So, here you are."

Speak of the devil. I glance up and see Darya standing by the open gate, a pair of sandals dangling from her fingers. I can smell the pungent leather and tanning chemicals from where I sit.

"New sandals?" I don't really want to talk to her yet, but she's clearly not going to cut me any slack.

"Yours, in fact. Mr. Yusufi brought them by the school today. But you had already left." She crosses the courtyard to my chair and hands them to me.

The leather is supple, the workmanship exquisite, and I spend an inordinate amount of time examining every last tooled scallop on the straps, trying to figure out what to say to my best friend. I finally come up with, "I haven't paid him yet."

Dar waves a dismissive hand. "That is no matter. I took care of it."

"A peace offering?" I look up from the sandals to find Darya studying me.

She purses her lips. "Do I need one?"

Our eyes meet. "What I told Cerelli about, well . . . about my 'episodes,' I told him in confidence. I trusted him to keep it to himself. He shouldn't have told you."

"No," she says sternly, angrily, "*you* should have told me. I cannot believe you let eight and one half years go by without telling me what happened to you in Khakwali. What *really* happened. And I don't mean the ridiculously sanitized version you've been passing off all this time." She drags over a chair, the wrought iron legs clanking across the mulberry-stained bricks, stations it directly in front of me, and sits down hard.

Her message is clear. She's not letting me hide from her. Or from the truth behind my hallucinations and nightmares. *Oh hell, be honest,* I chastise myself—she wants me to confront what any

shrink would probably diagnose as PTSD. Not something I want
to do. Not here. Not now.

"Dar—"

She starts to hold up her hand, but stops. Instead, she takes
my sandals from me, drops them on the ground, then moves my
laptop to the nearby table. She scrapes her chair even closer, until
our knees nearly touch, and reaches for my hands. "No, you listen
to me. We are friends. You are my oldest and dearest friend. And I
am deeply hurt that you haven't trusted me enough to—"

"Stop!" I pull back my hands. Damn. I hate it when she plays
the victim card. Especially when she's not the victim.

"You used to tell me everything." She reaches for my hands
again and holds them fast. Encouraging.

"It was more like you used to beat it out of me."

"Annie! I never—"

"Get real, Dar. That's exactly what you did. All the time. Especially
in college. I'd get back to the dorm after yet another humiliating
critique session at the hands of the all-male *Crimson* photog staff.
They were always trashing my images in favor of their own. I
definitely didn't want to relive it, but you pounded it out of me."

"Yes, well, there was that. But there was a reason for it. I was
trying to toughen you up."

"What?"

"Your work has always been great, but you needed more
confidence. You needed to trust yourself."

I crook my eyebrow in disbelief. "Thank you. I guess."

She smiles gently, twining her fingers around mine. "Annie,
please. Trust me. Tell me what happened in Khakwali."

"You mean Cerelli hasn't already told you?" I instantly regret
the snarky tone that cuts through my question.

"No. Not everything. Just that there was an ambush, that people died. I've always known about Malalai, of course. You told me a little about her. But other people?"

I take a deep breath, and I tell her. Everything that I've kept locked away in a hidden corner of my heart. Buried deep so I could get on with life. Except over the last week, it's all been niggling its way back to my consciousness.

I tell her about Nic Parker Lowe and the guys and their asinine hazing stunt that could've gotten me killed. That did get me reassigned to FOB duty instead of going to the front.

About Murphy having the hots for me, taking me back to Khakwali for a second visit, hoping to impress me enough to get me into bed.

About the ambush itself. Holding Malalai's shattered skull in my hands. Lopez being shot nearly in half. Murphy bleeding out, joking that he wanted me to take a picture of him, asking if I would've gone to bed with him.

About Malalai's *anaa* rescuing me. Leading me to the goats' stable where I waited through the rainy night for the Taliban militants to come for me. And no, damn it, I didn't try to escape because the desert was booby-trapped with IEDs, and I couldn't bear to die that way. Or worse, not die, but go on living without my legs, my hands, the ability to work as a photographer. Maybe I should have risked it. Maybe if I had, I wouldn't be trapped reliving that night.

My voice grows ragged.

Her face pales.

We sit silently, both of us guarded about the horror I've just resurrected.

"Oh, Annie." She keeps her eyes locked firmly on mine. "You

listen to me. I know you. I know how you think. You are *not* responsible for Malalai's death."

I shake my head slowly. "That's where you're wrong. I *knew* something was off in Khakwali that day. I *knew* I shouldn't have taken that picture of her. But I did."

"It was your job."

"That doesn't make it right."

"You didn't pull the trigger."

"I pushed him to pull the trigger."

"No! You don't know that. You don't know *why* he pulled the trigger. Maybe it *was* because you were taking the picture. But maybe it was because she was *writing* in the sand. Or maybe he was aiming at you and shot Malalai instead. By accident. You just don't know."

She's right, of course. I don't know. Although the thought of Malalai as collateral damage is cold comfort.

"Tell me the rest," she says.

I tell her about Cerelli and his team finally rescuing me in the deep dark of the night.

She doesn't smile. Somehow she knows there's more horror to come. "And now the interrogation you've never told me about."

I nod. "He called it a debriefing. Ha!" I tell her about the grueling interrogation at the hands of the masterful and manipulative Commander Finn Cerelli and his sidekick, John 'Mr. CIA' Smith. Their insistence that I was colluding with the Taliban. Their threats to get me to confess.

"What kind of threats?" she asks quietly.

"To go after you. After I demanded an attorney and stupidly gave them your name, they were convinced you were involved."

"Bah! How ridiculous!"

"It didn't seem that way at the time. Not coming from Mr. CIA holding a gun in my face."

She narrows her eyes. "What else?"

"Guantanamo. Or Leavenworth, if I was lucky. They said I'd never see Emmy again."

"Oh, Annie."

I release my death grip on Dar's hands and look away. I don't want to see the grief, or maybe it's pity, in her eyes. I'm not even aware that she goes into the house until she's back with a tray of cups, a pot of *chai,* and some slices of *roat.*

"Drink," she says, handing me a cup. A few minutes later, "Annie, I cannot begin to fathom how you have lived with all this. Why on earth didn't you tell me? I could have helped. I could have—"

I meet her steady gaze. "But that's precisely the point. I *haven't* been living with any of it. Not until I came back to Afghanistan. Before that, I'd buried it. All of it. Pretty damn effectively, too." I comb my fingers through my hair. "Coming here, though, running into Nic, then Cerelli, and the bombing at Dalan Sang. It's all come back."

Darya cups her hand to my cheek. "Your episodes—what happens?" Her voice is soft, gentle. A mother's voice coaxing a child to tell all.

I think for a minute. "Malalai. Murphy. Lopez. They die. Again. And again. *Anaa* leads me away. To save me." I shrug. "Or maybe to set me up. I don't know." I pause. "In some ways, the worst part is waiting in the stable for the militants to come. I'm there, in the dark, and it's as if it's all happening again."

"Do you relive the interrogation, too?"

I sip my tea, nibble on the apple-walnut bread, and consider her question. "Just once," I say finally. "The second night I was in Kabul.

Since then, no. Damn, he was an absolute bastard during that interrogation, playing up to me so I'd trust him and spill my guts."

"But you didn't have anything to confess."

"Didn't matter." I laugh and then wince at the bitter sound.

"So, how did you finally convince him you weren't guilty of anything?"

I think about that for a full thirty seconds and finally shake my head. "I don't know. One minute they were threatening me with Gitmo. The next Cerelli was thanking me for picking out a few of my photos that matched up with one of his. It doesn't make much sense."

"So what you're saying is that Phinneas was doing his job."

"I guess."

"It's what prosecuting attorneys do. We're trained to beat up the defendant, to play with their minds until they slip up."

I stop mid-nod and stare at Darya until I'm nearly cross-eyed. "Except Cerelli's not a lawyer."

She smiles. "Well, not a practicing attorney at any rate."

Yet another secret. "You mind telling me?" The snarky annoyance is back in my voice.

"There's nothing to tell. Phinneas graduated from law school, then joined the Navy."

"Of course he did. That's exactly what lawyers do. Go for the big bucks the U.S. military pays."

Darya moves her chair next to me and reaches for my hand. "So, this is what you're holding against him? That he's a lawyer? That he interrogated you?"

I shake my head. Cerelli's a lawyer. So much for my powers of observation. But what the hell difference does it make that he earned a law degree once upon a time? "No, honestly, I'm not holding that against him. Although I probably should. But like I told you, since I've been back, he's been the perfect gentleman. Except for telling you about what's going on in my head."

I decide not to tell her about my nightly calls with the man. It's still all too new. I'm feeling too unsettled to know what to make of whatever is going on between us. *If* there even is something between us. *If* I want there to be. There are some things I'm not ready to share with Darya. Yet. We have the rest of our lives to talk about my love life.

28

A FEW DAYS LATER, THE GIRLS and I set out for the place along the river Dar told me about—just east of town where the bank isn't quite so steep, making it easy for girls to get water. And, more importantly, to hang out with each other. Much to my relief, we make it through the village center without seeing a single teenage boy. According to Darya, parents and the boys' school are on alert to keep all males far away until we finish our photo shoot. As we pass the last row of houses in Wad Qol, we wave to a woman sweeping her front stoop, but see no curtains flapping with anxious mothers or fathers peering out to see what we're up to. Finally, the village is behind us. The sound of the river calls.

Darya says that the girls who frequent the riverbank are those whose parents don't allow them to go to school. They fetch water in the morning. By afternoon, they're usually home, working in the fields or helping in the kitchen or watching younger siblings. She seemed relieved that we'd have the place to ourselves. I'd been hoping the girls would be there, willing to pose for photographs. Without them, I've got to quickly think up another assignment.

As it happens, we're wending our way along the narrowing path to the river's edge, skirting heavily laden mulberry bush branches that snag our clothes, when we hear the girls. Thank God, I don't have to come up with plan B. One girl is singing a *landay* with lyrics far different from any I've ever heard:

Father, you bastard! You sold my sister to an old goat.
May Allah strike down your sons.

Damn, Cerelli was right about the snake-like edge to some *landays*. But in this instance, I think it's the father who's the snake, not the poet or the poem.

"He did it!" We hear her shouting angrily in Dari. "Yesterday. He sold Sumayah to that toothless, farting old shepherd. Her life is ruined."

Walking in front of me, Bahar gasps. "I know that girl!" she says. "My mother tried so hard to convince her parents to let her come to school. I think the mother would have let her, but the father refused. He said that girls do not need an education. It ruins them for marriage. No man would want his daughters. And now, look. Sumayah is stuck with an old man for a husband. What will she do when he dies?"

Seema hooks her arm around mine. "Maybe she loves him."

"That's crazy, Seema!" Bahar sounds truly shocked. "She hates him. Everyone knows she wanted to marry Darvash. She begged her parents not to force her to marry that awful, smelly old man. Her father just wants the money."

"Maybe she changed her mind."

"Her sister obviously does not think so." Bahar glares at Seema and walks ahead to join Wiin and the rest of girls in the class.

We crest the edge of the bank, and there's the river. The current surges strong out in the middle but splashes more quietly over and around stones in the shallows closer to shore. That's when we see the girls from the village. More girls than I would have thought possible, clustered in small groups, sitting on granite boulders along the river. They all look to be in their teens, and they're clearly happy. I can see why: far from the watchful eyes of their parents and other villagers, they're relaxing on the rocks in the sun, chatting freely with their friends. I wonder how they got away from their chores?

They're wearing their very best. Traditional dresses with full skirts in bright yellow and red, soft peach and azure blue, green and gold. Intricately embroidered bodices with tiny, round mirrors sewn onto the sleeves that catch the sunlight. Pants of shiny satin. A few even have on fancy high heels. Which strikes me as an odd thing to wear to a riverbank. But then I realize these girls knew we were coming and they knew why. They're wearing their prized clothing because they want to be photographed. I wonder if they'll want prints to give to their sweethearts? Without their parents' knowledge, of course.

I gather my girls around me. "Here's the assignment. I want you each to make a portrait of one of the girls here. Tomorrow, be ready to tell the class what your image reveals about the girl's story."

Seema's hand shoots up. "I'm not sure what you mean by 'the girl's story.'" The rest of the girls look equally perplexed.

"It could be many different things. What emotion is the girl feeling? What are her dreams? What is happening in her life? You know, is she a great seamstress? Does she work hard? Be sure to include a detail or two in your image that reveals her story." The girls stare at me, still not at all sure what I want. "Okay. Did you all hear the *landay* as we walked up?"

They look sideways at each other, hiding smirks behind their hands.

"Well, that poem is a story about one of the girl's sisters. The girl is upset for her sister. And possibly fearful about the husband her father will find for her. Find out something that's going on in the life of the girl you photograph and make sure you capture that in your image of her."

Bahar brightens. "That is what you did in your portrait of Malalai! She knew how to read and write. You showed the letters in your picture."

"Exactly. The fact that she could read and write was part of her story."

More confident now, the girls move off to start their portrait-making. I find a flat rock, sit down, and watch. If the girls have questions, I'll answer, but I'm not making any suggestions. They need to be free to find their own way, not feel bound to copy me. Let's see what they can do without me directing them. Even though I want to tell Wiin not to shoot directly *into* the sun and Bahar not to settle for such stiff poses. And, oh God, I wish Seema wouldn't compose her shots so it looks like a tree's growing out of that girl's head. Although after three long days of her moping and dragging around, I'm happy she's into shooting anything. Tomorrow's critique session should be interesting.

An hour later, something in the air changes. The village girls are on their feet, kicking off their high heels and gathering in a circle on the grass. They sing and sway and clap in a slow one-two rhythm. I know this music, but it's been a long time since I've seen anyone dance the traditional *Attan*. Darya and Tariq's wedding. *Hama* Bibi led the dancers, and Dar and I joined in.

The village girls sashay in front of us. Their brown, calloused

hands flit and turn elegantly above their shoulders, then dip down
to cast imaginary flowers to the ground. A few even take off their
headscarves and wave them rhythmically through the air.

Clapping to the beat, my girls stop their picture-taking
and join the circle. Even Seema. As she one-two steps her way
past me, she grabs my hand, pulling me into the dance. I take
a second to whip off my boots and socks. My toes curl into the
sun-warmed grass. The singing thrums through my body, and
my feet find the steps. For a moment, I struggle with the hand
movements, but I watch Bahar on the far side of the circle, and
my hands remember.

I give myself over to the dance, and for the first time in days,
my thoughts go to Mel. How I wish she could see me now. No, I
wish she could be here, dancing with me, being part of this circle of
girls. She'd love it.

My thoughts stay with Mel until the skin on the back of my
neck starts to prickle. Oh, hell! It's him. After several fear-free days,
he's back. And all these girls are in his line of fire. Should I stop the
dance? Get them to safety? I keep dancing but look around me as
surreptitiously as I can. And see no one, but the girls. He could be
crouched behind the boulders. Or hidden in the trees. Where *is* he?
I have to know so I can get these girls away from him. Staying with
the beat, I make a spontaneous slow turn, craning my neck to see
as much as I can.

Seema touches my arm and whispers *sotto voce*, "Not yet,
Auntie. The spinning comes later!"

"Thanks!" I whisper. I turn again, even slower, but still don't
see him.

Then, oddly, the sensation of being watched vanishes. Did I
just imagine it? No. And I'm still wary. I also need to keep an eye on

the time. Dar wants the girls back to the village and home before the boys leave their extra-extra-long religion class.

The dance ends, and the girls dissolve into giggles. I'm still watchful.

Time to head back. Their groans tell me it's much too soon. They haven't finished yet. Just another few minutes, they beg. I give them five. Then round them up. Today I'm determined to get everyone home without a repeat of the street party. As we start back, the village girls treat us to another *landay*:

> *My father forced me to wed a toothless old goat.*
> *His cock is a withered cornstalk. I will use the bedpost.*

Very educational. But just a bit too much information. And, oh God, please let no other adult be close enough to hear this. *Landays* have been around for hundreds of years, conveying girls' feelings of love and despair, but I seriously doubt they sang poems that were quite so *provocative*.

Should I be shielding innocent ears? Looking around me, I see most of my girls smiling. A few are singing along. This *landay* isn't new to any of them. Neither is the sentiment.

Do their mothers realize? Probably.

But it's a sure bet their fathers don't.

I'M STANDING IN THE CENTER of the village, pleased to have the last of my girls headed safely home before any boys appear. Now, where is Seema? I clench my jaw in frustration. Another disappearing act. I think back to the riverbank. When did I last see her? During the dance. And after that? Shit. I clearly lost track of her. Well, she's definitely not meeting up with Bahar and Wiin to study. Not that she did any of the other days. Wherever she is, she's not with me, which means I get to make that long walk home by myself. Not something I'm looking forward to. Not something that will make Cerelli happy either. If I tell him.

I haven't gone very far when my nerves take over. The stalker could rocket out from behind a tree or boulder at any moment, take me out, and leave me dead in the road. But nothing happens. Absolutely nothing. *Just being paranoid*, I tell myself. *There's nothing to worry about.*

Just because you're paranoid, doesn't mean he's not out there. Cerelli's voice.

29

LATE THAT NIGHT, LONG AFTER everyone else has settled
to sleep, I'm still awake—thinking. Just a few more days left to
my workshop. And although today's field trip went better than
the first, I'm not feeling great about those two *landays* we heard.
Or even the dancing. Not that they were any of my doing, but
complaining parents aren't going to see it that way. They'll believe I
engineered the situations for their innocent daughters to have their
purity sullied. Even though this time it was other 'innocent' girls
leading the assault. No matter who was at fault, for the last field
trip, I'll have to do everything possible to protect my girls. And the
reputation of the school. This time, I'll have to steer my students
clear of boys *and* girls who don't attend the Wad Qol Secondary
School for Girls. Maybe Tariq will have an idea.

Then, after the final presentation of best images to the entire
school, the workshop will be done. So many years in the making.
Done. And despite Tariq's idea that the workshop will become a
regular part of the curriculum, who knows when I'll be back?

I'm planning out the possible parameters of the girls' final shoot when the gate to the courtyard creaks slowly open. My planning stops. My breath gathers in my chest. He's back. Whoever 'he' is. Please let it be the boyfriend. That cute boy from the village center who was flirting with Bahar, clearly in an attempt to make Seema jealous. Was that his plan to get Seema to give in, to have sex?

I listen intently for footsteps but don't hear any. Didn't the boyfriend's shoes squeak? The next thing I know, the leaves outside my window are rustling. They seem louder than the last time. Shit. I left the windows open, just a bit. It was warm tonight. Too warm to sleep in this small room without some air.

I lie motionless, not wanting to give away my presence by breathing. The leaves are still rustling. This is taking a lot longer than it should. I want to yell at the boyfriend to leave his fucking *landay* and get out of our courtyard. But maybe it's not the boyfriend.

The rusting hinges of my windows start to squeal. Whoever's out there is pushing them open more. So he can climb in?

I stare at the window, my eyes gradually getting accustomed to the darkness. To his shadow against the bush. Reaching for my flashlight, I'm ready to launch my attack.

"Seema?" a male voice whispers. "Seema?" A little louder.

The boyfriend. Well, I'm not dealing with him in the middle of the night. "*Gom shoo!*" Go away! I hiss, pitching my voice as low as I can. Maybe he'll think Seema's father is lying in wait.

The leaves stop rustling for just a moment. Then, he's battling branches to get away from the window. His feet pound across the courtyard. But I don't hear the gate creak closed. I wait for what feels like forever, then finally climb out of bed and slide my way along the wall to the windows. Shining my flashlight into the bush, I see a piece of white paper folded small and nestled among the leaves. I pluck it and read:

The riverbank is lonely,
Many girls here, but I want you only.

My skin crawls. Now I know who was at the riverbank this afternoon. Wait. He should have been in religion class. Or did he cut class to try to meet up with Seema? From the sound of this *landay*, he never got to talk to her. Well, the boyfriend is most definitely back, and he's gotten impatient. *But he's going to have to wait a bit longer,* I decide as I slide his love note into the pocket of the cargo pants I'll be wearing today.

I give up trying to sleep. The sky is turning gray with the dawn, so flashlight in hand, I wind my way along the hall to the bathroom. Best get done in here before everyone else wakes up. Minutes later, washed and dressed for the day, I'm rounding the corner back to my room when I see the fluttering hem of a white nightgown cross the hall from my room and disappear into Seema's. Of course, she's been going into my room when I'm not around. That much has been obvious. But actually seeing her do it upsets me. I pat my hip pocket. The crinkle of paper reassures me that the boyfriend's *landay* is exactly where I put it. So, Seema didn't get what she hoped to find.

First thing in my room, I check the mulberry bush. There among the leaves is a small bit of blue:

I waited at the river for you, my dearest sweet,
You never came. Take me now—a treat.

Clearly, these two got their wires crossed yesterday afternoon. But damn, I don't like the turn these last couple *landays* have taken. I don't care how cute this boy is. And I really don't like that she's ready to offer it all up. Which is absolutely the worst thing she could do in Afghanistan.

I crumple Seema's *landay* in my fist, then pace the length of my bedroom to the window and back to the door. Again. And again. Oh, Seema, do you have any idea what you're doing? Don't you realize that sex outside of marriage means you're running the risk of lashings, jail, even stoning if you're caught? Is this guy worth it?

Clearly, he's the reason she doesn't want to go to college.

But Seema, you're way too intelligent to be doing this. I stop mid-stride. Well, maybe book smart, but not so life smart. I pound my fist against my thigh. What can I do about this?

Tell Darya. Cerelli's voice.

I will. But first I want to talk to Seema.

Let Darya handle this. She knows what to do.

I shut down Cerelli's voice and press my fingers against the creases of Seema's blue stationery, but there's no way I can make it look pristine again. So, I just fold it into a small square and stuff it in my pocket with the boyfriend's.

Time to talk to Seema. I cross the hall and knock softly on her door, telling myself that if she doesn't answer immediately, I'll wait until after school.

She opens the door in three seconds flat, rubbing her eyes in a show of sleepiness which I'm not buying. "Auntie?"

"Could I come in?"

She looks surprised. "Now?"

"Now." I step into the room, which is barely bigger than mine but a lot tidier. Almost spartan—just a bed and desk, a dresser and a bookcase with its shelves crammed full of books.

Seema pulls the chair out from her desk, then sits on her bed. I start to straddle the chair, but a sudden vision of Cerelli and the guy from the CIA onboard the *Bataan* convinces me to turn the chair around.

"Is something wrong, Auntie?"

"We need to talk."

"We do?" She sounds wary.

I pull the crinkled blue paper out of my pocket. "I found this on my windowsill a few minutes ago." I figure she doesn't need to know I went snooping for it. "I'm pretty sure it's yours."

She gasps, her hand shooting forward to grab it. But I close my fingers and stuff it back into my pocket. I'm not showing her the *landay* from her boyfriend unless I have to.

"That's mine! You have no right."

"Seema, I want to know what's going on. What's really going on. I just saw you coming out of my room. Your boyfriend was staring in my window earlier this morning. I think I do have the right. And I think your parents will agree."

Her eyes widening in panic, she hunches forward. "Please, don't tell them! Please don't! You haven't, have you?"

"Not yet. I wanted to talk to you first."

She relaxes a bit. "I don't have a boyfriend."

I pat my hip pocket. "This *landay* says you do."

Seema's eyes dart around the room. She's clearly hoping to buy some time. Finally, she looks back at me and waves her hand through the air—just like her mother. "Auntie," she smiles, "it's just a *landay*—a poem. All the girls write them. Boys, too. In fact, you heard the girls sing a couple at the riverbank yesterday. It's no big deal. We call them into talk programs on the radio. Some kids even post them online."

"I did hear the girls singing the *landays*, and I think they *were* a pretty big deal. So is the one you wrote."

She bows her head, obviously hoping I'll disappear.

"Talk to me, Seema. What's his name?"

She shakes her head.

"Seema? I'm not leaving."

Head still bowed, she whispers, "You promise you won't tell? My parents, they'd never understand."

I hear the desperation in her voice. Damn it all. Just the position I don't want to be in. Gaining Seema's trust, then betraying her to Darya. Which is exactly what's going to happen unless I can convince her to talk to her mother herself. I ease off the chair and sit next to her on the bed. Putting my arm around her shoulders, I pull her close. "Just tell me."

She pillows her head against my shoulder, then whispers tearfully, "Awalmir."

"And he's the reason you're not so sure about college anymore?"

Her shoulders start to tremble. "Oh, Auntie, please, please understand. I love him, and he loves me. But if I go to the States for college, I'll lose him."

"No, Seema, I don't believe that."

She wipes her hands across her cheeks. "What do you mean?"

"Just that the right boy, the boy who really loves you, wouldn't walk away because you go to college in the States. And, if you think the States are too far, you could stay here and go to college in Kabul."

She isn't having it. "No, you don't understand. Boys here don't want a wife who has more education than they do."

Wife? Has this no-big-deal exchange of *landays* gone that far?

Of course, it has. This is Afghanistan. Young people here, especially in the countryside, don't do romance without marriage on the near horizon.

But that cute boy—Awalmir—looked so young. Way too young to marry.

Well, Darya and Tariq brought Seema here so she'd learn about her heritage, her culture, and now she has. Although what's happening isn't what her parents had in mind. *Tread lightly*, I caution myself.

"I just want what's best for you. So do your parents. They love you. I love you. And, I have to believe if your Awalmir truly loves you, he'll want the best for you, too." I feel her shoulder muscles tense. "Besides, in Islam, it's important for girls to be educated." She doesn't say anything, so I go on. "You know, a Muslim woman, Fatima al-Fihri, founded the very first university in the world."

"Are you sure?" Seema sounds surprised. And here I thought my book-smart girl would have known this factoid.

"Oh, I know it's true. It was in 859—the University of Al-Qarawiyyin." Darya drilled those facts into me back in college. I hope I got them right. "And it's still open to this day."

"Wow—I didn't know."

"So?" I massage her shoulder and notice the day outside the window lightening. I sneak a peek at my watch and nearly groan. It's almost time to leave for school, but I don't want to stop this conversation. I've just gotten Seema to open up. But to what end? I've got to convince her that Awalmir isn't the boy she thinks he is. That he'll crush the life out of her. And if I can't? Damn, then I'll have to tell Darya and Tariq. Either way, Seema's going to lose the boy she thinks she loves.

She shakes her head. "I just don't think that will change anything. Awalmir says—"

I really don't care what Awalmir has to say. He's already doing quite a number on Seema. Another glance at my watch makes me realize I need to hurry this heart-to-heart along. "Why don't you let me meet your Awalmir?"

She's quiet for a moment. "I'll talk to him," she whispers.

"Yes, please talk to him," I say, standing and moving toward the door. "And I'd like the two of us to talk more about this later. After school today."

"If you say so." The defeat in her voice guts me.

I look back at my sweet Princess Seema, slumped over on her bed, and let myself out of her room. I can see Darya waiting for me near the front door. Darting into my room, I grab my pack, then, stomach churning, hoof it down the hall.

Annie? Tell Darya now—while you're walking to school. Seema will thank you—eventually.

So, now you're an expert on teenage girls, Cerelli?

Let Darya handle this.

No. I promised Seema we'd talk after school, and that's what I'm going to do. What are the chances she'll actually show up? If she's anything like Mel, I'd say highly unlikely. But if she doesn't, I know exactly what I have to do.

30

AFTER SCHOOL, I WAIT for Seema outside the classroom door. Much to my surprise, she shows up right on time. She's chewing her lower lip, clearly steeling herself to speak to me. "Auntie? You said you need to see me?"

I smile encouragingly. "Why don't we go in and sit down?"

She looks behind her, then checks out the classroom across the hall where the science teacher is still working. "Um, do you think maybe we could go outside?"

Of course. She doesn't want to be overheard—by other girls, teachers, or least of all, by her mother. "You bet. How about the walnut grove next to the school?"

"Okay."

As we walk toward the side exit, I glance back and see Darya peeking out her office. Smiling. Because she thinks Seema and I are about to have a long chat. We are, but not about anything that's on Dar's radar.

I follow Seema through the greening walnut trees, their pods still very small, nowhere close to being ready for harvest, to the farthest corner of the grove, well away from anyone who could hear us. We sit on the ground in the cooling shade, neither of us saying a word. Determined to wait for Seema to start, I lean back against a tree and watch as she tugs at her headscarf to make sure every last strand of hair is covered.

Finally, she clears her throat. "Um, Auntie, I want you to know that I really am thinking about what you said this morning."

"And?" If I've learned one thing from dealing with my daughter, it's that I've got to listen. Not always the easiest thing for me.

"You think I'm too young to get married and that I should go to college." She sits up straight, shoulders braced.

I nod warily. Something tells me she's got an argument ready to launch.

"But, see, I've known Awalmir for a *long* time."

"How long?"

Another tug at her headscarf. "*Three* months."

Okay, so maybe that's a lifetime in a culture where many marriages are arranged in a few weeks. But it's not very long to my way of thinking.

"And Mom was just a little older than me when she met Dad."

So, that's the tack she's taking. *Stay quiet! Let her talk!* But instead, I open my mouth. "Seema, you know very well that your parents didn't get married right away. They waited years—until after your mom graduated from college and your dad finished med school."

Her lips pressed tightly together, Seema intently studies the walnut trees. Then, taking a deep breath, she turns back to me. "Awalmir says that to be good Muslims, we *must* marry."

That stops me. I read the *Qur'an* years ago for an Intro to Islamic Studies course in college, but I don't remember anything about Muslims being required to marry. In fact, I'm sure they're not. I palm the air between us. "Wait a minute, there's no rule that says you *have* to get married." So much for keeping my mouth shut and letting her talk.

She nods defiantly. As in, Awalmir says so, and he would know. But I'm not backing down either. "And there's certainly nothing in the *Qur'an* that says you have to get married at such a young age—before you finish your education."

"Oh, Auntie." She looks at me like I don't understand anything. "I talked to Awalmir about exactly that. And he says that only *boys* are intended to get an education. Girls aren't. All of *that,*" she waves a dismissive hand at the school, "interferes with our true roles as wives and mothers."

I'm far from being an expert, but that doesn't sound right at all. Then, from across the years, I hear my professor say, "Rest assured! The same command for education and learning applies to women just as it does to men. As do all of Allah's commands because women and men are considered equal in Islam, but each different with their own strengths." How many times have I heard Darya say exactly that?

Seema smiles smugly. "It's in the *Qur'an.*"

"You've read it?"

"Well . . ." She looks away. "Not exactly, but he told me it is."

I shake my head. "Seema, he's not right about that. In fact, education is an *obligation* for boys *and* girls. Men and women, too." Despite my strong words, my shoulders sag. Awalmir again. And the drivel he's spouting has nothing to do with the religion I studied. What he's saying sounds completely twisted. Still, Seema believes him, so I've got to steer us away from anything religious. I put my hand on her shoulder. "Seema, I know you love him." Or, at least, you think you do. "But why are you so certain that he's *the* boy for you? There could be someone else out there, someone you haven't even met."

She shakes her head and eases her shoulder out from under my hand. "I just *know*. He does, too. In fact, he knew right away. The minute he met me. Just like when Dad met Mom."

I retreat to the argument I tried to make this morning in her bedroom. "If you and Awalmir are so certain you love each other, why can't he wait? Four years really isn't a long time. It may seem that way when you're seventeen, but—"

"I knew you wouldn't understand." Seema turns away in tearful frustration. "You're just like my mother."

"Sweetie, your mother loves you. So does your father. They just want what's best for you. So do I."

Her jaw clenched, she stares up into the green canopy of the walnut trees. Then, taking a deep breath, she turns back to me. "They don't. They don't love me. They only love their version of me. They don't accept me for who I really am, for what I believe."

"What do you believe?" I ask gently. Then, too late, I worry we're headed back into the minefield of Awalmir's skewed vision.

She looks surprised. "Do you really want to know?"

"I do." I try to sound calm and engaged and open to whatever she has to say. Please let my face be conveying that, because my insides are churning like crazy.

"Well, for one thing, women and girls should cover themselves completely." She smooths her headscarf. "I don't mean just wearing a headscarf, but the *burqa*. Except my mother won't let me get one."

I shake my head. "The *Qur'an* doesn't say women have to wear the *burqa*. It says they should be modest. Believe me, my Islamic Studies professor drilled that into me in college. So did your mother."

Seema looks at me, her eyes now shining, earnest and intense. "You're wrong, Auntie. Awalmir says women must cover themselves completely. It's the only way for us to be chaste and righteous."

"No, Seema. *He's* wrong." And just that fast, I'm doing exactly what I shouldn't—arguing religion. But it's too late now, so I plunge on. "Granted, modesty rules are open to interpretation, but wearing the *burqa* is cultural, not religious." Even though I know full well there are many women like Gulshan who don't feel *forced* to cover themselves, I'm ready to go all out and tell her that *burqas* were mandated by Taliban men as a way to control women. But one look at her stops me. Going that route may win me debate points, but it sure won't win over Seema.

"That's not what Awalmir says."

Could I have screwed this up any worse? I conjure up the senior boys' religion teacher, angry and scowling, blaming me for the boys and girls consorting that afternoon in the village center. Is this what he's teaching? That education for girls is wrong? That they have to cover every part of their body, even their eyes? That men are right to oppress women? Whatever he's pouring into those boys is the antithesis of everything I know. It feels wrong. Dead wrong. Nothing short of perverted.

I picture the cute boy I'm pretty sure is Awalmir—laughing and flirting with Bahar. What a manipulative little creep! Oh, my Seema, you used to love school and reading. But I have the feeling you'll believe just about anything he wants you to. Because you want the love he's dangling in front of you. How I'd hoped your first love would be sweet and romantic, not full of ultimatums and impossible choices.

I look at Seema—her jaw locked, absolute certainty etched across her face. I remember that expression all too well. I wore it when I was eighteen, when I, too, was completely set in my new worldview. I wait for her to say, *How could you possibly understand?* Or, even worse, *How could my mother understand?* But she doesn't have to say anything. What she's thinking is written clearly on her face. She's not going to believe a word I say because in her mind, Awalmir is right.

"So, Auntie, tell me the truth. If I *were* to go to college in the U.S.A., would I be able to wear the *hijab?*"

"Of course. Many girls in the United States cover their hair."

"The *burqa?*"

I take a breath. "If that's what you believe, then yes. Certainly, in Boston, other big cities, college towns."

"And will they accept me? The other students, the teachers, they won't discriminate against me? They won't assume I'm a terrorist and arrest me?" The sneer in her voice tells me she's sure she already knows the answer.

Who the hell is this guy?

"You see?" she says quietly.

"No, Seema, I don't see. There are millions of Muslims in the United States. They're citizens. Americans. And yes, there is Islamophobia, but there are also many non-Muslim Americans who support—"

"That's just not true! Americans hate true believers!"

True believers? Is that how Seema sees Awalmir? Herself?

"So, Auntie, you tell me. What should I do? Give up what I believe to make my parents happy? Or am I allowed to believe something they don't?"

Damn! I'm in way over my head. I should have just given the *landays* to Darya and been done with it. But I didn't. And now, here we are: Seema's life is at stake. Really and truly at stake. And even though she thinks she's mature enough to make this kind of decision, I know she's not. In some ways, she's still a very innocent, very naïve girl willing to believe whatever Awalmir wants her to.

"Auntie? Please? Please help us. Talk to my parents so we can be together."

I take a deep breath and reach for her hands, holding them tighter than I'm sure she likes. "Seema, *you* have to talk to your parents. I can't do that for you."

Eyes glistening with tears, she shakes her head. "They'll never understand. I know them. They'll try to come between us. They won't let me see him."

Which is exactly what Darya and Tariq should do, of course. "Give them a chance," I say in my most encouraging voice, while silently begging her to run from this boy as fast as she can. "Please. I bet your mother is still in her office. Go. Talk to her. Now."

She bows her head. "Okay," she mumbles. "But please promise me you won't say anything."

"Talk to her."

Seema heads back toward the school. I watch as she stops for a long moment at the front door, then turns away and walks on. Where the school drive meets the main road, she looks toward home for only a second, then heads in the opposite direction to the village center. Off to find Awalmir, who's probably just now getting out of religion class and will have answers for any doubts she might have.

There's no way she's going to talk to her parents. I have to.

BACK IN THE SCHOOL, I wind my way through the darkened corridors to Darya's office. Empty. Funny, I didn't see her in the hall or any of the classrooms. But she must still be here. She wouldn't leave school without locking up. I'm turning around to go look for her when I hear her voice coming from the supply closet. "Dar? You here?"

"I'll be right out."

Another minute, and she's back in her office, double-locking the closet door behind her. Which strikes me as a bit of overkill for a supply closet that can't possibly have anything more than a few books, some paper and pens, maybe a few jerry cans of kerosene. She turns toward me and smiles, clearly expecting good news. "So, how did it go?"

I shake my head and watch Dar's smile fade. Since I've been here, I've read a flurry of increasingly explicit *landays* and listened to Seema tell lie after lie. Which is pretty ironic, considering she thinks of herself—and Awalmir—as truth-telling and righteous true believers. When she finally did tell the truth, it wasn't a truth I wanted to hear. I pull the folded blue and white papers from my pocket and sink onto the chair next to the desk.

"What are those?" asks Darya.

I tap the papers against the desktop. "I found these in the bush outside my bedroom window. A boy left the white one in the middle of the night, which I took. Seema hasn't seen it. She wrote the note on blue paper early this morning while I was in the bathroom. I intercepted it before the boyfriend had a chance to collect it. There were others, but they weren't as explicit."

Darya raises her eyebrows and holds out her hand.

"I'm sorry, Dar. I should have given these to you first thing this morning, but I thought—oh hell, I don't know what I thought." I lean forward and put the small white and blue squares into her hand. We both look at them for what feels like an eternity. There's a lot riding on those little bits of paper, and we both seem to realize it.

Darya weighs the paper squares on her palm. "You thought, my friend, that you could deal with it because Seema trusts you. She talks to you and listens to your advice. You wanted to help."

"Yeah, that went well, didn't it?" Seema trusted me, and here I am betraying that trust. "I don't think she's listening anymore."

"It's not always easy to take the right decision," says Dar with a knowing smile. She unfolds the white paper and reads. "You said Seema hasn't seen this?"

The riverbank is lonely,
Many girls here, but I want you only.

"Correct. But that won't give you any comfort when you read what she wrote."

Darya unfolds the blue paper and reads her daughter's lovely cursive:

I waited at the river for you, my dearest sweet,
You never came. Take me now—a treat.

She studies the words in front of her, seeming to read them again and again. "I'm not sure I understand," she says.

I rake my fingers through my hair, pushing back the headscarf until it pools around my neck. "That's the last of the *landays* that

Seema and the boy left for each other in the mulberry bush outside my bedroom window. There were a few others since I've been here. They started out innocent enough but built to these pretty fast."

She taps her index finger against the crumpled paper. "You talked to Seema?"

"Oh yeah. Several times."

"And?"

"At first she denied everything. But she finally admitted what I've been suspecting for the last week. There's a boy."

"A week?"

"I'm sorry. I should've told you sooner, but it didn't seem like anything serious. And I didn't have any proof. Until now."

"Does this boy have a name?"

"Awalmir."

"That's Pashtun. Does he have a family name?"

I shake my head. "That's all I know. From the way Seema describes him, he sounds pretty conservative in his beliefs. Strike that—extreme. I'm sure he's lapping up everything that crazy religion teacher is spouting."

Darya narrows her eyes. "You think he's a student?"

"I'm pretty sure he's one of the senior boys. I saw him—that day when the girls and I were in the village center. Dark hair, average build, and really cute. Studying religion," I snort, "but based on that note, it's pretty obvious he's pushing her for sex. Don't ask me why, but I don't think she's given in yet." I think back to her swollen lips. "Except for some kissing."

Darya taps the blue paper against her desk. *Click, click, click.* The sound echoes around the otherwise silent room. "But she's telling him 'yes' in this."

"Which I intercepted, so he never got."

"Oh, Annie, I've talked to her. She knows how dangerous it would be to have sex outside of marriage in this country."

"To be honest, I'm actually more worried about the marriage part. She's convinced that this boy is her one true love and that their marriage is 'ordained' by Allah. Awalmir says he'll leave her if she goes to college. So, as far as she's concerned, college is out of the question. All she wants is to marry this guy. And given how extreme he is, I'm sure he'll want her to have babies right away."

"Which, of course, is completely out of the question. She is only seventeen years old. A *young* seventeen. What does she know about any of that? She's not getting married. And she is most definitely going to college."

I hear Seema's plaintive, little voice again. *What should I do? Give up what I believe to make my parents happy?*

"I've talked to her a couple times, Dar. This morning. Just now. Both times I begged her to come talk to you. She promised she would, but as you can see . . ."

"She hasn't."

"No."

She studies me for a few moments. "And it's tearing you apart to have to tell me yourself." Darya knows me well.

"It is. Dar, I wanted her to—"

"And yet, daughters don't always do what we want them to. Annie, please don't think you've done anything wrong. You haven't—"

"I gained her trust. I *promised* her I wouldn't tell you."

"Listen to me: you haven't betrayed Seema. She is not nearly mature enough to make these decisions. If anyone has betrayed her, it is I—by turning a blind eye to what was right in front of me, by ignoring what she needed."

"So, what can we do?" I hear the desperation in my voice.

I watch the thoughts spinning in Darya's mind as she tries to figure out how to deal with a daughter who's suddenly discovered her hormones and a new world awaiting her. My attention wanders, and I'm staring at the locked door to the supply closet, a rim of light running across the threshold. Dar left the light on inside. And she was talking. But the Dar I know doesn't talk to herself.

"Annie?"

Something about the way Dar says my name tells me she's been trying to get my attention for a while.

"Sorry." I turn back to her.

"I'm going to call the boys' school and ask them to locate Awalmir. Would you recognize him?" She waves the *landay*. "If we can figure out who he is, Tariq could meet with the boy's parents and convince them to talk to their son. To leave Seema alone."

"Recognize him? I think so. It's worth a try."

Darya enters the number on her cell. Lucky for us, the director of the boys' school picks up. He doesn't sound pleased. In fact, in a voice that quickly escalates to anger, he clearly interprets the situation as Seema pursuing one of his virtuous students. When Dar ends the call, she looks at me with an arched eyebrow. "There is no student by the name of Awalmir at the school."

"Damn." My stomach churns in frustration. "Maybe Seema made up the name so I can't find him."

"Could it be anyone else? Maybe someone who isn't a student? Have you noticed any other boy hanging around?"

I think back through the days I've spent in Wad Qol, stopping at the afternoon photo shoot with my students in the village center. The young man standing on the outskirts of the crowd. He was sort of watching Seema, sort of not. Then, he vanished when I tried to get a shot of him. I tell Darya about him.

"Do you think he could be Awalmir?"

I shrug. "Who knows? He was clearly unhappy with the boy-girl fraternizing that was going on. But he didn't go anywhere near Seema. In fact, he didn't do more than glance at her a couple times."

"What did he look like?"

"I only saw him at a distance. He was across the road and at the far end of the shops. He was maybe a little older than the rest of the students, had dark hair and wore Western clothes."

"As do most teenage boys in Afghanistan." She sighs and turns in her chair to look out the window. A few minutes later, she looks back at me. "Seema has no idea you're talking to me about this?"

"As far as I know."

"I have another idea. She seems pretty engaged by your class, don't you think?"

"Definitely."

"It's only a few more days. I'm pretty confident she'll be okay while you're here."

I hesitate, then nod, not at all sure I'm as confident as Dar. "Probably. Maybe. I don't know."

"We'll let things continue until the workshop is done. Three more days."

"Actually, it's four days. But okay."

"*Four* days. So, take back this *landay*. Seema's, not Awalmir's. If she gets suspicious you might have said something to me, you can show her you still have the 'incriminating evidence.' You could even promise her you won't tell me."

I stuff the crinkled piece of blue stationery back in my pocket. "Then what?"

"When you finish teaching, we'll forego our little trip to Anabah. Instead, we'll tell Seema we're all going to Kabul for a long weekend to see you off. Tariq will come, too. From there, do you think you could take her to my parents in California? If Tariq goes with you?"

I laugh. "Seriously? Can you actually make all the arrangements, get tickets that fast?"

Darya swats at the air. "Don't worry about that. Will you do it?"

Just then, the school's heavy front door slams shut, the sound reverberating down the hall. Dar and I freeze. What were we thinking—talking about Seema like this with the door to Darya's office open? The school felt empty when I came back inside, but that doesn't mean it was. Anyone could have been listening. Even Seema. Could she have come back to school to talk to her mother and discovered the two of us planning a fate worse than death for her? Then, when she heard this last bit, she took off?

"Darya? Are you still here?" It's Tariq, his footsteps heavy on the wooden planks. Thank God. But shouldn't he still be at the clinic? I glance at my watch and see that it's already six o'clock.

"In my office," she calls.

A moment later, Tariq stands smiling in the doorway. "You two ladies look very serious."

Darya gestures for him to come in and close the door, then brings him up to speed. Leaning against the wall, Tariq listens, his expression thoughtful. "Is there no other option? What if we find this boy and convince him—"

"We don't really know what he looks like," I say. "Or even his name, for sure."

"I'm concerned about asking around any more than I already have." Darya's voice is firm. "The last thing we need is for Seema or him to suspect we're on to them. They might just take off."

Tariq rubs his jaw thoughtfully, then nods. "Yes, the more

people who know, the more likely it will be that Seema or the boy will hear something."

"We need to get Seema away from this boy." Darya isn't brooking any disagreement.

"Agreed. So, we would leave at the weekend." Tariq's voice has a worry in it that I've never heard before.

"I just don't know, Dar," I say, shaking my head. "Seema's smart. Even if we manage to get her to Kabul, she'll bolt the second she realizes what's going on."

Tariq darts a glance at Darya. She answers with the slightest of nods. But it's so quick that I'm not sure it really happened. "What if she does not know what is going on?" says Tariq.

It takes me a few seconds, but then I get it. "You're saying you'll sedate her? As in—unconscious?"

He nods. "That is exactly what I am thinking. I have evacuated patients to hospitals outside Afghanistan before. The authorities know me. They will not question it. In fact, they will probably be very sympathetic once they realize it is Seema."

I stare at Tariq, then Darya. Really? They'd do this? To their own daughter? Drug her, ship her out of the country. To get her away from this boy she swears she loves. Holy shit. Yeah, I know Darya and Tariq are faced with a serious problem, but this seems totally out of proportion. I can't imagine a scenario where I'd do this to Mel. "Isn't there any other way?"

"What would that be?" Darya looks at me as though she'd welcome a suggestion. But there's something else in her eyes— something I can't quite read.

"This is not as sudden as it seems, Annie. We have always had a plan." Tariq shakes his head. "We could not live here in Afghanistan without an exit plan." Again, that quick glance at Dar.

"Many families do," Darya adds.

Right. Families with means. But still. This is a lot to swallow. "So, we get Seema to California. Then what? Your parents are in their seventies. How are they going to handle her? Lock her up in a tower?"

Darya waves away my objection. "My brother and his wife live close by my parents. They will help. Besides, Seema is very impressionable. Once she's separated from this Awalmir, back in the States and in college, she'll forget about him." She sounds so certain this will work.

"I have a colleague in Palo Alto," says Tariq quietly. "He directs a residential program. He would be willing to work with Seema."

Is he talking a therapist? Or a deprogrammer? I shake my head. "I don't know . . ."

Darya looks at me and cocks her head. "You don't seem convinced."

"I think when Seema 'comes to' in California, she'll be so angry and feel so completely betrayed that you'll have lost your daughter."

Darya looks at me, her eyes penetrating. "I will do anything to save my daughter. Anything. If this were Mel, wouldn't you do everything in your power to save her life?"

31

SEEMA IS LAYING LOW. SHE'S back to being respectful and helpful and studious. No more *landays* in the mulberry bush outside my window. Not another word to me about Awalmir. Nor does she talk to her parents about him. Not a hint of moodiness. And even more amazing, she's talking about college—in Boston. Maybe even a visit with Mel and me in August. In other words, a total transformation.

Except I don't believe it.

Her parents don't believe it either.

I'm elbows deep in hot, sudsy water, washing up after dinner. Darya is rinsing. I glance at the closed kitchen door as Dar whispers, "Clearly, Seema and this boy think she should act like her old self to lull us into believing everything is all right."

I put a soap-covered index finger to my lips, walk to the door, and open it. The front room is empty.

The door closed again, Darya scowls at the dirty dishes in the sink. "My daughter is smart, we've always known that, but when did she develop such devious behavior?"

32

"DEVIOUS?" SAYS CERELLI, sounding incredulous. "Darya actually said that?"

"Her exact word." I keep my voice low in case Seema is listening from across the hall and curl deeper under my blankets to ward off the midnight cold of my bedroom. After several warm nights, we're back to freezing. The fire in the front room is banked for the night, and the tiny bit of warmth it gives off doesn't reach this far back into the house.

"I never would have thought it. Seema's always seemed like the perfect kid to me."

"I know. Even when she was little." *Seema always seemed—*
"Hold on, Cerelli, just how well do you know Seema?"

"Not very. She was around when I was there."

Yet again, I've got the feeling there's a whole Cerelli-Darya-Tariq thing going on that I don't know about.

"Is that before or after you went to law school?" I wince at the snarky accusation in my voice. And that I even said anything about it.

He chuckles. "You've been talking to Darya."

"I have."

"Is this important? As in, you have something against lawyers?"

"Not important. I like lawyers. Mostly."

"Glad to hear it."

"So, I've got a legal question."

"Shoot."

"Why did you and Mr. CIA let me go?"

I can sense his grin. "Simple. You didn't do anything wrong. Except get hazed and not level with the CO. Or me."

"Are you telling me you knew I was innocent? The whole time? You put me through hell—"

"We had a situation. The Marines at FOB Masum Ghar were accusing you and closing ranks in support of Murphy and Lopez. I had a pretty good idea what really went down, but I needed to prove it. Besides which, you did withhold information that would have made my job a lot easier. Oh, and Mr. CIA didn't share my opinion—at first."

I curl my fingers into a fist and pound my thigh. "What about those photographs you had me search for? Did they pan out?"

A few seconds pass before he says, "I can't talk about that."

"You mean if you tell me, you'd have to kill me."

"You do have a way with words."

"I believe those were *your* words."

"I still can't tell you."

"Yeah, well, I didn't think you would."

"Then are we good?" Cerelli actually has a note of concern in his voice.

What can I say? That I'm still obsessing after all these years? "We're good."

"Okay. Look, about Seema. From what you're saying, it sounds like Darya has this well in hand."

"Well in hand? She and Tariq have a plan, but I'm not sure I've got a lot of faith in it."

"Why?"

"For one thing, I don't like waiting until the end of the workshop to get her out of here. I know it's only four more days, but who knows what could happen in that time. Plus, once Seema gets to her grandparents in San Jose, she'll have them wrapped around her little finger in no time."

"Trust me, Darya knows what she's doing. And as much as I enjoy talking about her, I really called to check in with you. Any more bad guys following you?"

"Nope. The last couple days have been wonderfully calm. My fear factor is pretty much at zero. It's almost like the bad guys have left town." I pull the blankets closer around me. "You *do* believe me, don't you? That someone was following me?"

"I do."

"Thank you." I think. Knowing what he does about me—my nightmares, my 'visitors' at the InterCon—I wouldn't blame him if he chalked my Wad Qol stalker up to my imagination. Or even PTSD hallucinations. His confidence in me feels good, solid. I smile into the dark of my room.

"And you could be right: maybe the bad guy did leave town. Or, not to scare you, maybe he hasn't. You sure I can't talk you into coming home? Tomorrow? Tariq and Darya can handle Seema on their own. And I know I'll feel better when you're back CONUS."

I smile. "There you go with that sexy Navy talk again. You sure know how to get to a girl."

He laughs. "Is it working?"

"Not a chance, Cerelli. I've got a few more days of the workshop." I lower my voice to a whisper again. "Then, we begin Operation Seema."

"Then, you'll be coming CONUS."

"Damn it, Cerelli. Don't do that!" The flush starts deep inside me and rushes past my chest to my face. I push the blankets off. Even the chilled air in the room isn't cooling me enough.

"Do what?" As if he doesn't know.

"Say CONUS that way."

"Which way is that?"

"You know exactly what I mean. You're making me hot as hell."

"Good to know."

"Except you're 7,000 miles away."

"Not for long. Then, we'll get to see how hot you can make me."

"I make you hot?"

"Oh yeah. In fact, right now—"

"Jeez, Cerelli, are we having phone sex?"

"Do you want this to be phone sex?"

"If that's all I can get right now." I cringe. Did I really just say that?

And then the static of the broken connection buzzes in my ear. The satellite has moved on. Oh, fuck! Holding the phone close, I let my thoughts drift back to the Cerelli of eight and a half years ago in that torture chamber on the *Bataan*. In my wildest dreams, I never thought I'd be reveling in phone sex with him. Wanting more than long-distance coitus. Definitely more than *coitus sat-phonus interruptus*. For the first time since Todd and I split up, I feel like there's hope for my sex life. And my love life.

Hold on. Can I really let someone into my life? Do I even want to? Yeah. Maybe. Except the man I'm falling for is on the other side of the world. And sometimes he's so infuriating, I want to kill him.

33

FOR OUR FINAL FIELD TRIP, I'm taking the girls to the wreck of a Soviet helicopter from the war years during the 1980s—just a few kilometers outside of town. Tariq's suggestion. The clinic is quiet, he says, offering to drive some of the girls. He lines up Bahar's father, Ikrom, to help. Between them, they'll take twelve girls and me in the morning. The rest of the girls and I will go in the afternoon. We'll have an hour of good light for each group. Golden light in the morning, a rosy glow in the afternoon. Perfect for girls who are obsessed with making everything look soft and romantic.

"The helicopter wreck?" groans one of the girls.

"Look," I say, "when you're a photojournalist, you go where the assignment is. You don't always like it. But you make the most of it. You *find* the story, and you tell it."

The girls nod in reluctant unison.

"You may take as many photographs as you wish, but you may submit only three."

"Only three?" One of the girls gulps loudly.

"The three that tell your story the best. That's it. So, you need to think carefully about what you want your pictures to say and what you want your viewer to feel. Plan out your compositions, your lighting, your depth of field, your shutter speed."

"May we ask questions?" asks Bahar.

"Absolutely. I'll talk you through how to adjust your camera, but you'll have to do it yourselves. And I won't tell you which images are better or worse. You'll have to make your own decisions. Then, we'll critique your images in class."

"But this is our final project," says Seema. "What if we make mistakes? What if our photographs look terrible?"

"Good questions. Everyone makes mistakes. Even professional photographers." I chuckle. "Especially professional photographers. For every good picture I take, you can bet there are a hundred that aren't."

"But what if we fail?" says Bahar.

"You won't fail unless you don't do the assignment. And don't *worry*. I'm expecting there will be things you'll want to correct. Besides, you *know* this place. You've all been there. The meadow, the wreck of the helicopter. The mountains. Tonight, try to come up with a new and different way to picture it—the way that tells your story."

Twenty-three girls stare at me. Seema plays with the edge of her *hijab*. Bahar's fingers twirl some loose strands of hair. The classroom is thick with their anxiety and their need to impress.

As the last girls leave for the day, Seema stays behind. "Auntie? Would it be possible for me to make a portrait as part of my story?"

"Of course."

"What if I want to make a portrait of myself?"

"You'll need to use the timer on your camera."

"Could you show me?"

"Absolutely." Pleased that Seema is thinking outside the box, I tell her what to do.

She listens intently, following each step. "Let me see if I can do it myself." Positioning the camera on the front desk, she sets the timer and runs in front of it to pose. We look at the image—she's managed to chop off her head. She laughs. "I need to practice."

I smile. "Practice would be good."

"Thank you, Auntie." And then she's gone.

An hour later, my eyes blurring from looking at way too many images of Afghan teenage girl drama, I shut down the laptop and slip it into my backpack. After straightening my scarf to make sure my hair is covered, I head to Darya's office. "You ready?"

"You go on." She sweeps her hand above the mountain of papers on her desk. "I have a grant request to finish up."

"I can wait."

"That would be a waste of your time. I'm sure you have other things you'd rather be doing. The generator at the house should be working, so you'll be able to look at more of the girls' photographs."

I cross my eyes. "Please, no more romantic fantasies."

"They're photographing what they dream about."

"Which is why I'm taking them to the meadow with the helicopter wreck tomorrow. Something different from what they've been photographing up until now."

"Ah, the teacher gets tough." Darya nods approvingly. "You go on. I want to finish this paperwork."

"Later." I waggle my fingers and am out the door before I remember Cerelli's strict instructions to have someone walk with me. What the hell. It's been days of complete and total calm.

Annie—

I wave my hand through the air. Leave me alone, Cerelli. I'll be fine.

I'm halfway back to the house when I feel it—that horrible, all-too-familiar chill charging full-bore up my spine. The prickles on the back of my neck stop me mid-stride. *Not here!* This is the worst possible place—no one else is around. And it's another mile to the house.

The Sig. Cerelli's voice.

I don't argue. Slipping my backpack off my shoulders, I reposition it against my chest, then slide my hand inside the partially unzipped compartment. I dig down past cameras and the sat phone until my fingers lock on the Sig. Angling it to rest on top of my cameras, I start to flip off the safety but stop. What if it's a kid? Or one of the mules or goats that wander around the village?

No. I don't kill. I've had way too much killing in my life.

But what if it's not someone innocent?

Hand on the safety, I force myself to do a slow 360, searching the road, the trees, and the bushes as far as I can see. Nothing. Absolutely nothing. Not a mule, not a goat. Not even a chicken scratching its way across the road.

I don't hear footsteps or see anyone duck behind the clump of mulberry bushes. But something or someone has caused the dust along the side of the road to rise up and hover in the air. And that branch heavy with berries to shake. The hair on the back of my neck stands so rigid it hurts.

A breeze? No, nothing else is moving.

Nothing.

The air is painfully still.

It's not an animal. No goat or mule would run to hide when I turn around. Or be deathly quiet. Animals aren't that calculating. I'd hear something.

Sorry if I'm distracting you. Cerelli again. *But would you mind getting the hell out of Dodge?*

Yeah, well, I'm like halfway between Dodge and Virginia City. Should I go back to school or go on home?

Your choice. Just keep your hand on that Sig, and if you pull it out, make sure you're ready to shoot. This guy will shoot to kill. As in dead. And I don't want to have to load you into a body bag.

So you said before. I'm not too fond of body bags myself. But I won't shoot an innocent person.

Sometimes the choices are lousy.

I run, remembering to zig, then zag, making it home, but nearly dead on arrival.

I slam and lock the front door. Another step into the lounge, then I lean forward, hands clutching my thighs, and take deep gulping breaths, trying to pull air into my lungs. Because of a mile run? How did I let myself get in such terrible shape?

"Auntie?" Seema stands in the hall, staring at me.

"Seema!" I nearly jump out of my skin. "Oh, my God, you scared me half to death! I didn't think you'd be home yet."

She looks at me quizzically. "I'm working on my story for tomorrow."

"Good." I gasp for more air. "That's really good."

"I hope you like it." Frowning, she moves closer. "Are you sure you are all right? You look *scared*."

"I'm okay. Just out of breath." I set my pack on the floor. Badly balanced, it topples over, and the Sig slides out. Shit!

"Auntie?" Now Seema sounds scared. "Why do you have a gun?"

"No cause for alarm." I try to sound reassuring as I scoop up the Sig, make sure the safety's on, and stuff it in my pack.

"Auntie, I have eyes in my head. I can see something is wrong. Should I get Mom?" Seema moves toward the door, ready to run for help.

"No! Don't go out there!"

"I don't understand. What's going on?" She edges closer to the door.

"Nothing. Really. Everything's fine." Right. Even *I* don't think I sound convincing.

"I'm going for Mom." Seema sounds for all the world like Darya.

I know that if I don't tell her what happened, or at least a sanitized version of it, she'll be out the door and heading toward school. And that would put her right in the crosshairs of whoever's out there.

"Okay, this will probably sound a little crazy," I say, loosening my headscarf and pushing it off my hair. "I'm pretty sure someone followed me home from school. Every time I turned around, he hid behind a tree or a boulder. It was pretty freaky."

"Someone followed you? In Wad Qol?" Disbelief is written all over her face. Before I realize what she's doing, she's unlocked and opened the door. "Look, Auntie." Seema steps out and opens her arms, welcoming the empty space in front of the house. "There's no one here. Believe me, everyone in Wad Qol loves my parents. And they love you. We're probably the safest people in the safest place in all of Afghanistan."

I hold up my hands in surrender. "You're right." I try to laugh off my paranoia. "Maybe it was a mule after all." Not likely.

Seema leads the way back into the house. "Perhaps you would like some *chai*? I could make it for you."

"Thank you, sweetie, but I think maybe a nap would help." I scoop up my pack and retreat to my room, wondering about Seema. She's behaving like the sweet Seema of the past. Could she really have changed? Or is this all an act?

I eye my bed. A nap is a great idea. But I'll feel better if I change out of these sweaty, smelly clothes first. I rummage in the pocket for Seema's *landay*. And this time, come up empty. I check again. Nothing. I search both pockets, my pack, my other pants. Every drawer in the little dresser. What the hell did I do with it? When did I last see it? Did I have it this morning? This afternoon? I can't remember. But it's gone.

I turn in a circle, wondering where else to look. Could Seema have taken it? She knew I kept it in my pants pocket. I pulled it out and showed it to her—to reassure her I still had it, that I hadn't given it to her mom. Could she have snuck into my room and taken it? Maybe last night while I was taking a bath? Would she actually steal from me? Time to find out.

I cross the hall to Seema's room and knock, wondering how I can possibly approach this without accusing her. Without totally alienating her. She opens the door almost immediately, looking puzzled.

"Auntie?" She smiles solicitously and steps aside, an invitation for me to go in. "You look upset."

I walk over to her desk and glance down at several photos. A terrific shot of Gulshan with her arms around Bahar. Another of me in profile about to snap a picture. And one of a young man with dark hair and wearing a gray T-shirt, lips in a full-on seductive pout, thumbs slung through the belt loops of his jeans. Definitely not the cute boy in the village center. Maybe the older guy who was watching from the edge of the crowd, but I'm not sure. I never did get a clear view of him. I tap the photos. "Nice shots."

She smiles. "Thank you."

I turn to look at her. "Seema, I've lost something, and I'm wondering if you could help me find it." Better than an outright accusation.

"Of course. What did you lose?"

"Well, as it happens, I can't find your *landay*."

She stares at me. "What do you mean?"

"It's not in my pants pocket anymore."

"I don't understand."

"Seema, I've carried that piece of paper everywhere. Just like I promised. And now it's gone."

"Oh, no! What if Mom took it?"

"No, Seema, I don't think she—"

"She must have taken it! What am I going to do?"

"Seema, really—"

"What if she goes after Awalmir?" Her voice quavers.

I almost laugh. "Your mother wouldn't go *after* him." Which isn't true. She sure as hell would go after him, but not in the way I think Seema means.

Eyes wide and fearful, she backs into the corner of her room. "You don't know my mom. Not really."

34

I NEED TO TALK THIS THROUGH with someone. But Darya's still at school, and there's no point putting myself at risk to go back there. Late afternoons like this, Tariq stops on his way home from the clinic to pick her up. So, she'll be fine getting home. I'll talk to her then.

Cerelli. Nothing he can do about Seema helping herself to the *landay,* but he'll want to know the bad guy is back. I tap in his number, and the phone on his end rings. And rings. And rings.

Baffled, I look at the phone in my hand. I've always been able to reach someone on this phone. I try the number again. It rings. And rings.

"Cerelli."

"You sure took your time." The accusing tone in my voice makes me wince.

"Some women like it when a man takes his time."

My face flames.

"You're blushing."

"Your X-ray vision telling you that?"

"Just a lucky guess."

I let the silence ride between us. It's nice, knowing he's at the other end of this very long line. It would be even nicer if he were actually here in Wad Qol and could check out the deserted road. Of course, the bad guy would be long gone, but Cerelli could look for footprints, broken twigs, let me know if someone really *was* there. I want Cerelli here—with me. The realization takes me by surprise.

"Nice as this is, Annie, you called for a reason?"

Okay, back to business. "Two problems here."

"The first one?"

"He's back."

"What happened?"

I tighten my hold on the sat phone. "Just the facts. I was walking back to Darya and Tariq's after school this afternoon. There's this long road—"

"I know the road."

I hold the phone at arm's length and stare at it. Is there anything, *anything* this man doesn't know?

"No big mystery. Remember, I've been there."

"Do you have to do that?"

"Do what?"

"You know, read my mind. It's—"

"Distracting. Yeah, you've mentioned that before."

"Anyway, I was by myself *on that road you know so well*, and suddenly, I could feel him behind me."

"What did you do?"

"I followed your advice."

"Did I give you good advice?"

"As it happens, you did. Got my hand on the Sig, but kept it in my pack, and then jogged the mile to the house. And spent the next fifteen minutes trying to get my pulse back to normal."

"Fifteen minutes? I thought you were a runner."

"Yeah, well, there was a bit of an adrenaline rush. Not to mention that I'm clearly out of shape."

"Were you ready to shoot? Mentally, I mean."

"No, I wasn't ready to shoot."

"Scared?"

"Scared of killing an innocent person? You bet I was scared."

"I mean, scared of the bad guy who's out there."

"So, you believe me?"

"Oh, yeah. Once, I can chalk up to imagination. Twice, eh. But three times is too coincidental."

"And you don't believe in coincidences."

"I don't believe in coincidences."

I don't like the frustration that's coating Cerelli's voice. There might be a touch of doom, too, and I don't like that any better. "That leads me to problem number two."

"Seema?"

"You got it. That *landay* of hers I've been carrying around? It went missing this afternoon. But get this: when I asked Seema about it, she played the innocent card, flipping out like she's afraid Darya has it. Now, she's terrified Darya will *go after* her boyfriend."

Cerelli pauses briefly, just a heartbeat, but it's a heartbeat too long. "And?" he says.

"While I was in her room, I saw some photos on her desk. Only briefly. One is of a guy who could be the boyfriend—Awalmir."

"Awalmir's a Pashtun name."

"Darya said the same thing."

"You think that's his real name?"

"I don't know. That's the name Seema gave me."

"Did you confiscate the photo?"

"I couldn't. Not with her right there." I inhale the aromas of dinner that are suddenly wafting under the door into my room. And catch myself in a quiet moan.

"What?" he asks.

"You heard that? It's dinner. Dar's home. Cooking. I should go help her."

"Tell her about the photograph of Awalmir. Now."

I'M STILL HOLDING THE sat phone when I hear Seema's door click shut and her slippers slap against the tiles heading toward the bathroom. Peeking out my door, I see her bathrobe turn the corner. Telling Darya will have to wait a couple minutes. Now's my chance to snatch Awalmir's photo. Right, like Seema won't miss it.

Thinking like a photographer, I grab a spare SD card from my stash, sprint across the hall, and swap it for Seema's which, thank God, is in her camera. Which is good because the photos that were on her desk an hour ago are gone. Please, let that image still be on the card! In less than a minute, I'm back in my room, uploading her pics onto my laptop, hoping against hope I finish before she comes back.

Upload complete, and she's still in the bathroom. It takes me less than three minutes, and I've got her original card back in her camera.

I'M SITTING CROSS-LEGGED ON the bed, Awalmir's image staring at me from my laptop screen. Does he look familiar or not? His eyes are soft, seductive in this photograph. Can I imagine him with eyes that frighten? Hate? I just don't know.

I hear Seema return to her bedroom. The knock on my door a minute later almost startles me off the bed. Damn, please let it not be Seema. I lower the screen just as Darya lets herself in, along with some intoxicating aromas that make me salivate.

"Dinner is nearly ready." She smiles, closing the door behind her. "Two of your favorites."

I sniff the air. "*Ashak* and *khichri*." Vegetable dumplings with tomato yogurt sauce, and sticky rice with mung beans and onions.

"You're amazing!" Dar laughs. "Sometimes I think you really are Afghan."

"I should be so lucky." I wave her over. "But first, I have to show you something." Lifting the screen, I turn the laptop around so she can see.

She sits on the bed to get a closer look and lowers her voice to that whisper Cerelli has perfected. "Awalmir?"

"Could be. He's definitely not the cute boy from the school. It's possible he's the other guy, the one who was hanging around the village center the day I took the girls."

She brings her palms together and presses the edges of her hands against her lips. "I've seen him before. Somewhere. Not at the boys' school. He's too old to be in school. It will come to me." She looks at me over the screen. "Did you take this?"

"Not me. Seema. Her *landay* went missing from my pocket

today, which is a whole other story. While I was in her room quizzing her about that, I saw a print of this guy on her desk. As you know, I've been letting the girls use the printer—one image per girl per day. Dar, it's got to be Awalmir. I mean, look at the expression on his face, those eyes. Why else would she have made the print?"

"I'm sure you're right. It clearly means something to her." She studies the image, then shakes her head. She can't place him. "So, how did you get this? Obviously, you didn't help yourself to the print."

"Couldn't. Not without causing a problem—making her suspicious. I swapped SD cards—while Seema was in the bathroom. Uploaded her images and put hers back."

Dar raises her eyebrows. "You're very good at smuggling, you know. Could you copy this to a thumb drive for me?"

"Of course. What—" One quick shake of Darya's head, and I swallow my words. Some questions are better left unasked. I make the copy and hand her the small, red drive.

She smiles and pushes herself off the bed. "Time for dinner."

"It smells divine."

"Let's go eat," says Darya, holding up the thumb drive, "then I'll see what I can find out about Awalmir."

35

THE MORNING OF THE FIELD TRIP, Seema meets me in the hall between our bedrooms. "Please, Auntie," she pleads, her panic of yesterday afternoon apparently forgotten, "could I go with the afternoon group for the field trip? I've been thinking about it all night, and the rose-colored light will be so much better for the story I have planned."

"Of course." I put my arm around her shoulders. "It's great that you've thought this out so carefully." I manage not to cringe at her emphasis on a rosy glow and hope she'll go easy on the romance.

"I'm afraid you may not like my story." Seema has a look in her eyes that I can't quite decipher. Wistful? Sad? Worried?

"Seema, I love all your stories. I always have. You're a born storyteller." With any luck, that will continue. In a few days, Seema, Tariq, and I will be heading to California. Not that she has any idea of her impending trip. I cross my fingers that come fall, she'll be at college taking literature and creative writing courses.

She hugs me tight. "Thank you, Auntie. So, I'll go to my classes this morning, then meet you and the others later," she whispers in my ear. "I wish—"

"What do you wish?"

She waves away her words, then kisses me on the cheek and hurries back into her room to finish getting ready for school. As she shuts the door, I catch a glimpse of a mountain of periwinkle cloth on her desk next to her Rebel. A *burqa*? Really? Is she using that in her shoot?

Darya walks with me to school and unlocks the front door. "I am eager to see the pictures Seema takes this morning. Last night at dinner, she was in raptures about the golden light of sunrise."

"Big change," I say. "Before we left the house, she begged to go with the afternoon group. Apparently, the rosy light of sunset will be better for her story." I pause on the front step, wanting to ask Dar if she's found out anything more about Awalmir, but she hurries off to her office to finish up yet more paperwork. I wave at her retreating back and head to my classroom at the front of the school to wait for the girls.

I want them out in the meadow as soon as the morning sun crests the mountains and colors the Soviet helicopter wreck with golden softness. They'll have only an hour or so before the sun climbs high and the light turns bright and harsh. Then, they'll have to work with the sun so it doesn't burn out their shots. This afternoon, I'll do the whole exercise in reverse. The second group of girls will start with the sun glaring directly overhead and finish with the indirect light of sunset. The second golden hour of the day.

I ride out to the meadow with Tariq, four girls piled in the back seat. The other seven are in the flatbed of Ikrom's pickup. It's not far to the meadow, but the road is pretty much nonexistent. Just two long ruts, deep and uneven because of the heavy run-off from the snowmelt.

"It used to be a road," says Tariq, driving slowly. "The Soviets built it back in the 1980s when they tried to establish a foothold here. But after Massoud's men shot down the helicopter, the road was left to ruin. Each winter leaves it a little worse." The Corolla bounces so hard through the ruts, my head clunks against the roof.

Another ten minutes, and we see the wreck. A few more minutes, and the light will be perfect. Impatience gnaws at me. "How about we leave the car and truck here and walk? I don't want to lose the light."

"The light?" says Tariq. "But, of course, you and the girls go on ahead, and we will follow."

The girls climb out of the car and the flatbed, and we all hurry toward the rusting remains. The sun inches higher, and the girls start to chatter.

"I see it, Ms. Green!" Bahar shouts. "The light! I see what you have been talking about. It is amazing! Everything has turned gold."

I gather the girls in front of the wreck, the snow-capped mountains rising craggy and steep behind, barely discernible trails for goats and other livestock crisscrossing their way up the rock-strewn face. The helicopter, once desert camo, is now faded to the palest grays and tans with patches of rust corroding the edges. The upper and rear rotors are gone, salvaged for use somewhere in the village, but the glass in the portholes and the cockpit is surprisingly intact.

"Do you all have your stories ready?"

Looking at each other, then at me, the girls nod excitedly.

"Do you know what message you want to convey, what you want your audience to feel when they look at your photographs?"

The girls smile, bouncing from one foot to the other.

"Remember: take as many shots as you want, but you can use only three to tell your story. Okay, start shooting!"

The girls scatter, too intent on making each image count to talk among themselves. I watch them scurry around the wrecked helicopter, setting up shots, taking turns, posing for each other, trying to be patient as other girls step in front of them and ruin a picture.

My pack slung over my shoulder, I train my camera lens on the girls. White headscarves flitting back and forth in front of the golden-washed helicopter—a great study in contrast. There is Bahar frozen in concentration, considering her shot. I press the shutter. More images of the girls, then I swing around and focus on Tariq and Ikrom, sitting in the back of the pickup, watching the action. I zoom in on Tariq, his cheekbones prominent, nose hooked, his smile contagious. But my smile fades quickly as the familiar sensation of being watched, no, *stalked,* takes over my body and the hair at the back of my neck stands achingly on end.

Goddamn. He's out there. Again. Watching us.

I look at my students. Eleven innocent girls. In the middle of the meadow. We're sitting ducks, all of us. I keep my fear in check and turn in a slow and casual circle, sweeping my camera a full 360 degrees, determined to seek him out, to stop this insanity.

I'm expecting a man to suddenly appear in front of my lens. A man with an index finger pointing upward to the heavens. His angry, passionate eyes will pierce my camera lens. I expect his glare will race through my eyes and down into my heart where he'll discover my terror. Then, what? He'll shoot me?

I've been expecting him to come. The entire time I've been here, I've known he would. He saw me at the Dalan Sang checkpoint.

It's got to be him. Then, he tracked me to Wad Qol. That was him following me home along the lonely road on the first day after school and again yesterday. He wants me dead. Because I'm American? Because I'm a woman? A photographer? Because I could recognize him? Probably all of the above. Will I hear the bullet?

What I'm not expecting on this golden-light-filled morning in this peaceful meadow is for the eastern sky to suddenly crack open. For black smoke to erupt from the center of Wad Qol, rising up, obscuring the newly risen sun. For the ground beneath my feet to tremble and shift off its axis. For my ears to fill with the blast of a bomb.

The girls freeze in place.

Tariq and Ikrom turn to stare in the direction of the village.

The distant popping sounds like fireworks. Except it's morning. Not the time for fireworks.

It's the time for gunfire.

I fix my eyes on the black smoke rising above the village, my camera resting against my chest, the lens focused on nothing.

Wad Qol.

The school.

Oh God, please tell me everyone has gotten out.

I have to get back. To the rest of my girls. To Seema. To Darya.

"Stay down!" I shout to eleven girls crouching in terror. And then, I start to run.

My boots pound along the ruts. Faster. Why can't I run faster? My lungs deflate like punctured balloons.

Tariq stops the car next to me. "Get in!"

The Corolla rockets over the ruts, my right hand a death grip on the door handle, my left clutching the bottom of the seat. The cold morning air rushes into the car, slapping against my face.

Ikrom will keep the girls safe in the meadow. An honorable man, he'll protect them with his life.

"Keep them safe. Keep them safe," I whisper, staring at the column of black smoke high above sleepy Wad Qol. Above the Wad Qol Secondary School for Girls.

36

THE SCHOOL IS BURNING OUT of control. The heavy, wooden, blue front door has turned black and splintered out of its frame. Tongues of fire lick at the doorjamb, obliterating all traces of girls' dusty footprints on the threshold. Windows have exploded, shards of glass littering the ground. Flames soar and crackle out of the roof. Orange and red, tinged with black. Plaster melts off the mud bricks. The heat is unbearable, pushing us back. Black smoke billows toward us, burning my eyes, urging me to turn away, but I can't. I keep scanning the school—back and forth across the front of the burning building—looking for the girls, the teachers. Anyone. But I see no one.

Oh, God, the sound. I've photographed way too many fires—the aftermath of suicide bombings and bombs dropped from thousands of feet overhead. My focus has always been on what I see through the lens. But now I know just how far my images have fallen short. It's the roar of the fire—so loud, deafening—that locks me in place, consumes me.

An explosion from somewhere deep inside the school staggers

me. What if they're still in there—alive? I start toward the building, but Tariq grabs my arm, wresting me back in place. I pull and lunge, but he doesn't let go.

Another explosion rocks us.

"Another bomb?" I'm ready to dive to the ground.

"No!" he yells. "Cans of kerosene. Fuel for the generator."

"Why the hell are we just standing here?" I scream at him. "We've got to do something!"

"There is nothing we can do," yells Tariq angrily, not letting go of my arm.

I keep staring at the front of the school, hoping to God I don't see any sign of life, any girl, any teacher trying to escape. The remains of a pickup, now a charred mangle of metal, stick out from what used to be my classroom. Another explosion, and flames shoot out the front door. The ferocious heat and billowing black smoke push us farther back. No one could have gotten out that way. But someone must have gotten out. Darya, Seema, the girls, the teachers. They can't all be trapped inside. Oh, God. Where are they? I wrap my arms around myself, struggling to keep my body from splintering apart. Villagers are running up the road to the school, desperate to find their daughters, their sisters, their wives.

"Who would do this!" I scream. "What kind of monster?"

"It is like at Dalan Sang," shouts Tariq, his eyes on the wreckage of the pickup. "He set the explosives, then ran."

I'm not so sure he ran away. I feel him close by, watching, maybe training the sights of his AK-47 on this mass of people. On us.

Finally, the wind shifts just a bit, the smoke rises into the sky, and I can make out the teachers huddled together on the far side of the building, near the walnut trees, their black headscarves and *burqas* pressed over their noses and mouths. A human screen. Girls slowly emerge from the grove. Crying, faces and white headscarves black with soot, they rush past the teachers, past Tariq and me, and into their parents' arms.

"He didn't kill them!" yells Tariq with relief. Like me, he's looking for Seema, who hasn't come running with the rest of the girls. Like me, he's looking at the teachers still standing close together. I can't see Darya.

That's when I know.

The sudden emptiness where my heart used to be tells me so.

Tariq lets go of my arm. He's sprinting toward the teachers, his black medical bag in hand.

No. No. No. I beg as I run behind him, my pack still slung over my shoulder, pounding against my hip with each step.

The teachers move aside. There she is, lying contorted in the bloodied dust. The familiar headscarf covering her face. Darya.

Unable to look away, I stare at the black scarf edged in finely embroidered gold filigree. "Pull off that scarf! She needs to breathe!" I scream above the roar of the fire.

Gulshan puts her hand on my shoulder. "No."

Tariq kneels next to Darya. His fingers probe her neck, searching for a pulse. Then, he reaches for her wrist, feeling for any beat of life.

Find it! Find her pulse!

Bowing his head, he lays her wrist gently next to her body, then lifts a corner of the scarf for the briefest moment before he lets it flutter back down.

Don't give up! Save her! She's got to live!

Gathering Darya in his arms, Tariq cradles her to his chest. Holds her. Rocks her. His lips move, whispering words for Darya alone. He holds her until first one hand, then the other slip lifeless from his arms to the dirt. He presses his lips to her headscarf, then returns her to the dust.

He looks to the teachers for answers. One after another, they tell us what happened.

"First, the truck came through the front windows. Then, the bomb exploded," says Gulshan. "It was so loud. Suddenly, the front of the school was on fire. I led the girls into the back hall and then out the side door. We carried the three who were sitting closest to the windows, the ones who couldn't walk."

The other teachers add details, one by one. "The girls ran into the woods to hide."

"Mrs. Faludi, she stayed behind to make sure everyone was out. She knew all the girls. Everyone by name. She counted."

"Finally, she came out. Three men, wearing black ski masks, they stood right there." Gulshan points to a spot ten feet away. "All three. Right there. Waiting for her."

"Mrs. Faludi, she looked at them. Then one man, he took off his mask. She recognized him, I am certain."

"She told them to leave Seema alone."

"And the man without the ski mask, he laughed and laughed."

"Guns, they pointed their guns at her and yelled, '*Amrikâyëy kâfir!*' They said only a *kâfir* makes a school for girls."

"She walked closer to the man without the mask. 'My daughter!' she yelled at him. 'You will not take my daughter.' But that did not make sense because Seema wasn't here. She was on the field trip."

"Then, she raised her hand. It looked like she was going to grab his gun, and he shot—"

"No," I say, choking on my words. "Seema wasn't with us. She wanted to be in the afternoon group. It was a last-minute change. She was at school this morning."

Tariq looks sharply at me, then back at the teachers. "Where is Seema now? Has anyone seen her? And where are the girls who are injured?"

Gulshan leads Tariq to the wounded girls. The other teachers run to the walnut grove and around the back of the school, searching for Seema. No one can remember seeing her this morning. But they didn't expect to because she had told all her teachers she'd be at the morning photo shoot. It wasn't until today that she asked to change to the afternoon. And I told Darya.

Slowly, the pieces fall into place. Last night, Darya and I were looking at the photo of Awalmir, the guy we figured must be the boyfriend. She said he seemed familiar. But she couldn't place him. Then this morning, thanks to that picture, when the militant took off his ski mask, she knew exactly who he was. Awalmir. By that time, she'd also realized that Seema wasn't at school. She'd counted. And come up one girl short. Seema.

I sink to my knees in the dust next to her, refusing to look anywhere but at the gold filigree twining along the edge of her scarf. I can't lift it. I can't look at her face. I don't want to know. But her hand. It's in the dirt next to my knee. Gently, carefully, I lift it off the ground and clasp it between both of mine. Slowly, her warmth is seeping out of her body. I sit. Holding her hand. Until everything else fades away. Until it's just the two of us. Time stops. Maybe I'm meant to stay here forever, until the rains come and turn the ground beneath us to a quicksand that will suck both of us down into its depths.

It is Allah's will. That is what the people here will say.

No! God had nothing to do with killing Darya.

I look up when a pickup truck cruises into the schoolyard. Then watch as Tariq and several men carry the injured girls out of the walnut grove, laying them carefully in the flatbed of the truck to go to the clinic.

A while later, another pickup pulls up. Several women climb out. Tariq greets them, but they all stand back from Darya and me, waiting. It takes me a minute to realize why they're here. To carry Dar away for the ritual washing and then to wrap her in a white shroud for the burial. Too soon. I tighten my hold on my best friend's hand.

Sometime after that, when the sun is a little higher, I hear the distant roar of helicopters. They're coming closer. Tiny grains of sand pelt me, but I don't move. I won't move. Not until Tariq asks me to help take her away.

I hear a familiar voice. "Hey, Annie."

Nic? Nic's here? Why? I don't respond, don't move, just keep watch over Darya.

"Annie." Nic kneels next to me. His hand hovers just above my arm. "They've looked everywhere around the school, but they can't find Seema. Dr. Ghafoor wants us to check the house to see if she's there."

Seema. Oh God, Seema. How the hell could I have forgotten about her? Please, God, let her be at the house. Don't let Awalmir have taken her. I lay Dar's hand gently on the ground and take one last look. The hand that reached for the gun. The hand that tried to save her daughter. Seema has to be at the house. She has to be. I can't let myself think anything else.

Nic helps pull me to my feet. Together, we turn away from Darya, from the smoldering school, and start down the dusty drive toward home.

That's when I see Piera McNeil, microphone in hand, and a cameraman, videocam on his shoulder, filming Tariq and the village women as they gather around Darya's body. The Piranha catches me looking and hurries over, the cameraman right behind her. "Annie!" Relief coats her words. "I'm so glad you're all right. I understand Mrs. Faludi was a friend of yours? She was an American citizen, right? What can you tell us about her?"

Pulling my scarf across my face, I turn to Nic. "I don't care what you have to do. Get her away from me and get that frigging camera off. Off me. Off Darya. Off Tariq."

"Clear out, Piera." Nic holds me against his chest, the nubby wool of his jacket chafing my cheek, and walks me toward the mulberry bushes that line the dusty driveway. He's doing his best to skirt the Al Shabakat television crew.

But Piera and the cameraman aren't giving up. They stand their ground, blocking our way to the main road. "Don't cut me out of this, Nic. Just because she's a friend of yours."

"I said *clear out*."

Piera keeps pace with us. "Annie, tell me about Mrs. Faludi. What do you want the world to know about your friend?"

"Get her the hell away from me!" I yell into Nic's chest, my words muffled by his jacket.

"She was the director of this school, right? Please, tell us about her. Did you see them kill her?"

I look toward her. "Leave me alone!"

"What about her daughter? Seema, right? Where is she? Was she killed in the fire?"

"Get. Away. From. Me!"

The cameraman moves closer. Piera takes a small step back, probably to let him zoom in on me. Then her voice turns harsh and cutting. "Annie, can you tell me why both times there's been a truck bombing in the last two weeks, *you've* been front and center?"

What the hell? I palm my hand in the air in front of the camera. Probably not a good move. Probably makes me look guilty of something I don't even want to think about.

"Tell me." She closes the gap between us, sticking the mic in my face. "Why is a photographer purportedly working for TNN always *right* in the middle of the action?"

Fuck. I've got to get away from them. I've got to find Seema. Without Piera following me, without the cameraman filming Seema. Which means I'll do whatever I have to. I pull away from Nic and dig into my pack. My fingers close around the Sig. I think the safety is on, but I'm not sure I even care. Whipping it out of my pack, I turn, and then I've got a bead on the Piranha. "Try me," I say, two-handing the Sig.

The cameraman backs away, still filming.

Piera takes a step closer. Her microphone's an inch from my face, and she's smiling. Not exactly the reaction I was going for. "That's a Sig, isn't it? Weapon of choice for highly classified operatives. Maybe the guards at the InterContinental had it right all along."

"In case you haven't noticed, we're in the middle of a frigging *war*." My index finger rests on the trigger.

Her eyes lock on mine. "Who are you working for, Annie? CIA? Or does this whole thing go deeper than that?" She glances briefly over her shoulder and calls, "Keep filming."

"Got it." This, from the cameraman.

37

AS SOON AS I UNLOCK the front door, the cold emptiness of the house sucks me inside. I run to Seema's bedroom. The door is open. "Not here!" I call behind me to Nic.

He stands in the doorway, watching me turn in place looking for anything that can tell me where she is. The room is neat as always. For the first time, I notice that the walls are a pale pink. Princess Seema. I wonder why I didn't see that until just now. I turn to look at her desk. The photographs that were here yesterday are gone. Her schoolbooks are stacked in perfect order, edges lined up. I riffle through them. There's nothing hidden between the pages. I cross to the dresser and open the top drawer. A handful of underwear has clearly been scooped from the piles. The second drawer. The third. It's hard to know what's missing. In the fourth drawer, I find a mass of periwinkle cloth. The *burqa* that was on her desk this morning.

For some reason I'll never understand, I pull the *burqa* out of the drawer. Then sit on the bed with it draped over my lap. Why leave this? Unless she had another? I hold it up. Large, like mine. Way too large for Seema. And it's dirty. Mud, dry now, splattered around the hem. Snags running through the cloth. My stomach clenches hard as I remember the periwinkle *burqa* I saw at Dalan Sang. Running away. I quickly check the coarse fabric, searching for the telltale rip that will let me know who last wore this.

And there it is. I stare at the torn cloth, desperate for it not to be in Seema's room, for it to be whole.

I search the drawers again, more carefully, looking for the boy's *landays*. His photograph. But then realize that Seema would have taken them with her. There must be something she left behind, something that will tell me where she is, what to do next. I come up empty.

Afghan-American Girl Radicalizes?

No! This isn't politics for Seema. She loves this guy. So, what the hell does it all mean? She went willingly?

I turn again. Speak to me, room!

Her backpack. The Canon Rebel. Neither is here. That stops me. Why would she take the camera? It's hard to believe photography is high on a militant's list of acceptable activities for a young wife. *Wife?* Seema is certainly in love. But just because *she* is, doesn't guarantee *he* is. Could she really have wanted to go with him? Does she know what he did?

"Annie?" Nic, from across the hall. "I think you better see this."

"What now?" I hurry to my room, which is completely and utterly trashed. Everything I didn't have with me in my pack has been dumped on the floor. My clothes—everything I'm not wearing—slashed. The dresser drawers—smashed and piled on top. Of all things, my periwinkle *burqa* is untouched.

I stare at the ruin. "No. Seema wouldn't do this." My hand touches my cheek where she kissed me this morning. It seemed sweet at the time, impulsive. But now, it's clear she was saying goodbye. She knew what was going to happen?

"Oh, Annie!" Tariq is standing behind Nic, his face drawn and gray. He looks old, so much older than he did just this morning when he sat in the back of the pickup and smiled at the girls running around the meadow snapping photos.

It is too much for this man. He shouldn't have to see this. "Tariq, let me make you some *chai*. I'll take care of this later."

He holds up his hand. "*Chai* will not bring Darya back. It will not help us find Seema. *Chai* is for later. When we mourn. Now, we have to assess what has happened here. What did they take?"

How can he be so strong? I do a quick inventory, talking as I work. "My camera gear's in my pack. So is my passport and my registration card. The rest of the gear and the laptop are at the sch—" Tears fill my eyes. I hold up my savaged *Take Back the Night* T-shirt, shrug, and drop it back on the pile.

"Did you see this?" Nic kneels and points to some splintered and singed wood sticking out from under my ruined clothes. "It looks like someone wanted to start a fire."

Tariq steps over to the pile and picks up a piece of wood. He runs a finger along the charred edge, then with a single, loud groan, snaps it in two.

"We're lucky it didn't catch." I squat next to Nic and poke at a few bits of cheap, lined notebook paper that haven't burned completely. I know that paper. The *landays* from Awalmir. So, she didn't take them after all. That doesn't feel right.

"What are those?" Tariq asks.

For a split second, my thoughts go to the romantic *landay* that passed back and forth between Darya and Tariq so many years ago. "Love notes. The ones Awalmir wrote to Seema. Or, at least what's left of them."

"Seems queer for a girl to leave love notes behind," says Nic.

Unless she didn't know. Unless Awalmir was making a statement. "Damn! If we'd only done something sooner. We shouldn't have waited for the workshop to end. We should've put Seema on a plane to California days ago. I should have taken her."

Tariq sinks onto the bed. "Annie, you will listen to me. Please. I cannot bear for you to think this is your fault. It is not. Seema's unhappiness, her anger, they have obviously been building for a long time. Darya and I were blind to what has been right in front of our eyes. We thought we could wait a few more days. We were wrong, horribly wrong."

"But I—"

Tariq shakes his head. "You saw the truth. But we didn't want to believe the danger was so imminent."

"Tariq—"

Nic puts his arm across my shoulders, pulls me close, and whispers, "Now isn't the time, old thing. Let it go."

I stare sorrowfully, angrily at the charred *landays*. Oh, Dar! How could you let this happen? You always knew what was going on. You always figured out how to solve problems. Always. And the one time that was most important, the one time you had the most to lose—why couldn't you figure out what was going on with Seema? Before it was too fucking late.

Nic puts his hand on the middle of my back. "What do you think that's about?" He points to the window.

I look up sharply. A sheet of blue stationery folded several times is sticking out from between the latched windows, clearly intended to catch my attention. I push myself to my feet and take two steps to the windows. Then, holding my breath, I unfold the paper to reveal a *landay* in Seema's flowery cursive, written in English. To make sure I understand?

I am in love. I will not lie.
Cut out my tongue with a knife. My heart is safe.

"No. I don't believe it." The Seema I knew couldn't possibly have written this. Good God, she kissed me goodbye this morning.

Tariq holds out his hand for the *landay*. After reading it, he looks first at me, then at Nic. "Could my daughter have written this? It does not seem possible. You told us she loved this boy, but there is no love here."

"Perhaps," says Nic, "she was coerced?" He turns toward me. "We might want to finish up here and decide on our next steps."

I stare at the blue note in Tariq's hand. "I can't believe she wrote that."

"I, too, find it hard to believe. But perhaps none of us know what is in her heart now. I thought I knew my daughter, but—" Tariq pushes himself wearily up from the bed. "I should check my study and see what has happened there." His feet scuff against the tiles as he trudges up the hall.

"Is there something they wanted here?" asks Nic. "Or is all this just lashing out?"

"Because I didn't help Seema run away with this guy like she hoped I would?" I scan the disaster that used to be my bedroom, stopping at the gaping dresser.

"My money," I say aloud. Then, a quick check under the bed reveals another item missing. "And my duffel."

"The money hurts, I'm sure. But the duffel?" says Nic with a shrug.

"This one said USMC."

"And?"

"That could make for one nasty package bomb."

"Bloody hell."

"Bloody hell is right."

TARIQ'S STUDY IS AS bad as my room. No, worse. Books cleared from the shelves, bindings broken and pages ripped, all dumped in the middle of the room. Nic sifts through a few on top that are nothing but ashes. Luckily the fire didn't catch here either.

Tariq sits at his desk, amazingly composed. "They were able to get in the safe. All the money is gone, as is Seema's passport. And Darya's. And mine."

"Tariq, I—" My voice cracks.

He lifts his hands. "This is my doing. I knew Seema did not want to come to Afghanistan. Darya was so sure this would be good for all of us. But to put a young girl into such a place where we knew something like this could happen."

"No, Tariq. I don't believe Seema did this because you moved here eight years ago. She could just as easily have fallen for a guy like Awalmir if you'd stayed in Boston."

Tariq sighs wearily. "I do not know what to do next. Where to look for her."

"Did Seema have any friends here? Any girls she was especially close to?" Nic asks. "Maybe one of them knows something."

I take a mental roll call of the senior girls in my workshop. Seema didn't hang out with any of them. Not anymore. Although both Bahar and Wiin were clearly covering for her.

"She is best friends with Bahar," says Tariq. "You remember, her father, Ikrom, drove some of the girls this morning."

Best friends with Bahar? I don't correct him.

38

"OF COURSE, YOU MUST SPEAK to Bahar," says Ikrom when Tariq explains what has happened, why the three of us have come. "She and Seema used to be good friends."

I register Tariq's surprise at this news.

"But first, we will have *chai*."

"No," says Tariq, his face haggard and drawn. "We need to talk to Bahar."

"My friend, before talking, you need *chai*. It will help you understand what Bahar has to say."

A few minutes later, Gulshan, a black *hijab* covering her hair, eyes red and swollen, appears in the doorway of the lounge carrying a tray with four cups of steaming tea that she places on a low table near the men. I start to sit near the men, but she shakes her head, pointing me to one of the floor cushions at the other end of the room. She brings me one of the cups of tea, then heads toward the back of the house.

I inhale the aroma, let the steaming liquid warm me. Ikrom was right. Tariq needs *chai*. We all do.

When Gulshan returns, she doesn't come all the way into the room. Behind her, Bahar lurks shyly, pulling her white headscarf halfway across her face. I try to catch her eye, but she looks to her father.

"Bahar," I say, beckoning to her, "come, sit with me. Please. We need to find Seema. I hope you can help."

Bahar crosses the room slowly, reluctantly, and sits on a cushion next to me. "Please do not be angry with me, Ms. Green," she says softly, leaning close. "But Seema . . . you see, we used to be the best of friends. She told me things in confidence. I promised not to tell."

I know exactly how she feels. I also know there's no point in asking Bahar why she lied about studying with Seema over the past two weeks. What's done is done. "Bahar, Seema's life may be in danger. Please, tell us whatever you know."

She looks warily at her mother, who nods. "Seema changed a few months ago. You see, one day after school, a group of us senior girls went to the market in the village. We like to do that sometimes, to buy sweets. Only that day, Seema said she didn't have any money to pay. She was going to put back the sweets, but then suddenly there was this man and he paid for her." She looks toward her father, who has a serious look crossing his face. "But he didn't pay for the rest of us."

"Could you tell me about him, Bahar? What was he like?"

"He told us his name was Awalmir, and he was very handsome. We all thought so. He had dark hair and a curl that flopped onto his forehead. Also, he had the most wonderful brown eyes. And his smile . . . But he only wanted to talk to Seema. He was so romantic. He told Seema he'd been looking for her his entire life, that Allah had brought them together." Bahar's voice is full of despair, as if she wishes she'd told someone sooner.

"The day we all went to the village center for our first photo shoot, did you happen to notice if he was there?"

Bahar cups her chin in the palm of her hand, clearly concentrating on that afternoon nearly two weeks ago. "Yes. I am sure he was there," she says finally. "He was standing off to the side of one of the shops. He looked very angry. He wasn't even smiling at Seema."

My shoulders sag. Even though I've pretty much pieced this part of the puzzle together, hearing Bahar confirm my assumptions is painful. But there it is. Awalmir is the older boy. The one in the picture I saw on Seema's desk. The image I copied for Darya. The boyfriend. And also the militant who killed Darya, who destroyed the school. Struggling not to cry, to keep my voice calm, I ask, "What else can you tell me about him?"

Bahar thinks for a moment. "He is much older than us. Maybe twenty-five. Or even older."

Darya said he looked older, too old to be in school. But damn! Twenty-five puts a very different spin on things.

"I don't think he is from Wad Qol or even from the valley," says Bahar, sounding more certain that she's right to reveal Seema's secrets. "None of us ever saw him before. Seema liked that he was a stranger. Someone her parents did not know."

"How do you know that?" Tariq sounds angry. Of course, he does.

Bahar shrinks against me. "Seema told me," she says for my ears only.

I put my arm around her shoulders. "You're doing fine."

"Do you know where he is from?" asks Tariq, struggling to control his voice. "From Kabul maybe?"

Bahar thinks for a moment, then shakes her head. "No, I do not think so."

"Why?" I ask.

"There is something different about the way he talks. He speaks Dari, but he makes a lot of mistakes. I am thinking he is Pashtun." She tilts her head to the side to consider what she just said. "Yes! That day we first met him, he said he was from a village near Kandahar and that he worked for his uncle." Pashtun—that fits with what both Darya and Cerelli said about his name.

"Was he planning to go back there?" I ask.

"Was Seema thinking to go with him?" asks Tariq at the same time.

Bahar looks back and forth between the two of us. "Maybe. But she never said." She shakes her head. "She was always telling us how much she loved him. And she was certain he loved her, too."

"Yes," I whisper for her ears only. "She told me the same thing."

"At first, all of us girls thought it was wonderful. He was so handsome and friendly. And *so* romantic. He was always looking at her with these dreamy eyes. We were so happy for Seema."

I'm betting they were envious, too. "Did something happen to change your mind?"

She nods. "Seema changed a lot. All of a sudden, she wanted to wear the *burqa*. Then she stopped studying. She said she wanted to marry Awalmir instead of going to college. She even said girls don't need an education." Bahar shakes her head. "And that just didn't sound like Seema."

"No, it doesn't." I glance over at Tariq. He's staring at his hands clasped tightly in his lap, struggling to come to terms with this new side of his daughter. On either side of him, Ikrom and Nic look faintly shell-shocked.

"There is something else," says Bahar, picking nervously at the hem of her tunic. "A few weeks after we first met him, he started to change, too."

"What do you mean?"

"He would look at us in this scary way, like he disapproved of us. And a few times, when Seema wasn't looking, I saw his eyes turn hard and mean when he looked at her, too, like he didn't really love her. Then, when she'd look at him again, he'd get all romantic. I started to think that maybe he didn't really love her, that he was faking it. I thought maybe he was only trying to . . ." She looks at me, trying to find the right word.

"To seduce her?"

"Yes."

Tariq and I exchange glances. Why Seema? Of all the girls in the Panjshir Valley, why seduce seventeen-year-old Seema? He clearly picked her out from the group of senior girls in the market. Could he actually be in love with her? She's beautiful, of course—she looks just like Darya. Or, did he somehow figure out she's American? Was the plan to kidnap her and hold her for ransom? One of the Taliban's favorite ways to raise money. Is her rich American father supposed to buy her back? Oh God, if that's the case, wait until these guys find out that Tariq is far from wealthy, that he's put everything he ever earned into the girls' school and the Wad Qol clinic.

"I tried to talk to her. I warned her not to trust him." I can hear the sadness in Bahar's voice. "But that only made her angry. And then, we stopped being friends."

"I wondered about that." I squeeze her shoulder, my heart aching that I didn't push Seema harder about her boyfriend.

"There's something else." Bahar sits up straight and turns toward the men, as if she wants to make sure they can hear her. "He didn't want to meet Seema's mother, or you, Dr. Ghafoor. And that was not right. All the girls said that. But Seema made excuses. She said he was embarrassed about his Dari and his poor English. Then, one time, I saw him in the market. Mrs. Faludi was there shopping. He walked right up to her and spit on the ground. *Amrikâyëy kâfir!* That is what he said. Then he took off one of his shoes and threw it at her." Bahar looks stricken. "How could someone insult Mrs. Faludi in such a way?"

From the corner of my eye, I see Tariq turn ashen.

So, that's where Dar first saw him. The village center. That's why he looked familiar. And that's where I first saw him, too. No. Wait. It's not. I saw him before that afternoon of the photo shoot in the village center. I know I did. But where? I sift back through my days in Afghanistan. Kabul. Dalan Sang. And I stop. Could he have been the man in the picture I took at the Dalan Sang checkpoint? Was it Awalmir who was staring at me before he detonated the bomb? Was he the man in the periwinkle *burqa?* I struggle to conjure up the image. Something's not quite right. That man had a beard, and Awalmir didn't. But, he could have shaved.

"Is there anything else you remember?" I ask.

Bahar starts to shake her head. "No—yes, there is something. Right before you came to Wad Qol, Ms. Green, Seema told me that this man wanted to meet you. She was excited for you to come because she was certain you would help them be together."

I nod wearily. Seema saw me as the person who would help her get around her parents. Clearly, she told Awalmir. But why on earth would Awalmir have wanted to meet me? He probably didn't. He just wanted Seema. And Darya.

"Seema also said something about a captain," says Bahar. She pauses for a moment, trying to make sense of what she's remembering, but finally shakes her head. "I did not really understand what she meant."

"Did she say Captain Cerelli?" Tariq's voice sounds hollow. I can see the devastation eating away at him. His face turning even grayer. His body curling in on itself.

The tears that have been welling finally spill over and run down Bahar's cheeks. "I-I don't remember."

"Enough!" Gulshan's voice stops us all. "That is enough for tonight." She crosses the room and gathers her daughter into her arms, whispers something to her, and leads her out of the room.

Ikrom pushes himself to his feet and takes charge. "Go home, Tariq, my friend. Please, I beg of you, do not try to do this on your own. We cannot have more death. Not tonight. Not tomorrow. Let me talk to Ahmad Zia Massoud. He will know what to do."

39

WE JUST GET BACK TO the house when Nasrat Parsa's music blares out of my backpack. Standing at the front door in the falling light of dusk, Nic and Tariq stare quizzically at me.

"My sat phone."

"I remember Seema listening to that music." Tariq unlocks the door.

I push past them into the front room and dump my pack on the couch, hoping to get to the phone before Cerelli gives up.

"Annie?" Definitely not Cerelli. This voice is loud and annoyed and female. Catherine Elizabeth. Why the hell is she calling *now*? Has she already seen the Piranha's story on TNN? Did the cameraman get usable footage of me pulling the Sig? I can just imagine the headlines. I can also imagine C.E. refusing to let Mel see her lunatic mother anymore. I sink onto the low sofa in the front room. *Stay focused*, I tell myself, *and be as pleasant as possible*. And above all, keep it short. I need to get through to Cerelli.

"Catherine Elizabeth." I don't sound pleasant.

"Well, hello to you, too."

"Is there something wrong? Is Mel all right?"

"I'll say there's something wrong. Your *delightful* daughter shaved her head last night."

"What did you say?"

"I said she's bald! Completely bald!"

"Let me talk to Todd—"

"Do you have any idea how humiliating this is for me? And let me tell you, if she thinks she's going to perform in her recital or audition for that dance class at UWM, she's got another thing coming. I don't care how prestigious that program is, she's grounded until her hair grows back. Which means from now until school starts in September."

"Let. Me. Talk. To. Todd." *Hurry up!* I want to yell. I've got to call Cerelli.

Seven thousand miles away, Catherine Elizabeth continues to rage. "Todd, she insists on talking to you, and you better back me up on this. You know as well as I do, if she ever bothered to spend time with Emmy, we wouldn't have these problems."

I close my eyes, but her words burrow deep into my already flayed heart.

Finally, Todd is on the line. "Annie, look, Emmy really did it this time." He sounds exhausted. I imagine him trying to run interference between his wife and our daughter. "Why in God's name did you give her permission to do this?"

I open my eyes. "What are you talking about?"

"She came home with a buzz cut after school, saying you told her to go *bold*."

Well, that'll teach me. "She's right. That's what I said. I told Mel to go bold because she hated, *hated* the caca-shit hair color Catherine Elizabeth forced on her. Purple hair, teal hair, fuchsia hair, whatever fucking color she wants her hair to be is who she is. Mel is a free spirit. Don't you dare try to kill that." I take a breath. "So, I suggest Catherine Elizabeth do herself a favor and get used to it."

"Look, Annie—"

"No, Todd. You look. Mel *will* perform in her recital. And she has an audition coming up for that UWM dance program."

"I know, but—" I can almost see him shrug. "Catherine Elizabeth has grounded her, and I'm backing her up on this."

"Really. Do you have any idea what that dance program means to her? Our daughter is going to that audition, buzz cut or not. And if she wins a place, she's taking it."

"No—"

"Yes. My rules, Todd. If you don't like them, talk to my lawyer. Oh, and why the hell can't you and C.E. call her 'Mel'? Is that asking too much?" And I power off. A second later, I realize that I didn't tell him about Darya. I should have. She was his friend, too. Then, just as quickly, I know I couldn't have. Not now. Not when Catherine Elizabeth is going berserk over Mel's hair.

Almost immediately, Nasrat Parsa starts singing again. No, I am not up to dealing with hair anymore. Not today. I let the music play and head to the kitchen. It stops. Eventually.

And is replaced by the sound of sobbing. Stopping in the doorway, I see Nic holding Tariq, his big hands rubbing Tariq's back. I step slowly, quietly out of the room, thankful Tariq feels free to cry, grateful Nic is there for him with his strong arms and nubby jacket. Back in the front room, I wander aimlessly, unable to sit, wishing someone would hold me and let my tears soak his jacket.

There's no time now to cry, Darya's voice sounds in my head. *You must find my daughter.*

Ten minutes later, the Afghan music starts up again. I grab the phone, ready to tell Todd or Catherine Elizabeth or even Mel that I'm done with the hair drama.

"Annie?"

"Cerelli? Thank God."

"You're all right?"

I lose it. I hear Tariq weeping and Nic's soft murmur. I smell the lingering aroma of last night's *ashak* dinner wafting in from the kitchen and the acrid odor of burnt paper from my room and Tariq's study. I can't hold the tears inside me anymore, no matter what Darya says.

"Annie?"

I sink onto the sofa and pull my knees against my chest. One hand still clutching the phone, I hold the other over my mouth to catch the gut-wrenching sobs. I lean back against the painted plaster wall, the cold creeping through my tunic, through my skin, searching until it finds my bones. There it burrows deep and fast. I wrap my arms around my knees and hug tight. But nothing helps. Nothing matters anymore.

"Annie," Cerelli says softly, "my God, there are no words. There's nothing I can say."

"Cerelli—" I just manage to say his name, and then I'm sobbing again.

"Listen to me, sweetheart. Carefully. You've got to put off crying until later. Right now, I need you to talk to me."

I try. I really try to stop crying. To stop trembling. To start thinking.

"Cerelli—"

"I'm wheels up to Kabul as we speak. Sawyer and I should be with you by early tomorrow morning. Pack your stuff and be ready to go."

"No."

"Annie, this isn't negotiable. I've got tangos out there. We've finally, goddamn *finally*, picked up some chatter, and I want you out of there yesterday."

I pull off my headscarf and wipe my face. But more tears flood silently down my cheeks. "Cerelli, I can't go. They've got Seema."

"They what?" Cerelli's voice is deadly quiet.

"We think," my diaphragm spasms, and I struggle to push out the words, "they took Seema. Or maybe she wanted to go. We don't know."

"What *do* you know?"

"That guy? Awalmir? She says she loves him and swears he loves her. From what the teachers told us, I'm certain he was one of the militants who blew up—" And I'm crying again.

"Do you know anything else about him?"

I try hard to stop my tears, but they keep on coming. "I don't have a family name. Maybe he doesn't have one. I got a picture of him. I could—"

"The one you gave Darya last night. I've got that. What else?"

"Darya sent you—" I can't even begin to sort through this piece of information.

"I'll explain another time. What else do you know?"

I try to sift through what we learned from Bahar, but what Cerelli just said about Dar has thrown me off-balance. "Seema's friend thinks he's Pashtun—maybe twenty-five—and that he works for his uncle in a village near Kandahar. That's about it. No, wait. That periwinkle *burqa* from Dalan Sang."

"What?" His voice is stone-cold—all business.

"I found it in Seema's room."

"What makes you so sure it's the *burqa* from Dalan Sang?"

"It's big enough to fit a man, it's dirty and snagged and torn. Damn it, I just *know* it's the same one."

"Show me when I get there. They take anything important, besides Seema?"

I know he's asking about the Sig. "I've still got the gun, but they took all the money in the house, my USMC duffel, and Seema's passport. Tariq's and Darya's, too."

"Goddamn, this is a total clusterfuck." He sighs. "Look, I'll see what I can pick up on Seema. But I'm not putting you in danger. And I know damn well Darya and Tariq would back me up on this."

"Cerelli—" But he's right. That's exactly what they'd say. Not that I'm going to tell him that. And not that I agree. We'll discuss it when he gets here.

"Yeah?" His voice is military-officer brusque, waiting for me to argue.

"Stay safe."

"Will do. *You* stay in the house. Don't let anyone—and I mean *anyone*—in. You're there with Tariq?"

"And Nic Lowe."

"Shit!"

"He's helping, Cerelli. He's here as a friend."

"Yeah, right. This'll be all over the cable networks before I get to Bagram."

"There's more." I hesitate. "There may be footage of me pulling the Sig on Piera McNeil from Al Shabakat."

"You have any other fucking joy to lay on me?"

"No."

"Twelve hours, Annie. Don't do anything until I get there."

TARIQ FINALLY, BLESSEDLY, falls into a restless sleep in my bed. He couldn't bring himself to be in the room he shared with Darya. And Seema's room was off-limits, too, for obvious reasons. It's after midnight, but Nic and I are still awake, sitting in the kitchen, elbows perched on the old wooden table. Waiting. For what, I'm not sure. Cerelli and Sawyer won't be here for another few hours. But, thank God, I've got Nic. I lift my arms off the table and try to massage some feeling back into my deadened limbs.

"Cold?" Nic sounds exhausted, but he's clearly not going anywhere.

I shake my head. "Numb." I rub harder. "Like the rest of me."

But I *am* cold, colder than I've ever been. As I well know, the nights here can get frigid, even in late spring, but this is the kind of cold that warm clothes, blankets, and *chai* can't help. Nothing can.

Nic takes off his sports jacket and drapes it over my shoulders. "I don't think this will do all that much good, but it's a start." He leaves his hands on the jacket shoulders, weighing them down. His touch helps more than the jacket.

"You're a good guy, Nic. Thanks."

He sits down and pulls up the time on his phone. "Hate to say it, old thing, but I'm done in. Maybe we should try for some sleep. You take the sofa. I'll spread some blankets on the floor."

Neither of us mentions the other two empty beds in the house.

"You take the sofa." I pull the Sig out from my pack, make sure the safety's on, and put it on the table. "Someone should stay awake."

Nic's eyes widen. "I assume that's real?"

"It is."

"I wasn't sure. Earlier. You know, with Piera."

I look at him, wordless, waiting for what he's going to say next. Disapproval. Censure for having pointed a gun at a colleague.

But he surprises me. "You know how to shoot that thing?"

"I do. Word is I'm pretty good."

"You've used it before?"

I shake my head. "Only for target practice."

"They tell me target practice is one thing, but actually shooting to kill is an entirely different matter."

"They're probably right."

"You think you could do it?"

I put my hands on the table, palms down, fingers splayed. These hands have cradled my newborn daughter, gathered a dying Malalai to my breast, and held Darya's hand until it grew cold. These hands have captured thousands of images. These hands are so in sync with my eyes that they tell me when I've gotten something really good. Could these hands kill a human being? "Before Afghanistan, I would've said *no*. Now? I don't know."

I HAVE TO CALL MY DAUGHTER. I've got to hear her voice, know that she's safe. And I've got to tell her what happened to Darya. Thanks to the satellite hovering in the heavens, the call goes right through.

"Mommy?" Mel is packing a lot of tears into that one word. "Are you okay?"

I blink back my own tears, which aren't going to help Mel. "I'm—wait! How do you know?"

"It's on TV." She chokes out the words. "Oh, Mom. This is so horrible. I can't believe they killed Auntie Dar. They just— oh, God—this is the worst thing that's ever happened. And you couldn't save her?"

No, I couldn't save my best friend. My heart clenches until my chest hurts. "I wasn't there when it happened. I got there right after."

"But that's not what the reporter is saying."

"Which reporter?"

"That Piera woman."

Piera. Damn it all. I wait a few seconds to stop seething. "What's she saying?"

"That you tried to stop the militants from blowing up the school and killing Auntie Dar and some of the students. They're showing you leaning against some guy. He looks like he's holding you up. Is that Captain Cerelli?"

So, Al Shabakat cut the scenes of me pulling the gun. Thank God. Not one of my finer moments. But why the hell did Piera make up that story?

"Mom? You still there? Was that your Captain?"

"Sorry." I sit up, bracing my elbows against the table. "Cerelli? No, that was Nic."

"Nic, huh?"

I know that tone of voice. "It's not what you think. Nic's a friend. Besides, he's gay."

"Oh. Well, that's good. So, you were able to save Seema? Right? And Uncle Tariq?"

I take my time. What in God's name can I possibly tell my daughter? That for all my running around with a gun, I didn't save anyone. That I don't have a clue where Seema is. That she may have been kidnapped. Or, oh God, that she may actually have run away with the militants who killed her mother and destroyed the school.

"Mom?" Her voice pulls me back to the present. "What aren't you telling me? Has something happened to Seema?"

I make a split-second decision. "Uncle Tariq is fine. He's sleeping in the other room right now. But . . . we think . . . we think the militants may have . . . taken Seema."

"They took *Seema*? As in *kidnapped*?"

"We think so."

"Oh my God, Mom!" She chokes on her sobs. "Will-will you be able to find her?"

"I hope so. Captain Cerelli should be here in another few hours, and then we're going to try." Which isn't exactly true. Not if Cerelli has anything to do with it.

"You've got to find her, Mom. You've got to kick ass and get her back."

"We'll do what we can, sweetie."

"Then you're coming home. Right? Please?"

My heart skips a beat. It's the first time she's ever asked me to come home.

"Soon. Very soon. I promise." A cold chill runs up my back as I end the call, making me wonder if that was a promise I should have made.

IT'S NEARLY OH-SEVEN-HUNDRED when the rumble of a pickup truck pulls me out of my restless sleep. I lift my head off the kitchen table and ease over to the window but can't see a thing. A minute later, a muffled knock on the front door. Moving soundlessly out of the kitchen and through the dark lounge, the Sig down by my side, I hear voices. A lot of voices. Cerelli said he'd be coming with Sawyer. He didn't say anything about other people.

"Annie? Tariq?"

Nic is up now and by the window. He shakes his head. "There's a bloody lot of men out there."

I trust Cerelli with my life. Sawyer, too. But what if the Taliban or ISIS have overpowered them, have guns to their heads?

"Annie? It's safe. Let me in."

"Who are all those guys out there with you?"

"Ahmad Zia Massoud's men. Friends. They've been standing guard around the house and the village since last night."

Standing guard? Damn! We've needed armed guards?

Tariq emerges from the hallway and peers out the window. "It is all right," he says. "Massoud's men are all right. I have dug out a lot of bullets and set a lot of bones for these men." He unlocks the door and welcomes each man with a bear hug.

In short order, the front room is teeming with the smell of sweat, unwashed clothes, and testosterone—Afghan men in baggy pants, collarless tunics, heavy vests, and *pakols* with such thick rolls around the edge, they look like cloth helmets. They're armed with handguns and AK-47s. Sawyer's there, too, dressed like one of Massoud's men. With his longer hair and beard, he fits right in. Cerelli, though, in his blue jeans and leather jacket, stands out. His hair is maybe a little shaggier than the last time I saw him, and he's sporting a couple days of stubble. But everything about him screams U.S. military.

Cerelli motions me to the kitchen. As the door closes behind us, he wraps his arms around me. "You're okay," he whispers against my hair.

I hold on tight. "I'm okay," I whisper back. "Now."

Then, Sawyer joins us. "We would've been here sooner, but we got lucky. We picked up a lot of chatter. From what we can pinpoint, they've got people all over the valley. I'm guessing fifty, at least. The tangos who've got Seema are *tweeting* about it. Which let us get a GPS fix on them. Hard to tell if they're bragging or setting a trap to draw us out."

I'm confused. "But the teachers at the school said there were just three of them."

Cerelli shakes his head. "Maybe at the school. But they're part of a much larger group that's coming together." He lowers his voice. "So, here's what we don't know. Is Seema a hostage or one of them?"

"I wish I could tell you."

Sawyer speaks up. "The Captain said this guy's name is Awalmir, probably from near Kandahar."

I nod.

"I'll be honest with you." Sawyer sounds discouraged. "The only Awalmir we're coming up with is a pretty bad dude. Originally Taliban, he could be ISIS now. Along with his cousin—an even scarier guy—and some other clan members."

"Oh, God. Seema never said anything about the Taliban or ISIS. But she's certainly convinced he's going to marry her." I pull the *burqa* I found in her room off one of the chairs and spread it out on the table.

"This what I think it is?" Cerelli reaches for it.

"I'm afraid so." I point out the snags and the tear. "And this is the *landay* she left in my room."

Sawyer takes the paper from my hand and reads out loud, "Cut out my tongue with a knife."

Hearing the words again makes my blood run cold. "But the

girl who wrote this isn't the Seema I've known all her life. Seriously, he must have brainwashed her."

Sawyer gives Cerelli a sidelong glance.

"Brainwashed is a possibility," says Cerelli. "I agree with you that Seema always seemed like a good kid. But this sure makes it sound like she's one of them. Although she may end up as the battle prize for some other lucky fighter."

I close my eyes. Tight. Oh, Seema. What kind of living hell have you gotten yourself into? "So, what do we do?" I look at Cerelli, silently pleading with him to work one of his miracles and get Seema back.

"We've got Massoud's men," he says, "and they want these guys for the Dalan Sang bombing. You don't kill a member of the Massoud family and walk away. Plus," he nods at Tariq, who's come to stand in the doorway, "they won't let your wife's death go unanswered. They know these mountains like nobody else. We'll do what we can to find them. And Seema."

40

"YOU ARE *NOT* GOING WITH us to get Seema back." Cerelli has me backed against the kitchen wall, his hands on my shoulders.

We're alone for now. Massoud's men have cleared out of the house and gone back to their guard duty. Sawyer and Nic are helping Tariq figure out what's missing and what can be salvaged.

"Don't tell me what I can and can't do." I lift my chin just enough to lock eyes with Cerelli's. "This is something I have to do. I owe it to Seema. But more important, I owe it to Dar."

"Annie, don't give me a hard time." The muscle at the corner of his eye is pulsing like crazy. "There's no telling what we'll run into, and I won't put your life in danger. You know damn well Darya wouldn't want that. She'd kill me if I let you go."

I take a couple deep breaths to bring my pounding heart under control. It's not working. He's right, and I know it. To get Seema back, Cerelli and Sawyer and Massoud's men will have to deal with the Taliban or ISIS. God only knows what will happen. I may be a *war photographer*, meaning I've seen my share of battles, but this is a spec op. Not a photo op.

"Annie?" He says my name softly, firmly. "I'm driving you to Bagram and putting you on the first plane CONUS."

"Then what?"

"Then, I'll double back to meet up with Sawyer and Massoud's men."

"So, why bother driving me? Why don't you just call in a helicopter to take me to Bagram?" I stare into the depths of his eyes, but I honestly can't understand what I'm seeing. Sometimes, it just too hard to read this man.

"Not an option."

"Right." I push my way past his restraining arm and out of the kitchen, then head down the hall to my trashed bedroom.

Damn, he's right. I have no business being part of this operation. And if I'm really honest with myself, there's nothing I can do to help. Nothing. The last thing they want or need is a photographer along for the ride, getting in the way. But knowing that doesn't make it any easier to accept. I have to help find Seema. There's no way I can live with myself if I don't. No matter that Tariq says I'm not to blame, I am. At least in part. I should have told Dar as soon as I suspected what Seema was up to. Instead, I waited. Why the hell did I wait? To get more proof? To be sure? To avoid embarrassing myself? And now look where we are. Darya—dead. Seema—if not dead, maybe living a fate worse than death.

I thump down cross-legged on the floor of my room and sift aimlessly through the pile of rags. The rags that used to be my clothes. Nothing great. Except for the copper *shalwar kameez* Cerelli gave me. My heart aches as I stroke the silky fabric, my index finger tracing the gold threads. It was so beautiful, and I'll never get to wear it.

"I'll buy you another."

I nearly jump out of my skin. "Damn! You scared me. You're like a ghost, you know."

Cerelli leans against the doorjamb, his arms crossed over his chest. "You told me that once before."

"Yeah, on the *Bataan*. Not something I particularly care to remember. Much like this." I hold up what's left of the copper tunic.

He crosses the room, squats next to me, and carefully examines the charred splinters of what used to be my dresser and the partially burned scraps of Awalmir's *landays* atop my savaged clothes. "Anything worth taking home?" He pries the *shalwar kameez* from my hands. "I meant what I said. I'll buy you a new one."

"Cerelli—" I can feel the tears gathering in my eyes. Stupid to cry over something like this, but there you are. "It won't be the same."

"Going sentimental on me, are you?" He drapes an arm around my shoulders and pulls me close.

"Thank God my *burqa's* still intact." I point to it on the bed and offer a half smile, which probably comes off as more of a grimace. "My personal favorite."

"And the last thing I want to see you wearing. Believe me." He presses a kiss to the side of my head.

I lean against his chest, dry my tears on his shirt, then turn my face up to his. "You told me that once before."

"I meant it then, too." He kisses me lightly on the lips.

I'm ready, more than ready, to respond, but before we can explore that possibility, I hear Sawyer making his way down the hall. "Finn? You back here?"

Cerelli exhales sharply, then puts a few inches between us. "Later," he whispers, then calls, "in here."

Sawyer stops short in the doorway. He looks from Cerelli to me. "Sorry to intrude. Captain. Annie. I—yeah—just checking to see what you've found in here."

"We're working on that," says Cerelli, more to me, it feels like, than to Sawyer.

"Okay then." Sawyer rubs his hands together, then takes a step backward. "Let me know if I'm needed." We listen to his feet slap against the tiles as he hurries up the hall.

Cerelli trains his eyes on me. "Later?"

"Most definitely."

"Anything in this mess you want to take home?"

I shake my head. "Just my pack and my cameras."

"You still have the Sig and the sat phone?"

"Yeah."

"Take them. The *burqa* and the sandals, too. Just in case."

41

CERELLI AND TARIQ DISAPPEAR about an hour before sunset. Sawyer isn't talking. Nic isn't either. And neither of them will look me in the eye. I've got a pretty good idea what's going on. Which is confirmed when they return in Cerelli's white pickup just as the sun dips behind the mountains. I'm standing in front of the house. Waiting. Tariq's face is drawn, his eyes red. His grief permeates the air. I step aside to let him by.

And look back at Cerelli, who nods toward the courtyard.

I follow him, and we sit side by side on the wrought iron chairs. I can't help but think back to a week ago when Dar and I were sitting here. Right here. Arguing. When I thought we still had a lifetime ahead of us.

He reaches for my hand. "We buried her."

"I wanted to be there." Tears well and burn.

"We did exactly what she told Tariq she wanted."

Dumbfounded, all I can do is stare at him. Really? Dar didn't want me there? She actually said that? Finally, I choke out, "Where?"

"An unmarked grave."

I turn away. *She felt called home.* Tariq's words as we drove to the Panjshir Valley. To Wad Qol. Was that really only two weeks ago?

The sun settles behind the Hindu Kush. Rose and mauve streaks quickly give way to sapphire blue. Then the night sky settles on us. And still we sit. At some point, Cerelli leaves off holding my hand and rests his arm across my shoulders, pulling me close.

42

THE NEXT MORNING, AN HOUR before sunrise, our caravan
of aging Toyota pickups passes the charred remains of the school,
invisible in the darkness, and pulls slowly out of the village. No
headlights. No light at all. The moon has dropped behind the
mountains. The stars have faded back into the firmament. When
we reach the river and the Panjshir Road, we all turn southwest.
From the little I've overheard, I think Sawyer and Massoud's men
will eventually veer off the river road and head north into the
Hindu Kush Mountains—where Sawyer's GPS has pinpointed
the source of the chatter about Seema. But whether she's there, no
one knows for sure.

As for Tariq and Nic—they've stayed behind in Wad Qol,
packing up whatever needs to be shipped back to the States. Which
is where Tariq will be heading. With or without Seema. They
weren't happy about not being part of the search, but apparently,
they obey orders much better than I do.

Hours later, Cerelli and I are still driving. Not talking about
much of anything. He's clearly thinking about the operation ahead,

after he drops me off at Bagram. And I'm staring out the passenger window, trying to escape my worry about Seema. But there are only so many rocks and so much river I can stand to watch. So, I go back to thinking about Seema and Dar and my role in everything that's happened.

He breaks the silence. "It's not going to help to beat yourself up about it," he says gently. He doesn't need to spell out what 'it' is. We both know. "'That way madness lies.'"

"Ah, that sounds like Shakespeare. *Macbeth?*"

"A good guess," he grins. "But it's *King Lear.*"

"You know, for a Navy guy, you're suspiciously well-read."

"Suspiciously? I just happen to like to read. It keeps me sane."

Yet another Cerelli mystery solved. "So, Captain Shakespeare, tell me if I'm wrong, but I remember King Lear making some pretty stupid decisions because he couldn't see the reality in front of him. Kind of like what I've done these last couple weeks."

"Not you." He reaches for my hand and twines his fingers around mine. "Darya. She and Tariq weren't seeing the Seema that was in front of them."

"Yeah, well, I sure didn't help matters."

He squeezes my hand. "I talked to Darya about exactly that the night before she was killed. After you uploaded Seema's picture of Awalmir. She sent it to me, hoping we could ID the guy. She was adamant that this was her screwup. Not yours."

Sounds like a cozy chat. Clearly, the two of them were a lot closer than I suspected. I shake my head. "And maybe one day, I'll believe that. Maybe." Then, because I don't want him probing my thoughts anymore, I struggle to change the subject, saying the first thing that comes to mind. "Dalan Sang. How much farther?"

He shoots me a look. Probably wondering if that's what I'm

really thinking about. "Another few miles. Nothing to worry about there. The hut's gone, but everything else has been cleared—" His attention shifts. He seems to be staring about a half mile ahead. At a small bridge over the river where several Toyota pickups are stopped. Frowning, he slows the truck.

"What?"

"Our guys." He pulls to the side of the road behind the last of the trucks. "I wasn't expecting to catch up to them. Or for them to stop."

"Engine trouble, maybe?"

"Maybe." He opens the door and climbs out, then looks pointedly back into the cab. "You stay here."

No argument from me. I'm getting ready to slide down and huddle on the floor if necessary. Up ahead, I see Sawyer and two of Massoud's men climb out of the other pickups. Cerelli joins them, his back to me. But I can see Sawyer's face, and he doesn't look happy. He points up the road toward Dalan Sang, then across the bridge, toward the mountains. Hoping to hear some of what they're saying, I scoot over to the driver's seat and roll down the side window just as Cerelli shakes his head. But the roar of the water drowns out their words. All I can do is watch Cerelli as he shakes his head again. And again.

Finally, he heads back to our pickup. Taking one look at the lowered window, he leans in. "You hear any of that?"

"Not for lack of trying, but the river is way too loud."

"There's been a change of plan."

"Oh?" I wait, hoping he'll clue me in. But he's thinking. Then, he's next to the flatbed, lifting out his duffel.

"There's a problem at the Dalan Sang checkpoint."

"What kind of problem?"

"Tangos. Not sure if they're Taliban or ISIS. We're taking a different route. From here on out, I need you to be Afghan, not a photojournalist," he says, measuring his words carefully. "The less attention we attract along the way, the better."

"Cerelli—"

The muscle at the corner of his eye twitches. Clearly, he's expecting a battle.

I swallow the protest I was about to make. This is definitely not a battle worth fighting. I climb back over the stick shift onto my seat, unzip the Lowepro, and pull out my periwinkle *burqa*. "You happen to have my sandals and dark socks in that duffel?"

He tosses them onto his seat. I change out of my military-issue boots and white socks first, then slide out of the truck. I tie the periwinkle headscarf Darya gave me around my neck. Just in case. Next, the *burqa*. In an instant, my field of vision is reduced by ninety percent. It's every bit as awful as I remember from my practice session with Fatima.

Cerelli nods toward my pack. "You have the Sig?"

"I do."

"Can you put it in your waistband? And walk like it's not there?"

I hoist up yards of fabric and tuck the gun in my pants. "You tell me." I walk to the end of the pickup. *Be invisible*, I tell myself. Like a ghost. Like Fatima. Like Malalai's *anaa*. I glide around the truck to Cerelli. "Satisfied?" Under this mountain of fabric, my voice sounds muffled. Even to me.

"Not bad." Cerelli nods thoughtfully.

And that's when I see that he's changed clothes as well. Gone are the brown leather jacket and the jeans. He's wearing his Taliban clothes from eight years ago. One whiff tells me they've never been washed. My eyes stop at his face, at the stubble that's far short of being a beard.

"Do I pass?" He raises an eyebrow.

"If no one looks too closely."

"One can only hope."

WE CROSS THE RIVER, WELL behind the other pickups. I'm waiting for Cerelli to share some details of this little detour, but he's not talking. Since I'm not the most patient person in the world, I finally ask, "So, what's going on?"

"Better you don't know."

Hemmed in by the *burqa's* thickly netted eyepiece, I have to make a full ninety-degree turn to see Cerelli. "No."

He glances over at me.

"That's not the right answer. I deserve to know what the hell's going on. What I've landed in the middle of."

He stabs his fingers into his too-short hair, hair that will be a dead giveaway if we get caught by any insurgents. "Have I ever told you how infuriating you can be?"

"Oh, yeah. You going to answer my question?"

He drums a tattoo on the steering wheel. "Sawyer's been picking up a lot of chatter during the drive this morning. Groups of Taliban and ISIS are moving around this part of the valley. Dalan Sang, among other places. They're referring to Seema. She may be with them. Or not."

"So, now we're going after Seema?"

"Not if I can help it. You and I are going the long way around to Kabul. The very long way around. But it's not always the safest route, so we need to be ready for anything."

"Oh."

"We could meet up with some militants. If we end up on the losing end, I want you to know there's nothing, *nothing,* those tangos can do to me to make me talk."

He clearly expects me to connect the dots. "And you're not so sure about me—whether or not I'll talk."

"Sweetheart, if they threaten to kill me—or Seema if she's with them—I wouldn't blame you for telling them everything you know."

"And that's why you're not telling me the plan." I nod. "Smart man."

He crooks an eyebrow. "Now you've got me worried."

"What?" I've been doing my best to be totally cooperative.

"I'm not used to you agreeing with me. Remember, I saw you in action all those years ago on the *Bataan*. And over the last couple weeks. There's not much that scares me. But *you* being cooperative? That scares the shit out of me."

"Are you saying I have a bad reputation?"

"You're a legend."

A legend. Tariq said that about me my first morning in Wad Qol. I helped save Massoud's son and grandson, and within hours everyone knew. That's an impressive intel pipeline.

Intel pipeline.

I freeze mid-thought. Darya? Tariq? Darya knew everything—often before it happened. And she always made sure I was away from the firing line when she was discussing real business, dangerous business. My questions come fast and furious. So, why were Tariq and Darya really in Wad Qol? To help rebuild Afghanistan, Darya told me. But both Darya and Tariq were from Kabul. That needed rebuilding, too—probably more than Wad Qol. Suddenly, the pieces of the puzzle shift into place. Damn, they were in Wad Qol because that's where their section of the intel pipeline was.

I almost laugh out loud. No way. This is insane. Darya was my best friend. We shared a dorm room for four years. We knew everything about each other.

Except we didn't share everything. Not really. I didn't tell Dar about what happened at Khakwali until just last week. What if I didn't know Darya and Tariq as well as I thought I did? What if—

Cerelli. How does he really know Darya and Tariq? Then it hits me: when he called me the day before yesterday, he already knew about Dar. *The intel pipeline.* Tariq. He must have called Cerelli. Their handler? A clusterfuck, Cerelli said when he talked to me. Not something he'd say about a school director being killed and a school being firebombed. Darya and Tariq are, were, intelligence agents. Spies. And holy shit, Cerelli was running them. A girls' school director and a physician. The perfect covers.

Only Dar's cover wasn't so perfect.

You don't know my mom. Not really.

Seema knew. And the militants found out. Because of Seema.

Please, let her not have given up her mother. Not intentionally. Maybe she said something to pique Awalmir's interest, so he seduced what he wanted out of her. But no, that doesn't fit with what Bahar said. She told us the girls met him at the market, and he had eyes only for Seema. The tangos already knew about Darya. Probably about Tariq, too. They came looking for Seema to get more information. To find a way to get to Darya and Tariq. And Seema fell in love.

You were so late. Mom went to the school. Darya went to the school to call Cerelli. Or Sawyer. To see if they knew what had happened to Tariq and me. At the time, it made no sense. What kind of equipment did they have there? A sat phone? A radio? Whatever it was, Darya kept it double-locked in the supply closet in her office, and that put the school and Darya and Tariq right smack in the ISIS and Taliban crosshairs.

So, what the hell is really going on now? A spec op? No, there's nothing officially sanctioned about this. A black op. Cerelli and whoever's above him up the chain of command need deniability. And there's more to this than going after a band of militants and rescuing Seema. This is about shutting down a long-running undercover field operation and getting Tariq the hell out of Afghanistan.

And me.

Damn it, Dar. You knew there was a problem with Seema. You said she was moody, but I picked up right away that she was beyond moody. She was sneaking out at night, passing messages, lying. Nothing like the Seema I'd always known. I should've said something sooner, told you what I suspected. Would you have believed me? Oh, Darya, you were her mother. How could you have missed it? You should've gotten her out of Afghanistan and back to California a long time ago. You should've taken her yourself. How could you have played this so wrong?

This way madness lies. Indeed.

What about Seema? Oh, fuck. Cerelli and Sawyer, Massoud's men. That's a lot of firepower. Are they trying to get her back? Or are they planning to kill her along with the militants?

We could meet up with some militants. That's what Cerelli said. They catch us, just the two of us, Cerelli dies. It's a simple equation. And they're going to assume I'm part of it, too. Photojournalist—a cover any Taliban or ISIS militant will assume is fake. They'll kill me, too. But first? They'll rape me—and make him watch. Oh shit. I bury my hands under my legs to try to keep them steady.

Are Cerelli and I really going to Bagram?

Or are we the bait?

WE DRIVE A FEW MORE HOURS on unpaved roads that get narrower and more deeply rutted until finally they seem more like animal trails passing through one small village after another. Each one filled with the ubiquitous yellow mud-brick houses. Most have mosque-blue doors. Each village looks a little more run-down than the last. The winding road climbs gradually. Pine trees cling tenaciously to the steep slopes of the mountains soaring above us.

Around noon, aging motorcycles begin to proliferate in the villages we pass through. Motorcycles—a Taliban favorite. The few women we see are clad in *burqas.* There are many more men than women out and about, and they all look like they could be Massoud's soldiers. Or Taliban. Hard to tell which.

Cerelli pulls to the side of the road next to one of the larger houses we've seen. He doesn't say a word, just drapes his arm over the steering wheel and studies the road ahead. I follow his eyes and make out a bend in the road and something else. Something white.

"What's that up ahead?" I ask.

"Rear bumper of a white Toyota pickup." Cerelli's trying to keep his voice light, but I hear that deadly calm. "Not one of ours."

"How can you tell?"

"Because all of ours are pulled off the road, hiding behind houses." He points off to the side. "There. There. And over there."

I count. And get to ten. The number of pickups that left Wad Qol. "So, what's that up ahead?"

"My best guess? A roadblock."

Not good. I close my eyes only to blink them open at the sound of Cerelli rolling down his window. I twist my requisite ninety degrees to see Sawyer and one of Massoud's lieutenants. Their whispered confab is impossible to hear. And it's short. After only a minute, Cerelli puts his hand on my shoulder. "You ready?"

"For what?" He's not seriously thinking of crashing through that roadblock, is he?

"Another change in plan. From here, we hike." He nods toward the shadowy mass of earth and granite looming over us. "Based on what the guys are picking up, we've got more tangos moving in. Behind us and up ahead. It looks like climbing that mountain is our best option. Just so you know, it'll be slow going. You up for this?"

I scrunch down so I can see the upper reaches of the mountains. The waterfalls cascading down from the snow pack on high. It looks brutal. And cold. "That's where Seema is?"

"Could be, but I don't know."

"I'm in."

"That's what I thought you'd say. So, these are the rules. From here on out, you do not speak. Not a word. You need some water or have to take a leak, wave your hand."

"Got it."

"Your name is Ana. Don't answer to anything else, especially not Annie."

"Okay."

"And until we get to where we're going, you're mine, as in *my wife*. If we get stopped, and I have to prove it, I will. So, I apologize in advance. Just know I'll do whatever I have to do to get you home safe and sound. I don't mean to sound like a pig, but if you're in the game, you're in all the way. You do what you have to, to stay alive. You play by my rules."

WE STUFF CERELLI'S DUFFEL and my Lowepro under the seat, then set off into the mountains with Sawyer and Massoud's men. But after an hour or so, it's clear I'm slowing everyone down, and the rest of the guys move ahead. Then it's just Cerelli with his MP7 slung over his shoulder and me climbing the nearly vertical trail.

Hours later, after hiking through the hot sun and now the chilling dark, my feet are screaming. With each step, blisters bite. My new leather sandals, which I never bothered to break in, and the scratchy wool socks are rubbing my skin raw. Plus, my legs are about to give out. It's been a long time since I've been on a trek like this, scaling a mountain, and my calf muscles are burning from the buildup of lactic acid. I'm breathing hard, struggling to pull enough of the thinning alpine air into my lungs, struggling to keep up.

Cerelli's in the lead, climbing slowly, for my sake, but also to make sure neither of us sends any stones or shale skittering. The last thing we want to do is call attention to ourselves. At least Sawyer and the others are out here with us. Somewhere. I try to keep that in mind—that Cerelli and I aren't totally on our own.

The shadow ahead of me suddenly stops and crouches. I do the same. Making myself as small as possible, leaning into the boulder next to me, I try to imagine we're not really in the Hindu Kush Mountains high above the Panjshir Valley, climbing for our lives. It can't be real, any of this. But then the image of Darya's body in the dust as the Wad Qol Secondary School for Girls burns to the ground flashes before me. It's real. All of it is horrifyingly real. And 7,000 miles away, Mel is waiting for me to come home.

From somewhere off to the northwest, moving across our path, comes the crunch of footsteps on shale, the occasional cascade of stones, and the whispered back-and-forth of voices speaking a language I can't quite make out. Then, I hear a word I do know. *Mashuqa*. Girlfriend. Followed by soft chuckles. It's got to be Seema they're talking about, and she must be with them or someplace close. Or, they've picked up on the tweets.

We stay frozen in place, not moving a muscle for twenty minutes at least. Long enough that my left leg starts to cramp. I don't know how much longer I can stay crouched. *Please don't fail me*, I pray to my legs.

Then, we wait longer.

Finally, Cerelli rises slowly, palming the air behind him for me to stay down. He stands in place, barely moving, intent on listening for the slightest sound, the whisper of a voice, the chink of a stone rolling under a footstep. The sky lightens as a full moon rises. Finally, he motions me to get up. My legs actually wobble as I stand. My feet nearly refuse to take another step.

We continue to climb, but it's painfully slow. I place each foot carefully, like he showed me, exerting no weight until I lock the downhill knee and am absolutely sure no rocks are going to slide. We're gaining altitude like crazy. My lungs are starving for oxygen, and my breathing is ragged. Too noisy.

The wind is picking up, blowing down across the snow farther up the slope. It's getting colder, a lot colder, and my *shalwar kameez* is damp with sweat. Neither my heavy sweater nor the *burqa* are doing much to keep me warm. But we can't stop.

A raven call catches me off guard. Unusual at this hour. Even more unusual for there to be an answer, and then what seems to be a conversation. Not ravens, I realize, people. I stop climbing and listen.

Another raven call, and then I almost laugh out loud from relief.

Cerelli. A few meters ahead of me, standing against an outcropping of boulders, his hands cupped around his mouth.

An answering call. Then Cerelli's shadow moves soundlessly away from the rocks. I squint into the darkness. Yeah, I'm pretty sure he's waving me forward.

As I pull even with him, he grabs my upper arm. "Follow my lead," he breathes through the netting of my eyepiece, "and don't say a word. No matter what happens."

Making a particularly steep ascent even more slowly than the rest of the climb, we approach a cave. The lookouts standing guard are the good guys. And Sawyer. Cerelli's shoulders relax. But my shivering gives way to full-out shaking, and it's not from the cold. I'm scared. No, terrified. I can't stop thinking about the men who crossed our path a while back. Militants, I'm sure.

Cerelli leads me into the night-dark cave. Still in my *burqa*, I can't see a thing, can't even make out shadows. He somehow guides me around the dim outlines of men who are eating or trying to catch some sleep.

No one says a word.

I follow him deeper into the cave, limping over the uneven floor. His hand steadies me, sitting me down on the hard rock. I pull the *burqa* back over my head. He gives me some rice—cold now. But I haven't eaten in hours, and the rice is something.

"Drink!" he whispers, putting the tube of his Camelbak in my hand. I need to hydrate—the only way to keep high altitude sickness at bay.

Then, he leads me farther into the cave, winding deep into the mountain, turning and turning like we're in the Minotaur's labyrinth. When we reach the very back, he stops me with his hand and moves away into the dark.

"Cerelli?" I whisper.

"Right here." He reaches for me. "This way. All fours. Watch your head."

On hands and knees, I feel for the narrow opening in the rock face and wriggle through after him. Incredible. A cave off the main cave. "How the hell did you find this?" I feel around me. Sand. I pick up a handful and let it spill grain by grain back to the cave floor.

"Wish I could take credit, but Sawyer found it. Listen to me, if anything happens, you hunker down here, and you'll be safe."

"What's going to happen?"

"Tonight? Probably nothing."

"Should we be talking?" I'm back to whispering.

"No worries. We're so deep inside the mountain, our voices won't make it to the cave entrance."

"Will you stay?" I ask.

"I need to do some recon first. But I'll be back as soon as I can. Try to sleep. Tomorrow could be brutal, and I'll need you on your A game." And then, he's gone. I listen hard for his footfalls, but hear nothing. The man truly is a ghost.

I pick up another handful of sand. Seriously? He thinks I can sleep while he's out there in the mountains? With Seema God only knows where? But relieved to be off my blistered feet, I curl into the hollow already formed in the sand, the memory of someone else's body. One of Massoud's men? A wife or a daughter Massoud ordered into hiding?

I pull the *burqa* back over my head and wrap it tightly around me. Nauseatingly hot during the day, it's keeping me a little warmer now. Warmer than the men standing guard outside. Definitely warmer than Cerelli out there on the mountain.

But it's not coming close to driving out the cold buried deep inside me. The pain that's got my heart clenched so tight, I'm afraid it could shatter.

Oh God, Dar, you can't be gone. One minute you were going to your office to finish some paperwork as I headed off on the field trip. An hour later you were dead. Killed, trying to save Seema. Or was it because they'd discovered you were a spy? A *spy*? No, no, no. This doesn't happen. It can't happen. Not to you. You're too strong, too smart. You're the one who always kept me going through all the crazy turns my life took. You're the one who pushed me to be a photographer, to take chances with my life. Please, Dar, listen to me! You can't be gone. I can't do this on my own. I need you here with me. We were supposed to grow old together. The two of us.

Tears prick the back of my eyes and then spill out, streaking down my cheeks, wetting the coarse cloth of the *burqa*. I wrap my arms around myself and burrow deeper into the sand, wishing it would open up and take me, too.

Dar—

There's no time now to cry, Darya's voice sounds in my head. *You must find Seema. She's out there.*

43

I HEAR SOFT RUSTLING. A hand finds its way around my neck, and I'm instantly awake. "Annie," a voice breathes against the coarse cloth. Cerelli.

"You're back." I whisper, not questioning whether he can hear me. Cerelli hears everything.

"I'm back," he breathes. "You did great today."

"Liar. I'm so out of shape. I held you back. Maybe you didn't notice, but I almost got us captured."

He tips my chin up so our lips are just a fraction of an inch apart. "You did good."

His lips find mine. Through the *burqa*.

"You warm enough?" he asks.

"I am now."

He lifts the hem of the *burqa*. "Then, would you mind terribly taking this off?"

"Not terribly."

"And while you're at it, you might try removing the rest of your clothes. Including that thing around your neck with the ammo clips."

"Lazy, are you?"

He chuckles softly.

"Are you sure you're up for this?" I whisper.

He helps pull the *burqa* off me. "Sweetheart, I've been up for this a lot longer than I want to admit. Let me count the years." He pauses. "The real question is: are you?"

I hesitate. For a split second, I'm back to the time right after my divorce. The occasional guy I'd meet on assignment who found his way into my bed, always leaving while the night was still heavy to avoid any morning awkwardness. But that was a long time ago. There hasn't been anyone in years. Cerelli is different, though. Not someone who's going to leave. It amazes me to realize that Darya knew it. Way before I did.

He puts his finger to my lips. "Sorry, but I'm not making any promises for the long term. This op is going sideways fast. I may not have a long term to promise. So, if you're not up for what may be just here, just now, say the word."

I push aside the last of the *burqa,* then pull the passport bag with the ammo clips over my head and strip off my clothes. The chilly air takes me by surprise. Cerelli's hands warm my breasts, my waist, my hips. I lift my mouth to where I hope his still is.

It is.

AFTER, HE GATHERS ME to his chest, his arms warming me. Then, he settles the *burqa* over us. Just the two of us.

"We need to sleep," he breathes.

"You can sleep after that?"

"Sweetheart, you rocked my world. But I just hiked up a mountain, so yeah, I can sleep."

Only he doesn't. Soon, his hands are back at work. "You are so beautiful. And so unbelievably brave," he whispers, kissing me lightly on the lips. "If you were Pashtun, your grandmother would have insisted on a crescent moon tattooed right here." His finger draws a tiny crescent at the corner of my right eye. He kisses the spot for good measure. "Or maybe some tiny stars along this eyebrow. Or maybe here." He draws a star on my breast. I gasp at his touch.

Then, for a few seconds, I'm back in the stable in Khakwali. The goat is nibbling my hair. Malalai's *anaa* pushes her *burqa* back over her head, long enough for me to see her face, to witness the grief we share. And there is the crescent moon, three stars.

I tell Cerelli about the woman and her tattoos. "Someday," I say, "when it's safe, I'd like to go back there. To see the villagers. Malalai's *anaa*. The children are all grown up, of course. Probably unrecognizable. Those girls must have little ones of their own."

Cerelli doesn't answer right away. Finally, he says, "Annie, the village isn't there anymore."

"What?"

He puts his index finger against my lips. "It was neutralized. Years ago."

"Neutralized?"

"We bombed it."

"And the people?"

"Annie."

I stare at him through the dark. Impossible. Inconceivable. All those innocents. I struggle against his arms.

"It wasn't my call."

"Does it matter?"

I feel his arms tighten around me. Flesh against flesh. His hot. Mine ice-cold.

"It was a war. It's still a war."

"What if it *had* been your call?"

"Don't go there."

I elbow him in the side, and he loosens his hold, letting me slide to the sand next to him.

"*Lâr sha!*" I hiss.

"Annie." His voice cracks.

And I know I hurt him a lot more than I meant to. I also remember that years ago, I sat in the debriefing room on the USS *Bataan* praying that the Marines, the SEALS, the entire U.S. military would do exactly what they did. Bomb the fuck out of the bad guys in Khakwali. But I didn't mean for them to kill the women and the children. Or Malalai's grandfather.

44

THERE'S MORE COLD RICE FOR breakfast, but I push it away and pull on the *burqa*. Cerelli in his Taliban clothes and *pakol* studies me carefully. "I can see your hair through the netting. It's got *Amrikâyi* written all over it." His voice is all business. "You still have your headscarf?"

"Yeah."

"Wear it under the *burqa*."

What I said to him during the night was wrong, dead wrong, and it's poisoning the air in the cave. But I don't know how to fix it. *Burqa* off, a periwinkle puddle at my feet, I pull back my hair, then wrap the headscarf the way Darya showed me.

A few minutes later, Sawyer emerges out of the darkness from the back of the cave. I have him check to make sure none of my hair is visible. Then, he grabs my wrist and walks me farther into the cave. "What the hell happened last night? Between you and the Captain?"

I wrench my hand away from him. "Don't. Just don't—" I seriously do not want to feel any worse than I already do.

"Why do you think he's here?" Fury radiates off Sawyer. "This is no military op. The man's here because of you. To get you out of here. To save your life. Think about that, Annie. And think about this: we've got tangos out there, and I mean right out there. They found our position during the night. People are going to die today, and the Captain could be one of them. So, if you've got any feelings for him, you let him know. And you better let him know now."

I pull the *burqa* over my head, shutting him out. But I can sense him following me to the front of the cave where Cerelli looks me over, careful to avoid my eyes. Finally, he nods.

"Not quite." I lift the front of the *burqa* past my face and bring my lips to his. Sawyer and Massoud's men turn their backs. I keep my mouth on his, demanding. His answer is quiet at first, then deepens. His arm circles my waist, resting strongly, protectively on the small of my back. "I'm sorry," I breathe into him.

Then we step away from each other. I rearrange the *burqa* to drape over me the way it should. His eyes meet mine through the netting of the eyepiece. "That your Sig tucked in your pants?"

"Yeah."

"When the time comes, keep it in your hand. And the MK3." He hands me a knife. "You ever gut a pig?" He smiles, but there's no joy in his eyes.

"No."

"Find the bottom of the rib cage, stick in the knife as fast and as hard as you can, then straight up to the heart. Think of the tangos out there as pigs. Don't humanize them. It helps."

My heart clenches. He's wrong. Nothing's going to help.

"Comfortable?" he asks.

"Not so much."

"Good. Don't get comfortable. I want you totally focused. This is the way it's going down." He puts his hands on my shoulders and turns me toward the front of the cave. "They've got a human shield right out there."

My knees go weak. There she is, about fifty yards away. A girl in a black *burqa* kneeling out in the open. "Seema?"

"They sure as hell want us to think so. But believe me, if that girl were Seema, they wouldn't have the *burqa* on her. They'd want us to see her and try to rescue her."

"Then, who is she?"

"No idea. But whoever she is, they've wrapped her with explosives."

"How can you tell?"

"She's a small girl. The *burqa* looks too bulky on her. That, and one of the tangos happened to mention it before we neutralized him."

That word again. "What's going to happen to her?"

"You don't want to know."

"Try me."

"Let's just say they're using her to get who they really want."

I lick my dry lips. "Who do they want?"

"Darya was at the top of the list. Now? Tariq is up there. Sawyer. Me."

"They think Tariq's here?"

"From the chatter we picked up last night, that would be affirmative."

"So, what happens next?"

"Massoud's men have been out since before dawn. They've taken out maybe half of the fifty we estimate were there. But so far, they haven't been able to pick off the shooters there, there, and there." He points to three enormous piles of boulders that form a wide arc in front of the cave.

"So, we're pinned down."

Cerelli puts his arm around my shoulders. "Also, affirmative."

"So, why are Massoud's men doing all this to help us?"

"They don't want Sawyer or me dead. Or you."

"Why exactly is that?"

Cerelli pauses, probably deciding whether or not to let me in on his secret life. "You know Ahmad Shah Massoud was assassinated just before 9/11?"

I nod. "September 9th."

"I was with him. So was Sawyer. I lobbied against letting him meet with the so-called 'Belgian reporters.' And when the shit hit the fan, Sawyer and I were the ones who tried to save his life."

"But he died."

"We did everything we could. Sawyer did a field transfusion. I took out the assassin who survived the explosion. His people will never forget that. You saved his son's life and delivered his grandson. They consider all three of us family."

"And now there's today. I just don't see how Massoud's men can get us out of this."

"Here's the plan," he says. "Massoud's men can't take out those guys, not from their current positions. They're hemmed in over there." He points to a few more rocky outcrops. "So, Sawyer and I are going to do it."

"Why don't we wait them out? At least until night."

"They're not in a waiting mood. They've been moving steadily closer, and I want to do this on my terms. Best chance to get you out of here."

"Cerelli, I so don't want to hear this."

"See that ridge?" He points to a rock formation that's a good hundred meters from where we're standing, maybe more, with a lot of open ground in between. "That's where we're going."

"You can't be serious. I can't get all the way over there, especially in this tent, not without getting shot to pieces."

He pulls me close. "Sweetheart, you're staying here."

"What? Then why do I have the gun? The knife?"

"Listen to me carefully. You're going to the very back of the cave, into the cubby. The bad guys may come looking, but they won't find you. Stay in there. Don't even breathe. Sawyer or I will get you when this is over."

"And if you don't?"

"Decided to be a realist, have you?"

"I think maybe I should have a plan B."

"You heard the raven calls last night?"

"Yeah."

"You hear that raven, you're okay. Let's hope it's Sawyer or me. But, it may be one of Massoud's men. If you don't hear it, wait as long as you can. They might just move on after—" His voice turns gruff. "Wait. As long as you can. If they're still hanging around, try bluffing your way out. Wearing the *burqa* and with your fluent Dari, you might get past them. If not, have the gun ready, aim for body mass, and remember what I told you about pigs."

"Cerelli—"

"It shouldn't have come to this, Annie. I'm sorry. And I'm sorry about Darya. More than I can say." He hugs me tight to his chest and then lets me go. "Get back there."

Ten feet in, I turn around and look at the mouth of the cave, but he's already gone.

I turn to face the winding darkness ahead of me.

"*NE!*" The girl's scream pierces the heavy silence. "*NE! Gom shoo!*" She keeps screaming.

Relief washes over me. It's not Seema. Then I freeze, my heart aching. Damn. What kind of person am I? There's a girl out there terrified she's about to die, and I'm relieved it's not Seema? Why is she screaming? Does she see some of our guys moving into position? Is she warning the militants? Does she know what it means to be a human bomb? That as soon as someone gets close enough to rescue her, the triggerman pushes the button and kills her along with the guys trying to help her.

Don't even try, Cerelli. Sawyer. You guys listening to me?

The girl stops screaming. Oh goddamn. They must have killed her. But no. There wasn't any explosion.

I make my way along the bends of the tunnel, then stop. Cerelli would kill me if he knew, but I can't bear the thought of going to the heart of all that darkness to wait for a raven call I'm afraid is never going to come. Or for militants who probably *will* find me, no matter what Cerelli says, then gut *me* like a pig after they take turns with me.

Don't be stupid, I tell myself. *Cerelli is putting his life on the line to get me out of here. To get me home to Mel. For once, listen to him.* So, I feel my way along the walls, winding deeper and deeper into the mountain until the passage narrows, then ends. On hands and knees, the *burqa* pulled up to my waist, I inch my way along the stone wall until I find the narrow opening into the cubby. Turning sideways, I push myself through the slit, then crawl into darkness so complete, I feel its weight press heavily down on me. Then, I wait.

And think about the very real possibility that I could die here, today, in this cave high in the Hindu Kush Mountains. No need for a body bag because no one will ever find me. Not in this secret little room inside a cave. No one will ever know what happened to me.

Damn. How can I do this to my daughter? All she'll ever

know is that I went looking for Seema and disappeared into some dark void. Oh God, sweetie, I'm sorry—I can't believe—I know I haven't exactly been the best mother. Hell, I've been a terrible mother—

Stop it! I hiss at myself. Then curling into a tight ball, I close my eyes against the darkness of the cave.

Time must be passing. But I have no idea how long I've been here. Or what the hell is going on outside. Did Cerelli and Sawyer make it to the ridge? Or did the militants pick them off? Is Armageddon raging outside? Or is everyone hunkered down in a stand-off? The good guys have to win because I can't imagine ending my life here in this nothingness.

Sometime later, I listen for a raven call. I'm desperate to hear it.

There, I do hear something. Footsteps. It must be Cerelli. Making his way back to me, to tell me all is well, to get me out. Now, I can hear the rustle of his clothes as he inches closer and closer to the back of the cave. To my cubby. I'm ready to call out. I can sense him right outside the cubby. I reach out my hand.

Then, I smell him. My lip curls at the overwhelming stench of sweat and testosterone and hate. And more hate. Such a sharp, horrible odor.

But no raven call. It's not Cerelli. Or Sawyer. Or any of Massoud's men. Fuck! What does this mean? My heart clenches. Have they killed Cerelli? Sawyer?

Don't even breathe. Cerelli's voice.

Not breathing isn't an option. Neither is stopping my heart from thundering in my ears. I cower underneath the *burqa*, praying the cloth muffles my sounds and keeps me safe.

"*La hagha zäy tsakha räwoza!*" he hisses. Pashto, I'm sure, but I don't know what he said.

"*Az änjä beron äyed!*" Dari this time. His accent marks him as an outsider, but I understand his words: *Come out of there! Does he know I'm here?*

"Tariq Ghafoor!" he says louder.

A second voice, saying something that could be in Arabic. The click of a gun. The faint beam of a flashlight.

Oh, shit! They'll find the opening to my cubby. Slowly, soundlessly, I reach for the Sig. But stop. If I miss, the bullet will ricochet off the walls and into me. The knife. How quickly can I gut a pig? Two pigs. Probably not fast enough to take both of them out.

The light is suddenly gone. I hear footsteps moving off. But the smell lingers. Have they gone? For all I know, they're sitting close by the cubby. Or somewhere along the winding tunnel to the entrance. I tighten my hold on the knife. And keep my other hand on the Sig.

There is no sound. Not the scratch of a mouse. Not the glide of a spider touching down to the sandy stone of the floor. Only the pounding of my heart.

I count. And reach 1,000. Still no call of the raven. Another 1,000. And another. Until I lose count.

What if they're all dead? My heart stops at the thought. How long will I wait? I see myself, days from now, staggering out of the cave to a field of bodies. Searching for Cerelli and Sawyer. Finding them. Or worse, not finding them. Knowing they've been captured, taken away to be tortured, beheaded. Because they were trying to save me.

More noise out in the main part of the cave. My fingers encircle the knife.

"Annie?"

"Sawyer?" I exhale my relief.

"It's over. Come on out."

I sheathe the MK3, slide the Sig into my waistband, and crawl out from my hiding place. Into Sawyer's arms. "Thank God, it's you."

"You okay? We saw them go in. What happened?"

"They thought Tariq was hiding in the cave. They got all the way back here, just inches away from the cubby."

"But they didn't find you. That took guts to wait that out. You are one tough lady. If you're okay, let's move out."

I stumble along behind him. We're almost to the mouth of the cave before I sense that something's wrong. Why is Sawyer the one who came to get me? My stomach tightening in fear, I grab his arm. "Where's Cerelli?"

"Behind the ridge. He took a bullet in the leg, but he'll be okay. I called in a dust-off. Chopper should be here in thirty."

"Sawyer!" calls one of Massoud's fighters when we emerge from the cave. He's standing over the body of one of our guys, sprawled on the ground, and gesturing for Sawyer's help.

I gather the yards of *burqa* to my waist and take off in the opposite direction, the blisters on my feet screaming as I slide down the hillside of scree. Skidding to a stop at the bottom, I look for the girl in the *burqa*. But she's not there. I scan the field, back and forth. No, she absolutely isn't there. Did one of our guys manage to rescue her? Or did she somehow break loose and get away? The next thought makes my blood run cold. Or is she one of the militants? Or, oh my God, what if Cerelli was wrong. What if that girl really *was* Seema?

I wade out of the loose stones. Finally, on firm ground, I run as fast as I can toward the ridge. I skirt around dead and bloodied bodies, praying they're militants, not Massoud's men. I've got to get to Cerelli. Sawyer says he'll be okay. And Sawyer would know.

But when I make it behind the ridge, Cerelli's lying on the ground, trying to rip the leg off his baggy Taliban pants. What the—?

He looks up at me and grimaces. "You okay? I saw two tangos go in the cave. About killed me when they came out again. You didn't gut them."

"Kind of hard to gut two pigs at the same time."

I throw the *burqa* back over my head, then kneel next to him and stare as his Taliban pants slowly darken. Red. Blood. So much blood. Too much blood. What the hell? "Sawyer said you were okay."

"Must've nicked an artery. Got worse when I tried to stand up. You happen to have a tourniquet?"

My head starts to spin. Don't do this to me, Murphy. I'm not going to let you die. Not this time. I close my eyes tight, then open them again and stare at the man on the ground next to me. Cerelli. This is Cerelli.

I reach for his hand. "Listen to me. We're getting you out of here."

Cerelli squeezes my hand. "A tourniquet?"

A tourniquet. I need a tourniquet to stop the frigging bleeding. I grab a handful of the *burqa* and use the MK3 to cut two long strips of fabric. Then I lift Cerelli's left leg just enough to slide the cloth underneath.

"This is going to hurt," I say, more to myself than to him.

"No shit." He grits his teeth. "Just. Do. It."

I tie the strip of *burqa* around his leg and pull it with all the strength I've got. Then, the second strip.

"Weakling." His voice is so quiet, I'm able to hear the click of a trigger behind me. Cerelli hears it, too, and looks sideways toward his gun. Just out of reach.

"Captain Cerelli." The man's voice is heavily accented, and from where Cerelli is looking, I'm guessing he's maybe ten, fifteen feet behind me. "I have waited a long time for this moment. Shooting you. This I will enjoy. I cannot tell you how much," he says in grammatically challenged Dari.

My breath catches in my throat.

"Let her go." Cerelli answers in Dari, his voice quiet, firm. He's not begging for his life. He's demanding mine.

"*Ah-nie*, the photographer. We meet again."

I'm that suddenly back in Khakwali. Malalai is running across the open space in front of dilapidated mud-brick houses toward the Humvee. "*Ah-nie!*" I blink, then swallow hard. *No!* I refuse to go back there. Not now. I glance at Cerelli. But Cerelli isn't looking at me. He's not taking his eyes off whoever the hell this guy is. Who *is* he? And how the fuck does he know my name?

From the corner of my eye, I see movement. The pig is sidestepping around, easing into my line of vision. The black balaclava concealing his face scares me to death. The pounding of my heart thunders in my ears. It hurts to breathe. He pulls off the ski mask, letting me see his hard eyes, pouty lips, and the dark hair flopping onto his forehead. So like the portrait Seema made of him. Except for the beard. *The beard.* Just a week ago, Awalmir didn't have a beard. There's no way he could've grown one this fast. Then, I freeze. His face. He's letting us see his face because in another minute, both Cerelli and I will be dead.

"Awalmir?" I say, pulling my hand slowly, oh so slowly, back from Cerelli's leg. A little more. An inch at a time. Almost under the *burqa*. Closer to the Sig tucked in my waistband. All the while, I'm staring at the man in front of me, willing him to keep his eyes on my face, not to see my hand disappearing under the *burqa*. No,

I'm positive. He's not Awalmir, even though he looks a hell of a lot like him. Same lips, same hair. But not Awalmir. So, who is he?

"Awalmir?" he sneers. "He is my cousin. You do not recognize me? I am disappointed."

"Why would I recognize you?" My voice quivers. Sweat trickles down my back.

"You forget what you did in Khakwali?" he hisses, shifting the aim of his AK-47 back and forth between Cerelli and me. "It is that easy for you?"

I wait a beat as my hand, moist with fear, closes around the Sig. God almighty, I hope I left the safety off. Slowly, I ease the gun out of my waistband and slide it to my side, still hidden by the flap of the *burqa*. I keep my eyes fixed on his. Those eyes. I know those eyes. Angry. Fanatical. Triumphant. The shepherd who took the Polaroid camera, who slapped Malalai, who blackened her eye. Ghazan.

"Malalai," I whisper.

"You *do* remember. Your Captain." A quick glance toward Cerelli, checking that he hasn't moved. "He has told you what he did to my village? My family?"

Neutralized. I take a deep breath and block out Cerelli.

"Yes. The truth, it is on your face. I alone escaped. Because when your dirty American bombs came, I was with the goats and the sheep in the upper pasture. Everyone else, *my family*, they were killed. Murdered. By your people. So many innocents. There were not even bodies left to bury."

I narrow my eyes and tighten my hold on the Sig. "What about Malalai? Someone in your village killed her!"

"Malalai!" He spits. "My sister. She was always begging to learn to read, to write. To be like a boy. She brought dishonor to our family. Her killing was just."

Focus! I tell myself.

"It was for *her* you came back to our village. You brought death to my family."

I can't get caught up with Malalai. I've got another battle. For a girl who's still alive. I hope. "Where is Seema?"

"Seema." His eyes flit back and forth between Cerelli and me. "The little rosebud no longer smells so sweet."

My finger tightens on the trigger.

"She is a fool. A plaything," he laughs. "Awalmir, he will tire of her soon."

I stare at him, refusing to let myself cry.

"But her mother. Darya Faludi. American spy. Teaching godless Western ways to innocent girls. Turning them against Islam. She was a blasphemer. Allah demanded her death." His words, like bullets, pierce my heart. He gloats and all but points his index finger above his head to paradise. "And now you. For this day, I have waited. Today, I will have *Nyaw aw Badal!*"

My heart races, the roar of blood pounding in my ears almost overpowering. It's all I can do to stay focused, steady, and not grovel in the sand and stones at his feet. Trembling, my hand grips the Sig. My index finger flexes the trigger. Can I do this? Can I shoot? Kill this man. *Not a man. A pig. Don't humanize him.*

"Where *is* Seema?" I say, doing my best to keep my voice from trembling, from cracking.

"Even if I spare your life, you will never find her." He slowly raises his gun, pointing first at Cerelli, then me. Toying with us. Doing his best to terrify us before he kills us. Then, he laughs and steadies his gun on Cerelli.

Bad move. I swing the Sig up from my side. Two hands. *Don't think! Aim for body mass!* Pulling the trigger is hard. But I do it and feel every moment of killing him. After the first shot, I keep shooting and shooting. Every single bullet hitting its mark as he flails and jerks his way to the stone-covered ground.

A hand clamps on my shoulder. "You got him." Sawyer walks past me and probes Ghazan's neck for a pulse. "We've been trying to nail this asshole for years."

"Not quite." I stand and take careful aim at Ghazan's gonads.

"Annie." Cerelli reaches for me. "Don't. You shoot him now, that's mutilation, and you'll have to live with that."

My rage continues to roil in my chest. My finger tightens on the trigger. *Just pull it!* I scream at myself. For Darya. For Seema. For Malalai. But my finger eases off. Turning, I meet Cerelli's eyes. Then slip the safety into place.

45

Bethesda, Maryland

STANDING AT THE BANK OF windows in the waiting room, I look out over the grounds of Bethesda Naval Hospital. Green. Peaceful. A far cry from four weeks ago at Bagram where the military docs stabilized Cerelli before shipping him to Landstuhl for surgery. Then here.

I press my palm against the glass, cool despite the June heat and humidity blasting the East Coast. Beside me on the windowsill, my new smartphone shows a texted photo of a figure in a black *burqa* staring into the camera. Seema? I can't make out her face, but the *landay* underneath the image stops me cold.

Tell my mother to dry her tears.
The pomegranates will blossom early in the new year.

I read the lines again and again until my heart aches. "Oh, Dar," I whisper, "I don't know where she is, but I won't give up. Ever. I promise."

Footfalls stop at the open door. I look over to see Sawyer. Mel, her hair now an inch long and dyed a particularly vibrant shade of peacock, stands next to him. Even taller than she was in May— if that's possible. She didn't win her audition, but she's certainly gained more confidence. And if I didn't know better, I'd say she has a major crush on Sawyer. God help me.

Sawyer shakes his head in obvious frustration. "He doesn't want to see you." He clearly isn't used to failure, especially where Cerelli is concerned.

"He tried, Mom. We both did." Mel crosses the room and circles her arms around me. "I'm sorry."

I manage a small smile and run my fingers through her hair.

"Annie, give him time." I can hear the pleading in Sawyer's voice. "He's willing to see the two of you."

"That's different, and you know it."

"No. No, I don't know that."

"Come on, Annie. The man lost a leg. He doesn't want you to see him like this."

I think about that for a minute. But it's no good. "Too fucking bad." I try to strong-arm my way past Sawyer, but he grabs my wrist, stopping me dead in my tracks. This, from the man who was once my guardian angel.

Still gripping my arm, he steers me toward the elevator. "Let's go down to the cafeteria. I'll buy you a cup of coffee, and we'll talk."

I stop struggling and let my shoulders sag in defeat. "Sawyer—"

Something about the way I say his name gets to him because he lets go of me. Just long enough for me to ease past him and head down the corridor to Cerelli's room. Five nineteen.

Stopping in front of the closed door, I take a deep breath. What am I doing? If the man doesn't want to see me, well then, he doesn't. I can't force him. I turn to leave and see Sawyer and Mel watching from the other end of the hall.

Sawyer looks pissed.

Mel calls to me, "Mom, don't screw this up!"

Yeah, well, this is Cerelli. I've been screwing up with him since oh-six. What difference will once more make? Heart pounding hard against my ribs, I push down on the handle and shoulder open the heavy door.

Cerelli is sitting on his bed, wearing a *Boston Strong* T-shirt and jeans that are a soft and faded blue, one leg cut short to allow for what's left of his actual leg, swathed in bandages from thigh to the stump below his knee. Seeing it for the first time stops me in my tracks. I don't know what I've been imagining—but it wasn't this.

When the door closes behind me, Cerelli slaps closed the book he was reading—a collection of Rumi's poems I see from the cover—and shoots me his fiercest glare. "I told Sawyer—"

"Glad to see you, too, Cerelli." Damn. I should've listened to Sawyer.

He doesn't say anything, so I wait him out.

"Why are you here?" he says finally, his voice steel—like his MK3 knife—hard and deadly.

"I have something to show you."

He doesn't answer.

Leave, I tell myself. *Get the hell out of this room, out of the hospital, and leave the man in peace.* Instead, I stand my ground and decide it's past time to kill the fucking elephant in the room before it gets any bigger. "How's the leg?" I cringe as soon as the words are out of my mouth. It's pretty damn clear how his leg is. Gone. Or at least part of it is.

"Not so good. Transtibial amputation. Just below the knee."

Which nearly does me in. "Cerelli, I—goddamn, I'm sorry."

He looks confused for all of two seconds, then I see recognition dawn in his eyes, and he actually curls up the corner of his mouth. "Let's get something straight. *This* isn't your fault. This is on the fucking Taliban."

"I know that." And I do. He came back to Afghanistan to get me out, but also to shut down the operation and track down the militants who killed Darya. He would've ended up in that firefight whether or not I'd been there. For once, I'm not feeling guilty. It's just that looking at Cerelli with half his leg gone is tearing me apart.

"And Annie, another thing. The last thing I want is your pity. I sure as hell didn't want to lose my leg. I hate it, but I'll deal with it. Being your charity case—that's definitely not in any deck of cards I want to be dealt in on." He draws a sharp breath.

I take a step forward, but he waves me away. "The pain can get pretty bad at times. Phantom pain. But there's nothing phantom about it." He glares at me, obviously ready for me to clear out.

"Should I get the nurse?"

"Nah. They gave me this." He lifts the small automatic pain meds dispenser lying next to him on the bed.

I shake my head, already knowing the answer before I ask the question. "You going to use it?"

He arches an eyebrow.

"Right. Of course not." Big bad SEAL. "So, when do they think this pain will resolve?"

"Tomorrow? Next week? Maybe never. They don't know. And neither do I."

How can I begin to respond to this? I don't have a clue, so I just say the first thing that comes to mind. "I may have a lead on Seema." I pull out my smartphone and show him the texted image of the girl I'm betting is Seema. Okay, this has nothing to do with his leg or his phantom pain, but if I know Cerelli at all, this could be a welcome diversion.

He looks at the snapshot, then reads the *landay*. "Sawyer didn't tell me about this."

"Sawyer doesn't know." I meet his gaze and count my lucky stars that this text has taken his mind off his leg for a minute or two. And also diverted his fury from me. "So, what do you think?"

"The picture? Hard to tell. The *landay*, though, could fit. Any idea who sent it?"

"I'm thinking Seema. I texted back, but no answer."

"If it's Seema, it sure sounds like she doesn't know Awalmir killed her mother."

"I can only hope."

He reads the lines again. "It also sounds like she's pregnant."

"Yeah. That's how I read it, too."

"We could try to trace it, but it's most likely a burner phone." He looks at me, his eyes narrowing. "You will *not* go after her."

I cross my arms and raise my chin a fraction of an inch. "I don't answer to you, Cerelli. I *will* find Seema. I'll do whatever I have to. For Darya."

"Don't give me a hard time. She sure as hell doesn't sound like she even wants to be rescued."

"But—"

"Annie, it's too damn dangerous." He sets my phone down next to his book. Then, "Did you hear what Ghazan said there at the end?"

"He said a lot."

"He said, '*Nyaw aw Badal.*'"

"Yeah." I nod warily. Where's he going with this?

"Justice and revenge. One of the tenets of *Pashtunwali,* the code every Pashtun lives by, swears allegiance to."

"Your point?"

"The war, these killings—it's *jihad.* Which was particularly ironic for Ghazan since his name means 'holy warrior.' But it's more than that. It's personal. Part of *Pashtunwali,* their way of life."

"But I killed him," I whisper. "He was the only person left from his village. That's what he said. It's over." Even as I say that, I realize it's not over. Far from it.

"His cousin Awalmir's still out there. So's his uncle. And who knows how many other cousins and uncles there are in villages all over Kandahar. They've all sworn *Nyaw aw Badal.* The whole tribe has. They'll never give up. A life for a life. Their sons, their grandsons—it's the same thing. They'll all swear *badal.* For generations to come. That's one of the reasons why I don't want you going after Seema."

I swallow hard. Nothing I can do about Pashtuns taking a vow of *badal.* "What's the other reason?"

He studies me intently, silently. Finally, he says, "You're still hallucinating. Aren't you." It's not a question.

"How the hell—"

"I take it that's a 'yes.'"

"Yeah, I am."

"You seeing anyone about it?"

"I will."

"When?"

"When I get back to Milwaukee. Satisfied?"

"I'd be *satisfied* if you'd already gotten some help."

"I said I'd do it, and I will. But right now, I'm here." In between assignments. In a few days, I'm off to Nigeria. Boko Haram has kidnapped some more girls. Not that I'm telling him any of this.

The muscle next to his eye quivers. A sure sign he doesn't believe me.

"Look, Cerelli, my hallucinations may resolve. Eventually. Or I may have to deal with them forever. But I refuse to let them stand in my way. If I do, I'll never go back to Afghanistan. Or any other war zone. But I *have* to go. I take photographs of war, conflict. I have to *be* there. It's not just what I do, it's my life. You don't get to make that decision for me."

He keeps his eyes on me, but I don't turn away. Neither does he. Then, with the muscle at the corner of his eye pulsing wildly, his voice turns that scary quiet I remember from the *Bataan*. "Do you have any idea what it took out of me to see that pig getting ready to kill you? And I couldn't do a goddamn thing to save you."

"Cerelli—"

"You don't get it. It was my job to protect you, and I fucked up. I should've had my gun in my hand."

"No." I put all the steel and flint and iron I can muster into that single syllable.

He frowns. "What's that supposed to mean?"

"It wasn't your job to protect me."

"Annie." He stabs his fingers into his hair. "There's no way—" He turns away from me and stares at the closed blinds for a long thirty seconds. Finally, he looks back at me. Locks his eyes on mine. "You said you had something to show me?" His message: show me and get the hell out of Dodge.

Oh, Cerelli. What am I doing here? Maybe I should just leave. Save myself a lot of heartache. Instead, I walk to the side of his bed. Not exactly the way I'd hoped to do this, but you go with the cards you're dealt.

It takes a few moments, but he finally looks at me. "What?"

I bend forward, take hold of his hand, and guide it to the small tattoo nestled in my hairline. "There. See?"

"See what?" Maybe his voice isn't quite as angry.

"Look."

He takes a few seconds but then surprises me by combing his fingers through my hair, pulling me a bit closer. Like he really wants to see. "A crescent moon." He traces it gently with his index finger. "To ward off the evil eye." His voice is definitely warming. "When?" His voice cracks. "When did you get this?"

"A couple weeks ago. It's still pretty raw." I don't tell him that I got the tattoo in memory of Malalai. And her *anaa*. But most of all, I was thinking of our night in the cave high in the mountains. I'm pretty sure he's figured that out.

His eyes linger on the crescent moon inked on my scalp, hidden from everyone except him. Then, in Dari, he says, just loud enough for me to hear,

One perfect crescent moon rises,
Jasmine opens laughing, stars fade into the night sky.

"For me?"

"For you."

I feel the heat rising in my cheeks. "It's beautiful. I love it."

"Do you, now."

Glossary

There are two official languages in Afghanistan: Dari (often referred to as Afghan Persian), spoken by 77% of Afghans in the west, north, and northeast of the country, and Pashto, spoken by 48% of the populace in the southeast. There are more than forty additional minor languages and many dialects. Dari is written in the Persian form of Arabic script; Pashto in a modified form of Arabic script. As a result, the Dari and Pashto words included in *Behind the Lens* are transliterated into English script based on Nicholas Awde's *Dari Dictionary & Phrasebook*, Nicholas Awde and Asmatullah Sarwan's *Pashto Dictionary & Phrasebook*, and *Dari/Pashto Phrasebook for Military Personnel*, compiled by Robert F. Powers, (Dari Editor) Edris Nawin, and (Pashto Editor) Subhan Fakhrizada. Many words have multiple variations in spelling in English. Most words and phrases are translated within the story or their meaning made obvious in context. Those that are not, I have listed below.

Adhan (var. adhaan, azan) — Islamic call to prayer recited by the *mu'adhdhin*; derived from adhina (to listen, to hear, to be informed)

Amrikäyëy; Amrikâyi (Pashto) — American woman; American man

Amrikâyi (Dari) — American

Anaa (Pashto) — Grandmother

Assalâmu alaykum, Wa 'alaykum assalâm — Peace be unto you, to you peace (a simple Muslim greeting with many variations in spelling; in Dari: *Asalâmu alaykum*)

Attan (Pashto) — Originally a Pashtun folk dance performed in times of war or at engagement announcements, now considered a national dance

Balê (Dari) — Yes

Bamb-e-motor (Dari) — Car or truck bomb

Bebakhshid (Dari) — Excuse me!

Borani banjân (Dari) — Sliced, sautéed eggplant served with garlic yogurt sauce

Burqa — A long, loose garment covering the body from head to feet, concealing even the eyes and the hands, worn by many Afghan Muslim women in public. Wearing a *burqa* is cultural and is not required in Islam. Some Muslim women see the wearing of the *burqa* as a way to show modesty. Others see it as a mandate by Taliban men to oppress women.

Chai sabz (Dari) — Spicy green tea

Che bahaaaal! (Dari) — Cooool!

Deewäna, var. dêwâna (Dari) — Insane, crazy

Gom shoo! (Dari) — Go away!

Gwâram kâmra (Pashto) — I want a camera

Hama or *Ama (Dari)* — Aunt (father's sister); in Dari, Pashto, and Arabic, there are different words to specify how an aunt or uncle is related to an individual—for example, father's sister as opposed to mother's sister.

Hijab — A head covering worn in public by many Muslim women

Ho (Pashto) — Yes

Inshallah — If Allah wills it

Kabuli pulao — a lamb and rice dish for special occasions

Kâfir (Pashto) — Unbeliever

Keffiyeh — A Bedouin Arab's kerchief, worn by men as a headdress

La hagha zäy tsakha räwoza! (Pashto) — Come out of there!

Lâr sha! (Pashto) — Go away!

Lotfan! (Dari) — Please!

Loya Jirga — A grand tribal council that has legislative function in Afghanistan

Lutfan! (Pashto) — Please!

Mashallah — What Allah has willed, to express appreciation, joy, praise, thankfulness

Mëebakhshêed! Mazerat mekhwaham (Dari) — I'm sorry! (Excuse me!) I apologize.

Mu'adhdhin (var. mu'ezzin) — The Muslim official who summons the faithful to prayer five times a day

Mujaheddin (var. Mujahideen) —The Arabic term for one engaged in *jihad* (struggle); guerilla fighters; fighters led by Ahmad Shah Massoud against the Soviets and the Taliban

Na (Pashto and Dari) — No

Nân (Dari) — Bread

Ne (Dari) — No

Nyaw aw Badal (Pashto) — Justice and revenge (part of the Pashtunwali Code)

Pakol — Soft, round-topped hat worn by Pashtun, Tajik, and Nuristani men

Qormah, chalau rice (Dari) — A meat and vegetable stew, often with lentils or beans and yogurt

Roat — Afghan sweet bread

Sabzi (Persian) — Literally means "green"; it is an herb and vegetable

Salah — The second pillar of Islam, which is prayer, occurring five times a day

Shalwar Kameez — Traditional trousers loose at the waist and narrowing to a cuff at the ankle worn with a long shirt or tunic, worn by both women and men

Shomâ (Dari) — You

Tashakor (Dari) — Thank you

Zë në pohesham (Pasto) — I don't understand

Zmâ dë kâmra wasâyêl (Pashto) — I lost my camera

Zmâ kâmra pêkar di (Pashto) — I need a camera

Author's Note

War photographers are daring and courageous individuals committed to capturing images of what's happening on the front lines and, perhaps even more important, well behind the lines. Their pictures tell the stories of military and insurgent forces as well as those of ordinary people who are just trying to get on with their lives as best they can. Far too often, life and death collide in the same photograph. One of the most compelling images I came across during my research was a single pink patent leather shoe—the size a five-year-old girl would wear—atop a pile of rubble that had once been a house. The death rate of journalists in conflict zones is frighteningly high. As the Committee to Protect Journalists reports, in Afghanistan alone, from 1992 to 2020, forty-eight journalists have been murdered, killed by crossfire, or by dangerous assignment. For further reading on life as a female war photojournalist, I recommend John Garofolo's *Dickey Chapelle Under Fire: Photographs by the First American Female War Correspondent Killed in Action* and Lynsey Addario's *It's What I Do: A Photographer's Life of Love and War*. Addario's *Of Love & War* includes photographs of life under Taliban rule.

In the process of researching for *Behind the Lens*, I discovered *landays*—twenty-two-syllable couplets that have been part of the Pashtun literary tradition for hundreds of years. As soon as I started reading them, I knew they had to be part of Annie's story. Women composed these short poems anonymously and often sang them to the beat of a handheld drum. But they never wrote them down, quite simply because girls and women were not allowed to read or write. Or love. Even in marriage, usually an inter-clan business transaction, love was an emotion forbidden to women. But women did love, sometimes a man who wasn't their husband, and they risked their lives to compose these poems for their "beloved." And they still risk their lives to create these poems. As recently as 2010, Rahila Muska's brothers beat her severely for dishonoring the family with her *landays*. In an interesting twist, some boys and even men now compose *landays*, and teens call them into radio talk shows. Anonymously, of course. For full histories of *landays* and many wonderful poems, see collections made and translated by Eliza Griswold with photographs by Seamus Murphy, *I Am the Beggar of the World: Landays from Contemporary Afghanistan* and *Songs of Love and War: Afghan Women's Poetry*, edited by Sayd Bahodine Majrouh and translated by Marjolijn de Jager.

Landays provide rich insight into women's lives in Afghanistan, and they also raise the all-important question of girls' education, which is central to this novel. Having gained control of most of Afghanistan by 1996, the Taliban issued a number of decrees restricting the lives of women and girls in every way imaginable, including bans on work, the *hammam* (traditional public baths—critical for personal hygiene in a country where many houses do not have indoor plumbing), and education. Girls younger than eight could study the *Qur'an*, but nothing else. Girls older than eight were not allowed in school at all. By 2001, when coalition forces drove the Taliban out of large sections of the country, the new Afghan government promised that all girls would go to school. Starting in primary school for grades 1 to 6, boys and girls would progress to the lower level of secondary school (or high school) for grades 7 to 9, then upper level for grades 10 to 12. According to Human Rights Watch, however, as of 2017, an estimated 66% of girls are still not in school. With parts of the country now reverting to Taliban control, the insurgent commander responsible for education asserts that Islamic *Shari'a* forbids the teaching of adolescent girls. Many religious clerics argue exactly the opposite—that Islam values the education of all girls. Ironically, although the Afghan government pays teachers' salaries in Taliban-controlled areas, it is the insurgents who manage the schools and control the curriculum. Since 2001, Taliban insurgents have blown up hundreds of schools not under their control and attacked the girls who try to get an education.

I have taken several liberties in the writing of this novel. Most notably, I have given first names to Afghan women and girls. As recently as 2017, it has been considered inappropriate to refer to females by their first names. Not only is a woman's name left off her wedding invitation and the birth certificates of her children, the inscription on her headstone when she dies reads 'Mr. X's mother, wife, sister, or daughter.' A group of activists in Afghanistan has launched the #WhereIsMyName campaign on Facebook, challenging people to say Afghan women's names out loud.

I have referenced a number of locations and events that are real, including Forward Operating Base Masum Ghar, various streets in Kabul, the attack at the Dalan Sang checkpoint which actually occurred in May 2014, the Panjshir Valley, and the village of Wad Qol. The Massoud family is also real. Ahmad Shah Massoud was, indeed, assassinated on September 9th, 2011. His brother, Ahmad Zia Massoud, continued the fight against the Taliban and Al Qaeda. Massoud's son, Ahmad, was not targeted at the Dalan Sang checkpoint bombing. The rest of the locations, characters, and events are completely fictional.

A portion of the proceeds will help fund girls' and women's education.

Behind the Lens Discussion Questions

1. What did you know about Afghanistan and Islam before reading *Behind the Lens*?

2. Annie and Darya's friendship is central to *Behind the Lens*. How do the secrets they keep from each other affect their relationship?

3. Both Annie and Darya have teenage daughters. In what ways are mother/daughter relationships key to this novel?

4. When Annie survives a Taliban ambush in 2006, she manages to go on with her life and her work with few ill effects. Yet, when she returns to Afghanistan in 2015, her memories come back to haunt her. What impact does Annie's apparent PTSD have on the story?

5. Why are Annie and Darya both so committed to helping girls in Afghanistan get an education?

6. *Landays* appear throughout *Behind the Lens*. In what ways are they integral to the story?

7. Annie is a war photographer. How are her photographs and photography important in the novel?

8. Throughout the novel, Annie becomes more aware of the distinctions between Afghan culture and Islam. What are some of those distinctions, and how do they feature in the novel?

9. There are several images, such as the crescent moon and the burqa, that are recurring motifs. What meanings do they conjure up for you? How do they enhance the story?

10. Annie and Cerelli have a complicated relationship. In what ways do they bring out the worst in each other? The best?

Jeannée would love to join your book club discussion! Please contact her at jeanneesacken19@gmail.com.

Acknowledgements

Heartfelt thanks to . . .

Shannon Ishizaki and her wonderful team at Ten16 Press, whose vision and creativity brought *Behind the Lens* to life. Lauren Blue made the editing process a dream. Kaeley Dunteman designed the perfect cover. Veronica Davis-Quiroz marketed the book in ways I never thought possible.

My brother, Erich P. Sacken, a former U.S. Navy Lieutenant, for sharing his expertise of all things Navy, including the sound a safety makes—or not—when being disengaged.

Members of Masjid Al-Huda in South Milwaukee, for explaining the differences between Islamic religious beliefs and sociocultural norms. Sue Obeidi, director of the Hollywood Bureau of the Muslim Public Affairs Council, for finding the perfect person to read the novel. Heba Elkobaitry, cultural and sensitivity reader *extraordinaire*, for correcting and refining my portrayal of Islam.

Judy Bridges, who took me under her Redbird wing many years ago when I became a member of her writing studio. She read multiple drafts, helping to shape characters and the story. Sara Rattan provided invaluable suggestions and kept me afloat with a U.S. Navy SEAL T-shirt: *The Only Easy Day Was Yesterday.* Beth Huwiler, Maura Fitzgerald, Kim Parsons, Aleta Chossek, Sharon Nesbit-Davis, Anne Rooney, and Amy Waldman—talented writers all—commented on drafts.

Nancy Backes, who understood the importance of memory and helped sharpen Annie and Cerelli's relationship. Elizabeth Jonas posed crucial questions at exactly the right moment.

Rochelle Melander spent countless hours over cups of blueberry rooibos tea, talking with me about Annie and Darya.

Shauna Singh Baldwin, Kim Suhr, Myles Hopper, Jennifer Rupp (writing as Jennifer Trethewey), and Carol Wobig for reading the book and offering wise counsel.

Roi Solberg, quintessential writing partner, whose help has been incalculable. She read too many drafts, threw too many strands of spaghetti against the wall, and engaged in too many conversations to tally.

My husband, Michael Briselli, with whom I have traveled to the ends of the earth, sailed the seven seas, climbed the highest mountain in Africa, and shared amazing adventures. He helps carry my camera gear and almost always understands when dinner doesn't happen.

A former English professor, Jeannée Sacken is a photojournalist who travels the world documenting the lives of women and children. She lives in Shorewood, Wisconsin, with her husband and cat, where she's hard at work on her next novel also featuring Annie Hawkins Green. Follow Jeannée at jeanneesacken.com.

CPSIA information can be obtained
at www.ICGtesting.com
Printed in the USA
LVHW051531170723
752377LV00009B/324/J

9 781645 382331